MW01142267

SUZANNE

A Novel

Nicholas Mills

"Quem dues vult perdere prius dementat"

*We are all travellers in what John Bunyan
calls the wilderness of this world – all, too,
travellers with a donkey; and the best that we
find in our travels is an honest friend. He is a
fortunate voyager that finds many. We travel,
indeed to find them. They are the end and
the reward of life. They keep us worthy of
ourselves; and when we are alone, we are
only nearer to the absent.*

Robert Louis Stevenson 1879

The characters in this novel and their actions are imaginary. Their names and experiences have no relation to those of actual people, living or dead, except by coincidence.

First Published in 2012 by Nicholas Mills

ISBN No. 978-1-4717-6482-0

www.nicholasmills.org

Somewhere in the distance the Cathedral clock struck mid-day. The surrounding trees reached down, straining to touch the endless flow of the Cherwell wandering a tortuous course through the wood lined meadows towards its senior neighbour, the River Thames.

Appreciating the tranquillity of the sunlit riverside walk, while watching the swans glide effortlessly downstream, students and visitors to the City strolled. On grassy banks away from the path, in small groups of two and three, sat friends, students and lovers; talking, silent, crying and laughing, but all enjoying the peace and privacy on offer a stones throw from noisy cosmopolitan Oxford. The warm June weather seemed to dispel pressure and in this quiet corner of a City brimming with energies old and new, people were gathering their breath, all momentarily trying to escape from the demands of everyday life.

With head down, a lone figure hurried along the path from the direction of Magdalen College. Half spectacles resting on the end of his nose, the middle-aged gentleman was dressed in collar and College tie and wore a tweed suit that most certainly had seen the best of its wearable days. Nobody gave him a second look as glancing at his watch he seemed to accelerate, muttering to himself as he did so.

Coming to a junction in the gravelled walkway he turned left, past tended flowerbeds and ornamental bushes, to follow the inclined path away from the river. At the top, encircled by further trees, was a wide-open green space where, surrounded by four dozen or so spectators, the University team was on the third and final day of their cricket match against a visiting County side.

The man stopped. Leaving the path he crossed the grass to reach an empty wooden bench. Although realising the result of the cricket match was of no significance today, tomorrow or ever likely to be, his boyhood passion for the game had never left him and he decided that there was time for an hour of self indulgence before his afternoon duties called.

Henry Patterson was fifty-five years old and weary. A Professor of Greek Civilisation at Oxford University, in younger days he had considered he was lucky to be working at one of the greatest centres of learning in the western world, but now after thirty years of the academic treadmill he was so very tired.

A brief ripple of applause came from the sparse group of spectators as a youthful spin bowler from the University team managed to claim his third victim of the morning. Soon the game had once more settled into its seemingly apathetic pace. Bird song, blue sky, mid-day sun and the distant hum of City traffic drifting across the University Parks; it all seemed such a long time ago now.

He had been married to his wife, Elaine, for twenty-three years, at the time she had been eight years his junior. They first met at the end of 1949 in a still expectant post-war England. Following one of his early lectures this extremely attractive student with long legs had first approached him, enthusiastically questioning on matters from the preceding talk. The younger Elaine entranced Henry; the invitation for her to take afternoon tea in his rooms the next day had been readily accepted. This was quickly followed by evening visits to the Oxford Playhouse and numerous musical concerts held throughout the City; soon the disciple was seen never to be far from the master's side.

Within six weeks she had moved into Henry's bachelor apartment and within three months they had become man and wife. According to those who came to know them they were an unlikely couple, but well suited. Elaine was lover, student, wife and protector to her new husband, passionately they seemed to be made for each other, but outside the confines of the bedroom and academic stratosphere offered by the University it was Elaine who drove the new partnership forward. Her energies allowed the quiet husband to rapidly improve his status as a humble university lecturer and two years ago he had been offered, and accepted, the Professorship, but by then it was too late.

Henry rose from his shaded seat; the clock sitting on the roof of the cricket pavilion situated in the far corner of the green arena was showing a quarter to one. His only appointment that afternoon was at three fifteen. He would return home, little chance Elaine would be there he thought, make a light lunch and perhaps be able to take an hour-out resting.

Crossing the open spaces of The Parks, he made his way into the Banbury Road, an artery feeding directly into the heart of Oxford. A straight tree lined route with large Victorian houses built on either side many of which, especially at the end nearest the City centre, had been converted into independent English Language Schools or seedy crammer colleges, all of which traded on the University's good name and were seemingly attractive to the less discriminating student. At the Summertown end of this bustling route building renovations appeared less tasteful and the properties clearly not so well maintained.

It was not long before Henry turned right into the peace and quiet of Norham Gardens where the trees seemed smaller and closer together so creating a leafy tunnel down through the length of the Victorian backwater. The tall red brick houses were all residential and the majority appeared to be occupied by ex-military officers or gentlemen returned from serving the far-flung corners of the former British Empire. In truth, most of the houses were homes for the current intelligentsia of Oxford University for whom the choice of Norham Gardens was clear; it was convenient and accessible for matters of both town and gown. The habit of animal species to live in herds close by each other for the purpose of primeval protection would, of course, have had a part to play in their choice of residing in this select neighbourhood known as North Oxford.

A third of the way down the street Henry stopped.

Observing the absence of Elaine's red mini parked next to his car in the pebbled driveway, he made his way through the overgrown garden and climbed the three steps to the front entrance of 225, Norham Gardens. Closing the door quietly behind him he repeatedly called her name. Henry did not really expect a reply and was not disappointed when there was no response.

Settling into the large armchair in his study, Henry breathed a sigh of relief and sipped at the full glass of claret he had poured. He looked though the window and on to the empty roadway beyond; no people, just cars. A solitary figure made its way past 225, an elderly woman heading for residence unknown. A Royal Mail delivery van drove by at high speed without stopping. Henry quickly finished the large glass of wine, he thought he shouldn't but then decided he would and poured himself another drink. Returning to the chair his mind started to drift.

Henry thought it odd that the City should allow the parking of vehicles in Norham Gardens. Despite the close proximity of the Banbury Road, in response to local complaints the Council had made the area one of the first in Oxford to be restricted parking for residents only and yet the road always seemed full of strangers' cars, nowhere free. It was just as well his aging Volvo was parked on the driveway close to the house. Who knew where Elaine's old red mini was? Tiredness and the effects of the wine were encouraging sleepiness and the net curtains at the window were beginning to act as a misty veil.

Was it five, six, maybe seven years ago the earlier passion of their relationship had quelled? Elaine for the first eight years of their marriage had found time to develop her own career. At first, on graduation she had fulfilled a minor role within his own faculty of the University until deciding, although much devoted to Henry and his work, she still wanted to have a career of her own. Buckland, the independent college situated on Boars Hill just outside the

8

City limits, was delighted to give her the opportunity and offered Elaine a position where for six years she had prospered and was very highly thought of by the owners.

Her zest for life was given a severe setback when just over eight years into their marriage Elaine suffered an unexpected nervous breakdown. Overwork, the hidden pressures of living with Henry or perhaps the longing to have a family of her own, no one knew the true reason. Perhaps it was a combination of all those circumstances, but Doctors came to the conclusion that she was spent; they said it was a sad case of personal burnout. Despite her employer's pleas she resigned the position at Buckland College and friends quickly rallied round to give their loving support. Henry? He insensitively totally withdrew into his academic world, now attending his College functions and dinners more often than not alone and without his wife. Elaine tried, oh he remembered how she tried, but the love and feelings that had been there in the first years were sadly withering and dying. A wall seemed to have been erected as a replacement.

Henry was now fast asleep in the chair.

Friends did not initially desert the pair, but those that remembered the gregarious Elaine found it hard to understand what had happened to the couple. Most mornings she could be found on the coffee circuit, otherwise known as the blue rinse round of North Oxford. Older than her, the majority of participants remembered Elaine as the attractive, highly strung young woman who used to appear at cocktail parties on the arm of this dour University fellow who, although quite pleasant to have a conversation with, never had the same captivating personality as his wife. In due course the idle chatter of those elite coffee mornings was expanded to include its twin, the more sinister and damaging gin and tonic circuit. Both groups are hidden to prying eyes by the curtains of North Oxford, but at his peril Henry Patterson had chosen to ignore the dangers of both.

In September 1972 Elaine Patterson gave birth to her only child. Those few people close to the couple hoped events would save the marriage, which at the time had seemed as a rudderless ship heading directly for the rocks.

On the 26th at Oxford Maternity Hospital, weighing 6lb 2oz, baby was born; fit and well, it was a little girl.

Friends visiting Elaine at the hospital told her how lucky the couple should consider themselves and poured praise upon them both. Henry was not so forthcoming with the superlatives. He visited his wife and appeared to do and say all the right things. The doctors tending Elaine had told him it was a minor miracle as pregnancy and birth was against all expectations. Six years previously tests had shown that due to his infertility the couple should not expect to become the parents she longed to be. The apparent mistaken judgement by the doctors was attributed to the inaccuracy of the testing carried out at the time. Offering as further explanation much progress had been made and nowadays similar tests could be made with more precision, leading to the possibility of totally different results. Henry was convinced even more than the medical staff that it was a miracle. He had not slept with his wife for over eighteen months and certainly not made love to her for over two years.

A telephone rang within the house.

Henry stirred, stretched, and moved out of his chair and into the hallway. Before he could lift the receiver it stopped ringing. It was just after two o'clock, he went though to the kitchen. Cutting a large slice from the cheddar he removed from the refrigerator, Henry sat at the kitchen table and pensively started to eat a passed over green salad which he coupled with a portion of last week's stale French bread. Drinking a cup of black coffee, he asked where did it all go wrong and what had he done to deserve it? Why, oh why? He rested his head in his hands thinking.

It did not escape Henry's notice that for the first two months of 1972 his wife had acquired a German friend, a biology student studying at the University and some years Elaine's junior, but at the time Henry was never formally introduced as Elaine had probably thought it unwise. Her friends were invited to meet the younger man at the 1971 New Year's Eve Party held at a mutual acquaintance's flat situated in the low life area of Oxford known as Jericho. Trying to escape the mundane way of life she considered herself trapped, Elaine was yet again drunk.

She now thought Henry so boring. He had no wish to attend any party or social gathering together, telling her before she had left home that evening in no uncertain terms how he hated parties and her current choice of friends would not be his. Out of sheer defiance of her husband, Elaine was therefore even more determined to enjoy herself.

Henry later learnt how a one Boris Jaeger had been telling everyone of the wild woman he had taken to this New Year's Eve Party. She was the wife of a University Professor, very attractive and likened her body to that of a Goddess. They had left the party together and he had taken her to the banks of the nearby Oxford Canal where he had made uncompromising love across the arm of a lock gate. To meet her sexual appetite when she demanded more and more, time and time again he had entered her. Finally, in the early hours unable to satisfy her drunken lust, Boris took her to his tiny flat in Walton Street where they again repeated erotic actions the likes of which he had never before experienced. It was well into the afternoon before Elaine finally slipped away, walking alone to the refinements of Norham Gardens while leaving her conquest of the previous night asleep across his unmade bed.

The story on reaching Henry's ears had no doubt been greatly embellished, but the truth was clear and he felt the woman he once adored had betrayed him.

In February 1972, the young German who in the previous six weeks had often been seen in the company of Elaine vanished from view and her life permanently. The evening they had met for a quiet drink at the *Eagle and Child* in St Giles and Elaine announced that she was pregnant by him had been too much for her lover.

Following Elaine's initial protestations at his reaction to the news, Boris rose in silence from his seat. He did not look back as he left the weeping lone figure at the corner table and walked out into the cold night air of the City and despite Elaine's numerous later efforts to make contact with him Boris disappeared for good. He never returned to his squalid student flat in Walton Street and a stony wall of silence met her whenever she questioned known acquaintances of his whereabouts.

"Where is he living?" "Is he still studying at the University?" "Has he returned home to Germany?" Nothing, and if they did know anything they were not saying.

As with Boris, hearing the news she was pregnant a lot of her personal friends also disappeared. It was as if a sense of guilt had hit them, they were only too aware over recent months of the frequent illicit liaisons that had occurred between the two. Her remaining friends were those from previous years, those that remembered the Pattersons from easier times.

Henry cast his mind back. It had not been a hard decision, after all he told himself Elaine was his wife and, whatever he considered the child must have a father. He only confronted her once with the situation and that was after a heated exchange Henry experienced with a pompous work colleague who, following an argument over a totally unrelated matter, had retaliated by exclaiming at least he had been aware of what his wife was doing at midnight on December 31st last. She was not making New Year rumours for her husband's pupils to gleefully discuss over their tepid pints of beer in the student bars and clubs of Oxford.

The late February evening he had challenged Elaine with the sordid detail which had been relayed to him earlier in the day Henry remembered she had said nothing, just letting him finish what he had to say. An agonizing silence of several minutes followed and it was only then Elaine had whispered it was worse than he had described, much worse; she was pregnant.

And so it was Suzanne Patterson was born into a very uncertain future.

Once more Henry sighed and shook his head. Clearing the dirtied plate and mug from the kitchen table, he prepared to walk back though The Parks and his afternoon rendezvous at Magdalen.

Chapter 2

Upon the birth of her daughter, Elaine Patterson seemed to regain some of the vitality and dignity she had lost at the time of her breakdown. The newborn child could not have wished for a better mother and both Pattersons idolized the little girl.

Elaine now had the one thing that she always wanted and thought she would never have. After the traumas of the past year Henry was happy to see his wife contented and it did not seem to bother him the girl had blue eyes and Germanic blonde hair, to him she was his daughter.

For the first five years of her young life Suzanne's mother cared for her immaculately. All Elaine's time and attention was given to seeing the child wanted for nothing, she was the model mother, but once again it was at Henry's expense and, enveloped in the comparative security of his academic world, he was just pleased to see mother and child so happy.

On reaching the age of five, Suzanne started at the pre-preparatory department of Greycotes. The independent school was situated just off the Banbury Road and within walking distance of the family home at 225, Norham Gardens.

With daughter now out of her life for long periods of the day it was perhaps inevitable that mother's previous problems would return. Drink soon replaced her child as the main attraction.

It was slowly at first, but her addiction gathered pace as more and more of the time she came to rely increasingly on alcohol for support. In avoidance of Elaine, Henry just withdrew further and further into the world surrounding him at the University. It was after the daughter had been attending Greycotes for just over eighteen months that he was compelled to act to protect the child from the excesses of her mother. Henry was forced into employing a series of live-in nannies which on the whole seemed to serve

Suzanne well.

The nannies ensured the girl was well dressed and following breakfast in the morning took her off to School, but always after an affectionate kiss and hug from her father. He would then tend to his day at the University, whilst invariably Elaine would be left in her bedroom recovering from the drink of the previous evening.

It was the nanny who met Suzanne from School at 3p.m. and it was the nanny who looked after her for the rest of the day. Henry would always ensure he was home for bedtime when Suzanne would always feel much cheated if the day did not finish with a story read by father.

Surrounded by innocence, she lay in bed, oblivious to the fates ready to befall her in later life. To say mother was present would have been a gross exaggeration for often she was not. On the occasions she was, if sober enough, Elaine was constantly skirmishing with Henry. Nannies looked after Suzanne well in what could be best described as difficult circumstances.

Elaine was not unkind to her daughter, but for the second five years of her life Suzanne was left in a bemused state. Following the initial period of unadulterated love and attention, the thought of having to share her daughter with an outside world was too much for mother and the drink problem from small beginnings grew. Elaine, amongst the matrimonial differences with Henry, came and went from the house at will. She hardly gave a second glance to the child who longed once more for her attention, but the woman she called mother asked for and in return gave no love or affection, whilst all the time Henry's love for Suzanne was constantly reciprocated.

On March 3rd, 1983 Henry and Suzanne were alone in the house at Norham Gardens; as usual mother was not there. Rachel was the latest in the long succession of nannies, for many before her the strains of the Patterson household had been too much and however much the attractive and well mannered daughter enchanted during the day, the constant verbal battering they were subjected to from the gin-soaked Elaine usually proved too much and eventually they all moved to pastures new.

Henry employed the girls through an agency that had its offices in the St Aldate's area of the City; they were invariably of a high quality and Rachel was not an exception. As her employer had returned home earlier than expected she had been given time-off to go out with friends for the evening and as usual the whereabouts of Elaine was unknown.

It was 7.30; soon he would put Suzanne to bed and continue the nightly reading of her latest book which as usual was full of child fantasies. Henry readily admitted to others he enjoyed these evening sessions that always ended long before he had finished reading with Suzanne fast asleep on her pillow. He would kiss her lightly on the cheek and quietly slip out of the room, softly closing the door behind him, but tonight before making his way up the stairs he had something to tell her.

Henry called.

"Suzanne, Suzanne, come down to my study, we have to talk before you go to bed. It won't take long and then I will be ready to read to you."

From her first floor room, without waiting to put a dressing gown over the pretty nightdress she was wearing, Suzanne excitedly hurried down the stairs to where her father was calling.

With her feet unable to touch the floor, she settled into the worn leather chair in front of his large oak desk. Expectantly she waited; Suzanne always enjoyed it when daddy called her into his book-lined den. The place had a sort of musty smell about it, a mixture of polished wood and old books.

Henry looked her straight in the eye and slowly started to explain things to his ten-year-old daughter.

"Suzanne this coming September, after the summer holidays, I have arranged for you to go away to boarding school."

The statement brought a quick retort from the diminutive blonde girl sitting opposite him.

"Daddy what is a boarding school and what happens there?" In her innocence she had no idea.

Henry continued by explaining in some detail.

"The school I have chosen for you is called St Bernadette's."

The next question he faced from the by now stone-faced child was one of the location of St Bernadette's.

"It is near Bournemouth. Bournemouth is by the sea, on the south coast in Dorset." As if to convince himself he quickly added, "It is situated in very pretty countryside, you will love it."

A cold silence followed and it was Henry that spoke first.

"You know how much I love you, and your real home will still be here in Oxford where I will be waiting for you every holiday-time."

There was once again silence while what her father had explained registered in the young ten-year old mind.

"What will happen to Rachel?" she said. "I like Rachel more than any of the others who have stayed and looked after me."

Henry smiled to himself. She had said that in the past about most of the young nannies who had worked in the house and there was always childlike sorrow when they left. Suzanne soon discovered the replacements were usually just as fun loving and nice as the previous incumbent.

"Sadly, Rachel will have to go, but I am sure she will have no problem finding another position. Anyway, she will not be leaving us before you set off for school in September and you can have lots of time together in the summer holidays. It you wish, you can go shopping with Rachel and buy all the clothes necessary for your new School."

Henry's enthusiasm for the future scheme of things was beginning to show as his speech slowly gathered speed.

"I can make arrangements for her to visit us in the school holidays" he said. "I intend talking to Rachel about the arrangements for her future when she gets in this evening."

The building atmosphere of euphoria, like a pricked bubble, evaporated into nothing with Suzanne's third and final question.

"What does mother think of the matter?" she nonchalantly asked.

There was no reply, just silence

*****

Set in just over forty acres of parkland, St Bernadette's Covent had a pupil roll totalling around two hundred girls, of which just over half were full boarders, eight aging nuns and a dozen or so teaching staff.

The centre of the School was a Queen Anne mansion, designed by the same architect as the splendiferous Blenheim Palace in Woodstock, just outside of Oxford. The School had been lovingly cared for over the previous twenty years by the Order, but it was clear from the fabric of the building that expenditure on upkeep was a losing battle as with the passing years wear and tear were taking their toll.

Standing on the green outskirts of the seaside town, the mansion had once been part of a far larger country estate long present on the Dorset border before the urban sprawl had developed which today constitutes the twin holiday resorts of Boscombe and Bournemouth. Approximately half the School's acreage was taken by coppice woodland, the rest being given over to tree filled parkland on which room had been made for tennis courts, hockey pitches and other recreational areas associated with a girls' minor independent boarding school.

Originally Henry had chosen St Bernadette's not because of any religious beliefs, but on the recommendation of a colleague's wife. When asked in passing, she had told of her wonderful school days in a small boarding establishment in the west country. Details of this heavenly institution for young ladies were enough to start Henry thinking the best for Suzanne was to send her away to continue her growing-up in an environment which would be more conducive to the fulfilment of her potential than 225, Norham Gardens. Away from an unstable mother to a place which had far more to offer than Henry had time for and where a strict regime would be imposed while at the same time letting her develop with a well-rounded education.

He had to make a choice so six weeks prior to the first evening talk with Suzanne Henry started the search for a suitable school for her to attend. Following the conversation he had with the colleague's wife, he checked-out St Bernadette's and following a visit immediately fell for its old fashioned charm.

As promised that evening in her father's study, Rachel stayed until Suzanne started at her new school and the first time she had been delivered to St Bernadette's, Rachel was still waving from the car as Henry drove away down the long driveway.

She wiped a tear from her eye. Suzanne hoped it would not be the last time she saw Rachel, who had already told her in ten days time she would be taking up a new position with a family in Yorkshire and in forty eight hours would be leaving Norham Gardens for good. Father looked on as she hugged Suzanne goodbye and promised to come and see them all at Christmas.

Suzanne was quite right to have deep doubts in her young mind in thinking this really was going to be the final farewell. After the first three weeks the letters became more infrequent and November came and then there had been no more. She had written again and again asking when Rachel would be coming to stay at the home in Oxford, but still there was no reply. Rachel had moved on with her life.

Neither did she hear anything from her mother who, devoid of any feeling, had kissed Suzanne goodbye the evening before she set out for her new school adventure. The morning the three of them had departed for Bournemouth, Elaine was nowhere to be found and when Suzanne did go home in the holidays it was always father picking her up from St Bernadette's, never mother.

She still adored father and when at home frequently asked him questions.

"Please could Mummy spend less time in her room? I would like to see her more often" or "Why isn't mother ever here? Why doesn't she spend more time at home?"

She soon came to understand the meaning of the words when father repeatedly told her, "Unfortunately, most of the time your mother is not sober and when she is chooses to spend time with her so called friends."

At holiday times Suzanne also quickly came to realise things were no different at home than before she first went to boarding school and as time went on if anything they seemed to be getting worse. She missed the older companionship of Rachel, but most of all Suzanne just longed to get to know her mother and be given the opportunity to explain what her seemingly irrational behaviour was doing to both husband and daughter.

Suzanne's early school reports seemed to indicate she was not an academic child, neither was she outstanding at any particular sport. They stated she was very quiet, polite, neat and tidy and very practical in all domestic matters. The strongest praise of all had come as a great surprise to Henry; those early reports indicated she possessed an undisputed artistic talent, particularly for drawing and painting. Time without number her artistic creativities were acknowledged and soon her abilities were spoken of throughout the School as outstanding. Those that knew said without question, she was the best young artist St Bernadette's had ever produced.

At holiday time she came and went from Norham Gardens, still adoring her father, but how she wished her mother would not have those seemingly constant fearful arguments with him over matters that seemed so trivial to Suzanne.

Despite Henry's loving attention, while both at School and in Oxford, Suzanne was lonely. A quiet child, some may have said introverted, her friends were few, but at sixteen those observing her development agreed the butterfly was emerging. Some said her looks were those of a plain child, but it was in that plainness the beauty of the young woman seemed to lie.

Chapter 3

It was on a delightful spring Sunday afternoon that Henry
Patterson had driven to Bournemouth to meet Suzanne; he
turned from the Oxford ring road on to the dual
carriageway of the A34. As he drove towards Newbury he
reflected on the events of the previous two weeks.

He had telephoned St Bernadette's and spoken to the
Reverend Mother. Whilst accepting it would not be easy for
him, they had agreed Henry should break the news to his
daughter; it was his wish. He made good time, stopping
only once for petrol at a garage just off the A4, whilst there
he also bought a small bunch of flowers for Suzanne. Ten
minutes later he was back in the old Volvo heading towards
the market town of Newbury. The car radio was playing the
most popular of English oratorios, the one which
compendiously tells of the coming of Christ, His death and
resurrection, Handel's *Messiah*. Henry was oblivious to the
music, his mind now totally focussed on the message he
was about to deliver in the afternoon.

He turned into the driveway and past the twin
sentinels standing either side of the entrance, *St
Bernadette's, Girls' Independent School, 11-18 years,
Boarding and Da*y. The notices had recently received a
welcome coat of paint and the blue gloss with gold
lettering shone in the afternoon sun. Henry drove up the
metalled surface before turning on to the gravel car park in
front of the main School building.

Entering the hallway, he made his way to the left of
the large fireplace, his footsteps sounded hollow as he
walked across the highly polished surface, past the staircase
which swept its way to the top floor and into a darkened
passageway; during their long history these dark oak panels
would have had many tales to tell. On reaching the end he
was faced with two doors, one was closed, clearly centrally
set at eye level it carried a brass sign *Secretary*. The second,
on the left-hand side, was ajar; this he knew from previous

visits was the Reverend Mother's study. Pausing, he looked at his watch, 3.28, and knocked once.

A woman's voice invited him to enter.

"Please come in Mr Patterson, do come in, you are two minutes early!"

Henry did as he was bid.

Sitting behind her desk he found the bespectacled, small greying figure of Sister Veronica, looks belied the energies resting beneath the black habit. She quickly rose from her seat and politely shook his hand before showing him to a chair. Seated, the offer of afternoon tea and biscuits was declined. Having disposed of niceties the Reverend Mother, from the second of two telephones on her desk, spoke to some unseen person or persons unknown.

"Is Suzanne Patterson there please? .....Good.....Would you ask her to come to Sister Veronica's study straight away, I wish to speak to her...........Thank you."

She gently replaced the receiver.

Three minutes later there was another knock at the door and upon direction Suzanne entered. She had been warned the previous day by her housemistress that father would be calling-in sometime on Sunday afternoon, but was still a little surprised to find him already there in the room.

Declining the Reverend Mother's offer to leave them, Henry said if there was no objection he would like to talk alone with his daughter whilst walking in the School grounds.

Soon they were passing the rose garden on the east side of the mansion; past the tennis courts - two of which were in use, under the spreading cedar tree and on to the wooden footbridge crossing the ha-ha which surrounded the limits of the original buildings and away from the hearing of others making the best of the spring sunshine. It was only then Henry spoke to Suzanne and once started he did not hesitate.

"In the hope they would be able to find a solution to her illness, which seemed to be getting worse by the day, sadly, ten days ago your mother was admitted to a private nursing home in Hertfordshire. They will treat her and try to find an answer to the problem surrounding the continuing abuse of alcohol. With a little persuasion from the doctor she took herself off there; they are experts in such matters and I am positive they will be able to help her sort herself out."

Suzanne said nothing.

"Believe me, it's for the best. In your absence the situation at home has been getting worse and if your mother had not followed through with this course of action who knows what may have happened. It really was for the best."

Looking to be comforted the sixteen year old threw herself into her father's arms. She held on to him tightly, sobbing aloud. After a full five minutes Suzanne bravely repeatedly whispered in his ear.

"Perhaps it is for the best."

Next, abruptly and without warning, she pulled back from Henry.

"When will I be able to see mother? Whatever you feel, it is now she needs not only my support, but also that of her husband. After all father she is your wife."

He paused. Holding his daughter by the shoulders, he looked into her eyes, Henry waited before he gave his reply, "Soon", before repeating the single word, "Soon."

It was in silence for the next ninety minutes they walked through the parkland and woods surrounding St Bernadette's. Upon reaching the front of the House, Henry announced to Suzanne it was time for him to return to Oxford. When making the original arrangements, he had warned the School it would only be a fleeting visit, but had insisted it was to be him, no one else, that imparted the sad news regarding her mother. Henry took the bunch of flowers he had left on the back seat of his car and gave them to Suzanne. She reached across and kissed him on the cheek, quietly thanking her father for his kind thought and as Suzanne whispered her simple "Thank you" a lonely teardrop slowly ran down the side of her face.

"The Easter holidays will soon be here" he explained, "When the three of us will be at home together."

In truthfulness, he did not think Elaine would be back in Oxford by then, there wasn't a chance. Henry had lied. Clutching the flowers to her breast, Suzanne turned and ran across the gravel towards the front door. She did not say goodbye, she was too upset.

Watching, as the green and white of her school uniform disappeared into the interior darkness of the building, he thought it best to leave St Bernadette's as soon as possible. As his car went down the driveway towards the School gates, Henry did not see the lone blond haired figure in a top floor window observing his hurried departure.

To accompany him on his lonely drive back to Oxfordshire, he instinctively turned on the car radio; fittingly the music being performed was Mozart's *No La Morte*.

*****

April and the Easter school holidays soon arrived. Suzanne found it strange with the house to herself. Despite his earlier promises, father was not there for three of the four-week vacation. Henry was in Cambridge at one or other of those conferences at which he was always being asked to speak.

As Suzanne lay in bed that morning, all she knew today was Tuesday, her father was in Cambridge and he would not be returning until the weekend. She had written several letters to her mother since the Sunday nearly six weeks ago when he had made the short visit to the School giving her the awful news; the news which everyone who knew Elaine, apart from Suzanne herself, had accepted as inevitable. He had not left her with an address so she sent the letters to her father, asking him to forward them to mother.

In the correspondence, Suzanne begged Elaine to write to her at St Bernadette's, but to-date she had received no reply. In her naivety she thought the absence of any news meant her mother must be well on the way to recovery. It did not even cross her mind that upon receipt of the letters from Suzanne, Henry, rather than redirect them to his wife, had destroyed all evidence of them having ever been written.

If he was to be believed, she was still in Hertfordshire. Perhaps, once again due to her innocence, Suzanne did not think it strange that since giving her the news Henry had hardly mentioned her mother. It was as if in some strange way he wanted her to forget all about Elaine.

The Easter holidays came and went.

*****

The summer in any boarding school is considered by staff and pupils alike to be the best of the three term yearly cycle; at St Bernadette's the first half of the summer term 1988 was no different.

Warm days, the idyllic setting, the expectancy of the long break at the beginning of July, it all added to an environment which would have been hard not to enjoy. The only minus point, especially for the girls in the fifth and upper sixth, was the yearly examinations. By the second week of June all exams had petered-out and the whole School was in a more relaxed mode for the last four weeks. Only when the results were received at the end of August would costs through the lack of individuals' efforts have to be counted.

That summer the half-term week came at the end of May.

Excepting two old spinster aunts, her father's sisters,

who lived somewhere in the Lake District and were rarely heard of let alone visited, Suzanne to the best of her knowledge had no other living relatives. Due to father being "On another of his beastly trips" she did not return home to 225, Norham Gardens, but spent the break away from the School at the home of the art mistress' family. In her early thirties, Mary Bowron, between having three children, depending on her line of pregnancies had taught at St Bernadette's for the previous eight years and in that time worked in both full-time and part-time capacities. She took a great interest in all of her pupils and their efforts, but none more so than Suzanne Patterson. Mary had soon recognized of the many girls who had passed through her hands at the School Suzanne was by far the most talented. The art mistress had also acknowledged to herself the potential of this attractive sixteen year old was far beyond that of her tutor and should be put to good use; the pupil's horizons should have no bounds.

As half-term approached Mary had come to the rescue. Whilst sitting in the staff room drinking a cup of coffee, she had overheard housemistress Selby speaking to Sister Josephine.

"With mother away and father endlessly engaged in his work, what are we to do with the child? There will be nobody at the School and most of the staff normally resident want to take advantage of the seasonal fine weather and go away to friends and relatives for a few days."

Mary listened as Selby continued.

"Reverend Mother said she will look after Suzanne for the week, she has done it on the odd occasion in the past, but to me it hardly seems fair on her. Next week when she stays with her sister in Teignmouth it is her intention to take the girl with her. Likewise, it hardly seems fair on the young girl; the sister is an elderly, house bound, spinster of ninety three!"

Before Sister Josephine was able to respond to the

housemistress, Mary interrupted their discussion.

"Excuse me for breaking into your conversation, but I could not help over-hearing the problem, it started me thinking. I would be quite happy to give Suzanne a home for the week and I am positive my husband would not have any objection. Our three children would love to have her around the house, for the youngsters it will be like having an elder sister about the place. If everyone approves, I could make the arrangements this evening. I will start by telephoning Mr Patterson to let him know there will be no need for him to worry about his daughter's welfare this half term. We will take charge of Suzanne after lessons on Friday afternoon and I will return her to School early on the Monday morning following the break."

Housemistress Selby needed little convincing the art teacher's plan was a splendid one. The worrying problem of Suzanne Patterson returning to Oxford and an empty house had suddenly evaporated.

*****

Mary and Tony Bowron lived in Willowbridge; a small village situated five miles north east of Bournemouth. He was Assistant Manager at the Boscombe branch of the National Westminster Bank.

On Friday evening, Tony drove directly to the School from his office picking Mary up on the way. He was over six feet tall, dark suited and a good-looking figure who, when introduced to Suzanne, certainly made an impression on the other girls waiting around for their parents to collect them from the car park.

His fresh, smart appearance was in sharp contrast to his accompanying wife's rather dowdy appearance which the pupils were used to.

Having an afternoon free of teaching, Mary had spent the time at the home of her husband's parents, where their three children were to spend the night. Suzanne would have to wait until Saturday morning before she was introduced to them.

With his masculine charm, Tony greeted Suzanne as if had known her all his life. He carefully placed the small suitcase into the boot of his Ford Cortina and it raised on-looking youthful eyebrows when, as if a handsome family chauffer, he had held open the rear door and showed her into the car. As he pulled away down the driveway, sitting next to her husband in the passenger seat Mary could not help an unseen triumphant smile.

The next morning Grandfather delivered the three Bowron children home, Rupert, Ian and Philip, aged ten, eight and four respectively. It didn't take Suzanne long to realise all three were blessed with the same charm as their father and after the introductions was soon playing with them in the extension built as a playroom at the rear of the 1930's style detached house.

Mary explained to Suzanne that Ian normally had a bedroom to himself, but quite happily had agreed to move and sleep on the spare bed in his older brother's room, so his room where she had slept the previous night was hers for the rest of the week. If she wanted anything else all she had to do was ask.

"It's not 'Miss' or 'Mrs Bowron' while you are a guest in our house, it is Tony and Mary," she told Suzanne for the umpteenth time.

The week was going well. At the weekend they had all walked for what seemed miles in the surrounding countryside and on the Monday Tony had started his new working week, whilst Suzanne was in her element playing with the three young boys.

It was early on Wednesday, Mary and the children had gone to visit her parents leaving Suzanne alone and still in bed. Mid-morning she decided perhaps now was the time to look around parts of the house that still remained undisclosed to her. Starting with the attic, peeping her nose around every closed door, floor by floor she investigated. It wasn't until she was in the kitchen and at the end of her exploratory tour a terrible sense of guilt overtook her.

"What are you doing Suzanne Patterson? Here you are a guest in this house and all you can do is slink around nosily taking everything into your gaze, acting as if you are a petty criminal. You should be ashamed of yourself!" she angrily muttered to herself.

Opening the back door, she ran out of the kitchen and into the garden. Taking a deep breath and if as to escape the imaginary hideous crime she had just committed, Suzanne started to run around the outside of the house. In her child-like mind, she considered the Bowrons' hospitality had been abused and their privacy invaded. Suzanne circled the building until the double garage doors were reached.

As if drawn by some unseen force, unable to help herself, she stepped from the clear sunlight of the midday sky into the cooler shadows of the garage. Empty of the two Bowron cars, inside it was as one might find any normal garage space; stored on the racks and shelves arranged on two sides were garden tools, hoses, step ladders and various boxes.

At the back of the central clear area, a narrow wooden staircase led up to a closed door. Not sure of her own feelings and confused by the earlier thoughts of dishonesty, Suzanne moved slowly forward and started to climb the steps. Reaching the top, she tried the handle; it turned. Tentatively she pushed the door open; Suzanne was not ready for what met her eyes.

Inside the large loft, one side of which was totally of glass and angled by the steep pitch of the roof, lay a room the contents of which clearly showed it served as an artist's studio. Paints, easels, canvases, frames, they were all there. She breathed a sigh of relief.

Here at least, Suzanne felt she was on familiar territory and it was with great interest she looked at what surrounded her. Eventually attention was drawn towards the three large paintings hanging from the wall facing her.

All three were of women, all wearing no clothing, or at best very little, and all in similar poses, erotically placed over upright chairs. Suzanne did not like it and very quickly decided this would teach her in future not to pry into the privacy of others.

She quickly turned to go and was faced by two further paintings. In each of the pictures there were two naked women, lying, kissing and fondling each other, the sensitivity of the paintings gave off an uncanny realism.

Suzanne was stunned, turning she looked once more at all the paintings surrounding her, it was then she saw the only other work in the studio. Partially covered by a large dustsheet, it sat on an easel alone in the far corner. She hurried across and in one movement removed the cover. Immediately a look of horror spread across her face.

The exposed canvas was smaller than those hanging from the walls, but showed another well-shaped female body. Younger than the women in the other pictures, it too was completely naked, partially in a foetal position, long blonde hair was falling over the left shoulder covering one of the small, but well rounded breasts.

The following gasp was not for the figure or beauty of the subject, but the sight of the young woman's face. Suzanne was horrified! Without doubt she recognized it to be an image of her own.

Hastily replacing the dustsheet, clumsily hurrying, she slammed the door of the studio shut, fled down the wooden steps and away from the garage, leaving the dark secret resting above.

In the evening, it was at the supper table Tony spoke to Suzanne.

"How have you spent your time today? Have you done anything nice? The weather was gorgeous, wasn't it?"

"Oh, I spent most of it reading", she casually replied. "I have written two letters, one for father and the other to a friend at School and then I walked to the village Post Office

31

to mail them. It was a very restful day."

Mary, seated at the opposite end of the dining room table, raised an eyebrow and said nothing.

"I hear that you paint and have considerable talent" Tony said, "Mary is always talking about you as her star pupil." Suzanne blushed as he continued, "Perhaps you should ask Mary to take you to the forbidden territory of her studio, even I'm not allowed into the room over the garage." He chuckled. "Then perhaps you will be able to tell me what really goes on up there."

Mary quickly rose to clear the supper plates.

"Really Tony you are such a bore, don't you think our visitor has enough of me during school? There is no way Suzanne wants teacher pushed down her throat at holiday time as well."

Once more Tony laughed aloud, while Mary quickly changed the subject.

"Come on boys it is well past the time you should be in bed, if you hurry by the time Rupert and Philip have been in the shower, Suzanne would have finished reading Ian his bedtime story. If you two older ones are good perhaps she will also read to you."

There was a mad rush for the door.

Tony smiled, "Perhaps you should stay with us more often."

No more was said by anyone about secret things over the garage, but on the Friday morning, finding herself once more alone in the house, Suzanne had mustered the courage to surreptitiously try the door again at the top of the stairs, only this time to find it firmly locked. Considering the matter best forgotten, Suzanne thought maybe she should just continue by enjoying the rest of her time with the family.

In the evenings, Tony often seemed to be away from the house at meetings concerning one community based group or another he was associated with; Rotary, Village Hall Committee, PTA of the children's School, the Squash

Club of which he was a member, the list seemed endless.

He did not seem to notice for the week Suzanne was staying with the family, sounds of quiet contentment seemed to be coming from his wife rather than the normal noises of complaint. Mary thought the week had gone well, if only her damn husband had not returned earlier than usual from his regular Friday evening visit to the Golf Club, events may have even delivered what she considered her ultimate goal.

Not wishing to offend his wife and their young visitor, Tony had returned ninety minutes before his usual punctual eleven o'clock. He found both women had been drinking from the drawing room cabinet. At the time, he considered due to her age Suzanne had just been unable to take the alcohol. What he did not realise was that for the previous hour Mary had been plying her with a cocktail of spirits any hardened drinker might have found difficult to handle. Tony had not thought it particularly strange his wife seemed perfectly sober, but Mary's apparent large intake of gin had consisted mainly of pure tonic water.

He decided it was time for someone to help Suzanne; Mary looked on grudgingly as Tony led her from the room.

At the entrance to her bedroom, in a fatherly tone, he said, "Young lady, I think it is time you were in bed, have a good night, sleep well."

An induced grin spread across her face. She opened the door to the room and with a drunken wave of her arm Suzanne returned the compliment, reminding Tony in a loud stage-like whisper.

"Sshh, the children are in bed asleep, Mary will be very cross if you wake them."

With that she fell into the bedroom, slamming the door behind her with a loud bang!

Re-entering the drawing room Mary did not seem to be there. He crossed to the side window to close the curtains and through the glass Tony saw the light shining over the garage door. Thinking she had retired to her secret refuge, he shrugged his shoulders; the matter of what had gone on in his absence earlier in the evening could wait until her return.

Much to the disappointment of the children, the next morning Suzanne rose late. She drank a mid-morning cup of black coffee. Alone with Tony in the kitchen she waited for him to say something about her behaviour of the previous evening.

"How did you feel this morning?"

"Oh, I'm fine thank you" Suzanne sheepishly answered. Blushing, she clasped her hands tightly around the hot cup.

Fortunately, at that point the three children burst through the kitchen door, each one of them trying to be heard above the other as they noisily asked Suzanne if she would come with them into the garden and play. Putting down the half finished mug of coffee, she tentatively placed one hand to her forehead, before smiling kindly at them.

"Of course I will."

Behind the backs of the children, Tony winked at her, smiled, turned and left the kitchen, happily humming an undistinguishable tune.

On the Monday morning, when it was time for Suzanne to leave there was much sorrow amongst the children and they demanded she promise to come and stay again. Mary had no lessons until midmorning, so it was her who took the two older children to the village school and left the youngest at his Grandparents for the day. Tony dropped Suzanne at St Bernadette's where waiting housemistress Selby told him it was what Suzanne had been in need of, a week in a caring and kind environment.

Chapter 4

By Thursday of the following week written examinations at St Bernadette's were nearing conclusion, they had gone well. Following supper, Suzanne was making her way down the corridor towards the house common room in preparation for her last two exams the next day; in the morning it was English Literature and finally in the afternoon it would be the second of her two Geography papers.

As she passed Amanda Dick, one of the School monitors, stopped her.

"Suzanne Patterson, Selby is looking for you. She has just asked if I saw you to send you to her office."

"Thank you, thank you I'll go straightaway. I wonder what she is after at this time day?" said Suzanne to the older girl. With a puzzled look on her face she turned to make her way back down the corridor, all the time wondering what she had done wrong to justify a summons from Miss Selby.

Suzanne stopped on reaching the office door of the housemistress. She heard voices' coming from inside, one clearly that of a man. Knocking twice, she heard the mumbling conversation stop. A brief silence was followed by the order to go in.

To her surprise, upon entering she found not only Miss Selby, but the other occupant of the room was a very straight faced and sombre Henry Patterson.

Accepting the housemistress' invitation to take a seat, she joined her father; their wooden chairs were placed side by side in the middle of the room facing the stark bare desk behind which sat Miss Selby.

She appeared to be picking her words carefully as she addressed Suzanne.

"Your father has something important to tell you."

Next, as if by some prearrangement, readying herself to leave the room, the speaker slowly rose from her chair behind the desk. Both pairs of eyes followed as the housemistress crossed the floor, before leaving and carefully closing the door behind her.

With a warm hug and a kiss on the cheek, Suzanne belatedly greeted her father.

"What brings you to School on a Thursday and particularly at this time of day? What is the matter?"

As if searching for an explanation, unable to express himself, her father did not answer. There was silence between them. Suzanne spoke first; it was as if something was slowly dawning upon her. Rather than just asking another question she started to make a statement.

"It's news of mother that has brought you......."

Before she could continue any further with a trace of a tear in his eye, Henry Patterson started to tell his daughter of the news from Hertfordshire. Finding it hard to explain he started slowly.

"After many years of alcohol and drugs use, tormenting and abusing her own body and mind, your mother has finally given up the fight."

The face said it all and in answer to the non-verbal question Henry quickly reassured Suzanne he did not mean her mother was dead.

"Your mother is in a place where she can do no one any further harm, including herself. A week ago she physically attacked a Doctor. He had just told her that for the foreseeable future his recommendation would be she stayed with them. For some weeks previous your mother had been trying hard to convince those looking after her she was much better and had made a full recovery from the nervous exhaustion which took her there in the first place. Goodness knows what supportive medication the Doctors had put her on, but all I know is whatever had been achieved was without her using illicit drugs or booze."

Henry waited a short while before continuing.

"Unfortunately, following the Doctor expressing his views to your mother, her loud screams and shouts of anger brought two nurses racing into the room. Nobody seems to know where she got it from, but as a hunted animal cornered before the final kill, she proceeded to attack all three occupants of the room with a sharpened kitchen blade. I am told it was a pretty awful scene."

Henry had spared Suzanne the horrific detail, but now openly upset, he steadied himself before once more speaking to Suzanne.

"One of the two female nurses suffered serious injuries, which, thankfully, in time she should make a full recovery from. With the help of three other members of their staff they eventually overpowered your mother. Sedated, they then took her by ambulance to secure accommodation, situated near Cardiff in South Wales, where for a time she was under lock and key and strict observation. Various Consultants who have since examined her think her mind has gone and the chances of a full recovery to her old self are pretty slim."

Another silence followed.

"What I consider the most hurtful part of this terrible affair was when they told me my wife, your mother, for her own well being was to be committed."

Suzanne said nothing. Straight faced, ignoring her father, she stared straight ahead and all the time negatively shaking her head. Summoning strength to address his daughter, Henry waited.

Finally, unable to suppress it any further, he blurted out "In the Doctor's opinion your mother should be classified as insane!"

Suzanne immediately besieged her father with pleas.

"I want to go! I would like to be taken to Cardiff! I demand to see my mother who I have not seen her for nearly five years. You have tried to let me forget, but rest assured I haven't. Please, I would like to go, now!"

However much she pleaded, the answer from her father was always the same.

"It is not possible and no matter how much you ask

me the answer will remain the same, for the time being it is well left alone. Your mother is safe where she is at present and in the best possible place if there is to be any chance at all of her recovering."

Shortly after giving Suzanne the news about her mother, Henry Patterson left St Bernadette's to return to Oxford, leaving his daughter with the caring housemistress. He left Suzanne wondering why, unlike her father, she had found it impossible to shed tears over a woman she was desperate to spend time with and get to know, the same woman her father had once loved so much.

On the day of Henry's visit, news of Elaine Patterson's problems had been discreetly given to a gathered St Bernadette's staff during their afternoon break. There had been many murmurs of sympathy as Reverend Mother had told all of them about the situation. It was to their credit Suzanne's fellow pupils did not get to hear of the matter for there were a few of her own age who would have delighted in telling "the high and mighty" Miss Patterson her mother was locked-up in "The nut house", where, together with all of those damn paintings, Suzanne would end up! Adolescent girls can be very cruel.

It was Mary Bowron who offered to take her star pupil to Bournemouth that Saturday afternoon. "To do a little shopping with the girl," she told her colleagues.

"Examinations will be finished and in celebration of Suzanne having completed the year's studies under very difficult personal circumstances I will buy her a present."

*****

"Next year you will be in the Sixth Form" Mary said, "And then, after A levels, it will be Art College, but that shouldn't present you with too many problems, everyone expects you to do well. After College you..........."

As she continued, Suzanne smiled at Mary's future plans for her.

She looked at herself in the dress shop's full-length

mirror. It was a short, off the shoulder, blue, see-through cotton dress that clearly defined her shapely young body. Pulling her long blonde hair back to the top of the head and, pushing her left leg forward, she suggestively pouted her lips. Laughing once more, Suzanne felt she had not had so much fun for such a long time.

Mary told her she preferred it with her hair down. Suzanne let it drop to rest over her shoulders, protesting when told by the other woman she looked so beautiful. The flimsy blue dress was the last of many Suzanne had tried on and her protestations grew when Mary insisted she would pay for it, saying she was buying the dress as a gift and there would be no further argument over the matter.

"It is a present, the least I can do for my star pupil!"

Leaving the shopping in Mary's car, they strolled alone together on the beach and kicking off their sandals, they made their way along the shoreline in the warm afternoon sun. Mary did not mention her family while laughing, joking and appearing not to have a care in the world Suzanne skipped her way through the shallow water.

"Where are Tony and the children this afternoon? Are they at Tony's parents? How are they all keeping?"

Mary remained silent and did not answer the questions knowing her children would be very upset if they knew where she was and even more so if they had any idea in whose company.

"I did enjoy the half-term holiday and the time I spent with your family." Suzanne had clearly forgotten about the secrets discovered in the forbidden room over the garage at the Bowron's house.

The laughing girl ran on along the beach leaving Mary well behind. Following repeated distant cries from her elder companion, Suzanne waited for her to catch up.

An out of breath Mary spoke, "Suzanne Patterson I protest! You should not have done that! I am not as fit as I used to be, remember, there is nearly twenty years difference in our ages. In future do not even consider leaving me on my own ......ever!"

She smiled as Suzanne agreed never to repeat anything like that again.

"May I suggest that perhaps we return along the beach? I know of a very nice tea-room close to the town centre where we can take afternoon tea before I take you back to School."

Surprised at the distance covered in the previous hour, they turned and started to retrace their steps. The return started in relative silence only broken after fifteen minutes by Suzanne.

"I am really thankful for the support you have given me, not only with my School work, but also your personal efforts in trying to help me overcome my family problems. You have been very sweet, but however can I be expected to repay your kindness? I owe you such a terrific debt of gratitude."

"If that is what you want, but now is not the time, not this year. Perhaps next, or even the following year, but one day, sometime in the future, I am sure you will be able to repay me."

They walked slowly side by side along the sand, close enough for Mary to smell the sweet fragrance and feel warmth radiating from the young body. Taking Suzanne's hand she gently entwined their fingers as they progressed along the beach.

Following a hurried afternoon tea in Bournemouth, it was just before five when Mary Bowron dropped her favourite pupil back at St Bernadette's and following goodbyes and thanks, hurried off to tell her family of the afternoon she had spent working hard at School.

It was the middle of the next week when a letter addressed to Suzanne arrived at St Bernadette's that was to seal the eventual fate of both her and Henry Patterson.

*****

Having eaten very little at breakfast Suzanne returned to the

40

house common room and was surprised to find a blue envelope sticking-out of her pigeonhole; it was immediately recognised as the type her father used to correspond with. Removing it, Suzanne went out into the cobbled courtyard, past the small stone cottage which acted as the School sanatorium and where the Matron, Sister Patricia, lived and worked. On she walked, through the wrought-iron gate and into the open grounds.

Suzanne stopped under an aged walnut tree. Her bedroom was on the uppermost floor of the old mansion from where, peering through the stone balustrade surrounding the top of the building, she always had sight of its spreading and gnarled shadow. As indicated by the painted warning sign nailed into the trunk about ten feet from the ground half of it was dangerously dead, but this also acted as a home for a pair of noisy Screech owls. The sound of their nocturnal adventures through the open bedroom window would often awake her from a deep sleep in the middle of the night. Away from the School, alone and with back resting against the tree, she sat on the ground.

Before opening the envelope Suzanne looked hard at the handwriting on the outside; it was the familiar black ink scrawl of her father. She had only received a letter from him on Monday, as was his usual correspondence it had been very short, but intuition told her today's was something very different than the normal. She paused before hurriedly tearing it open while thinking that after all this time perhaps it contained news about her mother. Slowly Suzanne began to read the contents, she noted twelve pages, more than six times the usual length of his letters.

It started with the rather stunning news that Henry had resigned his position at the University and in less than six weeks at the end of July would be leaving. He apologised profusely for not having discussed the matter beforehand with Suzanne, but went on to explain he had had no wish to put her under further pressure. Mother's ill health, examinations and the fact in recent months he had found so little time for his daughter were all given as excuses for not having communicated his intentions earlier.

Goodness knows what his daughter had been going through in the past year, but he admitted the strain had been too much for him. With his work at the University unrelenting, feeling at a point not far off of breaking, he was convinced the price of staying would be permanent damage to his health. When approached the Authorities had reluctantly agreed to his early retirement. After long discussion a decision had been made to replace him and he could go, but they felt it was almost certain the successor would be far less experienced.

Leaving with everybody's blessing meant, in addition to his sizeable pension, for recognition of the thirty-three years of his life given to work and research at Oxford, he would be receiving ex-gratia from the University a large tax-free lump sum.

What Henry Patterson did not tell his daughter was following a letter he had submitted over a year ago, he had been negotiating his resignation for the past twelve months.

"I will sell Norham Gardens".

Suzanne could not believe what she was reading; her mother and father had lived there for over twenty years. What madness had overtaken him? She read on.

The regular income provided by his University pension, the proceeds from the sale of the house, together with monies coming from astute investments made for him in the past by his solicitor, meant future finance should not prove to be a headache.

Suzanne turned the page.

She did not move, she read on, but did not hear the bell ringing from the top of the clock tower situated on the stable block at the rear of the old mansion. It was calling the girls to prayer and morning assembly.

He wrote about a recent lecture visit to Montpellier University in the South of France.

"But surely" she asked herself aloud, "That was eighteen months ago?"

She was puzzled, but tried not to give it another thought, perhaps she was mistaken. Suzanne continued reading.

When his leaving the University had been agreed, he set wheels in motion to buy a property he had seen on his visit to France. Such were the low house prices in those parts the University's payment more than covered the purchase.

Suzanne shook her head in amazement.

Henry wrote he hoped that her exams had gone well, now she could relax a little, it would be one thing less for her to worry about.

"As long as I do not get too many letters like the one I am reading," Suzanne thought aloud. She gave a wry smile before carrying on.

Her father said she was not to be disappointed if her results were not all at the top of the scale. If that was the case promising not to be cross, but still would like Suzanne to finish her schooling at St Bernadette's at the end of the current summer term. Henry wanted her to leave and go to live with him in the south of France. He assured her he would not be travelling or working all hours as in the past. Suzanne could paint all day and in-between times help him keep the attached small holding up-together, but only if she wanted to.

Henry wrote enthusiastically. He would have his books and she would have her paintbrushes. They would just enjoy each other's company in the Mediterranean warmth. She could spend holidays visiting her friends in England or the pair of them could go anywhere in Europe Suzanne wanted. The letter took her breath away. For a sixteen-year-old who as a young girl had travelled very little and never been outside the shores of her homeland, it seemed a very tempting proposition.

Money would not be a problem as he would pay

Suzanne a regular monthly allowance. If her pride stood in the way and she considered the money had not been earned, her domestic and culinary talents would more than compensate Henry for the payments.

"Compared with the fumes of Oxford, the fresh air in this part of rural France is as pure nectar" Henry wrote. *"An ideal place to sit and paint without the interruptions of everyday life, breathtaking scenery........."*

He spent a whole page of the letter reciting the various benefits to be gained if she joined him on *"This exciting journey to pastures new."* He need not have worried because she had already made up her mind.

As she came to the end of the letter, she was brought down to earth by the authoritarian voice of Sister Clare, who was standing over her as Suzanne looked up.

"Suzanne Patterson, do you intend going to Assembly this morning? Is it really necessary to hide behind a tree in the School grounds to avoid doing so?"

Suzanne jumped to her feet, apologetically spluttering a reply the kindly Sister Clare did not understand. As the rest of St Bernadette's staff she had heard of the girl's family problems and had no wish to upset the pupil further, especially as it was so close to the end of term. Assuring herself on this occasion there was nothing wrong or untoward happening, she told Suzanne to be on her way.

"Get yourself to the first lesson of the morning, but in future please ensure you do not miss Assembly and morning prayers, whatever the reason."

Suzanne thanked the elderly nun profusely and ran off towards the narrow wooden bridge.

She had noticed the letter the girl had been reading and guessed it was from her father, but did not press for any detail. As the rest of the nuns and staff, Sister Clare had been made fully aware of the circumstances presently surrounding the girl's mother.

In her haste to get away, Suzanne did not see what

44

the letter had failed to mention. What was to become of her mother? It begged the question, if husband and daughter left for France what would become of Henry Patterson's wife? It was written as if Elaine never existed.

Within the week, it was apparent from the Reverend Mother's actions the news of Henry's plans for Suzanne had reached the School. It was made clear to the staff at St Bernadette's that she was in full support.

".........the girl will therefore not be returning to do her A levels in September."

Within her small circle of friends, Suzanne kept her own counsel; none of them realising her future was to be different from their own and she would not be returning to the School at the beginning of the next autumn term. The staff, with one notable exception, was pleased for her and agreed she could happily leave without causing herself or St Bernadette's too much anguish. They all perceived her as a complex child with highly strung parents although it was unanimously agreed Suzanne had never been a great problem for them.

The exception was art mistress Mary Bowron. The week following the news having been given to a hushed staff room that Suzanne would not be coming back in the autumn, she reported in from home sick. Lacking the courage to say goodbye to her favourite pupil, she did not return to work at St Bernadette's until the beginning of the new school year.

*****

1989 was the last year in St Bernadette's history. The aging nuns who made up the Teaching Order and had responsibility for the running of the School were facing the problem of falling pupil numbers; this brought additional financial pressures on an already hard stretched School budget. All concerned, Accountants, Lawyers and Bankers sadly advised to save themselves the embarrassment of insolvency the School had no alternative but immediate closure.

In July of that year, nearly twelve months to the day after Suzanne had followed the same path, the last pupil was driven away down the driveway and by the following October the Order had been disbanded. In November 1990, a large part of the by then empty mansion was destroyed by fire and that is how today, over twenty years later, the building stands damaged, blackened by soot, roofless and open to the ravages of nature.

Chapter 5

Situated to the north east of Marseilles, the Cevennes is a rugged upland area of Southern France. It stretches from Anduze in the south to Le Pays en Velay at its northern extremity. From Florac in the west to St Ambroix in the east and while not supporting the high peaks of better-known French mountainous regions at the heart it is extremely isolated. In area the Cevennes covers in excess of four thousand square miles.

Because of the distance by road from Paris and La Manche, it is a region relatively unvisited by the British and there is no direct Autoroute access. The Cevennes is not an area gastronomically blessed and, compared with the vast majority of French cuisine, the food is plain and simple. The inhospitable terrain does not allow for extensive farming, but at its unmarked southern border it is less than forty miles from the Mediterranean Sea and therefore does not suffer the winter snows that plague other French mountain ranges.

For half of the year, from above the small town of St Jean du Gard the view looks damp and forlorn. Here cold winds of the mistral blow across the hilltops seeking the unprepared and for those six months the views are as daunting as any to be found in winter mainland Europe. For the rest of the year the hills, reaching as far northwards as the naked eye can see, lie parched by the summer heat.

Amongst these mountainous tops are many hidden valleys where fast tumbling streams and tributaries feed the rivers flowing south before they empty into the sea. Having escaped the extremities of the caverns and gorges of their highland sources, along the banks of the Gard, Hérault, Tarn and Lot the local population endeavour to grow vines and it is testimony to their efforts that in quantity, if not quality, they succeed as the region produces more wine than any other in France.

The majority of inhabitants in the Cevennes are of the

Protestant faith, but France is a Country where for centuries the population following the word of Rome has far outnumbered those with simpler beliefs. It was here, deep in the mountains during the Wars of Religion that following the misguided attempt by Louis XlV to unify his Kingdom, the Camisards, led by Fous de Dieu, secretly practiced their faith. It was to this mysterious region Henry Patterson turned, arriving with his daughter during the summer of 1988.

*****

Suzanne came to France exactly one month after the end of St Bernadette's term. Immediately School finished she returned home to Norham Gardens, whilst father took her cases from the Volvo, she climbed the steps and let herself into the house and was not ready for what greeted her.

Moving from room to room, on the ground floor Suzanne discovered although curtains still remained at the window the interiors were mostly bare; the exception to the denuded was the kitchen where some semblance of the previous order still remained. Dropping two large suitcases on the hallway floor Henry joined her. He saw the look of horror on Suzanne's face and quickly explained.

"I have already disposed of most of the furniture in the house, but your room remains untouched. I thought it was only right you should pack away your own belongings."

"I did not realise things would happen quite so quickly." Her comment was not one of anger but one of surprise.

She moved out of the kitchen and up the stairs to her room. Suzanne could see at once father was as good as his word as the room lay undisturbed and remained just how she had left it after the Easter holiday. Silently entering the room, Henry followed through the open door behind her.

He started to explain. "If we are to leave England for France in four weeks we have very little time to make all of

48

our arrangements. My work at the University is winding-down, but it still leaves me with a very tight schedule."

As at that stage he had no wish to upset his daughter, Henry did not tell her the house had already been sold to a Fellow of Jesus College called Savin. It seemed to him Suzanne had accepted most of what he had said without a large amount of question; maybe it was the ritual sense of adventure and the thought of starting a new canvas in her life with long days under the Mediterranean sun? Henry Patterson did not know the answer, but was aware of receiving very few questions since telling of his plans.

It did not take long for Suzanne to pack the few precious belongings as a sixteen year old she possessed. During the following three weeks, Henry arranged for the rest of the furniture to be removed and the few larger items he intended they should take with them were shipped-out via Paris and Clermont Ferrand.

The last week father and daughter were in England they stayed at the Cotswold Gateway Hotel. Situated in the Banbury Road it was convenient for Henry's final trips to the University and for Suzanne's numerous forays into Oxford City centre to purchase the little things considered necessary for the journey and their new life in France. Items somehow only the English abroad might want such as her father's *Marmite* and *Frank Cooper's Oxford Marmalade*; both of which she had heard it said by girls at School were unavailable in shops across the other side of the English Channel.

On the Sunday evening before the planned departure, following the Hotel's more than adequate dinner Henry spoke to Suzanne.

"I am going as promised to the offices of Adkins, the estate agents in the High to drop the keys for Norham Gardens through their letter box. Do you want to come?"

"No, I don't think so, thank you." Having declined her father's invitation she then asked "If I am quick would

49

you mind if I went alone for a few minutes to take one last look at the inside of the empty house?"

Somewhat reluctantly Henry agreed. Fifteen minutes later at twenty past seven Suzanne was letting herself in through the front door. She walked slowly though the echoing spaces, occasionally stopping as a particular room evoked one or other childhood memory. There was father's den, the drawing room, the attic bedroom where all the nannies had slept, including Rachel, who had been her own favourite. The separate bedrooms of her parents and her own room where in recent years it seemed so little time had been spent.

After nearly thirty minutes Suzanne crossed the hallway to the front exit and left the house for the last time pulling the door firmly shut and as a final act turning the lock. It was just past eight when Suzanne handed the small bunch of keys back to the waiting Henry.

He climbed into the newly acquired left hand drive Land Rover, having the previous week part-exchanged the two older cars at Hartwell's Garage in the Botley Road.

"In the terrain where we are going" Henry said, "Four-wheel drive vehicles make more sense, beside it is the perfect motor for moving our personal effects," which was clearly shown by its laden state in readiness for the next day's journey.

Returning by nine and parking the loaded vehicle into the hotel's garage, the receptionist told Henry his daughter had already gone to her room and left a message for him saying she was tired and tomorrow was an early start with a very long day ahead of them. On receiving the news Henry smiled to himself, perhaps he would allow himself one celebratory drink before he too settled down for the night. Moving through to an empty Hotel lounge he asked the waiting barman for a large Glenfiddich.

*****

Their new home was very isolated; situated some fifteen

kilometres from the nearest small village, Pont de Monvert, it was placed at the bottled end of a very narrow green valley where the rocky sides rose steeply towards the stunted evergreen oaks covering the ground like hundreds of similar hilltops in the Cevennes, all reaching towards the high-point of La Mejaric.

Standing at the head of the valley the stone constructed house which once had been part of a working farm was now set to become their new residence. In total, besides the moderately sized farmhouse, the property consisted of two barns and numerous smaller outbuildings. A further eight hundred metres away lay a small-disused cottage. Five kilometres later the trail joined the unclassified road running over the hills to Pont de Monvert.

Alongside the track, falling from a series of steep waterfalls situated in the woodland that rose behind the farmhouse, a fast flowing stream passed down the valley. The waters ran continuously throughout the seasons of the year and for a short distance there was a narrow strip of cultivable land either side of the watercourse.

Henry had been over to France in the previous months, buying, selling and making the necessary arrangements. After their two day car journey Suzanne arrived at the old farmhouse on 21st August and quickly decided it would need a lot of feminine attention before she could truly call it home, but on that hot sunny day could not help herself and immediately fell in love with the beautiful setting.

As her father unloaded the boxes and cases from the Land Rover, she moved around exploring their new house. One by one Suzanne inspected the rooms, they were set on three floors and most of the furniture that had belonged to the previous occupants remained; it was of traditional dark French design and most of it had seen many years of use.

The house had three bedrooms, one for father, one for her and the room which had been constructed under the roof, high in the space running along the upper part of the building. Henry said the beds were fine to use and had ordered new mattresses which he would collect as soon as possible from a furniture store in Florac.

The kitchen, with a large traditional pine table as its centrepiece, had a log-burning stove and oven on which she would have the new experience of cooking meals, but after a little practice it was something Suzanne was certain could be mastered. She carried-on exploring the surrounding buildings, whilst at the front of the house her father continued with the unloading.

"What do you think of what you've seen so far?"

"Wonderful!" was the joyous cry back from Suzanne as she slipped from one structure to another. At the third and best repaired of three single-story buildings she pushed open the door and called to her father.

"Your mahogany writing bureau and large oval oak table have already arrived from England."

Suzanne's father came to investigate.

"Obviously the French carrier was unable to gain entry into the house and has stored the furniture in the best place he could find available rather than having to make another tortuous journey back along the track."

Henry took her arm and guided Suzanne towards the barn standing at the rear of the farmhouse. Hurriedly he ushered her forward, explaining all the while.

"The building at the front of the farmhouse needs some repairs to make it storm proof; only then can it be used for winter stabling for any animals we eventually decide to keep." He reached the door of the rear barn, "but this is for you."

Pushing the heavy wooden door open, he pulled her though and exclaimed.

"This will be yours, your own studio where you can paint and work as long as you wish!"

Suzanne looked around the interior. From the direction they had approached the wall of the building had shown no windows, but it was clear from the light streaming from the open opposite side with the addition of glass, numerous window frames and very little interior work the place would make an idea area for her.

Henry Patterson was trying so hard to please his wife's daughter.

*****

The weeks passed quickly by and soon the summer turned unnoticed into the mellow time of autumn. The days gradually shortened from their long span, the nights began to lengthen and the change brought cool relief from the extremely hot month of August. By mid-November the bleak cold winter had arrived. Whilst none of the other utilities had reached the lonely farmhouse, surprisingly, electricity was the exception. This lack of services included telephone communication, whilst water had to be hand drawn from a deep well situated a short distance away in front of the disused cottage.

The first year passed very quickly. The interior of the farmhouse, although lacking the refinements of their former home, was in no time basically respectable. Suzanne kept it clean and in a very orderly fashion, making a perfect housekeeper and companion for her father. Henry spent most of his days tending and cultivating the land running alongside the ever-flowing stream. As with most houses in the poorer rural regions of France, the exterior maintenance did not match the loving care given to the interior and outwardly the building retained an air of abandonment.

One promise he fulfilled was to have the work completed on the barn so turning it into suitable premises for Suzanne to use as her own studio; renovations were complete six weeks after their arrival by Henry employing a local carpenter and his son. The senior of the two men was called Claude Ricard, his son's name, much to the older Patterson's amusement, was Henri. Daily the two

53

workmen drove from Pont de Monvert to make and fit window frames into the large gaps down the side of the farm building. Although simple in design, the work took over four weeks to complete.

Monday to Saturday, arriving before seven in the morning; each day promptly at noon they would disappear down the farm track in their battered Renault truck, only to re-appear four hours later in the afternoon. When questioned by Henry about their daily work pattern the answer would either be "La dejeuner!" or "La Soliel!" An afternoon visit to the shade of Madame Louiser's bar situated in a small village nearly twenty kilometres away would probably have been a more accurate answer.

The day the two of them arrived with large sheets of glass to fit also caused Henry a little consternation. They had bounced up the rough and uneven track with the fragile cargo loosely falling around in the back of their truck; the purchaser had visions of having to pay for the glass more than once if the job was to be completed satisfactory. Yet again, the older of the two Frenchmen just shrugged his shoulders. "Monsieur Henry, why do you Anglais always have to worry? The glass is safe, it has not moved and it is as when loaded. Exactement!"

After six weeks all the work was complete and Claude and Henri simply disappeared. In the following months and year no one else was to visit the isolation of the new Patterson home. Once a week Henry drove forty kilometres to visit Florac or Mende for their supplies, but he always made the journey alone.

About eighteen months after their arrival it was supper-time. Sitting in silence at opposite ends of the large pine kitchen table where they always took their meals together it was Suzanne who broke the silence and first raised the subject.

"Father, are you happy living alone as we do?"

Henry realising there must be a good reason for the question paused before answering.

"Why do you ask?" hurriedly adding, "The answer to your question is 'Yes'. I am very happy living here, but that is not to say very occasionally I feel lonely, life is very different from Oxford."

Suzanne sat in silence eating the rest of her meal while Henry stared down the table and asked himself what was bothering her. There must be a reason for her to ask the question.

She looked up, but still said nothing. He averted his eyes and continued eating. Five minutes later the silence was broken with Suzanne's explanation.

"I am nearly eighteen years old and although very happy living alone in one of the most beautiful places on earth with my father, who I love very much, I would still like to have occasional sight of the outside world."

Suzanne continued.

"I can live without radio and television, which since coming to France we no longer possess. I can also live without newspapers and magazines, but what I do long for is to see the shops. Yes, I agree you have been very kind in ensuring I have everything required. You fetch the grocery shopping every week and you buy the material so I am able to make my own pretty dresses. I like that because you are always so very clever in choosing the correct material and colours and get very excited to see you so pleased when I wear the finished garments. I enjoy being allowed to paint as I have never been allowed to paint before. I also enjoy the cooking, tending the vegetable garden and keeping house, but it is not the same."

She paused.

He shifted uneasily on his high-back wooden chair, empty plate pushed back and hands clasped in front of him, Henry glared at his daughter. He said nothing, but allowed Suzanne to continue.

"I feel as if I am a prisoner shut away from the real world and all I want really is to see other human-beings and walk down the street looking at goods displayed in shop windows, normal everyday things." Defensively adding, "I am sure that you are aware I would never use the situation as a reason for wasting our money, I would be very careful with anything I spent."

Chapter 6

The following Wednesday more than one Frenchman's
head turned to admire Mademoiselle as the arm in arm
couple, a middle-aged gentleman with greying hair and a
very attractive blonde young lady, walked along the main
street of Florac. The happy twosome laughed and joked
their way down the thoroughfare gaining people's attention
as they stopped in front of the various brightly coloured
stalls, looking, examining and sometimes buying the goods
on offer.

It was market day and Henry had come to the small
town to do the weekly shop. Prompted by Suzanne's
outburst at the supper table two days previously, he had
invited his daughter to join him and excitedly she had
agreed.

Sadly, Henry's future invitations did not extend to
every week as more often than not he would leave the
farmhouse early in the morning before sunrise and it would
be late evening before he got back. On his return there
would be no offer of an explanation or description about the
day, in silence he ate the meal put before him and kept his
thoughts to himself. Suzanne quickly came to recognise
these moods and thought that sometimes things were best
left alone, leaving the kitchen she would return to her room.
Suzanne would never challenge Henry about the events of
the day and soon learnt to accept things as they were.

After the initial twelve months, having sufficiently
repaired the barn at the front of the house to provide the
necessary shelter the goats and sheep required at the height
of the winter, her father started to keep animals. He also
succeeded in cultivating the rich area of soil between the
farmhouse and stream and soon was growing all the fresh
vegetables and soft fruit required.

It was late on a Wednesday afternoon in the spring of
1990. Henry Patterson had made the customary weekly
journey without her. Alone in the kitchen preparing their

evening meal she did not hear the Land Rover lurching back up the track and it wasn't until Henry called aloud as he entered the house to find her exact whereabouts did she know of his return. Wiping her hands on the clean white kitchen apron she was wearing, Suzanne immediately stopped what she was doing. Descending the single step from the passageway her father entered the kitchen and she threw her arms around his neck in greeting.

Seemingly very pleased with himself Henry spoke.

"And what sort of day has it been for you my dear?"

"Fine, but first I must tell you that at last I have finished the painting I have been struggling to complete, you know the one showing the view and the front of the farmhouse."

Henry just smiled, but did not reply. Suzanne was puzzled as her father appeared to be in an extremely happy and buoyant mood, something recently she found increasingly rare. Pleasantries dispensed with and before his daughter could speak again, Henry interjected.

"I have something very important to tell you. I want you to come with me and greet the two people I have brought home for you to meet." Puzzled by her father, Suzanne did not move.

"Come on don't be shy follow me!"

With that Henry turned and briskly marched out of the room. Curiosity aroused, she followed him from the kitchen to the front of the farmhouse. In the evening sunlight he stopped in the doorway and pointed to a couple standing some distance away next to his parked vehicle. With aplomb and as a Master of Ceremonies introducing two top performers to their audience, he waved and turned towards Suzanne.

"It is my great pleasure to introduce Jean and his beautiful wife Claudine!"

Speechless, his daughter remained on the top step

"Jean and Claudine are set to become our new neighbours; they will be moving into the vacant property over there!" With gusto and pride, he pointed to the dilapidated cottage standing opposite the well.

Before the two new arrivals had moved from their spot Suzanne hissed at her father.

"Whatever the reason for this intrusion it is breaking our agreement. However hard I sometimes find it, I have no wish to end our isolation by having people live so close by. If this is to be a permanent arrangement why didn't you consult with me beforehand?"

Oblivious to his daughter's protestations Henry continued.

" To begin with Jean will be working to put the cottage in order, he seems to have the necessary basic practical building and joinery skills and that is why I chose this young and unemployed Frenchman. Until he has repaired the roof and the cottage is ready for them to live in they will stay in the farmhouse. They can use the empty space at the top of the building and join us for their main meal of the day. Claudine, when not helping her husband with the renovations, will assist me by helping to tend our ever growing number of goats and sheep, besides helping you keep the vegetable garden together."

Suzanne stifled a cry of dismay, whilst with an air of firmness Henry continued.

"I would remind you, in recent weeks you have constantly been complaining to me about having to dirty yourself by looking after the animals and it is you who are always telling me you would much rather be doing something else than tending to the garden."

Her shoulders drooped with an air of resignation, saying nothing she stood firmly fixed to the spot.

Momentarily it was as if the whole scene being acted out at the end of their valley was frozen in time. Father, daughter and the two strangers, the only background sound seemed to be coming from the babbling stream and waterfall.

It was Henry who broke the spell, at the same time as

scornfully speaking to Suzanne, he removed from behind his back a large cardboard box.

"Perhaps you could put to good use this latest consignment of oil paints, but before doing so please be polite to our new employees."

He called Jean and Claudine towards him and in a very formal English manner introduced the young French couple to a very confused Suzanne.

Jean was twenty-six, dark haired, a little over six feet tall, physically very fit and, like his wife, of Algerian blood, the two of them seemed well suited. He was tall and handsome, the only blemish on his dark facial skin being a four-inch scar to the side of his right eye; Suzanne noticed it only when he turned his head towards her.

Claudine was shorter than her husband and in Suzanne's opinion not as physically attractive, she possessed a well-rounded figure, slightly over weight, but this was compensated by her very pretty facial features. With her shortly cropped hair Suzanne's immediate visual thoughts were of France's patron Saint.

Suzanne had forgotten, because none of the retailers in the neighbouring market towns stocked professional artists' materials, to acquire the box of paints her father would have had to journey a greater distance than was usual for a Wednesday.

The nearest such shop was to be found in a southeasterly direction in Alés which was on the road to the City of Nimes and the opposite direction to the regular weekly route he took. Henry had first told her about it some eight months ago.

What Henry did not tell Suzanne was that on one of his infrequent visits to Alés he had first encountered Jean and Claudine. He had found them sitting in a bar located in a rundown area of the City.

Over several glasses of wine he talked at some length and took to them immediately.

As many young people living in the region, he

discovered both were unemployed. Jean in his earlier days had served his time as a builder's apprentice and Claudine, a very practical and domesticated woman, had been brought up on her late father's farm which was situated some distance away in Orange. The pair had no ties Henry therefore considered they were ideal for what he had in mind.

"You can live at the farmhouse, I will pay a small weekly retainer and in time, when the work on the cottage is complete, you will have a home of your own. To begin with, whilst you are living under the same roof as my daughter and I, we will feed you."

"What will be expected of us?" Claudine had asked inquisitively.

"That is simple" Henry replied, "Jean will help restore the cottage and work on the small-holding. You can pay your way by practicing the housekeeping skills you learnt in childhood. The only other person living at the farmhouse is my eighteen year old daughter."

"I will return here at mid-day on Wednesday in four weeks time, but in the meantime you should both consider my generous offer. If you find other employment within the month or if for some other reason you decide you have no desire to join us just don't bother to keep the lunchtime rendezvous. If your decision is to accept, all you have to do is be here, together with any luggage you may wish to bring."

An hour after Henry had departed, Jean was still drinking alone in the Bar contemplating the offer that had been made. A returning Claudine rejoined him at the Bar.

"We have nothing therefore we have nothing to lose."

Jean smiled at his wife and chuckled, his eyes were smiling too, the scar showing more prominently as the skin creased. He spoke quietly to Claudine.

"Perhaps, just perhaps, it is our lucky day. Perhaps we have everything to gain."

Four weeks later shortly after twelve, a box of paints

tucked under his left arm, Henry strode through the beaded curtain covering the entranceway to the small Café-Bar. He had been sure the French couple would say 'Yes' and was certain he had done enough to convince the pair at the first meeting the proposed arrangements would be to a mutual advantage.

Henry Patterson was not to be disappointed.

Looking around the crowded smoke filled room, he saw Jean and Claudine sitting at a corner table awaiting their new Master's arrival, alongside them lay a single battered leather case containing all their worldly belongings.

The fate of Father and Daughter had been sealed.

*****

Suzanne thanked Henry profusely for the present of paints he had brought back and, whilst trying to avoid the scarred stare of Jean, kissed her father lightly on the cheek before making her way to the building at the rear of the farmhouse that served as her studio.

Jean watched as she strutted across the open ground towards the former barn. As Suzanne walked away from the other three, he could swear the girl was provocatively moving her hips for his benefit. Henry drew his attention away.

"Come on you two follow me and I will show you around your new home. Claudine, instead of struggling with that case just leave it at the front door of the farmhouse and later I will show you the way to your temporary room in the attic, but right now I want to show you your future home."

Henry marched away down the track, past the well, before stopping in front of the deserted building. Claudine followed closely behind him, but Jean held back before joining his wife, together the three pushed open the one-hinged door.

Suzanne had completed over thirty paintings since

her arrival from England, about half of them hung from the walls of the studio. She crossed to an old tea chest and sat looking at the shadows falling from the tall window and growing longer in the evening light.

"Why?" she asked herself, "Why, why do we need others to come and share their lives with us?"

She knew it was true her father could do with more help. The goats he had introduced were proving to be a great success and the cheese he had learnt to produce from their milk always found ready purchasers when taken to the market in Florac. She hated the animals with a passion

"But why hadn't he spoken to me before making any decision about bringing Jean and Claudine to live and work in our secret world?"

At eighteen years of age, Suzanne was beginning to feel it was only correct she should have some say in their joint future. As she grew older she also felt her father appeared to be slowly distancing her from any thoughts she might have of her mother and Suzanne was not sure if she liked that either.

With daylight finally disappearing Suzanne was alone in her bedroom. She unbuttoned her thin cotton blue dress and let it fall lightly to cover her bare feet. Stepping out of her underwear she stood naked in front of the full-length mirror on the front of the wardrobe that had just been another piece of the inherited aging French furniture.

Staring at the reflection in the glass, she ran her soft hands over the suntanned skin and combed her long blonde hair so it rested on her narrow shoulders; Suzanne Patterson had become very aware of the firm young breasts and the shapely curves of her upper body. She reached for the long cotton nightdress hanging over the end of the large double bed, put it over her head and adjusted the hair so it once more lay over her shoulders.

Suzanne again looked into the mirror; the outline of her young figure was clearly visible through the thin material. She saw a picture of beautiful innocence with a mind and body suffering the frustrations of wanting to express themselves, but discovering they were not in a position to do so. An hour later, alone in the darkness, Suzanne's tears slipped to the pillow as she slowly fell into the deep chasm offered by sleep.

Chapter 7

The weeks passed and life settled into a familiar if somewhat different pattern. The new couple soon proved to Henry he had made the right choice; they kept themselves to themselves and were extremely hard-working. Claudine was well organized and had soon taken over the majority of the day-to-day cooking duties, allowing Henry's daughter more time for her painting. Taking the tools of her trade with her, on sunny days Suzanne would walk into the surrounding hills and often could be found sitting working alone on the rocks, while far below her father could be seen happily tending to chores around the farm.

The young Frenchman, tall and good looking, worked swiftly and efficiently to restore the cottage and such was the speed Jean worked it was not long before he and his wife were able to leave their room amongst the rafters of the farmhouse for the less confining spaces of their new quarters.

It was a late June morning towards the end of the couple's first month in their new cottage residence and Suzanne was sitting facing the farmhouse in front of her easel. She was near completing a picture showing the buildings in the foreground nestling in the valley. The view was unusual as it faced away from the natural green backdrop and showed the track winding away from the house and into the distance. The colour of the lavender growing on the distant hills offered the picture a special aura which, together with the heat haze from the sun, gave the whole scene a feeling of lost in time.

Suzanne looked at her watch. With midday approaching the temperature on the hillside was nearly unbearable, it was time for lunch after which she could return to the shade and relative coolness of her studio; gathering her things together she slowly made the way down to the farmhouse. While still some distance from the building she watched as Claudine leant from the kitchen window and called.

"Suzanne! Suzanne! Please will you do me a favour? I am at a critical time with my baking preparation."

As if trying to justify her request she held up her two arms, both of which were covered to the elbow in flour. "Could you take Jean's lunch over to the cottage?"

Suzanne stopped in her tracks; she knew Claudine normally never missed a day taking the lunchtime food to her husband.

"Jean will be very annoyed if, because of my cooking, he has to break from his work and come over here to eat. I am already more than three-quarters of an hour later than usual getting it to him."

It didn't take long for Suzanne to agree.

After quickly returning her painting material to the barn, she collected the simple lunch from the farmhouse and made her way to the rear of the cottage, calling aloud as she entered the restored kitchen area. Receiving no reply, she shouted his name once more, but again there was no answer.

Suzanne left the covered plate and half-finished bottle of wine on a ledge at the side of the room before passing along the narrow passageway and leaving by the front door. Wherever he is working, she thought, Jean should be able to find the delivery left in the kitchen. Before reaching the gate at the end of the small overgrown garden she heard a muffled voice calling her name.

"Suzanne," "Suzanne," "Suzanne," once, twice, three times, "Ici!"

She turned to face the cottage and looked up; at a window to which he had been fitting a new wooden shutter stood the Frenchman. Suzanne quickly considered how long had he known of her presence in the cottage?

Stripped to the waist and wearing only the skimpiest pair of shorts, Jean was dressed for working in the hot mid-day sun. He suggestively stretched his seasoned torso across the opening.

"Merci ma Cheri, merci!"

Suzanne blushed and whilst her young eyes were still fixed on the scantily dressed figure, Jean mockingly blew her a kiss. Shocked, she turned on to the track and hastily made towards the safety of the farmhouse. Watching her from his raised vantage point, Suzanne could hear him laughing heartily as she ran all the way back without stopping, immediately going to hide away in the confines and security of her studio.

The strange thing about Suzanne's lunchtime experience was in following days she felt compelled to make herself available for Claudine, always offering to take his lunch to the cottage, but it was always from afar Jean admired the pretty Englishwoman. Never attempting to hold a proper conversation with his lunchtime visitor, never getting physically close to Suzanne, it was if knowingly he was tantalising the fantasies of her young mind.

Suzanne always took her own lunch with Henry; never at anytime mentioning to her father the pains of young adulthood she was experiencing. The days Suzanne had no need to make the excursion to the cottage always seemed to coincide with Jean being away from the valley. Having in the morning driven her father's Land Rover down the bumpy track, he was then always absent for several hours, and increasingly in recent weeks seemed to be spending more and more time away.

When one day challenged by his daughter, Henry explained.

"I am allowing Jean to use the vehicle to collect materials he needs to complete the restoration work. It is not for you to worry about what he gets up to and you would do best to mind your own business," he snapped.

In spite of Jean's journeys, Henry still completed his own weekly trips to market to fetch goods and supplies; only very occasionally taking Suzanne with him, sometimes he took Jean, but never together. It was during one of her father's solitary trips the storm began to break.

The French couple were both in the attic room gathering the last of their few belongings for the renovated building, where work was now complete.

Suzanne was on the ground floor of the farmhouse, but she heard it all.

First it sounded as if heavy objects were being thrown followed by a raised voice. It was Claudine screaming at her husband, and then came the calm, relaxed and deep tones of the Frenchman, followed by more female abuse and then there was silence.

A loud bump came next, it sounded as if Jean had thrown her across the room. Once more Claudine screamed at the top of her voice before yelling at Jean, from above there was a further dull thud on the floor and for the first time the sound of his voice raised in anger.

Suzanne hid in the drawing room at the sound of feet descending the ladder from the roof space before they noisily clattered down the first floor flight of stairs and into the hallway. The front door banged shut and finally she heard the sound of boots crunching through loose gravel as Jean made his way back to the cottage. Suzanne could clearly hear Claudine sobbing uncontrollably in the upper room.

Upon his eventual return, she said nothing about the incident to Henry, but that night noted Jean slept in the cottage whilst Claudine remained in the farmhouse attic. The next day Suzanne mentioned to her father she had noticed that Claudine and Jean had spent the night apart.

"The sleeping arrangements the couple have are their own affair. Jean was probably preparing and making arrangements for their permanent move out of the farmhouse" was Henry's seemingly disinterested view on the matter.

Unlike her father, she became very wary; he had not

heard the argument that had taken place during his absence. During the following days Suzanne watched as the French couple seemed to be working around rather than with each other. Henry appeared not to notice, but for the husband and wife team one night of separation soon turned into two weeks. Meanwhile, Suzanne purposely avoided going to the cottage alone by excusing herself of the daily lunchtime errand, naively she thought it might give Claudine opportunity for reconciliation with her partner.

As the weeks continued the unthinkable seemed to just happen. Henry Patterson's attention for the young Frenchwoman grew, watching it appeared Claudine was slowly seducing the older man, whilst Jean just stood by and said nothing. It seemed he was rarely to be found around the farm and when he was appeared not to notice the growing relationship between Henry and his own wife, but Suzanne was certainly becoming aware something had changed and was different.

Perhaps it was what Claudine had said to her husband the evening of the first day Henry had been absent, telling him she had watched from afar the way he looked at their employer's daughter.

"Yes, of course I am jealous. Once upon a time, not so long ago, you kept those sort of looks for me and me alone" she told Jean. "I was very foolish to let the English girl start to bring you your lunch, but I am more than positive your feelings about her are not reciprocated, you are wasting your time. You are nothing but a cheat and a liar!"

Jean's thoughts were far worse, angrily retorting "How can you make such accusations about me when you are having an affair with him? When you have been licking the dick of a much older man! You are an ungrateful bitch! It was me who found Henry Patterson and it was me that found the meal ticket, our pot of gold for the future. Patterson will not be around forever and then somebody else will have to run the farm. You are an ungrateful slut from the gutter and would do well to remember that without me you have nothing at all!"

The sad truth about Jean's ranting was prior to that evening Claudine had not even considered bedding the older man. The thought had never crossed her mind. Whilst for Jean the Englishman's pretty young daughter was just the latest of his many self-imposed challenges, convincing himself the girl was a sweet young virgin who inwardly was just wanting and waiting to be swept off her feet by someone with his physic and Mediterranean charm.

Finally, five weeks later, Claudine swallowed her pride and moved from the farmhouse, to live back with her husband in the now fully restored cottage opposite the well.

*****

The summer went by. In the Cevennes August is the hottest of all months, that year some days were unbearable. The winter, although cold, damp and windswept, was easier than previous years and with the passing of time all of their everyday lives became more established. Spring and its delights, including the first lambs being born on the farm, followed the dark months and before the four had time to think summer was once more upon them.

For nearly a year life followed an undisturbed routine and there was an air of normality about everything, but Suzanne purposefully went out her way to avoid Jean, ensuring she was never left alone with the Frenchman for very long. His smiling eyes and the crinkled scar just gave her a feeling of unease, but she found there was still this strange attraction to him over which she had no control. Just viewed from a distance his mesmerizing smile and magnificent physique alone was enough to make the uncontrollable feelings inside of her grow.

Henry went about his work whilst Jean and Claudine continued to fulfil their roles as hired help, but now the couple were ensconced in the cottage and living entirely separate lives to the Patterson's. Every day Claudine went to the farmhouse to carryout her chores, but Jean was never seen to enter the building. Although not as the same high level as when they first arrived in France, father's attention for his daughter was constant. Suzanne continued painting and living her life in the same style but was only too aware of one change that had taken place to their original pattern. The same problem confronted her throughout the winter months; it was the growing relationship between Henry and Claudine.

There was nothing positive she could identify, but daily she saw the looks the Frenchwomen gave her father, her eyes followed him everywhere, Claudine was unable to hide it. Bothering with her everyday appearance by dressing a little smarter, seemingly always doing small things to please Henry whilst he always pretended not to notice, perhaps he did, but at the same time thought Suzanne had not.

It was shortly after midnight on a particularly hot and sticky night towards the end of August. Suzanne alone with her thoughts lay on the top of her unmade bed and gazed through the open window up to the twinkling night stars.

"How long will I have to live here?"

From her deep subconscious came the unwanted answer she had no wish to hear,

"Maybe forever!"

Her thoughts turned to Elaine.

"Whereabouts and how is my mother? Father never mentions her."

Feeling guilty Suzanne balanced her own question.

"But I never ask him, does he know the answers? If so why is he not talking to me about her?"

She turned, trying to rid herself of the guilt that as a taunting demon had now entered her mind. Tossing and turning she was unable to sleep.

"What of father?" she asked herself, "In recent months he seems to be so much happier, maybe it's the attention Claudine is giving him."

Suzanne accepted the affection she was able to give him was bound to be different than that offered by the other woman. Once more she turned.

"And last year there was the row I heard between Jean and his wife." Suzanne asked herself, "What was all that about?"

She had not discussed with anyone, including father, what she had heard that day. She suddenly sat bolt upright.

Deciding it was hopeless and there was no way sleep would come to her in the sticky oppressive heat of the house she rose from the bed and dressed in only her thin nightdress went to the bedroom door. Exiting and tiptoeing forward Suzanne made no sound as she turned the corner of the corridor, pleased to see there was no light coming from under the door of father's room. Creeping by she assumed he had had less trouble than her falling asleep. Suzanne remembered during supper he had complained of being exhausted, subsequently retiring to his bed a full two hours before her. She went down the stairs and quietly let herself out of the house.

Thinking at the time how the stones were hurting the bottom of her feet, she walked down and across to the stream. Suzanne searched in the darkness for the shadow of the fig tree where she would often rest from the heat of the daytime sun, knowing her only company would be the sound of water running over its rock-strewn course. On the soft ground under the spreading branches she lay down to rest and in no time at all was sound asleep.

Uncertain of how much time had passed, she was suddenly awakened from a deep sleep. Quickly gathering her thoughts, away to her left she was aware of someone moving along the track from the direction of the well towards the farmhouse. Suzanne sunk further into the shadow of the tree, watching as the moon appeared from behind the solitary cloud to reveal a figure nimbly slipping by en route to the house.

"No!" was her stifled cry. She was not mistaken, dressed as Suzanne in only a thin nightdress; the barefoot figure was that of the Frenchwoman.

The astonished onlooker peered through the shadowy darkness. Claudine had now entered through the door Suzanne had earlier emerged from. A light came on in her father's bedroom and moments later shadows were cast by the bedside light on to the curtained window as the intruder removed her night attire and fell into Henry's arms. Within seconds the room was plunged into darkness and the images disappeared; Suzanne sank to the ground in total disbelief. Sleep quickly returned, overtaking the thoughts now starting to race through her head and it wasn't until first light she awoke, cold and hungry.

Suzanne had no idea of what the time was. To be alone with her anger she hurried across to the studio where, having no wish for intrusion, she immediately bolted the door from the inside.

An hour later she watched from a window as her father left the farmhouse to tend to the morning needs of the animals. There was no sign of anyone else, Claudine had returned to the cottage before dawn while Suzanne had still been asleep recovering from the shock of having seen the night visitor.

Once back in the relative safety of her bedroom, Suzanne dressed and prepared herself for the new day. Despite the anger she harboured within towards Claudine and the growing sense of betrayal by her father, she felt unable to speak to either party about their secret relationship.

Two weeks later, well into the night, Suzanne lay awake in her bed, confused about the still developing situation of which she had no doubt.

"What does father think he is playing at? This is not the bargain we made in England. Jean, is he aware of his wife's affair and if so why doesn't he put a stop to it? The original deal which father made with him surely did not include the Frenchman's wife as well?"

Suzanne considered there were many questions now requiring answers. Her thoughts were suddenly interrupted by the unmistakeable sound of a latch lifting. It was followed by the front door being firmly shut in a quiet and controlled manner.

"Where is father going? Is it his turn to visit his new found mistress?"

Suzanne went to the window wanting to see him making his way to a clandestine meeting place, but there was no one, nothing. Returning to her bed, she thought it was her imagination and the front door had not been opened because father had now been in his room for some hours.

Suzanne's heart sank as she heard the unmistakable sound of unsure floorboards moving below the pressure of someone creeping along the corridor, once more it seemed Claudine was making her way to Henry's bedroom. If confirmation were needed she heard the clear sound as the door of her father's room was quietly opened and closed behind the night visitor.

Having no intention of sleeping until the matter was resolved, she waited an hour and with an air of determination eventually left the bed and made her way towards Henry's room. On reaching the door she tried the handle and found it firmly locked so gently knocked on the wood.

"Father, father are you there? Father, please speak to me."

There was no reply. Again and again she knocked, each time calling to her father and each series of knocks being louder than the previous.

Eventually Henry's voice was heard from within.

"Go back to your bedroom Suzanne, go back to bed."

By this time in an uncontrollable rage, Suzanne was hysterically hammering on the bedroom door with both fists. "I demand you let me into your room! I want to see for myself who is in there with you, please unlock the door and let me in. What are you trying to hide?"

The charade continued for several more minutes and then there was silence. Suzanne, her back now resting against the door, had slid to the ground.

"I am not going away until you let me into your room."

After some moments there was the sound of the lock turning, movement of the latch and then the bedroom door opened three inches. It wasn't the face of her father, but the image of the Frenchwoman who appeared in the gap.

"Go back to bed, go back to bed, you do not understand" Claudine whispered softly.

Suzanne, sitting in stunned silence on the floor, looked up.

"Go back to bed and leave us alone, you can see your father in the morning. Suzanne, go back and sleep."

The door closed and once more she heard the sound of the key turning the lock.

Devastated, Suzanne fled to her room and flung herself on to the bed. She lay there sobbing, working herself into a climatic frenzy and only when spent did she fall into a deep sleep.

Chapter 8

After the troubled night daily routines seemed to carry on as before. Suzanne still did not have the determination or strength to broach the subject with Henry or Claudine, but did find some solace in the fact she was as certain as she could be the Frenchwoman no longer made night visits to her father.

What Suzanne did not realise was her father had no wish to bring an end to what he thought was a new found caring relationship, but at the same time neither did Henry Patterson have any wish to further hurt the feelings of his daughter. He was convinced in-time Suzanne would come to understand his position, but recognized he also lacked the courage to openly discuss the matter with her.

Alone in their stolen private moments Henry repeatedly told Claudine the truth.

"You must promise me you will never tell her, but Suzanne is the result of an illicit liaison between my wife and a German lover. At the time we were married, but, unlike our own relationship, things were extremely strained between us. For everyone's sake, yes my own as well, it was easier to assume the role of Suzanne's father...."

Henry's indiscretion would later prove to be very costly.

For days Suzanne sought the opportunity to tell Jean of his wife's behaviour and ask him if he was aware of Claudine's success in seducing the older man. In private Suzanne was constantly rehearsing what she might eventually say to him.

"Jean, please would you tell your wife to call a halt before somebody gets hurt further, surely it is in everyone's interest?"

It would be hard, but she decided it had to be said before the matter got any more out of hand.

Suzanne caught up with the Frenchman nearly two weeks after her night-time confrontation with Claudine; it was a Monday morning. She could see her father looking for stray sheep on the surrounding hillsides while Jean was working in front of the cottage splitting logs for fuel in preparation for winter. Untrusting, keeping her distance, she approached and forced herself to speak.

"Are you aware of the relationship that has developed between my father and your wife? Were you aware he and Claudine have spent nights together in his room? I do not approve of the situation and it cannot be allowed to continue. If you do not know about them, do you realise what Claudine is not only doing to my father, but also to me? She is destroying the bond between us so are you not concerned your wife has become the mistress of another man?"

Ignoring the person addressing him, Jean focused his attention on the growing wood pile and continued to split the larger pieces of wood into fire sized logs while Suzanne just continued to wait for his reply. After a further ten minutes of work the Frenchman stopped. Leaning on his axe, he wiped his sweating brow with the back of his hand and gathering breath spoke for the first time.

"Do not be concerned, do not bother yourself with matters you do not understand. The needs of a man are different from those of a woman and as you experience life you will begin to comprehend."

Axe raised, Jean once more turned to the pile, but in mid-swing stopped to lower the blade to the ground. Looking to Suzanne he shrugged his shoulders and gave the same-scarred smile she had to come to hate. It drained from his face in an instant as he began to speak, slowly and deliberately spitting his words at Suzanne.

"Of course I am aware, I have been aware for over a year!"

He turned and laughing aloud raised the large axe high above his head and with great feeling drove the sharp blade into the wood. With the sound of the laughter still ringing in her ears she moved away in disgust to go in search of Jean's wife.

She found Claudine on the east side of the valley helping her father move a number of goats from the lower to the upper slopes. As she had no wish to confront him and his newfound mistress at the same time Suzanne decided for now the matter should wait.

On Wednesday, Suzanne thought providence had made Henry take Jean with him on the weekly shopping trip. Surprisingly on Tuesday evening her father did not mention which market he would be attending, but said he was extremely pleased with their ever-growing supply of goat's milk. In the past weeks Claudine had helped him to produce a record number of cheeses, the quality and texture of which were outstanding and Henry was sure they would fetch a good price.

Early in the day she observed the Frenchwoman drawing water from the well and not having seen her husband around assumed Jean had left with father at dawn. By mid-morning Suzanne finally summoned the courage to speak to Claudine, deciding immediately after lunch she would seek out the young Frenchwoman who had trespassed into their lives. She would warn Claudine what had happened was disgusting, wrong and should father's feelings eventually be hurt it would be Suzanne she would have to answer to.

She searched the farmhouse, outbuildings and the barn, but Suzanne could not find Claudine anywhere. On reaching the gate to the cottage she could not bring herself to walk along the path to the front door.

Returning to her studio, Suzanne sat herself in front of the uncompleted picture. It was unusual because of all the scenes she had painted in the past of the surrounding countryside it was the only one looking down the valley; there was a sigh as she looked away from the picture towards the window. Through the glass was the stream and slopes, gradients increasing towards the summit, noting how quickly the lush green of waterside grass gave way to the rocks and scrub she pensively asked herself "What has gone wrong, why has father betrayed our idyllic world?"

She fought an argument within herself. An hour passed before Suzanne finally decided she just had to summon the strength that day to speak to Claudine; it could not be delayed any longer. She hurried from the studio and made her way down the track, approaching the well and still some yards from the building, she hesitated; there still was no sign of Claudine. Slowly she crossed the small garden before reaching the front door, it was ajar.

Suzanne had not entered the cottage for some months and was curious about the latest improvements the French couple may have made. Pushing the door open further, moving into the small sitting room, there was no reply as she called Claudine's name. She called again, but still there was no sound or sign of the occupant. Suzanne paused at the bottom of the stairs leading out of the kitchen and started to climb. At the top three doors faced her, from behind the middle one she could hear stifled cries; she pushed and under the pressure it freely swung open. Before her was a bedroom, central and the only piece of furniture in the room, an unmade bed in the middle of which lay two figures, a man and a women.

The man was fully clothed excepting his trousers, which lay around his ankles; his body was moving rhythmically as he repeatedly entered and satisfied the female figure spread beneath him whilst she seemed to be crying encouragement. The man carried through with the perverse act before Suzanne's eyes. The door being pushed open didn't seem to disturb the couple and not even bothering to completely withdraw, the man turned his head. A smile slowly and triumphantly crossed Jean's face as he realised the intruder was no less than "The high and mighty Mademoiselle Patterson."

Claudine barely raised her head from the pillow, only

momentarily glancing towards the door. Ignoring the presence of Suzanne, without another word they continued their passionate exercise. In horror Suzanne fled the cottage, already certain of what was necessary to enable father and daughter to resume their lives without further distraction.

*****

Deep in naïve thought, Suzanne lay behind the locked bedroom door where she felt safe from the evil Frenchman and his wicked wife. Looking at her watch it was nearly four o'clock and soon father would be back and immediately he returned she would tell him what awful things she had witnessed that afternoon. Suzanne told herself he must send the couple away immediately driving them to the nearest town tonight as she could not bear to have either of them anywhere near Henry or herself. She would tell father she was frightened of Jean and understood how Claudine had trapped and seduced him and finally that he could count on his daughter who understood the situation completely.

Having seen it all with her own eyes Suzanne decided to tell everything and that she would forgive him, Claudine was nothing more than a country whore and as for Jean, Suzanne doubted if they were ever man and wife. Father could find another couple, perhaps an older pair, to work for them and in a region with such low employment there would certainly be no lack of takers.

Planning the course of action in her mind allowed Suzanne some comfort, but in recent months she had gradually grown away from father and did very little for him in comparison with the beginning, Claudine had seen to that. Suzanne considered the situation, perhaps it was her own fault, she would have to play a big part in putting things right and would begin that evening by baking some of her father's favourite pastries. If the cooking was started immediately he would be able to eat them later when he returned from taking the French couple as far away as possible. She would prove to him they would not have to starve during the time it would take to find a replacement for Claudine. Suzanne tried to think positively and put the events of earlier that afternoon from her mind by thinking of how things would be in the coming weeks, but however hard she tried was unable to rid herself of the scene witnessed in the cottage and the thought of how her father had been fooled by the scheming Claudine.

Unlocking the bedroom door, she looked downwards from the small landing window towards the cottage; there was no sign of life. The door through which she had fled twenty minutes ago was now firmly closed, but Suzanne knew they were there, planning and scheming against father and her.

Trying to shut the couple from her mind, she gathered her bathrobe to shower, it was symbolic, but Suzanne thought washing the body would cleanse her of the wrong doings she had been witness to earlier. She made her way to the bathroom and fifteen minutes later was back in her own room.

Dressed in a fresh pink cotton dress, Suzanne combed the wet hair from her face and tied it back with a ribbon; it fell down her back in a long blonde ponytail, just as he liked it. She thought on his return it would please father to see her dressed like this, "My little girl". She looked at her own pretty face in the mirror, at the same time determinedly muttering to herself "Don't worry father, things will shortly be as they were."

Suzanne went downstairs to the kitchen to prepare and cook the surprise for Henry's return, now able to see ahead in her mind the end of the developing nightmare, she appeared to be a lot happier. Working swiftly, Suzanne found she was singing to herself the nursery rhymes of her childhood, tunes that Rachel had taught her all those years ago in Oxford.

She did not see him come in, but as Suzanne turned around from the kitchen sink he was there in the entrance leaning against the doorframe. Arms folded, Jean stood smirking, admiring the diminutive figure of Henry Patterson's daughter, looking so vulnerable in her thin cotton dress. The long hair tied back uncovered all of her pretty innocent face which due to the Frenchman's unexpected presence was now showing signs of anguish.

Suzanne asked him to leave, arms still folded Jean did not move or reply, but now he had the same smile across his handsome scarred face she always found so threatening. Leaning against the doorway he just stood there, blocking any thought of escape that Suzanne might have.

"Do you understand? I want you to leave the house!"

Again there was no response, but she didn't take her eyes off of him for one moment.

"You shouldn't be here; my father will be returning from market any time now, please will you go way."

The level of her voice rose.

"He will not be pleased to find you here, especially after the things I have to tell him about what I saw at the cottage. The duplicity of Claudine, your animal-like behaviour, I will tell him everything!"

Suzanne's voice had now reached fury pitch.

"All along I was certain you were aware of my father's affair with your wife and I would not be surprised if Claudine had originally been sent by you to seduce him!"

Her frantic speech was interrupted by the soft voice of the Frenchman.

"That is simply untrue." Silence followed.

Suzanne's face now had a quizzical look, answering the unasked question Jean was the first to speak.

"It will probably be another three hours before your father gets back to the farmhouse."

Suzanne said nothing.

"You must not forget besides the normal shopping,

he was going to make the arrangements, no doubt over several glasses of wine in some bar, for the proper marketing of the goats' cheese he is now producing. Henry will take hours bartering deals with the market stallholders, but if successful you can be sure the old man will drink himself drunk and then when he does arrive here you will have the pleasure of putting him to bed" Jean mockingly told her.

Noting his tone of sarcasm, Suzanne decided she hated the Frenchman more than ever, but still he did not move from the doorway and still he was looking at her with that awful smile. She quickly made up her mind the best course of action would be to ignore him altogether and then perhaps he would take himself away and perhaps he had lied and father would return sooner. Telling herself just to pay no attention to him, Suzanne turned her back and returned to the kitchen sink.

Silently Jean moved quickly. He came from behind, tucking his left arm around her narrow waist; he placed his right hand on her left breast. As she tried to scream, he took his arm from around her middle and reached for the tea towel that lay on the draining board at the side of the sink. Using the cloth as a gag to stifle any scream, Jean pulled it tight; she felt the heat of his body through her thin dress. As Suzanne struggled she also felt his warm breath breathing deeply on the back of her neck as Jean pulled the towel tighter.

Suzanne tried to pull the cloth away; frantically she moved her arms to indicate that she was having trouble breathing. Jean relaxed his grip, immediately she reached up and pulled the cloth out of her mouth and away from the face.

No longer having hold of her, he allowed a retching Suzanne to bend over the sink where she was left gasping for breath, but showing no remorse for his earlier action Jean just moved forward and kissed her lightly on the nape of the neck. Her instant reaction was to quickly turn and face the Frenchman. He took a step backwards.

"Please do not scream there is only Claudine to hear and she will not be interested."

Angered, but surprisingly not crying, her breasts and body ached as breathlessly she spoke to him.

"Are you completely mad? I will not scream as long as you don't do that to me again."

She was trying to hide her fright without much success.

"What are you going to do when my father returns? He will kill you."

Jean laughed and quickly replied.

"I do not think that is likely. It was in Alés when we met for the first time, Henry Patterson said he was looking for a couple to come and work for him and they would be paid well."

Jean slid onto a nearby kitchen chair and continued speaking.

"Your father has had the best part of the bargain. Oh yes, as promised he paid us for the work we carried-out, but he was greedy and wanted more than his entitlement."

Studying her attacker as he spoke Suzanne listened attentively. Jean had sunk his head across his arms that were now resting on the table. Any anger she had felt about the young Frenchman inexplicably had started to drain away, taking a step forward away from the kitchen sink she gently asked him.

"But why are you so aggressive?"

"All my life I have had nothing. My parents were very poor and I was their only child. I was only eight years old when they both died at which time I was sent to an orphanage in Marseilles. Alone in the world I experienced the hardships poverty brings. My life changed when as a lad of sixteen I met Claudine. Although no richer than me she was a lot cleverer, but with my charm and her looks we were able to make our way together and it was two years ago in Alés when we first met your father. It was the barman who first alerted me to an Englishman looking to hire help and at first Henry only wanted to hire me, but I managed to convince him he should also employ Claudine. I will admit to you we are not formally man and wife, but I do see Claudine as the only thing in the world I possess of any value; I could not stand being without her."

Jean was sitting, leaning back and relaxing on the kitchen chair as Suzanne once more started to ask him questions.

"But why have you been so aggressive towards me? Why have you just behaved as a caged animal? Why..."

Before she had time to finish the sentence Jean had leapt to his feet, his mood seemingly changed in an instant.

Suzanne immediately sensed danger, she had been lulled into believing the Frenchman was different than her first impression when briefly thinking he was looking for help and maybe she was the person to give it.

Now Suzanne was terrified as Jean started to bellow at the top of his voice.

"It is Henry who must carry the blame, he has taken what was not his to take and now I have come here to organize payment. It has always been Jean the world has used and denied, why shouldn't I also have treasured possessions? Your father owes and now I have come to collect the debt!"

It was soon over, resistance at first, but that quickly passed. As if a little child, he lifted her in one movement. One arm around her waist, the other behind her bare legs; she felt the strength of his arms and the sweaty warmth of his body as he lifted her from the floor and lay her roughly across the kitchen table. Frantically he tore away what little clothing she was wearing, forcing her legs wide apart as he allowed his trousers to drop to the floor. Jean mounted the table, painfully entering her with force. What little resistance Suzanne gave soon melted away as she pulled to remove the shirt on the body that lay across her, with indefinable pleasure digging her fingernails deep into the bare buttocks and skin on the back of the French debt collector.

Chapter 9

It was growing dark when Suzanne awoke and wondered how long she had been asleep; looking at her bedside clock it showed just after seven thirty.

Going as swiftly as he had arrived, Jean left her sitting on the floor in the corner of the kitchen naked, with knees under her chin, crying, distraught and ashamed. She could have resisted him, but somehow Suzanne had not wanted to and now she was thoroughly disgusted with herself. The pain and his body scent were still with her and Suzanne could still see in her imagination the closeness of the scar on his face as he lay across her, kissing lips and body as no other had done before, only to be followed by the pleasure he had shown on reaching his climax, a shared shameful excitement.

Showered, having washed away any last trace of the Frenchman and wearing fresh clothes Suzanne now felt totally cleansed. The dress she originally intended to be wearing when her father returned was beyond redemption as it lay in pieces where she had earlier thrown it across her bedroom in disgust.

She brushed her long blonde hair and with her sad blue eyes looked once more into the mirror, Suzanne was no longer in any doubt what had to be done.

*****

Suzanne called as she went down the stairs "Father! Father! Are you here?" No reply, she called again and again, but he had not yet got back. Inside of herself she could feel the pent-up anger, it was unbearable and could wait no longer; action was needed before father's return.

Making her way towards his study, she stopped at the large mirror hanging on the wall in the hallway and what those blue eyes saw in the reflection frightened her. Where so many tears had passed since her terrible sinful act was a red face looking many years beyond its true age; a

87

slightly stooping, nervous figure stared back at Suzanne. She reached upwards to the top edge and awkwardly ran her fingers along before removing what she was looking for.

The key was to the small recessed cabinet where Henry Patterson, like all good Frenchmen from rural communities, stored his guns and ammunition for hunting. Past the mirror and further along the hallway she tried the door to his study and was relieved to find it was not locked. Entering, she made her way to the corner of the room and the partially hidden cupboard; Suzanne hated it when her father had shown her how to load and use the shotgun. In the past she had not been able to reconcile herself into using it to kill the birds and animals, living things of the countryside she had to come to love. Henry just laughed at her.

"But this is different" Suzanne told herself.

In the gathering gloom there was no sign of the returning Land Rover as she made her way from the farmhouse. However irrational he might find her actions, she considered by the time father came back they would be irreversible. With a loaded shotgun tucked under her arm, Suzanne turned towards the track. On reaching the cottage she found the door shut, but on trying the latch mercifully discovered it unlocked. Standing in the sitting room Suzanne could hear the sound of movement from above. Now carrying the gun in both hands she moved swiftly across the darkening room and into the kitchen before climbing the wooden stairs.

She stopped and considered where the sounds were coming from and made her way to outside the bedroom visited earlier in the day. Eyes tightly shut with back to the door Suzanne muttered, "Forgive me Dear Lord."

With no further hesitation she burst into the shuttered room. In her frenzied anger briefly opening the eyes she saw the outline of a man lying under the bedclothes, point blank Suzanne pulled the trigger. The recoil from the first barrel discharging knocked her backwards; picking herself up with eyes still closed she fired the second.

Not wishing to see the results she immediately dropped the shotgun and fled from the room on to the landing where she was shocked to find Claudine emerging from the bathroom dressed only in a towel.

Suzanne took the narrow stairs two at a time and rushed out into the fresh air; running towards the stream to wash her soiled hands. She was aware of loud hysterical screams coming from the cottage; Claudine had entered the bedroom. In her muddled state of mind Suzanne could not help herself.

"He asked for it! Jean entered our lives and destroyed everything between father and me. What about earlier, did he not rape me? He deserved to pay the price!"

Uncontrollably sobbing Suzanne lay motionless and still on the grassy bank.

Claudine tried her best to clean him up, dress his injuries and make him comfortable, but with the severity of the gunshot wounds and the amount of blood he had already lost, without available transport to the nearest Doctor or Hospital, she knew it was a hopeless situation.

Within the hour he was dead.

As soon as he had given-up the will for life she lifted a clean white sheet over the head of the motionless figure. Claudine looked around the room. In one corner, where she had thrown them in her vain attempt to restore order lay crumpled soiled bedclothes and the walls were bloodstained, smeared and pockmarked with the lead from the shotgun discharges. The shutters were open to catch the last glimmer of light from the day; Claudine moved to the window and looked towards the outline of the farmhouse. Her eyes stared past the well where she had often drawn cold water to quench his thirst after a day's hard work. Claudine's eyes came to rest upon the small crumpled figure lying on the banks of the stream beneath the spreading branches of the fig tree and soon realized it was Suzanne who following her murderous actions was now probably in a state of great shock.

Shaking nervously, Claudine pulled the shutters together and made her way out of the bedroom intent on speaking to her as soon as humanly possible.

She was woken with a start; Claudine was now kneeling beside her. Suzanne was frightened as she sat up and tried to back away without speaking. Having no need for words, Claudine put a single finger to her lips and as the two young women sat in silence she placed a calming hand on Suzanne's slender shoulders, her head eventually came to rest in the Frenchwoman's lap.

Some minutes later she rose and took Suzanne's hand and tried to guide her towards the cottage, but there was resistance. Claudine held it tighter and now being pulled Suzanne had no option but to follow.

At the entrance there was firmer resistance, but unyieldingly Claudine took control and did not let go until they had reached the sitting room. She again indicated there was no need for words and started to move towards the kitchen, beckoning Suzanne, who once more was beginning to show signs of agitation, to follow.

Feeling she could no longer stand the morbid charade, Claudine started to climb the stairs to the first floor while Suzanne moved to leave, but upon reaching the kitchen door was stopped in her tracks by a loud cry.

"Arrêtez!"

Suzanne froze and turned; arms outstretched Claudine was now standing at the bottom of the stairs.

"I beg you to stay and not go, please, follow me, please."

It was as if a hidden force had drawn her away from the door and back into the kitchen; Claudine once again started to move up the stairs, but this time she followed. They stopped outside the bedroom door which Suzanne had already ran from on two occasions, but by now Claudine

90

had taken a firm physical grip on her wrist to prevent any thought of retreat.

She was taken unaware by the sudden mood change; the gentle look had disappeared from the Frenchwoman's face to be replaced by one of unmitigated wrath. Suzanne shouted and tried to pull herself away from Claudine's vice-like grip.

"I demand you let me go! I want to leave this wicked place!"

Claudine half-pulled and half-pushed her into the bedroom. Standing in the doorway she threw the sobbing Suzanne on to the floor of the darkened room and barked an order to the English girl.

"Open the shutters, now!"

Suzanne crawled across the floor to reach the window and struggled to re-open the wooden covers. As the half-light entered the room Suzanne saw as she had crossed the floor her dress had been smeared with sticky blood, there was also blood on the palms of her hands. Suzanne was now shaking and crying uncontrollably.

"Claudine I am now begging you to let me go, I didn't mean it, besides do you know what he did to me this afternoon? Please, please, I will be sick if you continue to keep me in this room."

The answer to the request was an emphatic.

"Non!"

Claudine pointed at the bed, the body lay covered just as she had left it, but now a number of dark red patches had appeared on the white sheet. Suzanne pleaded again and again to be freed; Claudine refused and moved to the bottom of the bed. With one movement she pulled the covering from the slain body. Suzanne turned her head away, expectantly covering her eyes in horror. Claudine moved in behind her, forcibly turning Suzanne's head towards the bed and in the same movement pulled the hands away from her face and as she did so she hissed in

Suzanne's ear.

"And now you can see what you have done!"

She slowly opened her eyes, but was not ready for what greeted her. On the bed before Suzanne was the dead body of her father, Henry Patterson.

Her scream was stifled as she lost consciousness and sank to the floor.

Jean did not show until the next morning

*****

At five thirty the previous evening Suzanne had not heard her father return; following the Frenchman's vicious and unprovoked attack she had been fast asleep in her locked bedroom. Jean had met Henry as he had driven up the track towards the farmhouse, waving him down to stop at the well.

He was certain Suzanne would not tell her father as she would find it too humiliating and what was more important, that afternoon before leaving her naked body stretched across the kitchen table, he had explained to her in some detail what terrible things would happen to the English couple if she should dare mention the incident to anyone at all.

"I will seek revenge on your father for the crime he has committed; I mean the matter regarding the theft of Claudine."

Stepping in front of the Land Rover Jean addressed Henry.

"My cousin who lives in Anduze has been taken seriously ill. Would you be kind enough to lend me your vehicle for the evening? I want to drive over there and return early tomorrow morning in time for work."

Having no knowledge of the day's earlier sordid events, Henry could see nothing wrong with the Frenchman's request as he had often let him use the Land Rover to collect items for the farm from neighbouring towns and villages. He could hardly wait for him to turn the vehicle full circle, Henry watched in a cloud of dust as Jean drove away at speed down the track.

Now smiling to himself he made his way not towards the farmhouse, but directly to the cottage; he could not help thinking Jean must take him for some kind of fool.

"Sick cousin in Anduze, indeed! It is the first time the Frenchman has mentioned he has family living only sixty kilometres away, more likely the man has a whore he wishes to pay an overnight visit!"

*****

Uncharacteristically for September it was raining hard; it was running through her hair and down her face and like the earth it was cold. Suzanne once more dug the spade into the ground as she toiled to dig deeper the dress clung to the outline of her body, but she no longer noticed the damp rain against her delicate skin. She lent on the shovel, three by one metres and one and a half deep, Jean had told her. He had wanted no part saying she must do it, so hidden away on the hillside behind the farmhouse an hour later the task was complete. The rain stopped.

She waited, a pathetic limp creature with bowed head, Suzanne stood back from the newly completed gaping hole in the earth. She was wet, red eyed, drawn and exhausted, crazed by the thoughts racing around her head. The same thoughts that had been denying her sleep for the past forty-eight hours, but now she had completed what the French couple had told her to do.

Soon they emerged from her studio where Jean had placed the body the day following her father's death. They carried between them a bundle of blankets which was tied in the middle and both ends. Climbing upwards to where Suzanne was standing, Jean and Claudine stumbled over the uneven and open ground, slowly progressing towards her and the crudely constructed gravesite that in the earlier downpour Suzanne had struggled to finish. She raised her head at the morbid sight and unable to handle events any longer Suzanne fled in fright towards the open rear door of the farmhouse.

Jean and Claudine lay their burden at the side of the newly dug grave and looked towards the first floor window of the building from where a lonely sad face now stood watching. Without speaking a word, Jean lifted one booted foot and placing it behind the blanketed figure he unceremoniously rolled the dead Englishman into the unwelcoming gap in the sodden earth.

"The girl can finish the job later" he muttered.

They walked slowly back towards the cottage, stopping only to pick-up the solitary battered suitcase sitting outside the front door, before continuing their way down the track.

Jean leading, Claudine obediently two steps behind carried their small case of worldly goods.

She watched as they disappeared around the first bend. Suzanne Patterson was never to see the French couple again.

Chapter 10

Like Rome, Bath is built on seven hills, the Romans named this English City Aquae Sulis after the Celtic Goddess Sul and with their numerous idyllic villages to the North lies the Cotswolds while to the South are Blake's "England's Mountains Green", the Mendip Hills. It is where the mineral springs originate which surface in the centre of the City that since the 17th century has allowed Bath to become a medicinal spa of international repute. An elegant place of parks and open spaces and yet, because of the talents and visions of Robert Adams, Thomas Baldwin, both the elder and younger John Wood and more, the architecture of its past has brought many to consider it unsurpassed in the British Isles. The eighteenth century also brought here the most famous of all Masters of Ceremonies in the form of Richard 'Beau' Nash, whilst the Irish playwright and Member of Parliament Richard Brinsley Sheridan had cause to focus more than one of his stage plays in the City.

That February day the rain was sweeping across the open paved square as she crossed in front of the Abbey Church of St Andrew, the comparison between here and the hot dry Cevennes could not have been starker.

The surrounding shops were from another era, *Green's Umbrella Emporium, Howells* the photographers and nestling over the top of *Filkins-* the obligatory Estate Agents, a single winding wooden staircase led to the premises of Robert Miller, as the well polished brass plate on the doorway announced to the outside world, *Dentist.* Opposite the shops was the public entrance to the City's number one tourist attraction, the subterranean experience of the Roman Baths, there appeared to be few takers on a cold winter's day.

Under the shelter of the columnar entrance to the area, known by all as the Abbey Churchyard, the hoarding of the newspaper vendor selling the day's edition of the Bath and Wilts Evening Chronicle announced *Latest IRA*

Outrage in Belfast, whilst the gloom of another approaching English night threatened to envelop everyone and everything, Suzanne hurried on.

Twenty-four hours later the weather had improved little, but at approximately the same time she crossed the Churchyard before making her way into one of the narrow pedestrian passageways which help to make Bath such an interesting place for the hordes from home and abroad who descend every summer as filings to a magnet, seeking to discover the hidden treasures the City holds.

She moved past numerous brightly lit shop windows shining through the evening light, all hoping to attract custom for their wares in this the traditional low point of retailers' annual cycle. Past the *Tea-Shop*, except for an ordinary couple seated in the inglenook it was empty, onwards, until she reached *Serendipity*. Suzanne stopped outside what she had always considered the rather old-fashioned toyshop despite the slogan on the sign over the doorway clearly meant to convey the feelings of the proprietor, *The Present Shop for Present People*.

Luckily she had remembered tomorrow was Robert's birthday, one of her employer's two children and he would have been extremely disappointed if Suzanne had forgotten. The bustle of a City making its way homewards was lost on her as she stared into the brightly lit window at this Aladdin's Cave of children's toys. In the confines of the narrow pedestrian way people brushed by as Suzanne moved towards the door.

Some way behind a figure stretched its neck trying to attract the attention of the young shopper, pushing forward against the growing flow of bodies, all the while calling Suzanne's name aloud. Determined to purchase the boy's present and return home away from the damp and cold night air she detested, Suzanne at first did not hear.

Reaching the entrance to the toyshop she stopped, through all the noises of evening activity she finally heard her name being called. Turning, she listened, there it was again, yes, someone was repeatedly calling her name, "Suzanne! Suzanne! Suzanne Patterson!"

As it burst from the crowd Suzanne was confronted by a breathless figure. Surprised, both women stood as statues looking at each other and there was a moment's pause before she recognised her former art teacher from St Bernadette's, Mary Bowron. In unison they exclaimed each other's name before laughing and warmly embracing.

Following the initial excitement of greeting each other it was Mary who spoke first.

"After all these years, what a surprise to find you here in Bath!" without giving time for a response she continued, "I thought you were living in France with your father, how are you? What are you doing in England? You have changed so very little since leaving School, where are you living now?"

Without warning, Suzanne burst into tears.

"I'm unable to stop," she told Mary, "I have to go."

Abandoning any thoughts of entering into the toyshop and without further explanation she pushed herself out into the evening rush.

Taken aback by the outburst, Mary tried to follow, calling as she did so.

"Suzanne, I would like to meet-up again, how-about afternoon tea later in the week?"

Mary had to think quickly as she could see Suzanne appeared to be making better progress than her through the flow of people. Again, she called after her.

"Thursday afternoon? The Pump Room?'

Suddenly Suzanne stopped and with tears still running down her cheeks faced the approaching pursuer.

"I am sorry, so sorry, I apologise for my behaviour and yes, I would like to talk, and maybe we could meet tomorrow?"

"Tomorrow is OK by me, yes, tomorrow is fine."

Mary gave a sympathetic smile.

"Is three-thirty a suitable time?"

There was no answer.

Passing heads turned to see Suzanne standing openly sobbing. Mary moved forward to comfort her, but when she reached out she was caught off guard as Suzanne turned quickly away and again moved swiftly into the crowd. Rooted to the spot, Mary thought she had caught the response "Tomorrow at half-past three," but all she could do was watch as her former pupil once again disappeared into the evening throng.

*****

Afternoon tea taken in Bath's Pump Room is like making a journey back in time. As a daily ritual, throughout the year the niceties modern day living appears to have forgotten are acknowledged here. The interior décor, the Georgian architecture, the unfailing smiles of the immaculately dressed waitress service, whilst a string quartet makes a final topping to the setting's splendid ambiance

Standing in the foyer, Mary looked at her watch.

"Five minutes to four and still no sign of her." She asked herself, "Was it my imagination? Did I not see Suzanne Patterson outside the *Serendipity* toyshop and when she left was it not agreed that we should meet today? Perhaps I was mistaken; she was terribly upset about something so perhaps decided to stand me up or as I originally suggested could have meant Thursday." Reluctantly Mary turned to go.

"At least today it isn't raining!"

Suddenly through the glass she saw the familiar figure of Suzanne making her way across the Abbey Churchyard from the direction of Orange Grove.

Before she could give a reason for her lateness or had chance to have second thoughts about being there, Suzanne was whisked away into the interior of what must rate as one of the most lavish tearooms in England. Settled with tea and buttered scones before her, as if pupil to teacher, she hesitantly apologised to Mary Bowron.

Suzanne explained.

"Arriving home yesterday I felt very foolish, there was no excuse for my behaviour. The only explanation I can offer is for the first time in a number of years somebody has mentioned my father."

She continued.

"Yes, you were quite correct, up until five years ago we lived in the South of France, and then, unfortunately and rather unexpectedly, he suffered a massive heart attack and passed away. The isolation of where we were living did not help, it was all so sudden."

"I am so so sorry." Mary reached across the table and placed a comforting hand upon that of her former pupil. "I am truly sorry for you."

"I am grateful for your kind thoughts, but all that is now in the past. I think what really upset me yesterday was the shock of seeing my former art mistress standing right there and after all these years too. It was rather clever of you to spot and recognize me, but please tell me, what are you doing in the City? Bath is a long way from Bournemouth, do you no longer teach at St Bernadette's?"

Avoiding the question surrounding her own past, Mary answered, "Recognition was easy you have not changed at all, excepting these days you are even more beautiful than when we first met."

Suzanne began to blush, but sensing the girl's embarrassment Mary continued the conversation.

"You must tell me, what has happened in the intervening years? Why are you here in Bath?"

Mary listened attentively to Suzanne's reply.

"As you already know, directly after leaving St Bernadette's I moved to France with my father. Living in a small isolated farmhouse near Montpellier, we were very happy, that was until five years ago last September when father died."

Mary was by now intrigued by Suzanne's tale.

"How have you managed on your own since?"

"Father collapsed and died whilst making his weekly visit to market. That day I was patiently waiting at home for his return and it was only when a group of his friends, usual fellow visitors to the market, returned up the track to the farmhouse driving his Land Rover I learnt of his death.

They offered to stay with me, but I refused help. Another man accompanied the two bearers of the sad news in his own transport and they all eventually departed together and I was left alone to grieve. I grieved for three weeks after which I walked the miles to the nearest town where I arranged the immediate sale of the livestock, all the sheep, goats and chickens from the farm. One of father's same friends who had brought the news of his death dealt with all the details for me."

Suzanne continued by adding some authenticity to her fabricated story.

"I am not sure how honestly the arrangements were made, but the same man who in the end arranged the sale of the animals for me, perhaps not surprisingly, bought most of them himself. Pleased with the deal made with a naïve young English woman, he and his wife returned the following week to transport the animals away."

She paused, as if trying to recollect the full details.

"I was also told they would be pleased to buy father's aging Land Rover and it was the same couple who came back ten days later and gave me the final lift back to town. I caught a train to Nimes and then, via Paris and Dieppe, to England. Those first weeks after father's death were a lonely existence and I did not venture beyond the confines of the farm and its buildings."

What Suzanne did not say was her isolation had been purely voluntary, in those early days being extremely fearful someone would discover details of the frightening and sordid events that had taken place. Slowly, partially through painting, partially through her beliefs she found herself conquering those fears and, unable to drive, eventually walked the distance to Alés.

Mary listened in silence.

"I withdrew most of the monies in our joint Bank Account and journeyed by way of Alés on the local train service to Nimes. Money was not a problem, in addition to the 100,000 francs I received in cash for the livestock and vehicle in my lone travelling holdall I carried a certified Euro Cheque. You can imagine the enquiring looks I received from the Assistant Manager at the Bank in England when I handed over a piece of paper which had a cashable value of 300,000 French francs. Father and I were the single authorized signatories to our French account, but my previous need to use it had been pretty limited."

Suzanne explained.

"In France it is a requisite to owning or renting a property to be the holder of a French bank account and to live and work in the Country, as we did, for more than three months in any one year required a Carte de Sejour."

In truth, rather than draw unnecessary attention to herself, she did not close the account completely, Suzanne left nearly 15,000 francs deposited with the Bank.

She went on to tell of her journey back to England.

"From Nimes I caught the TGV through the Rhone Valley, Valence, and Lyons, onwards to the French Capital. An overnight stay in a small, rather seedy Paris Hotel, then I took a taxi to La Gare St Lazare and the not so swift boat train to Dieppe."

Suzanne did not mention to Mary how, alone with her thoughts, somewhere in the middle of the English Channel she had disposed of the French property keys over the side of the Sealink Ferry.

"On reaching Newhaven and English soil, I caught the connecting train to Victoria, where after my tiring journey I sought refuge for the night in a small hotel of the type which abound in that area of London.

The next day, for no other reason than a childhood visit here, I set out westwards to Bath. Even at a very young age I had enjoyed the City's elegance and charm; I travelled by the regular coach service running from Victoria Coach Station."

With happy childhood memories in her mind and thoughts of the girls employed by her parents to look after her own personal welfare, Suzanne told of how within the week of arriving in Bath, she had found a job as a live-in nanny.

"And what has happened about your painting?"

"I still try to do some, but both my time and space are very restricted."

What Suzanne was not asked and did not tell for fear of being questioned further and worried she might have difficulty in providing Mary with acceptable answers was the fate of the French property.

The day of leaving the farm she had locked the house, cottage and studio, leaving everything as it stood. She left not only the contents of the farmhouse and the cottage, but also the paraphernalia of her studio, this included paints and canvas plus finished and unfinished work, with the exception of one painting which she wrapped and tied in a piece of sackcloth. Tucked under one arm, Suzanne carried the parcel away with her leaving no forwarding address behind and before the Authorities and Bank had time to realise she was gone never to return. Her intention was to lose her recent past and after many painful battles with her conscience decided she had no further use for her former life. Suzanne concluded the only sensible route of escape was to leave the past locked behind and endeavour to forge a new beginning.

"And what has happened to yourself and your own family?"

"My husband Tony is still working for the Bank; we moved from our house near Bournemouth two years ago when he was transferred to their Regional Office just outside Bristol at Almondsbury. We actually live in Bath; home is a large family house along the Newbridge Road, it is conveniently situated on the west side of the City and really en-route to Bristol. It takes Tony less than half an hour to reach his office in the morning. The children are fine, Rupert and Ian are at a boys only boarding school, Phillip is at a local prep school and all three appear to be prospering; Rupert is doings his A levels next year."

Before Mary ended, Suzanne commented on how the years had flown.

"Thankfully they are all in good health and all three boys, the older two particularly, are growing-up fast."

"So if you finished teaching art at St Bernadette's what are you doing with your days now?"

Mary told her about the demise of the old School and how in 1989, a year after Suzanne had left, for a combination of commercial reasons coupled with the lack of novice recruits into their Teaching Order, at the end of that Summer Term the Nuns were forced to admit defeat and close the doors of the School for the last time.

"Come the following September it was strange at first when there was no excitement or expectations of a new academic year at St Bernadette's to look forward to."

She was now staring hard at Suzanne's youthful beauty sitting in front of her, something Mary had long given-up hope of ever seeing again.

"It was never the same at the School once you had left," she whispered to her former pupil.

Lost in thought, Suzanne did not hear the passing words. Raising her eyes from their fixation on an imaginary spot somewhere on the polished floor in front of her, she looked into Mary's eyes and asked.

"Does that mean you have given up painting?"

The reply came quickly.

"I most certainly haven't. Following the closure, by the time Christmas had arrived, I had more than enough private students, both young and old. In addition, when time allowed and right up until Tony's move, I tutored evening classes at the Technical College in Bournemouth. Shortly after arriving in Bath I obtained a part time position at the Royal Crescent School, like St Bernadette's, it is an all-girls boarding school. The hours are reasonably flexible and my employers are quite understanding, in truth I would like to cut back on my time, but that would inconvenience the School which I have no wish to do."

After exchanging further pleasantries, they both said it would be nice to meet again in the not too distant future and it was agreed it should be the same place at the same time the following week.

"I promise not to be late again."

"Next time would you bring some of your paintings for me to see?" There was a pause. "Would you? Please, I would like that."

Mary waited expectantly for the reply.

"OK, but only if you really want me to, I will bring what I can, but ought to warn you I haven't a great number to show. You understand all of them have been completed since my father's untimely passing and my arrival back in England."

As the two exchanged addresses and telephone numbers Suzanne spoke.

"As you insisted on settling the bill, a condition of our meeting next week is that it will be my turn to pay."

Mary looked longingly at her younger friend and smiled.

"If that is the only condition I have no objection, I agree."

Outside the Pump Room Suzanne declined a lift home and before Mary could raise any objection the figure of her desires had gone. Before making her way to the nearby car park, she pondered.

"How wonderful after all this time, because of one fluky chance, I have once more met Suzanne Patterson."

Her feelings for the girl ran deep; it had been an extremely painful time when the attractive young woman had suddenly disappeared from her life.

"There seemed a lot of the past six years Suzanne had no wish to talk about perhaps that will come later. I will have to be very careful if I am not to force her away from me again, yes, I will have to be very careful."

Chapter 11

The following Thursday Suzanne arrived on-time at the
Pump Room for afternoon tea with Mary. Her former art
mistress noticed immediately much of the tension from
their earlier meeting seemed to have disappeared; Suzanne
was a lot more relaxed and under her right arm carried a
large art portfolio.

It was late into their teatime meeting when Mary
opened the folder for the first time and looked at the two
dozen watercolour paintings inside. Suzanne apologized.

"Sorry, I was unable to carry anymore."

"Water colours?"

"Since my return I have found them easier to use, I
have completed a handful of oils, but nothing like the
number I finished whilst living in France where I had both
the time and the space."

Mary brushed aside the apologies, the quality of the
landscapes was unquestionable, over half of them being
recognizable as pictures of Bath and the surrounding
countryside.

"Your talent, as your beauty, has certainly blossomed
in the years since I last examined your work."

Still sitting at the table, Mary continued to study the
pictures carefully.

"Are you free the Saturday after next?"

Not bothering to ask why her companion wanted to
know, Suzanne paused before reaching into her shoulder
bag and taking out a pocket diary. There was an expectant
silence as Mary waited while the pages turned, watching
the face of her young friend closely and the silence was
only broken when Suzanne looked-up.

"I have the complete weekend free to myself. My
employers and their children are away from Friday evening
until late on Sunday afternoon, they are visiting relatives in
Suffolk..."

Before Suzanne could continue Mary asked "Would

you like to come to Bournemouth with me? Just the two of us, we can visit all the former haunts, including the site of the old School and we could even do a little shopping, it will be a sort of a girls' day out. I will pick you up at about ten on Saturday morning from the address you gave me in Camden Crescent. We can have a leisurely drive to Bournemouth and stop for lunch on the way, returning in the evening at supper time."

Suzanne's reaction to the proposed outing took Mary completely by surprise. As if startled by a ghost entering the room, she leapt from her chair. Forgetting her previously made condition of her being there she thanked Mary profusely for the afternoon tea and without giving an answer to the weekend trip offer rushed from the room, into the foyer and the gathering dusk of the Abbey Churchyard.

Mary was left standing at the table, alone with her thoughts and looking aghast at the empty chair opposite her. What had she said that once again triggered her former pupil into running away without explanation? Why was she so volatile? This was not the Suzanne she remembered, always so quiet, attractive, shy, maybe timid, but certainly not as a long extinct volcano, prone to eruption without warning. Mary stood there alone, searching for an answer.

Was it something that had happened during those in-between years? Perhaps it was the unexpected death of her father and what of her mother? There certainly had been no mention of her, neither had there been any specific mention of a member of the opposite sex. Maybe there had been or, even worse, there still was a man friend in her life; she prayed to God this was not the case, her Suzanne deserved better.

"Unfortunately, it is a fact of life some things are best left unsaid, if Suzanne wants to tell me what is troubling her she will, but in her own good time."

Mary decided to leave it a day or two and then to try and phone her to suggest they should get together again.

She reached across the table and straightened the contents of the portfolio which in her haste to get away Suzanne had left behind.

The waitress speaking startled Mary.

"Was everything alright madam?"

"Yes thank you, fine, very nice, but please could I have the bill as I wish to leave."

*****

She did not have to wait long. Having regained her senses and calm, Suzanne phoned Mary to apologize for her extremely rude behaviour of the afternoon.

Tony took the call instead of Mary.

"I am sorry she isn't here, it's a fifth form parents evening at the School where she teaches. She won't be in until later."

Relieved she would not have the immediate embarrassment of speaking to Mary she continued to talk with Tony.

"Oh, never mind it doesn't matter, I will call back another day."

He thought the caller was no doubt one of Mary's pupils as they always seemed to phone the house after the School day had ended. It had always annoyed him a little, but he spoke politely to the anonymous caller.

"Would you like to leave her a message? My wife should be back sometime around nine-thirty, otherwise is it possible to call her again tomorrow?"

There was a brief silence and only then did Suzanne explain who she was.

An air of excitement was detectable in Tony's voice as they exchanged pleasantries and he asked how she was keeping.

"After all this time it is truly nice to speak to you again."

The ice having been broken, the two of them were soon engaged in conversation, but having been briefed on

108

what had happened to Mary earlier in the day, Tony did not mention the matter as he didn't want the young caller to hang-up on him.

"Yes, I can confirm on Saturday week Mary is planning to make a trip to Bournemouth......No, the children and I will not be going. Unfortunately, after a long illness, eighteen months ago my mother died and we soon found my father could not cope with living alone and he has moved to Malvern in Worcestershire to live with my sister. When Mary indicated her intention to make the Bournemouth trip it hardly seemed fair to take the boys all the way there and then for them to be traipsed around the shops; it isn't the time of the year for them to spend very long on the beach. It was therefore decided my sister should bring father to visit us and as Saturday is the final day of *Tom Browne's Schooldays* at the Theatre Royal, the six of us would go to the matinee performance and round the day off with a restaurant meal before my sister takes him home."

"I am very sorry to hear about your mother, she was a lovely lady, it must have come as a great shock to you all. I am so sorry."

"Thank you for your kind thoughts, but her death was not totally unexpected, she had been ill for some time beforehand. What is more worrying is my father who suffers from multiple sclerosis and is slowly deteriorating; it is very hard for my sister who looks after him. Mary and I would like to do more, but with our own family we find it nigh impossible."

Suzanne again said how sorry she was. Tony did not reply for a moment, but when he did it was in a jaunty manner and it was if something bothering him had been lifted from his mind.

"Are you going? Do you still want to join her for the trip? If you wish I can tell her as soon as she gets in this evening, any arrangements Mary has already made with you can stand and if they are any different she will call you in good time."

Regretting her earlier melodramatic exit from the Pump Room, Suzanne's reply was immediate.

"Yes I would love to go."

Suzanne was pleased it was Tony rather than his wife speaking on the phone as at this time she had no wish to search for an excuse to cover her apparent frequent irrationality.

Suzanne decided to cut the conversation short.

"Tony, I hope you will not think me rude, but I have been talking for nearly an hour on my employer's telephone and although I have free use of it, I have no wish to upset them when they receive a very large quarterly bill on account of me."

"Of course not" he said laughing. "I don't want to be the person to get you into trouble!" Adding as an afterthought, "Mary has the paintings you left behind this afternoon. Unless you want them back before, I will get her to return them when she calls for you on the Saturday."

She hadn't wished to lose her paintings, Suzanne was thankful Tony had brought the matter-up. Having telephoned the Pump Room only an hour and a half after leaving, she had been told they were nowhere to be found, so was very pleased to discover that Mary had taken them with her.

"Yes that will be fine; I will collect them when I see Mary."

*****

It was dry and sunny, if a little cold, as shortly after ten-thirty they left Bath, arriving in Salisbury just before midday. A quick visit to the Cathedral with its crooked spire was followed by lunch at the nearby White Hart Hotel where the food served was as fine as the building's Georgian portico.

After their splendid meal, while sitting in front of

the warm open fire drinking coffee, Mary cast her eyes around.

"I have stayed at this Hotel several times in the past, I cannot remember if the first time was before or after I met my husband, but I am sure it wasn't him I stayed with in a four-poster under the big oak beams."

Suzanne seemed not to hear, the wonderful lunch coupled with the warmth of the lounge's log fire was making her feel soporific.

By two o'clock they were on the road again heading towards the south coast and by three they were driving by the grounds of their former School.

Mary stopped the car in front of the rusting, chained and padlocked wrought iron gates standing at the bottom of the driveway, unable to advance further both women got out of the vehicle.

The cold winter air greeted the soft skin of Suzanne's face, waking her from the drowsiness caused by a mixture of inner contentment and warmth of the car's heater. A quarter of a mile away at the end of the drive, she could see between two old cedar trees the blackened outline of the now roofless school. Cattle were grazing in the surrounding parkland; a local farmer had rented the grass keep, but could find no use for the fire damaged building.

To stop further vandalisation, closer attention showed a high wire fence now surrounded the house; all items of any value having long been removed. There was an air of quiet desolation, but to Suzanne the fence seemed purely symbolic. Looking up the overgrown drive towards the gnarled walnut tree she recalled reading the all-important letter from her father, only to be discovered by the kindly Sister Clare. It seemed like only yesterday.

Mary interrupted her thoughts.

"I am sorry we are unable to get closer. I told you previously about the fate of the School, but I did think we would be able to get nearer to the buildings."

They stood as two complete strangers, locked-out and looking into a different world now passed on its way in time leaving nothing but memories behind.

"What happened to everyone once the School closed?"

"The Reverend Mother and Housemistress Selby retired; regarding the rest of the staff I have no idea. Two or three of us corresponded for a while, but with moving away from the area I lost touch and I did not hear from any of the former pupils excepting one, Nicola Adams. She was a year younger than you, an artist and pretty, but not nearly as proficient"

"I remember Nicola, tall, slim, dark haired and very attractive. How strange of all the girls you taught at St Bernadette's only one besides me, and I am not sure if I really count, kept up with their former art teacher."

"I was very fond of Nicola, we regularly wrote to each other and then just over two years ago she came to visit us for a few days during the boys' school holidays. She was a great help as Tony had been working in London for a couple of weeks and having Nicola with me was very useful, helping to look after the children during the day and good company for me in the evening."

"Where and what is she doing now?"

"Shortly after staying with us I believe Nicola moved with her parents to live in Brussels, her father worked there for one or other of the Secretariats of the European Commission. It is funny, but after that visit Nicola never wrote to me again. In the past year I have received a single, if rather formal, letter and last Christmas a card from the whole family. I miss the regular contact, as I miss all the other girls from the old School."

There was a pause. The only sound was coming from the wind moving through the bare over-hanging branches.

"I am cold and I want to leave this place now" Suzanne forcibly said to Mary, "It no longer has anything to offer me."

112

Without replying Mary made her way to the car and started the engine and Suzanne quickly joined her.

The rest of the day was spent window shopping, followed by a walk along the seafront, but the strong breeze coming off the water was too cold to enable the lone figures to take full advantage of the now sunny afternoon and soon they retreated back into the bustle of the Town shoppers.

The couple walked and walked, finally into Westover Road and past the Ice Rink, opposite the Pavilion Theatre they entered Pavilion Court, it was five o'clock. After some teatime refreshment they made the short walk back to the car park and returned directly to Bath, arriving at Camden Crescent shortly before seven forty-five.

"I am late" Mary said, "I promised the children I would be back by seven and it is a quarter to eight already, so, sadly, I will have to decline your invitation to come into the house, but I am sure there will be other opportunities."

They both agreed the day had been fun and a great success.

As Mary kissed Suzanne goodbye on the cheek, she remembered the portfolio lying on the rear seat of the car. Reaching from the pavement into the back she passed it across to Suzanne.

"Why don't you come over to Newbridge tomorrow and join us for Sunday lunch?"

"I would love to, but you have already been very kind and I couldn't possibly impose myself on your family."

Mary would have none of it.

"You have already told me the people you work for are away until later in the day on Sunday. Tony and the children will call for you at about Eleven-thirty. That is it then, settled!"

Before Suzanne could argue, Mary reached forward and kissed her once more on the cheek before climbing back into the car. She called for her to wait; Mary wound the window down expecting to hear further protestations, but Suzanne spoke to her in a hushed voice.

"Thank you once again for such a marvellous and enjoyable time" momentarily pausing before continuing, "I am very sorry for my terrible behaviour the other day at the Pump Room, it was really very very rude of me."

Mary smiled sympathetically.

"Don't worry, I understand."

Still smiling, she began to wind-up the car window and with a wave of the hand started to move-off.

Suzanne was also waving as she shouted after Mary.

"Thanks a lot and thanks for returning my paintings," which were now safely tucked under her left arm.

The last words Mary heard through the partially closed window were "Half past eleven is fine; I will be ready when Tony and the children call for me."

Chapter 12

Driving down the hill towards the City centre, Mary thoughts turned to what she had just said, "Don't worry I understand", if only it were true. She had just spent the whole day with the girl and her time living in France was not mentioned once.

Suzanne found Sunday as enjoyable as the day in Bournemouth. She discovered Mary, Tony and the three, now not quite as young, Bowrons were all delightful company to be with and in turn they all found their attractive guest equally so.

It was after the splendid lunch Mary had taken most of the morning to prepare, the three adults had settled down to coffee in the drawing room and the boys had disappeared somewhere upstairs when Mary made the proposition.

"I hoped you wouldn't object, but I showed the paintings you left behind to some of my friends. They considered the pictures extremely good, so much so that those same friends wanted to purchase a number of them."

Suzanne abruptly put her coffee cup down on the table beside her.

"My paintings, you mean my watercolours? Are you sure? I can do much better…."

With a smile on her face, Mary tried hard to indicate to Suzanne now was the time to be quiet and let her finish what she had to say.

"Perhaps what you will find more interesting is the monetary value those people put on your work" she said, "They would be willing to pay quite handsomely and my friends are interested in at least half a dozen of your pictures."

"But the paintings are watercolours, as you already know I prefer working in oils, I do not consider my best work is achieved with watercolours and I think it would be dishonest to suggest otherwise."

Knowing full well from the past Suzanne had a

passion for painting, Mary asked the question outright.

"Have you ever thought about making your living as an artist?"

Suzanne cautiously answered the question.

"If I did paint full-time where would I live? At least with my present employment I have a roof over my head. I do not have a proper studio facility and once I have completed the pictures where would I sell them? I hardly have enough to support myself at present and what about the start-up costs of a professional artist?"

Having rapidly fired the questions, she then started to qualify what had been said.

"Of course I would like to paint fulltime, but I have not even considered it because I do not have enough money behind me to get started." Negatively she told Mary "So it would be out of the question."

Her former art mistress was allowed to continue.

"Your reasoning is flawed. With a little determination and lots of talent anything is possible. Both my husband and I are aware you have an excess of both qualities so you should give the matter serious consideration. The monies you will receive from the sale of those watercolours could be a great start."

There was silence.

"So, how about it?" Mary asked

Suzanne hesitated.

"Before saying 'Yes', I would have to be sure I am able to support myself, although I am aware there are no guarantees. No, I think it is probably too risky."

It was Tony who spoke next.

"Forget the risks, the whole of life is a lottery and believe it or not this is a banker speaking, the question is if you had the opportunity would you like to make your living as an artist? As Mary has already said, you have the talent and we are both convinced people would flock to your door."

"It is very flattering the pair of you have that sort of

confidence in me, personally I am not so sure about my own abilities, but yes, of course, I would like to create all day and be paid for doing so."

With a smile on his face, Tony nodded his approval as Mary continued.

"Eighteen months ago my uncle passed away, he had lived alone in a small cottage in North Devon. He had no children and I was his only surviving niece and so in his will I inherited the cottage, which is situated in the tiny coastal community of Lynmouth. The village is best remembered by those a lot older than you for the disaster that struck in 1952 when, following weeks of torrential rain, parts of it were wrecked by flood waters rushing from the high ground of the Moor that rises way to the south. It was a terrible disaster, but today people do not know of those events from nearly forty years ago as all the buildings have long been replaced or repaired. The picturesque village and harbour are very popular with visitors and holidaymakers, especially during the summer months."

"When Mary initially inherited the property our intention was to retain it as a holiday home. Because of my work with the Bank and Mary's teaching, not so much at the Royal Crescent School, but her tuition sessions with private students which seem to go on year long and are taking more and more of her time......."

Mary interrupted her husband.

"Of course the financial gain I make from lessons is not great, but I do so much enjoy giving them. It is exhilarating to see my students, what ever their age, getting so much pleasure from painting and for the first time the self-discovery of their own creative talent is a joy to watch. In addition, especially with our own boys' long school holidays, having a situation where one can work to suit is good, a lot of my lessons are in the evening after Tony has returned from the office and in my absence he is able to look after the children."

Tony was then allowed to once more take up the

story.

"We therefore discovered finding the time to regularly visit our newly acquired seaside property was nearly impossible and maintaining the garden and the outside of the building has become a real nightmare for us. We thought about long-term letting, but after much consideration it was decided to own a cottage in such a beautiful spot and not have regular access was a bad ideal. Then we considered shorter lets, the holiday hire business, asking others to pay for the use of the facility when the family had things planned and the property would otherwise have been standing empty. Living miles away from Devon and operating at arms length seemed to have more minus points than plus ones so that idea never really got off the ground. The third option was to sell the property, but even with an attractive cottage in such a desirable location it was clear to us owing to the depressed state of the housing market now is not the time to be selling residential property of any sort. Who knows? Two, Three, maybe five years and the position will have altered for the better."

There was an expectant pause as if Tony was waiting for Mary to continue with the narrative, he was not to be disappointed.

"Tony and I would like to put forward a proposal, part of which is the suggestion you should move to Lynmouth. You can live in the cottage rent free until you become so rich from selling your paintings you could afford to pay a modest rent."

There was further silence, until with great enthusiasm Mary continued.

"The large attached conservatory at the rear would make a terrific studio. To begin with it would be like babysitting the cottage, but I can see you would not have a problem selling your paintings as there is no shortage of visitors to Lynmouth, especially in the summer months. We could come to an arrangement about visiting, if last year is anything to go by you should see very little of us, although of course we will regularly keep-in touch.

Time has not allowed us to take advantage of the good fortune that came our way when we inherited the property and it being in such a beautiful place too." Mary paused. "When can you come and see it? Next week? You will say 'Yes', won't you?"

There was a stunned and complete silence, Suzanne was lost for words and did not know what to say.

Chapter 13

She was dead on arrival at the hospital.

The ambulance paramedics had done their best, but, in the words of the policeman who attended, the injuries were horrific and amongst the worst he had experienced in his twenty years with the Devon and Cornwall Constabulary.

The cars had met head-on, the other driver who was a male octogenarian lost it on the bend at the bottom of Trentishoe Hill taking the short journey from Bagworthy to Barbrook; he had just descended the steep one-in-five incline.

It was later said he was travelling far too fast for the road conditions. A dark and dismal winter's evening, it was just after seven and it had been raining heavily for most of the day. The locals all knew in such weather conditions water always ran down the surface and at the bottom of the hill it spewed left to right across the road before disappearing over the edge and into the fast flowing stream that carried the water away from the Moor and through the deep wooded gorge.

As she approached the sharp right hand bend before the ascent up the hill the torrential rain was no doubt partially obscuring her vision. From there it was only five minutes and she would have reached her final destination and the warmth and security of home.

The oncoming vehicle hit the driver's side, the door panel collapsed under the force. The car was pushed off the road, toppled over the edge and had continued rolling down the steep rocky bank before coming to rest on its crumpled roof. It was left partially submerged in the ever-increasing water flow of the normally sedate and picturesque stream. Upon impact the male's car slewed around and came to rest half-on, half-off, the narrow unclassified road.

It was nearly an hour before another traveller passed that way, Bob Newell, a farmer from Blackmoor

120

Gate. He found the ageing Ford still parked at the side of the road, nothing had moved, including the driver. It was soon clear to the farmer the man was in shock and a closer examination of the situation soon revealed what or whoever the driver of the damaged vehicle had hit was now off the road and had crashed through the flimsy wooden fence and lay somewhere in the dark far below.

He scrambled down the slope and his fears were soon confirmed when the beam of light from the powerful torch he always carried in the back of his van picked out the upturned black Metro. In the shadowy light he could see the outline of a figure in the driver's seat; still strapped in, upside down it was not a pretty sight.

Hurriedly climbing back to his parked vehicle he used the mobile phone fitted to his dashboard to call for the emergency services. Before returning to further investigate the situation at the bottom of the ravine, he took the blanket normally reserved for when Jack, his faithful collie, wanted to travel in comfort with the master and placed it over the shoulders of the white haired driver.

By the time the police had arrived fifteen minutes later, Bob Newell had released the crumpled unconscious body of what he thought must have been a very attractive young woman. His attempts to stop the bleeding from her facial cuts were proving to be futile as he was not carrying a first aid kit in his van and his inappropriate dirty handkerchief was totally inadequate.

Soon in the distance he heard the eerie wail of the summoned ambulance, he hadn't even noticed, but at least it had stopped raining.

He had removed the frail figure from the upturned Metro and carried it to the bottom of the rocky slope. Later Bob Newell recalled the shock felt as he recognized the diminutive female lying in his arms.

At the scene there were now two ambulances with their paramedic crews, two police patrol cars with three uniformed officers and a police motorcyclist. He could see clearly into one of the ambulances, the back doors were open and in the interior white light, sitting between one of the policemen and a green uniformed paramedic, was a hunched figure that he nonsensically noticed was now wrapped in a more presentable blanket.

He watched as another of the ambulance crew disappeared through the ominous gap in the roadside fence. Bob Newell thought it strange no other traffic had used this route since he came this way, unaware the police had closed the road in each direction once they realised the severity of the accident. Looking at his watch, eight forty-five, not wishing to worry her about his late arrival home, he called his wife. The farmer didn't want her unduly concerned before he got back, especially if she heard of the accident through the local radio station news.

Leaning back in the driver's seat, he stubbed out his cigarette and tried hard to relax. Tired, damp, cold and hungry he just wanted to get home, but the policeman had asked him to wait in the van so that in due course details could be taken of what Bob Newell had found immediately upon his arrival at the scene.

There was movement away to the right; he momentarily turned on his wipers to clear the windscreen. A policeman and a paramedic emerged from the gloom carrying between them a stretcher on which there was a strapped blanketed figure. Of the other paramedics, one was holding an intravenous drip while the other was tending the covered victim, the group hurried forward towards the waiting ambulance. Blue lights flashing, the stretcher and cargo loaded, it sped off into the night.

Bob Newell sat quietly observing from his van as a figure came towards him. He wound down his window to speak to the approaching police officer.

The second ambulance drew away, to be followed moments later by the motor-cyclist. Immediately a strange silence fell over the surrounding area, broken only by the sound of dripping vegetation and the fast flowing water below. Speechless, the two men looked at each other.

It was the policeman who spoke first. "I will be requiring a statement from you sir, where were you making for?"

"I was on the way home" was the reply,

On hearing Bob Newell only lived twenty minutes away the policeman suggested if he was OK to drive he should return there and get changed from his wet and soiled clothes.

"After I have radioed a report to Divisional HQ in Barnstaple to let them know what we propose to do, I will follow you."

Bob Newell nodded his agreement.

As he turned to leave the side of the van the policeman asked a question.

"As you are local, by any chance did you recognize the young lass involved in the accident?"

Before answering he paused.

"Yes, she was a young, recently married, teacher from my village, a lovely girl, very pretty and popular with kids and parents alike."

"A great pity" replied the policeman; looking the driver in the eyes, he put his head back in through the window to quietly address him.

"As you saw for yourself sir, she was in a pretty bad way. It isn't only the cuts; I am told there are serious head injuries as well. It will be touch and go…if you would like to lead I will follow. My colleagues here will arrange for the removal of the two damaged vehicles."

With no more ado, the policeman straightened and walked away.

*****

Rock, sand and soaring cliffs are all to be found on the North Devon coast, the relatively unspoilt the scenery is truly magnificent. It is only when travelling around Britain's other coastlines and seeing the unsightly developments that one realises just how lucky this part of the world has been. Caravan sites, marinas, large asphalt car parks and the hideous amusement arcades, here there is very little.

Fishing villages and tiny ports were the only settlements to be found along the North Devon shoreline before the Napoleonic wars put pay to people holidaying abroad. Wealthy travellers then discovered the treasures on their own doorsteps and word soon spread of a remote and unknown place called. Lynmouth.

In years past Lynmouth only comprised of a cluster of fishermen's cottages built around the mouth of the river Lyn, its rocky foreshore and a small pier. Until the early nineteenth century virtually the only living for the inhabitants had come from the catching of herring, thereafter the tourists arrived and with them the hotels and tea rooms. Gradually the coast was opened-up and the locals found themselves objects of curiosity to their holidaying visitors and this is resented just as much now as it was then, present day attitudes having changed very little from that of a hundred years ago.

Lynton, high up on the hillside above Lynmouth, owes its very existence to the influx of Victorian visitors. Large Hotels, parades of shops, level walks and viewpoints were all constructed to keep the summer visitor happy.

Close to Lynmouth is where the waters of two rivers, the East and West Lyn, converge. On that fateful day in history, after weeks of monsoon-like rain, their swollen contents met and a forty foot high wall of water swept towards the village where in its centre it swept aside numerous buildings and carried many helpless victims far out into the Bristol Channel.

Now the beautiful scenery of the East and West gorges are one of the area's principal attractions, the rush of the rivers is short but spectacular. Rising on Exmoor they have sliced their paths through an area deeply populated with wooded scrub oak. The different seasons of the year offer many varied visual attractions. After the ravages of winter comes the spring vegetation and foliage, to be followed by autumnal shades and sights of colours unmatched in North Devon.

Home to numerous species of birds, Watersmeet is a popular tourist haunt where visitors flock to see the waters bursting over a million rocks and boulders, but now the former Victorian fishing lodge acts as a shop and café, like most of the surrounding hinterland being in the ownership of The National Trust.

*****

The solitary male figure followed the footpath that was only partially distinguishable though the undergrowth and scrub covering the ground in Six-Acre wood. As he had been walking for over an hour with the warm air of the mild late-spring day refreshing his face, the going had gradually become more difficult as he left the easier ground of the cliff path and had taken the trail leading into the wood.

He was alone, that was the way he wanted it; he came here to be alone. Very few people knew of the deviation from the well-worn path regularly followed by the local population and many holiday visitors to the area. With the sun beating through the Larch and mature Sycamore trees he pushed onwards. Where the Scotch pine towered the daylight was totally obscured, only to re-emerge with a blinding ferocity; here the primrose, wood sorrel, cow-wheat and golden saxifrage grew.

With the exception of overhead squawks from cormorants and guillemots, the only sound was of the undergrowth as it lightly brushed the legs of the onward-bound walker. Left, right, and then right again soon the little used track was on a downward incline. Through another green tunnel and then without warning, as the path broke from the cover of the woods into the sparkling of an afternoon sun, the sight of open sea where the waters of Atlantic Ocean and Bristol Channel meet.

He inhaled deeply as the cooler air blowing inwards towards land hit him. Picking up another ill-defined track, he quickened his pace, stumbling over the now rocky terrain. From six hundred feet below the waves could be heard breaking on the shoreline, the path now became noticeably steeper. Picking his way between the exposed boulders away to his right he could just make out the small sandy beach of Lee Bay where in the height of the summer season visitors to the Abbey would often bathe, but his planned route was away from that area. Rounding the protruding cliff face he looked behind; alone, alone with nature and the sea, it was as he wished.

About two hundred feet above the sea he reached his destination, this was a place he often visited when wanting to be alone with his thoughts. Grass covered and boulder-strewn Meldrum Rock, a headland jutting out into the sea, a place where during the winter storms it was possible to stand looking seawards and feel spray thrown upwards as below the full force of angry water hit the bottom of the cliff face.

He stopped and looked northwards at the expanse before him. Miles away across the water in the distant mist he could just make-out the shadowy outline of the Welsh coastline. Turning his head slowly around, he surveyed the scene that over recent months had become so familiar, at first failing to notice today he was not alone, but was then taken aback.

No, he was not mistaken, this hidden world was his own territory and away to his left someone else was present. When taking the higher cliff-top route he occasionally met walkers who were on the long distance footpath that stretches around the southwest peninsula, but here was his territory. Feeling the intruder into his privacy was worthy of investigation, swiftly and silently he covered the ground to where the trespasser was sitting.

On approaching, he could see the offender was an artist, sitting on an exposed rock, back turned and apparently unaware of his presence. Now he was close enough to see the picture being painted was of the view facing him of rocks, cliffs and onwards out into the glistening waters.

He was unable to see the face, only the back of what was clearly a female figure. The wide brimmed hat and the delicate hands making the brush strokes on to the easel-mounted canvas suggested to him any confrontation he was about to have would be with a member of the opposite sex.

Not stopping to consider if his upcoming actions might be seen as unreasonable, in his own mind they were unquestionable, after all how could anyone dare to gatecrash his secret world?

Mesmerised, he stopped and watched the brush directing paint on to the canvas; the emerging picture had an uncanny likeness to the real thing.

At first she did not hear him approach and for a full ten minutes worked on appearing to be unaware of his presence. In the end it was he who was taken by surprise when she spun around and came face to face with the man standing directly behind her.

"Don't you know it's rude to stare? You have been there at least fifteen minutes, you could have frightened me."

In standing up she forsook the shelter offered from the sea breeze by the surrounding boulders and rocks, the wind caught the wide brimmed straw hat and blew it five or six yards away from her up the incline of the hill.

Three, four, five nimble steps and then reaching to the ground to pick-up her displaced headwear; he was taken aback, rooted to the spot and lost for words.

On the slightly higher ground and fifteen feet away stood a young woman, around mid-twenties in years, but he was never one to judge the age of another and would readily admit so. When he first approached from behind it had been gathered-up underneath, but as she stooped down to retrieve the lost hat it shook loose and the long blonde hair fell over her shoulders. Dressed in a full-length black skirt, high-necked white blouse and a quilted olive green jacket, the diminutive figure was given false height by the elevated ground on which she was standing.

The young woman spoke again.

"Don't you think it was rude and rather ungentlemanly to creep up on a lady, especially given the isolated nature of this place?"

He was unable to answer as before him stood the most beautiful woman one could wish to meet. The forceful elegance left him speechless; she also considered this her private domain so who was this man with the audacity to disturb her while she worked? Glancing towards the nearly finished painting sitting on the easel, he wanted to apologise for taking her away. He wanted to tell her he had been watching her re-create on canvas the real-life beauty of nature which spread out before them, but instead, shaken by their encounter, moved forward and with a weak smile embarrassingly mumbled an apology.

"I am sorry, I am truly very sorry."

With that he turned and hurried away, making his way over the same route so expectantly used fifteen minutes previously. His mind was topsy-turvy, who was this demanding young woman? Why had she intruded into his private world? Even to his inexperienced eye her painting was good, and like many a person before him he had been instantly captivated by her beauty. It was understandable because he had just encountered Suzanne Patterson for the first time. She watched as he disappeared up the path to the cliff top towering above her.

Satisfied the stranger of a few words had finally gone Suzanne returned to her painting, less than an hour later a passing cloud covered the sun bringing a rapid drop in temperature and an early end to her working day. The painting in progress remained unfinished and she would have to return another day.

Chapter 14

The next day it rained, the following day and the next, in fact there was foul weather for the next five days, but then it was a complete transformation. The high winds that had been blowing a gale dropped and if by a Royal Command the sun appeared, it was Saturday. By Monday the weather was very summer-like, bright and warm. Suzanne decided the time had come for her return to the hidden cliff-top ledge to continue painting the sea pounding away at the North Devon coastline.

Suzanne took the Cliff Railway to Lynton. On reaching the top she strode out, taking the mile long trek known as North Cliff Walk that in 1817 had been carved from the face of Hollerday Hill. Past the daunting Castle Rock and the junction with the footpath that went to Wringcliffe Bay, soon she was on the grass track which eventually passed close to the misnomer of Lee Abbey. Suzanne had already covered half the distance to her secluded spot.

At the stile, where the weathered *Lynton* signpost stood she paused for breath. Suzanne reached into her shoulder bag and took a single refreshing swig from the bottle of clear mineral water. The pace she had set herself in the first half of the walk had been quite demanding and, although well before mid-day, the sun was very warm. Suzanne continued walking and was soon amongst the carpet of spring flowers covering the floor of Six Acre Wood, she trod carefully as she made her way towards her final destination.

Emerging from the trees and making her way down through the grassy boulders with an air of contentment she quietly hummed to herself.

There was a solitary stillness and the only sounds were of the ocean breaking on the rocks below with the occasional shrieking of gulls as they sped outwards to sea seeking food for their cliff-top young.

And there he was!

As she rounded the final protruding rock he was standing alone with back turned and legs apart looking out across the water, one hand shading his eyes from the sun. Suzanne was surprised to find him back again; surely his last visit to this lonely spot, which she discovered by pure accident, had also been chance? Their encounter of the previous week had been very brief, but she was in no doubt about the identity of the figure ahead, it was the same stranger.

Suzanne did nothing to disguise her approach, as she hurriedly descended several loose stones clattered downwards from her path. The sound of the tumbling objects startled him and whoever it may have been he quickly turned to face the on-comer. His face showed a little faked surprise at seeing the blond haired Suzanne bearing down. Inwardly an excitement that had been missing for so long was aroused. Immediately he felt good, a hunch the beautiful creature encountered on his last visit to the isolated place would return was correct, but at the same time a voice from within seemed to be telling him how wrong it was.

Unlike the first time they met he was the first to speak, greeting Suzanne as if he had known her a long while and acting as if it was perfectly natural the two of them should be meeting in such a lonely spot. She returned the greeting, but chose to ignore his rather frivolous remarks about the day's beautiful weather, instead she just looked at her watch; it was nearly a quarter past twelve. Suzanne moved to the spot where she had been previously painting, unpacked her portable easel and prepared the incomplete canvas. She ignored the offer of help. Moving to another rocky outcrop, five feet above her, he sat with his knees pulled up under his chin and watched as Suzanne started to go about her work.

Nearly an hour went by and not another word passed

between them, Suzanne was only too aware of the casually, but well dressed man sitting behind watching her every move. As first she was a little concerned, although the distance from habitation was not overly great, perhaps it was being a little naïve and foolish to remain there with a complete stranger.

As she sat at the easel Suzanne could feel his eyes undressing her. She stopped and lowered her brush from the canvas and placed it on the edge of her paint palate, her hand now resting in her lap she took a deep breath ready to question the stranger. Before she could speak, without moving he quietly spoke.

"My name is David, David Burge. I know what is going through your mind, but you have no reason for concern. I come here regularly to get-away and be alone because it is such a beautiful place. No, no, please don't move."

As he had been speaking Suzanne was slowly rising to her feet, now once more sitting she turned to face the man who at least she now knew the name of.

"I have been watching, even to my inexperienced eye you are very good, do you paint for a living? Are you local? Where do you live? I have been around these parts all of my life and if you had been I am sure I would have noticed someone as beautiful as you before now, I used to work for the Post Office so there aren't many people I don't know."

He was firing the questions with a sudden newfound confidence. "What is your name and if you don't live in Lyn where are you staying?"

He was taken aback and his jaw dropped when rather than reply to his questions Suzanne just roared with laughter, she was laughing so much tears were rolling down her face.

He tried to stop her, asking hesitantly "What have I said that's so funny?"

"Nothing, oh really nothing, it isn't your fault, it's me!"

132

She stopped laughing, a warm smile now radiating in a very English manner from her pretty face, Suzanne held out her hand to shake his.

"I am very pleased to meet you" she said, "You must pardon me for being a little guarded I am a newcomer to the area and it isn't everyday one meets a complete stranger in such an isolated spot. Especially, as I am sure you will agree, if one is female and alone."

"And a very pretty female I might add"

"You flatter me!"

"I hardly think so," pausing before repeating himself, "I hardly think so."

"My name is Suzanne, Suzanne Patterson and I live in Lynmouth, Mr Burge."

"Please call me David; 'Mr Burge' sounds so formal."

There was a further pause as the two, now standing at a distance of only three feet apart, looked into each other's eyes. It was David who spoke first.

"Where do you live in Lynmouth? I thought I knew most of the residents of both Lynton and Lynmouth and yours is not a name I recognise."

Suzanne thought before she answered, her newfound friend stirred something inside her body. He was young, maybe a few years older than her, yet his face was so sad, but more important was that she did not feel threatened by him. David Burge had the air of a warm and gentle being. As she smiled at him a mischievous glint entered her eyes, while he waited expectantly and held his breath awaiting the reply.

"First things first, David!" As if trying to mask a point she spoke with emphasis on the word 'David'.

"To begin with you must tell me a little about yourself and what makes you return regularly to such a lonely spot?"

It was his turn to smile...

"I returned here in the hope of meeting the beautiful young lady I was fortunate enough to encounter last week. It seems the Gods have been gracious enough to grant me their favour."

He smiled again, but Suzanne noted the note of sarcasm in his voice.

"Please, Mr Burge do not mock me, you asked a question and I had the courtesy to answer truthfully. Even in this present day is it not correct a gentleman should nail his colours to the mast and it is certainly not fair to leave a lady at a disadvantage."

She was retaliating with an equal amount of sarcasm, the understanding of Victorian-like virtues having been well taught in childhood by her father.

A look of horror spread across his face.

"I am sorry, it wasn't my intention to offend and it will be well past my lunch time if I do not hurry," but instead of departing he just stood rooted to the spot.

Now straight faced, she in-turn stood looking at the worried figure before her, Suzanne had no wish yet to lose the company of the young man she surprisingly had rediscovered. Over the few days since their first meeting he had entered her thoughts more than once and this morning she was very pleased to have met-up with him again.

Suzanne's face relaxed as she broke the impasse by moving back towards the easel, he stood carefully watching as once more she sat herself down on the boulder facing him.

"You appear to be tetchier than me David."

She patted the rock beside her.

"Whatever you were going to do can wait, come and sit here and tell me a little bit about yourself, I give you my word I won't bite and then perhaps I will tell you a little about Suzanne Patterson and what brought her to Lynmouth. If it is lunch concerning you, come here and share mine, whatever plans you had for this afternoon can wait."

Once more she demandingly patted the rock face by her side. After a moment's hesitation he stepped forward and in two movements was sitting on the same boulder, a few feet from Suzanne.

A relaxed smile now on his face, he held out his right hand in greeting.

"Welcome to Lyn Miss Patterson. Please tell me, what would you like to know about David Burge?"

*****

Suzanne had left Bath with more than a little sadness in her heart for the family who she had been working and lived with for the previous five years. They, like everyone else she encountered, had a fondness that steadily grew in the time they had known the refreshing and girl-like Suzanne. Taking the girl into their hearts they gave her both a home and a job without realising the importance of their actions.

Initially she did not know why she had chosen the City to be her bolthole, but on reflection at the time it had probably seemed as good a place as anywhere. Suzanne had been responding to the advertisement placed by the Employment Agency in *The Lady* magazine she had purchased at Victoria Railway Station.

Suzanne reached Nimes five weeks after that fateful day, once there she had spent nearly another four weeks hidden away in a seedy back-street hotel contemplating what to do about her future. It was the sort of French boarding establishment where no one, especially the management, asks too many questions of the guests and there she slowly came to terms with her grief and the growing sense of abandonment.

She caught the early morning TGV service to Paris, the journey wound its way along the Rhone Valley, through Valence, stopping at Lyon, before making the 450 kilometres dash to Gare de Lyon. Suzanne did not wait in Paris, but immediately took a taxi across the City to

Gare de St Lazare where she had bought a single ticket and ninety minutes later boarded the mid-afternoon semi-fast service to the Channel fishing port of Dieppe.

It was shortly after six when the train on the final leg of its journey started the crawl from Dieppe Ville through the streets of the seaside town before finally coming to a halt at the harbour-side station of Dieppe Maritime.

The ticket Suzanne had purchased in Paris was to take her directly to London Victoria. It was along with seven or eight fellow passengers she stepped from the carriage and crossed the rails to enter into the station's shabby waiting room to await the next scheduled departure of the service to Newhaven and England.

She breathed a sigh of relief when nearly an hour later the cross channel ferry *Stena Londoner* eased its way through the dredged passage adjacent to the houses and along the watery route leading from the harbour mouth right into the ship's berth deep in the busy commercial centre of the Town.

The white painted vessel passed the end of the outer harbour wall as the flashing navigation light shone-out into the gathering dusk. This evening the sea was flat and calm, but in stormy weathers of winter many a sailor had been comforted to see the welcome indication of safe haven ahead. That night the red flashing beacon seemed to be bidding her farewell, goodbye to France, goodbye to unkind memories and goodbye to her past.

The ship made for deeper waters, Suzanne watched from the stern as on the horizon lights twinkling on the coast one by one slowly disappeared. Four hours later back on English soil having cleared Customs she boarded a paint-peeling train to take her direct from Newhaven Harbour Station to London Victoria.

Suzanne's original intention was to rest a while in London allowing herself time to decide which path should be taken at the crossroads of the Capital. With little difficulty she found what could be best described as a clean commercial hotel in which to stay, one of the many that seem to abound in the honeycomb of streets surrounding Victoria.

The first night she read the magazine bought earlier at the Railway Station. Suzanne did not know what drew her attention, but it had been placed in the centre of the classified ads and was an advertisement for an agency seeking suitable staff to fill numerous childcare and domestic positions. There was an address and telephone number to which interested persons should apply for more details, but Suzanne's intuition told her for the time being to ignore both.

And so it was the next day she caught the 9.35 a.m. National Express service from Victoria Coach Station to Bath. As Suzanne alighted at the end of her journey she enquired of the newsvendor selling the early editions of the evening newspaper outside the entrance to the Bus Station.

"Milsom Street?" she asked.

Advised the distance was too far for a young lady and her luggage to go on foot, it was a cherry-faced taxi driver who dropped Suzanne at number 46, a sign to the right of the front door announced *The Universal Domestic and Nanny Agency – second floor.*

In less than two weeks she had met the Bradshaw's and moved into their Camden Crescent address. It didn't really matter, they readily accepted Suzanne never talked about her past, because she was the best nanny they had ever employed and better still the Bradshaw children loved her too. There had been great sadness on all sides when Suzanne had eventually announced she planned to leave the family for pastures new.

The Bowron's were so correct about the cottage that had once belonged to Mary's uncle. About a half a mile in distance from the tiny harbour it was situated in a wooded combe, alongside a fast flowing tributary of the Lyn. With a low wood beamed lounge, two bedrooms, bathroom, a kitchen that also served as a dining room and a relatively large glass conservatory at the rear of the building, it was idyllic.

The move from Bath had been just over a year ago and at the time much against Suzanne's wishes Mary had lent her four thousand pounds enabling the former pupil to get started at the new artistic venture. It said much for her talent when within the first six months the loan had been repaid in full.

Chapter 15

Suzanne arrived in April. More often than not Mary came
to Lynmouth without the children, visiting regularly,
especially during the summer months. To begin with Tony
came with her, but after his first three visits Suzanne did
not see him, with the children it was an ever decreasing
number of times, but never Tony. The only response
Suzanne got to the question relating to his whereabouts or
well being was "Oh, Tony? He's fine, but he's busy today."
After a while she didn't even bother to ask.

Suzanne, "The blonde goddess that appeared from
nowhere", won everyone's heart with her looks, charm and
kindness. "The blonde woman who paints" and "The
mystery lass who is living up at Mike Edward's old place"
were only three of the many terms of endearment used in
the twin North Devon communities by locals when
describing the new arrival.

Slowly the wounds of the past were given full
opportunity to heal completely. She was just happy, very
happy at being allowed to do what she had always wanted
without distraction.

Because of their picture postcard appearances present
day Lynton and Lynmouth are never short of a steady
stream of visitors. The annual first quarter trickle slowly
builds to the rush experienced during the month of August
when, with car parks overflowing, the narrow streets are
thronging with people all seeking the unquestionable
atmosphere, but at the same time straining residents and
services alike.

The high season is past before it arrives, but through
all the crazy activity of the busy period one does not have
to travel very far to find the isolation that makes the north
coast of the south west peninsula so appealing. The final
three months of the calendar are a mirror image of the first
quarter and upon reaching Christmas the whole annual
cycle is repeated.

During the first year of her venture Suzanne soon discovered it was impossible to meet the demand and she could not produce enough of her work. With the kind permission of the vicar, and a handsome donation to parochial church funds, numerous exhibitions normally lasting ten days were mounted at the nineteenth century parish church of St Mary's in Lynton. It was June and at the second of these displays when she first met Mrs Molland.

It was a Saturday evening, Elsie Molland was just leaving the main door of the Church, Suzanne was returning to start the process of removing the twenty pictures displayed on the walls of the north and south aisles. As she approached the older woman recognized Suzanne immediately.

"You must be the person who painted these delightful pictures, Suzanne Patterson?"

"That is very kind of you to say so, yes, I am indeed responsible for the paintings; I have just come to remove them before tomorrow morning's service and am a little late. The verger will be here shortly to lock-up, but the vicar has very kindly agreed to me storing them overnight in the vestry. I have been very lucky though, this week I have sold eleven of the twenty on display."

"Twelve if I am not mistaken, are all those you have already sold marked accordingly?"

"I believe so", said Suzanne, looking at the other woman rather quizzically.

"There is a painting, half-way down on the right hand side, a picture of a half timbered building…"

Sensing maybe there was another sale in the offing Suzanne interrupted.

"The one of the *Lorna Doone Hotel* painted looking at it from across the harbour." As if embarrassed by the asking price, she lowered her voice, "It's two hundred and seventy-five pounds, or shall we say two hundred and fifty?"

"My dear!" the would be purchaser exclaimed,

"Cheap at half the price, I shall give you three hundred and fifty pounds, no argument."

Suzanne was lost for words.

"May I take it now?"

"Why of course, I will go and get it," hesitantly adding "That is if you are quite sure?"

"Of course I am sure! I wouldn't have spoken if I weren't. Oh, if you are to trust me to take the painting away I suppose I had better introduce myself, I am Elsie Molland and the sole proprietor of said hotel and restaurant. In recent weeks I have seen you at work around the locality and some weeks ago I came to the first of your exhibitions here at St Mary's, one or two of your paintings are the same, but it is the first time I have seen your picture of the Hotel, you are very clever."

Suzanne was blushing.

"Thank you, thank you very much, you are indeed very kind" hurriedly adding "I will get the picture for you."

Not believing her luck she disappeared through the door and into the church. Elsie followed and was standing behind Suzanne as she removed the picture from the wall; turning she passed it over to the elderly silver haired hotel owner.

"Thank you", Elsie paused before continuing, "If you are doing nothing this evening perhaps you would like to join me at the Restaurant for dinner, shall we say about eight? I will settle my debt of three hundred and fifty pounds then" and with an air of intrigue added, "I would also like to make a business proposition to you, but more about that in due course."

Suzanne waited before answering.

"This evening? That will be fine Miss Molland; I would be delighted to join you, as like every other evening I am doing nothing."

"I am surprised you are so readily free, I thought I would have to wait for the pleasure of your company at the

141

dinner table. Well, if that is all settled I must be off and make sure old Cheffy has got something special for us to eat on tonight's menu. Until later!"

She shook her enthusiastically by the hand and with the purchase safely tucked under arm, strode down the aisle, through the door and was gone before Suzanne had chance to add another word.

*****

The encounter at the Church, followed in the evening by the Restaurant meal, was the start of what was to become a strong and productive business relationship. Throughout the year Suzanne was allowed to display her paintings at the popular and picturesque *Lorna Doone Hotel and Restaurant* and in return she paid a percentage of the money earned on the sale of the paintings to the Proprietor, it was a constant and steady source of work for her and although the hotel itself closed during the winter months the high-class restaurant was open year-round. The clientele, many of who were local people, quickly came to appreciate the quality of the pictures on display and by autumn of the first year people were also starting to find their way to the studio at the cottage. It was inevitable the limitations on her time coupled with the overall standard of her work swiftly combined to push the purchase price of her paintings rapidly upward.

By the end of the first summer, Suzanne had repaid Mary's earlier loan besides forcing her former teacher to accept the second part of their original bargain by her starting to pay a moderate rent for use of the cottage both as home and place of work.

*****

Suzanne walked up the path to the front entrance. Unlocking and letting herself in, she made her way to the studio at the back of the house, missing the white envelope on the mat behind the door. With care she unloaded what she had been carrying and unwrapping the near finished painting placed it on an easel at the far end of the converted conservatory.

Suzanne took two steps backwards to examine her own work, satisfied she slumped into the old grey easy chair standing in the corner of the room.

He never talked much about himself, but she had found him so charming. He always let her get on with what she was doing, on reflection Suzanne thought she had probably said too much and hoped he wasn't completely bored, but at the time knew she had been unable to help herself.

"Silly really!" she said aloud, "David Burge, you appear so different from all the other men I have met since my arrival back in England and yet I know so little about you."

Suzanne smiled, at least when they met today she had had the sense to arrange a meeting next week and at his invitation to journey with him into Barnstaple for lunch. With a sigh she rested her head back on the chair; Suzanne had very quickly come to like her new friend and was still smiling to herself as she closed her eyes.

She looked at her watch; it was well into the evening and time to go and get ready if she was to dine with Elsie at the Restaurant. Since the purchase of the painting and the subsequent business arrangement, over the past weeks the older woman had become a close friend and Suzanne regularly dined with the hotelier at least once a week. It gave chance to discuss the happenings of the preceding seven days and Elsie always took the opportunity to introduce the young artist to Hotel guests, business associates and chosen friends. For Suzanne it created a new and fuller circle of contacts which in the case of Elsie Molland herself had soon extended into a firm friendship and shared confidentialities.

She made her way to the entrance hall to climb the

stairs to shower and prepare for the latest of her regular evening dinner meetings. It was only then she saw the single envelope which had been put through her letterbox at the time of the mid-day mail delivery. Suzanne immediately recognized the handwriting on the outside of the envelope; it was the familiar neat script of her former art mistress.

Sitting on the bottom stair, she used her little finger to slit-open the top of the envelope. Reading slowly, Suzanne found the content came as a shock and it was only after reading the letter a second time the sad truth started to dawn on her.

243, Newbridge Road,
Bath

23rd May, 1996

My Dearest Suzanne

I hope this letter finds you in good health, and, like your beauty, your work keeps being in such demand.

I still miss you as words cannot describe. We really must do something about getting a telephone line installed at the cottage and then we will be able to talk more often.

In your last letter you spoke of how well the arrangement is working with Elsie Molland, I do hope it long continues to be such a satisfactory situation. Having observed everything when last there with the children I see no reason why it should not. The visit was over two months ago and is one of the main reasons I am writing.

Because of circumstances, I am afraid it will be sometime before I will be able to reach and be with you again, a situation I am finding very hard to accept. Some years ago I thought I had lost you forever, but fate was to play a hand in getting us reunited, allowing me to care for you like I have cared for no other woman. During my recent visits to Devon I wondered when you questioned me to explain the absence of Tony how I would eventually have the courage to tell you the answer. I think the time has now arrived.

Tony was always suspicious of my love for you, but I must say, he realised with your innocence you were probably unaware of my true feelings and in his fatherly manner he is, as in their own way the children are, very fond of you.

When he first suggested the move to Lynmouth it was purely in your professional interest. Tony had no wish to face-up to the fact his wife had fallen in love with another woman.

Within a month of you moving to Devon he was made redundant. Tony lost his job with the Bank, modern day rationalisation was the reason given and he was shattered. Worse was to follow.

Ten days after being given notice by the Bank, Tony went into the attic to look for a box of family papers he thought he had put there when we first moved to Bath from Dorset. Whilst in the roof he came upon an old school trunk from St Bernadette's full of my paintings. I was so cross, by sorting through it Tony did something he had never done before with my belongings, one by one he removed all the pictures in the trunk and unwrapped the sackcloth individual paintings were wrapped in.

Everything was fine until he reached the ninth canvas; it was a picture I had painted during the time I was teaching at the School. Painted from my imagination it was of a young and slender girl who was erotically posing nude. The problem arose when Tony looked at the face of the beautiful female. He later said without any doubt it was a picture of you. It was as I intended.

Each time upon reaching this part of the letter Suzanne paused. She understood fully and remembered only too well seeing the same picture all those years ago when making the illicit visit to Mary's studio over the garage. She remembered being as a naughty schoolgirl who had no wish to be found-out for her mischievous trespassing and had said nothing to anyone at the time and the whole incident had long been forgotten. Suzanne continued to read the letter.

The shock of losing his well-paid job, coupled with the fact I refused to deny my true feelings for you, was too much for Tony. After weeks of continual arguing between us, he rented a flat in the Clifton area of Bristol and moved out of the family home. Three months later, together with a large redundancy package from his former employer, he moved back to Bournemouth.

The children visited their father, as they did not really understand what had happened between their parents and, together with pressure from Tony's sister, implored us to get-back together again. I really am surprised the boys did not talk about the situation when we last visited you

To cut a long story short, ten days ago Tony moved back to Bath and has found himself a part-time management position with a Company in the Larkhall district of the City. For the sake of the family we have decided to give things one more go, but with my feelings for you undiminished and our previous compatibility problems, truthfully I am not very hopeful for the long-term future of the relationship with Tony.

Unselfishly I have promised him I will not visit you either alone or with the children, however unlikely, Tony thinks this arrangement will give me a chance to forget how much you have come to mean to me. The one other sanction he imposed on me was in future our family solicitor should handle the arrangements relating to all matters arising from your use of the cottage. Please forgive me, but for simplicity's sake I agreed to comply with both of these conditions. I am so sorry about the morbid tone of this letter, but I will write to you again shortly. At the present time I do not think it would be in either of our interests for you to write to me. I will just have to get a telephone line installed for our use!

Until the next time we are in-touch, take care and please remember I will always love you

.

All my fondest love

Mary xx

Suzanne finished reading the letter for the third time and with her head in a spin slowly folded it, before climbing the stairs to prepare for her evening meal with Elsie Molland.

Chapter 16

For the time of the year the evening in the restaurant was relatively quiet and surprisingly to begin with very little conversation passed between them. It was only when Suzanne pushed the plate containing much of her duck à l'orange main course to one side the Proprietor spoke.

"Is there anything wrong? It is most unlike you, was the food not to your liking? You normally have a very healthy appetite and will eat almost anything Cheffy puts in front of us. Are you feeling unwell?"

Suzanne averted her eyes, as she spoke.

"It's nothing, nothing at all Elsie. I am fine, but I am so tired."

"Well if you are sure everything is alright. Now then…" said the older woman, who was trying with an exuberant tone to raise the sombre air that seemed to have settled between them, "I don't want any pudding, must think about my waistline, how about you?"

Suzanne shook her head.

"Good, shall we go though to the Lounge for some coffee then?" She paused before continuing, "If you feel unwell perhaps we should retire to my flat, it would be a little more peaceful there. Whatever, we should not be too long, coffee and then home early to bed otherwise if you are sick we could put you up here for the night, there are a couple of empty rooms."

Suzanne managed a smile.

"I am sorry, unusual really, but for some reason I am just not hungry, you always feed me so well Elsie, you are very kind. Tonight for once I will also manage without the sweet trolley otherwise I will be having trouble with my waistline!" She chuckled as she tapped her own shapely figure.

"That's better, you have cheered-up."

Suzanne smiled back at the older woman.

"Let's go to the Lounge, it looks fairly quiet so we

will be able to talk in peace. Afterwards I will get Chris the porter to walk with you up to the cottage just to make sure you arrive safely. I would hate anything to happen on the way."

"You really are very thoughtful, but I assure you I am, and will be, fine."

As the two women moved back from the table and crossed the dining room to go through into the Lounge, Suzanne did not notice Elsie studying her face and noting her worried frown, it seemed to be a face behind which lay a mind in turmoil. They were interrupted by the Head Waiter.

"Is everything to Madame Molland's liking?"

"Fine Philippe, fine!" She followed Suzanne from the room. "I would have soon let you know if it bloody well wasn't!" thought 'Madame'. While passing, she surreptitiously ran a finger over the small ledge by the door.

"In the morning I must remind the cleaner I pay her to clean!"

Having ordered the coffee, Elsie settled into a chair in the subdued corner lighting of the Lounge, table between them, Suzanne took the chair opposite. A brief discussion followed about the paintings sold at the Hotel over the previous ten days, two definite and one perhaps and both ladies agreed 'Not bad.' Forty minutes and two cups of coffee later Suzanne said it was time for her to leave.

"As you suggested, I don't want to be late. I feel a lot better than I did, but I would like to make an early start tomorrow, besides I have no wish to drag your porter all the way up the hill just to accompany me. I know it is a warm and dry night, but I am positive he has much better things to do than chaperon home his employer's friends."

"Are you sure? It really doesn't matter to him."

"I am quite sure, but thank you for the offer, the walk home alone will do me good. Before I go there is one thing you may be able to help me with though," pausing she

149

looked down at her hands, "I don't know how to ask you this really." She waited again.

Elsie came to her rescue.

"Why not try me, I can only say I am unable to help, you should know me well enough by now and realise if I can assist in anyway I surely will."

Suzanne started nervously, slowly gaining in confidence as she continued.

"Well it is like this, I have made the acquaintance of a young man. We have only met a few times, the first was by pure accident, the second occasion, I suspect, was a partially contrived situation on both our parts. The second time we met he told me he had gone there in the hope I would be painting in the same spot as when we first encountered each other."

"So you have been with this man earlier today?"

Suzanne looked at Elsie anxiously.

"Why yes, I was with him late this morning and most of the afternoon. Is there anything wrong? He was perfectly honourable, good-looking, cheerful and charming."

Realising perhaps she was overdosing Elsie on the superlatives Suzanne added, "The only thing is he seems perhaps a touch shy, quiet, one might even say a little too deep and certainly guarded in response to some of my questions."

Elsie laughed aloud.

"My dear you are incorrigible. In full flight you are indeed a very formidable young lady. Now before you go you must tell me about this new found boyfriend of yours."

Without realising how far off the mark she was, the Proprietor exclaimed so loudly that all the other guests seated in the Hotel Lounge turned their heads.

"I knew it! I knew as soon as you arrived this evening you had something on your mind. When you didn't eat Cheffy's meal it was proof, you are in love! Congratulations!"

Colouring-up, Suzanne had no wish to attract further

attention from the room's other occupants so did not attempt to put her friend straight about the real reason for the earlier uncharacteristic sullenness and apparent lack of hunger. With the letter tucked away safely at the bottom of her dressing table drawer she decided it was best for the present to play along with the partial truth, she spoke in a hushed tone.

"The thing is I have agreed to go shopping in Barnstaple with him on Market Day next week and he has offered to take me to lunch. The problem is I know so very little about him, I wondered if you may be able to help? You know everyone and everything there is to know in Lyn, do you know him?"

Elsie laughed again. She was pleased to see Suzanne radiating like her normal self; who ever this man was certainly seemed to have made an impression on her in a very short space of time.

"But you haven't told me anything about him yet, how can I help? There are many visitors to Lyn I never have the opportunity to meet, unless you are more specific I don't think I can be of any assistance."

A glum look reappeared across Suzanne's face.

"Sorry, I am asking the impossible; I just thought you might be able to help."

Watching her apparent rapid deflation Elsie asked, "I don't suppose you even got a Christian name? If we had that we would have at least somewhere to start searching or asking."

Suzanne excitedly looked across the table.

"How silly of me, didn't I say what his name was? How silly! I forgot, he told me earlier today." She blurted out "His name is David, David Burge! Do you know anyone of that name?"

There was a stony silence, which was only broken by Philippe entering the room. The Head Waiter came to his employer's elbow, bending over he whispered something

151

into Elsie's ear, before leaving as unexpectedly as he had arrived.

She turned to Suzanne.

"My dear will you please excuse me, I have industrial unrest, as one might with the kitchen staff, it happens from time to time even in the best Hotels. Please excuse me."

She rose and moved quickly towards the door. Halfway across the lounge Elsie turned and with a smile on her face raised her eyebrows, as did the listening heads of the other six occupants of the room.

"Oh yes, I know of him, nice lad, even if a little quiet," she slipped in the word "Understandably," but it was virtually inaudible in her sentence. "As you said, he is a charming polite young man, I approve. I am sure like many others who know him, he has my blessing to keep your company; long may it prosper."

With no further explanation, Elsie whisked herself through the door and silence followed.

Ten minutes passed. Suzanne sat alone in the lounge and keeping themselves to themselves the other occupants said nothing. An elderly couple rose from their chairs and wished everyone goodnight before making their way to the first floor and their bedroom. Not wishing to wait any longer for her hostess Suzanne followed. After collecting her coat from the lobby of the Hotel, she made her way into the street.

It was a clear night and Suzanne was looking up into the sky as she turned and started the half a mile walk to the cottage. The stars were twinkling their pattern above the rooftops as if smiling in the still night air at what lay below the shadows cast by the moon. As she walked Suzanne's mind turned to the future, very rarely thinking of her past terrors, she seemed to have naturally acquired the ability to shutout the preceding horrors of her young life.

There was the question she had to address of being able to meet the public demand for her paintings. Very nice it may be to currently have friendly support for her work, but in the future would she be able to keep up with the demand without the quality suffering? What was she to do about the letter she had received from Mary? Never thinking of her as anything different, she had previously thought of the former art teacher purely as a mother figure.

Suzanne considered the situation. Surely she had not misled Mary in any way? There was no doubt from the content of the letter and on reflection some of her past words and actions Mary was suffering from more than a middle-age infatuation. Suzanne had no wish to hurt any feelings as over the years Mary and her husband had been very kind to her and in time could see no reason why the friendships should not continue. She would just have to be very careful not to start something she could not handle and at least for the time being dealing with a solicitor rather than Tony or his wife would be a help. The length of time Mary is able to keep away should determine whether she is able to forget about the feelings expressed in her letter and with Tony's help she can do it, poor Mary.

Before turning into the narrow confines of Church Passage and starting the steep climb up the hill away from the shops and houses, passing the doorway of *Pomeroy's Antique Shop* Suzanne was startled by the shadow of two figures. They were moving in the darkness created by the recessed entrance, she stopped and peered into the gloom.

After a moments hesitation Suzanne breathed a sigh of relief as she realized the outlines were those of two young lovers oblivious to the watching nocturnal spectator as they embraced and passionately kissed. Having no wish to be accused by the two teenagers of being a voyeur, she continued her journey upwards leaving the couple oblivious to having been discovered.

As Suzanne walked her mind returned to the exercise of examining her future and what may lie in store for her in the months and years ahead.

"Ah yes, the mystery man! The mystery man whom

when questioned about earlier Elsie Molland had been very guarded about. Perhaps I will find the answer out next week, yes, certainly a challenge."

As the hill got steeper with determination her stride lengthened and she took the footpath leading away from the main thoroughfare. Now panting and short of breath she hurried forward.

"Yes, I think I will accept the challenge of David Burge" she muttered.

Within ten minutes Suzanne let herself into the comforting security of the cottage. Her mind was still awash as an hour later, now curled safely under the cover of her lonely bed she soon fell into a deep sleep.

*****

Following their planned lunchtime visit to Barnstaple, the friendship between Suzanne and David grew. Throughout the autumn they would meet regularly and could often be found arm in arm walking and talking together, obviously enjoying each other's company.

With wry smiles Elsie Molland observed from afar. As far as she was concerned the developing relationship was good news, David did not interfere with her protégée's work and if anything Suzanne's output seemed to be increasing without sacrifice to quality. The number of paintings sold at the Hotel had steadily increased and Suzanne appeared able to meet the ever-growing demand. He had injected even more creative energy into the young artist.

Elsie thought to herself why should she be the one to complain as it had made the *Lorna Doone Hotel and Restaurant* an even more popular meeting place for both visitors and locals. Long may the friendship last, it was good for Suzanne, it was good for Elsie Molland and meeting Suzanne had certainly been good news for David Burge.

Elsie was not too concerned, but she had not spoken

to Suzanne for nearly six weeks and it was nearing the end of October so the seasonal demand for local land and seascapes was past its peak. Soon it would be time to make arrangements with Suzanne for the winter and Christmas periods, besides she was holding nearly a thousand pounds in cash and cheques which Suzanne had yet to collect from sales of her work. It was unusual, normally Suzanne called into the Hotel once a week, occasionally it had extended to once a fortnight, but never six weeks. Three days ago Elsie made a call to Suzanne's newly installed telephone to enquire if all was well, only to be greeted by a confounded answering service and she hated talking to machines!

Perhaps she had gone away for a few days? Unlikely, Suzanne would have confided in her and one thing had soon become very obvious, Suzanne had very few family or friends to visit, the only people Elsie had ever heard her speak of was a family she knew living in Bath. Elsie's mind was very active as she relaxed in a corner of the empty Hotel lounge where the autumnal late afternoon sun cast beams of light across the room. Soon it would be time to close the Hotel for winter and yet another season would have passed. She sighed and collected the tray Cheffy had sent from the kitchen with her afternoon tea and scones; rising from the green velvet chair she came to the conclusion whatever the reason for Suzanne's absence it wasn't her problem.

Lucy, the front desk's young receptionist entered the room. "Ah, there you are Mrs Molland. I have a telephone call for you."

Not being used to being disturbed in her relaxation time, "Staff should know better," she always said. Elsie snapped at the short-skirted youngster.

"Who is it? Why couldn't you get them to call me later rather than disturb me at this time? And please note, in future I would prefer it if your hemline was more in keeping with the tone of this establishment!"

"I am very sorry Mrs Molland, but there is a very upset lady on the line asking for you…it sounded a bit like Miss Patterson and I thought that…" Before she could continue any further the young receptionist was interrupted.

"Put the call through to my rooms, I will take it in the flat."

Elsie moved swiftly across the lounge and was making her way up the stairs to her second floor accommodation before her young employee had time to react.

"Hello, hello, is that Suzanne?"

A timid female voice confirmed it was indeed Suzanne Patterson.

"I need to talk to you Elsie, I am sorry I have not been in touch with you for a couple of weeks."

"Nearly six." thought the older woman.

"What is the problem my dear? You sound very upset, what's wrong?" There was a pause and the line appeared to go dead. "Hello…Suzanne are you there?"

The caller was obviously in tears when she replied.

"Where is 'Here'? It obviously isn't Lyn…What do you mean by you have no wish to talk over the telephone? How can I help you if you won't talk to me?" A hint of annoyance had found its way into Elsie's voice, but as the answer came back she thought quickly.

"Make your way to the railway station…have you any money? …Good, I was only making sure…Catch the next train from Temple Meads to Taunton, I will meet you outside the station…There is no need to thank me now, you can do that later, just make sure you are on the train…What is the time now? …Good, with a little bit of luck you will be here tonight, just in time for dinner ….Yes I am sure, now hurry, I will meet you in Taunton."

The caller was still offering profuse thanks as Elsie put the receiver down, but her immediate curiosity was curtailed by the need to find the departure of the next train

156

from Bristol to Taunton and its time of arrival in the neighbouring County town. Having waited for what seemed like hours Elsie's telephone call was eventually answered, but once picked-up the response to her enquiry was efficient and prompt. The next train left Bristol in fifty-five minutes so it gave her two hours to make Taunton; she could easily handle that.

Elsie quickly made her way down the stairs to check everything was functioning as it should and tell the staff she would not be returning until around eight-thirty in the evening; it was now twenty minutes past four by her watch.

She met the 16.50 from Bristol Temple Meads to Taunton without any problem, excepting the train was seventeen minutes late arriving due to a signalling fault at Weston-super-Mare, but as instructed Suzanne was on it.

Greetings exchanged, the younger of the two women said it was extremely good of Elsie to meet her.

"No problem my child, but what of yourself? Why the mysterious telephone call this afternoon? Where have you been for the past six weeks? We have all missed you so much."

The last statement was perhaps a slight exaggeration, as with a few exceptions the majority would not have noticed her absence and assumed the artist was hard at work or even taking a well deserved break, but Elsie's intuition told her something was wrong.

"Later Elsie, later; please would you take me back to the cottage? Have no fear I am in good health and in part my absence has been due to a matter of the heart, I am afraid I've been very foolish. May I swear you to secrecy if I tell?"

"Why of course my dear, what other way is there?"

They reached the car where Elsie unlocked the doors and looked across the Peugeot's roof as Suzanne began speaking.

"I am sorry, there was no other way and it was wrong

157

of me to think there might have been, but over the past days my mind has been in a complete turmoil..."

Climbing into the car and pulling shut the passenger door Suzanne finished the sentence.

"... and I have not known which way to turn, I have needed time to think."

As they pulled-out into Taunton's evening traffic Elsie added "Poor Suzanne, poor girl, why didn't you ask me? I am sure I could have helped in some way."

"Yes perhaps, but I don't think you could have solved the awkward part of the problem. In his wisdom, God has thrust that responsibility upon my shoulders."

As she negotiated the rush hour traffic and reached the A39 leading all the way to Barnstaple and then home, Elsie Molland said nothing but just thought. Perhaps she was about to learn the answer to the question which had been avoided by the girl and been nagging in the back of Elsie's head since day one and their first meeting at the Devon church.

"I decided I had to visit the only person who could help me, the only person who would be able to begin to understand, but I am afraid I did not have the courage to complete my journey. Finally and out of desperation, I telephoned you from the Guest House in Bristol where I decided to stay..."

There were tears in her eyes as she stopped and turned her head towards Elsie.

"So .... Here I am now." Silence followed.

Despite the driver's attempts at starting conversations it remained the same way for the rest of the journey. Any response to Elsie's pleasantries seemed to be a polite, but monosyllabic 'Yes' or 'No'. In the end she gave-up trying to talk and the miles went by with nothing of any further consequence passing between them.

Chapter 17

Six weeks before, two days after the last meal at the Hotel with Elsie, was the first time Suzanne realised she was trapped by her own feelings and fear of the past. Suddenly the memories started to reappear; taunting and unpleasant memories she had no wish to relive.

For an hour after returning home from Taunton, Suzanne read and reread the letter.

"Why me?" she asked herself. "What are these feelings Mary has? Perhaps I should have recognized the unrealistic warmth shown towards me and she has been so kind, poor Mary. I certainly would not be in the position I am today with my painting without her support, she has been so kind. What about Tony and the children? They adored her, but I loved her too, so kind to all the girls at St Bernadette's, but never asking for anything in return. Why paint a picture of me? I did not recognize anyone else in the paintings hidden away over the garage. Why paint me unclothed and posing suggestively? Tony has reached the wrong conclusion because I certainly have not offered myself to his wife. What has Mary done and why has she left her feelings so exposed?"

With a large degree of personal naivety Suzanne sought answers to her own questions before she fell asleep exhausted having finally decided the problem could only be solved by seeking-out the art mistress and having a frank face to face discussion relating to the overall situation between them and in the long run how it would effect Suzanne's occupancy of the cottage.

On Thursday of that week she agreed to meet David. He also wondered where Suzanne had been over the past weeks, he told her it was imperative they meet at the first possible opportunity, as there was something important she should know.

They arranged to meet at the beginning of the cliff path as David said he would find it easier that way.

Whatever had to be said she had no reason to disbelieve him having already discovered he sometimes found difficulty in putting things into words.

Rising in the early morning before seven, she pushed Mary's letter to the back of her mind. The sky was clear, the risen sun was shining and she wanted to put the finishing touches to a near completed painting which, unusually for her own organized methodical self, was nearly three weeks over the promised delivery date. In this case the customer was the local tourist information office who because of her growing reputation had asked if they could commission a painting of the harbour mouth to hang in their reception area.

Spending nearly three hours in the conservatory studio, Suzanne packed away the materials she had been using and looked at the clock, ten-thirty; an hour to prepare a picnic and meet David at the beginning of their private and secretive route.

Cutting her delicate sandwiches she thought about the male stranger who had entered her life. Over the past months Suzanne and David had met a number of times, he had driven her to Exeter and Barnstaple and they walked and talked at length, all- the-while clearly enjoying each other's company. They met mainly in the afternoons as David worked in a supervisory position with the Royal Mail which invariably meant early starts to his day. Suzanne still knew very little about him including not knowing where he lived, but she did not press him, confident eventually he would tell all.

David had never been to her house except the night he had taken her to see the Bournemouth Symphony Orchestra perform at the Northcott Theatre in Exeter after which he offered to walk her home to the front door. It was an enjoyable warm summer's evening, declining his offer she walked alone light-heartedly up the darkening narrow lane to the cottage.

Oh, how she had enjoyed herself both the music and atmosphere, but best of all the company of a person who seemed to make no demands at all excepting she should just be there accompanying him. In the period of time since they first met there seemed to be an ever-growing understanding between them.

Suzanne packed away the last of the lunchtime food into the wicker basket and hurried down the hill and into the town centre where she made her way to the vertical railway to take her up the cliff face and the agreed rendezvous.

"I am sorry I am late" was the greeting David received.

He looked at his watch before replying.

"Five minutes, if that, you're forgiven. How could anyone be cross with you? As usual you look beautiful."

"Oh go on David Burge, flattery will get you nowhere. For your cheek you can carry our lunch!"

She thrust the basket forward, in doing so playfully pouted her lips.

"Lunch as well! Her thoughtfulness is second only to her beauty," he mockingly retorted and with a smile took the basket containing the goodies. With his other arm he reached around the trim waistline and pulled her towards him, before kissing Suzanne lightly on the cheek.

"Behave yourself David" laughing as she pulled away. "Do you always behave like that in public? I have my reputation to protect and it would not make good reading in the Exmoor Herald - *Devon Lass Attacked with Sandwich Box by Rampant Local!*" It was her turn to try and mock him.

A horrified look spread across his face.

"I don't find that particularly funny Suzanne. I wanted to tell you something important this afternoon, but how can I possibly if you are going to act in such a frivolous manner?"

"Oh come on David, don't be such a bore, the sun is

shining again and it is joy to be alive. Unless you are going to tell me you are a married man with three kids who all of a sudden has just found his conscience and thinks perhaps he should not be keeping company with a member of the opposite sex who, I assure you, sees your intentions to be nothing but honourable, I quite frankly don't want to know."

Leaving him holding the basket containing their lunchtime food, she turned and slipped away lightly skipping down the path.

"Come on follow me, catch me if you can and don't be such a misery because I am hungry and ready to eat."

Turning with a smile, Suzanne stopped and beckoned him.

"Come on you can tell me later, if you must" she chuckled, continuing to playfully skip along the high pathway.

David sighed and glumly shrugged his shoulders thinking at least he had tried. With a resigned air, "Wait for me" he called after the disappearing figure, "I'm coming."

*****

It was late afternoon; David and Suzanne were sitting some distance apart on the cliff top rocks, close to where their first meeting had taken place. They had spent a very pleasant time discussing the beauty laid-out before them. It was truly a special place, the angular definitions of the rock face below, the sparkle of the sun off of what was a pure blue sea and the sounds of squawking gulls and cormorants borne upwards by the warm air thermals. Both looked seawards towards the horizon, Suzanne with her knees pulled up below her chin, he with both legs resting over a large drop, they had not spoken for nearly an hour and it was David who broke the long silence.

"I have enjoyed being with you again, but perhaps we ought to be thinking of going, it is fast approaching

162

four o'clock and you said earlier you had to deliver the painting you finished this morning. I would not want you to be late on account of me."

"It can wait and I have no wish to go. I am just so happy here enjoying the peace and seclusion."

"Are you happy Suzanne? Talking to you it seems you are such a lonely person. You work and live alone and with the exception of Mrs Molland at the Hotel you appear to have very few friends."

She turned to face him before speaking.

"Let me assure you I am fine, of course, like everyone else in this world, I have my worries and my fears."

With an air of seriousness she lowered her voice, before continuing.

"Life has not always been kind to me and I have had more than my fair share of frustrations, disappointments and shocks. I have learnt to trust no one and in many ways, often through no fault of my own, this world has been very cruel to me. Please don't push me further David, but here I have been able to re-discover myself without being asked for too much in return and in helping me to establish my business people have been very kind and friendly."

As she stopped speaking a silence once more returned between them, only broken by the muted roar of the surf below and the sound of the birds above.

He pulled himself to his feet and moved across the craggy outcrop to sit closer to her.

"That was a very sombre few words, most unlike you, but can I assure you on behalf of all the people who have made your acquaintance here in Lynton and Lynmouth the luck is all ours."

He reached out and took her left hand into his and after a moment spoke.

"We all suffer disappointments at some time or another in our lives that have to be endured. Whilst not wishing to pry into your affairs, I very much suspect you too, but I have suffered monumental grief and at one time feared I might be scarred for the rest of time. It is a deep wound and you alone have started the healing process."

David Burge stopped speaking. As he held on tightly to Suzanne's hand his gaze was fixed far out to sea, the only sounds were those of nature. With the continuing silence she turned to face him, but he did not notice, his eyes were fixed on the distant horizon, Suzanne watched as tears slowly trickled down his face.

"What is it David? You can tell me." Whispering as she gently stroked his hand "What is it you are afraid of?"

He did not reply, but continued with his stare into the far distance. It was several minutes before he turned towards Suzanne and quietly spoke.

"You are very kind, beautiful and talented. It is you and only you who has allowed the healing process to begin and that is because ..." he stopped; tears were once more appearing in his eyes.

"Because? Because of what David?"

He continued, "Because of the most perfect person the world has known, irreplaceable, irreplaceable that is until you arrived in all our lives ... my life in particular."

Pulling away and now openly sobbing, he rested his elbows on his knees and placed his lowered head into his hands.

"I think you should leave me here alone."

She reached and placed her hand on his shoulders. Without looking up and in a raised voice he retorted "Leave me I said! Go!"

Rejected, Suzanne hurriedly sat back and then quickly got to her feet. David did not attempt to stop her as she scrambled over the rocky ground towards the cliff top path leading her back to the secure isolation of her home. Nearly four hours later she eventually once more made her way up the lane towards the cottage.

Initially when returning from the strange and abrupt

164

end to the afternoon, she gathered the completed painting and took the commissioned work to the tourist centre in the centre of Lynmouth. They had been more than happy with Suzanne's efforts and following proud introductions by volunteer staff manning the office, she spent over an hour in discussion with the late visitors. Although by then early evening, she decided to walk to the quayside and mingle with the crowds of tourists still seeking the exclusive atmosphere of the small seaside haven.

Suzanne made her way to the *Lorna Doone Hotel* intending to talk with Elsie Molland who she thought might be able to throw some light on the reason for David's earlier behaviour. On reaching the Hotel she was disappointed to hear her friend was not there, the girl on the front desk recognised Suzanne.

"Mrs Molland will not be back until later tomorrow at the earliest."

With an air of desperation, Suzanne asked quizzically "Where has she gone?"

"Don't know" was the half sneering reply "None of my business, Mrs Molland doesn't tell her employees all of her movements" and as if trying to justify the reply added, "After all it's none of my business so now is there anything else I can do for you?"

"No, no thank you, I'll call and see Elsie about this tomorrow. Please will you leave her a note to say I have been in today to see her" and with a sigh Suzanne added "That will be all thank you" turned and walked out of the door back on to the street.

As Suzanne left the previously short-skirted receptionist resentfully looked-up from the note she was already writing.

"Yes Miss! No Miss! Three bags full Miss! Anything you want Miss High and Mighty!"

Even if she had known about it, she wouldn't have understood the turmoil and confusion in the mind of her employer's young friend.

As Suzanne neared the cottage her thoughts once more turned to the letter received from Mary. What was she to do? Her feelings for the former art mistress were deep, but she did not understand the words of love expressed in the correspondence and even if she did not fully understand they seemed to hold a dark and sinister meaning. As she took the final steps to the gate at the end of her garden path Suzanne found that she was asking questions of herself.

"Oh Mary what am I to do? If you were only here to help, tell me what you want and allow me to tell you of my own problems. Perhaps Elsie has the answers? Perhaps she can advise on the course my life should take? Yes, I must talk to her first and as soon as possible. I will tell her absolutely everything because she always knows what to do…damn you Elsie Molland where were you? Why can't I talk to you this evening? Why must it wait until tomorrow?"

Pushing open the gate to walk the short distance up the cobbled path to the front door Suzanne was startled by a shadowy figure emerging from under the ivy covered porch. On hearing the approaching footsteps on the stones it rose from the narrow wooden bench on which it had been seated awaiting the return of the cottage's occupier.

Chapter 18

As she entered the gate to walk up the path, the figure moved from the long shadows being cast by the sinking late summer sun.

"Hello Suzanne, I thought I had better return this and apologize for my earlier uncalled for behaviour, I am truly sorry."

She stopped frozen to the spot, but no words came from her mouth as she tried to speak. The two of them stood in silence for what at the time to her seemed an eternity. It was the unexpected visitor who spoke first.

"I thought the least I could do was to return this to you."

Suzanne managed a faint smile as David Burge bent down and picked-up the picnic basket which earlier in the day he had carried to their lunchtime rendezvous. He held it at arms length towards her.

"I am sorry, my behaviour was uncalled for and I don't know what came over me. I should have known better."

Having recovered from the surprise of meeting anyone waiting on the doorstep at that time of the evening, let alone the person who after such a pleasant picnic lunch had acted in such an uncharacteristic manner, Suzanne composed herself.   Finally she spoke in a hushed tone.

"Thank you for bringing the basket back, it really didn't matter, but I am sorry I forgot and left it behind."

"Not surprising really, my behaviour this afternoon left more than a little to be desired. I don't normally shout at anyone, especially a person whom I have very quickly come to respect. I don't know what came over me. I shouldn't be here really, but I was afraid you wouldn't give me another opportunity to apologise so I decided to take a chance and hoped you would let me say sorry to your face. I am truly very repentant so please forgive me because I'm certain it will not happen again, I swear."

There wasn't a sound; a very straight-faced Suzanne was the first to speak.

"How can you be sure?"

"I promise, I swear, on my life it will not happen …"

Before he could finish his sentence Suzanne interrupted him, but by now there was a beaming smile across her face.

"I was going to ask just how were you going to get my basket back if you didn't return it to me in person?" Mockingly she asked "You mean, you now have shouted at me not once but twice and then you have the audacity to keep my very nice picnic basket for your own future use? David Burge I am ashamed of you!"

Again there was a total silence.

"Don't you think I had not already considered the odds that eventually you would find your way here? What I am surprised about is that you made it so soon."

Whilst David stood still with mouth agape Suzanne was chucking out aloud.

"But I have been waiting for over two hours! I do not think …"

"It serves you right young man, just be thankful the weather was kind to you and it wasn't raining. Remember in future not to be so hasty to condemn someone who is trying to understand and offer you some comfort."

Suzanne solemnly stepped down the path and moved across to kiss a very surprised David on the cheek before moving past to open the front door of the cottage. Still with a smile on her face she crossed the threshold and turned.

"Well now you are here you had better come in because for such long wait a mug of coffee or tea is the least I can offer you. Oh, and you had better pickup my basket and bring it in, please don't leave it outside!"

Before he could show any form of protest Suzanne had disappeared into the house and it was a bemused and dumfounded David Burge who slowly followed through the door leading directly into the small sitting room.

Once inside he cast his eyes around the simply but tastefully furnished area. Suzanne quickly disappeared into the kitchen-dining area calling to him as he entered the house.

"Would you prefer a glass of red wine rather than tea or coffee?" Hearing no reply she called again.

Still receiving no answer Suzanne re-entered the room carrying two glasses and a quickly uncorked bottle of wine. She found David, back towards her, in front of the rough stone fireplace staring at the painting hanging above the narrow slate mantelpiece. Without moving his head he asked.

"Was the picture painted in this area? It looks like as if it could be a painting of somewhere on Exmoor. I don't recognize it, but the ruggedness, the lonely farmhouse and the flowing stream could easily be any one of a hundred local views. Am I right? I presume it's your work; it really is quite good, quite atmospheric."

As he spoke he turned to find Suzanne sitting on the sofa, glasses and bottle of red wine on a small table before her.

"Having not answered my earlier question on whether you would prefer coffee, tea or wine, I am afraid you now have no choice in the matter" she said with a smile

"That's rather harsh; I didn't hear you and you weren't even in the room, besides you have just chosen to ignore a perfectly reasonable question."

"I did hear you. The painting is indeed very special to me, very special indeed." She lowered her voice, "Yes, it is my own work and yes it is a real place. I did it several years ago, it is the only painting I still have from that period of my life "sombrely adding, " I have managed to keep it close by wherever life's journey has taken me."

There was silence between them before David spoke.

"Was it painted on Exmoor? The scenery looks so typical."

"No, I am afraid you are wrong there, it was a rather

special place, but I will never return." Now sensing perhaps he was touching on delicate matters David's curiosity never the less got the better of him.

"May I ask where the picture was actually painted?" Quickly adding "You needn't tell me if you have no wish to."

Suzanne paused again before she replied.

"It is a real place, but it wasn't painted around here, in fact it wasn't even painted in England or anywhere else in the U.K. for that matter. Have you ever visited the Cevennes region of southern France? Unfortunately it's not an area regularly visited by the British as neighbouring Provence seems to get most of the tourists' attention, but they just don't know what they are missing. It truly is a very special region."

"No, sadly I must admit I know very little about the south of France, but tell me what were you doing in a little known part of that Country? You say this is only a sample of your early work, but how old were you when you completed it? Were you on a holiday or did you live there and if so why did you leave? Were your family with you?"

Before he could fire-off any more questions Suzanne interjected, once again her mood appeared very sombre.

"Not now David, another time. Maybe then I will tell you things I have never told anyone before, but I am not ready yet."

She looked towards the fireplace

"In the little time we have known each other I have come to trust you and I promise one day you will be the first to know the truth behind the picture."

He stood in silence across from Suzanne waiting for her to continue. When eventually she did her mood had changed dramatically and with a smile across her face Suzanne reached for the wine bottle.

"I am afraid if you want your glass filled you will have to put your bashfulness to one side and join me here."

She patted the vacant space beside her on the sofa.

"I am quite tame you know and I hate drinking wine alone."

David hesitated before seating himself next to Suzanne. Without looking-up from the task of pouring two glasses of wine she spoke.

"You see contrary to what you may believe I am harmless and have no desire to devour you!"

Suzanne rose from the sofa and put the drink on the small table at his side. She returned, this time seating noticeably closer to him.

"Really I know very little about you so now I have you here you can start by telling me a little more about yourself. To begin with, I think I have established you are single and there is no significant other, but where exactly do you live and how long have you been in the area? What other members of your family live close by?"

Glass in hand she turned to her right and kissed him lightly on the cheek.

"We have the whole night before us and in the kitchen I have several more unopened bottles of this cheap wine!"

*****

At daybreak Suzanne awoke, the sun had already risen and was shining brightly through the gap in her bedroom curtains. She looked around her at the clothes she had been wearing the previous evening that now lay strewn around the floor while her naked body was sending a loud and clear message to her brain indicating she had consumed more alcohol than was good for her. Hands behind her head, Suzanne lay on her back atop the duvet reflecting on what had happened after the initial glass of wine.

They had talked and talked; he had told her so much and appeared to be all too pleased to have the opportunity to tell her. Maybe it had been the wine doing the talking; after all she could remember uncorking at least three bottles as they chatted and talked and at the time it all seemed so natural. One thing she would have to remember to do is pull his leg as it must have been around three in the morning he finally stopped, dropping asleep on the sofa with his head finally coming to rest on her shoulder.

At the time Suzanne remembered being a little dazed in her thoughts, but she gently lifted his head and moved it to rest on the soft cushion beside him, by now he was sound asleep, hardly noticing as he stretched his arm around and cuddled into the soft fabric. How Suzanne wished he had made such advances earlier in the evening and cuddled her so lovingly, she had certainly given him enough opportunity.

Suzanne unlaced and removed his shoes before carefully lifting both David's legs onto the sofa. Going to the cupboard under the stairs she quickly found a woollen blanket and managed with some difficulty to spread it across his slumbering body and for the third time that evening kissed him gently on the cheek.

She had recollections of managing to climb the narrow wooden stairs and steadying herself at the top before quietly entering into the bedroom. Supported by and with back to the closed door, Suzanne sighed and through her muddled thoughts asked why he had not taken advantage of her knowing for sure there would have been no complaints if he had had his way.

Scattering clothing around the room she quickly undressed, dropped on to the bed and pulled the soft cover around her body, the last thing she remembered was glancing at the digital alarm clock and for some unexplained reason noting that it showed 3.24.

The time was now approaching seven o'clock, swinging her legs from the bed she reached for the bathrobe that lay across the foot of the bed.

"The shower can wait until later; at present there is a more important need for a generous input of caffeine." She thought, "Besides, where exactly is last night's unexpected guest to be found? David certainly consumed more than me and wherever, he is probably suffering because of it!"

Robe wrapped tightly around her, Suzanne opened the bedroom door and quietly started down the stairs; as she reached the bottom the recently installed telephone in the kitchen started to ring. Quickly she moved through and lifted the receiver, "Hello, hello… hello can I help you?" Three seconds of silence, which seemed a lot longer to Suzanne, were followed by an ominous click and the line went dead as the unknown caller hung-up.

"Who was that at this seemingly ungodly hour?"

Suzanne placed the handset back on the cradle and turned. Standing in the entrance, using the doorway for support, looking a little worse for wear after the night spent on the lounge sofa, unshaven, dishevelled and bleary eyed was David Burge.

"Good morning!" she said with an air of surprise. "It was probably someone dialling a wrong number, it is still a bit early in the day for somebody to be trying to sell me something I don't want and have no need for. I hate the telephone; although occasionally useful for business, I am sure I could manage adequately without."

Suzanne smiled.

"I think it would be better if you sat down at the kitchen table whilst I make us both a large mug of coffee, you look as if you could do with it"

Without a word of complaint, he dutifully shuffled across and sat himself down.

"I think that's a good idea, black with no sugar, I really need to wakeup properly! I have an appointment in Exeter at nine-thirty and I really need to go home to shave and shower before I set-off."

"I think you should let your stubble grow, a beard would suit you," turning towards David with a sparkle in her eye she said "It would be soft and very nice for all your girl friends to kiss" adding with a smile "What do you think?"

Without replying to the question he looked up at the

clock on the kitchen wall.

"Six-fifteen, is that the correct time? I must not be late my bosses would be very angry."

Back towards him, concentrating on the job in hand of making the eagerly awaited coffee, Suzanne nonchalantly replied.

"Oh no, really it is an hour later than that I never bother to alter the clock in the summer months, the clock is six minutes slow anyway, the correct time is just twenty-something past seven on a bright and sunny morning and who cares anyway if we both have tremendous hangovers from a very pleasant evening spent together in each other's company. Loosen-up, what would you like to eat?" she asked, putting a large mug of steaming hot coffee on the kitchen table.

Leaping up from his chair David exclaimed "What? Are you serious? That really can't be so!"

"Believe you me I have never been more serious in my life… what will it be bacon and eggs? …One egg or two and how would you like them done?"

Ignoring the coffee placed before him David made a swift movement towards the kitchen door.

"Suzanne I know you must think I always seem to be rushing to get away from you, but I really do have to be in Exeter by nine-thirty. Truly I am so sorry to be doing this."

Closely followed by Suzanne he moved through into the lounge and in desperation asked, "Where are my shoes? I really did enjoy last night, please forgive me for rushing off."

"Your shoes are where I left them, beside the chair over there." With a resigned smile adding "Don't worry I will forgive you, forgiveness has been the story of my life."

The last part of the sentence was lost on David as he sat on the sofa tying his laces.

"I have left your place in such a mess and now I am rushing off." He made a move towards the front door

"What is the time now? I must not…"

Suzanne followed David across the room and gently put a finger to his lips, not allowing him to finish what he was going to say, blocking his exit from the house.

He stood there in silence as she reached up and kissed him firmly on the lips.

"I have no wish to make you late, but I think my overnight hospitality has at least earnt me that because…"

Before she could finish David reached out and pulled her towards him, her arms embraced him around the neck as their lips met with passionate intensity. He could feel the heat radiating from her naked body beneath the softness of the long bathrobe and as he drew her ever closer she felt the excitement his own body was experiencing.

They broke away from the warm embrace and he held the delicate skin of her pretty face between his hands and looked deep into her eyes.

"I really have no wish to leave now, but whatever else we talked about last night I feel there is one last thing you should know about my past. Now is not the time or place, but I want you to know and want to tell you before anyone else does. I will get in touch with you within the next few days, please do not try and contact me beforehand; there is a place I would like to take you and someone special I would like you to meet."

Without giving Suzanne an opportunity to reply, David bent over and kissed her lightly on the forehead before turning quickly and letting himself out.

Suzanne stood in her robe at the front door of the cottage and watched him hurry down the path to the garden gate where he stopped, turned and called back.

"In the meantime Miss Patterson please don't forget I love you!" and with that quickly disappeared down the hill to where he had parked his car the previous evening.

Stunned by his parting remark Suzanne stood in the doorway for a few moments after David had left and realised perhaps the feeling between them was mutual and certainly she had never felt this way about any man.

She was brought back to reality by the sound of the telephone ringing once more. Closing the door Suzanne rushed through to the kitchen, this time the ringing had stopped before she had opportunity to lift the receiver.

Chapter 19

Elsie Molland was tired. In ten days time it would be her seventy-second birthday; she considered the time fast approaching for retirement and the need to slow down from the very active lifestyle followed for so many years.

Shutting behind her the outside door bearing the plaque *Ballard and Bailey,* she stopped to peruse the view of Lynmouth spread out below her. She had been using the services of the Lynton solicitors since moving to the North Devon community with her husband Richard over thirty years ago. At forty-five, he had just retired after an outstanding career in the Royal Navy, when they bought the rundown quayside *Lyn Harbour Hotel.* They used all their annuities and lifetime savings to embark on what at the time must have seemed to their family and friends as no more than a hair-brained scheme doomed to financial failure. Elsie smiled to herself as she muttered "But they did not have Richard's eye of vision or commitment."

The first five or six years had been so much toil, sixteen hour days were the norm, but with their hard work and incredible support from the Bank, after ten years the Hotel and Restaurant had been completely renovated and modernised. With the new image had come a change of name, from the uninspiring to the now familiar and visitor friendly *Lorna Doone Hotel and Restaurant.*

Sadly she recalled the time fifteen years ago when her husband had been diagnosed with stomach cancer and after a relatively short illness had passed away in a Barnstaple nursing home. That had been in October and immediately she had closed the business and decided without her partner to work with she would put it on the market and with the proceeds from the sale move away from the area.

The following three months were extremely hard as she came to terms with her bereavement, life at first had been so lonely and it was only then that she slowly began to appreciate the warmth and friendliness of people from the twin communities who rallied round with their loving support.

By the beginning of February, confident Richard would have been in full agreement, she made the decision. The business although having attracted a lot of interest from potential buyers was taken off the market and plans were put in place to enable the Hotel and Restaurant to re-open that Easter.

Now after more than twelve years of being on her own and running the business single handed, having weathered more storms than she cared to remember, Elsie had had enough. Hotel and Restaurant patrons loved her and several local charitable groups were so thankful for her involvement and seemingly boundless energy. Many more just wished to have an Elsie Molland to swell their ranks; in truth she was an inspiration to everyone with whom she came into contact.

Elsie sighed, looking at her watch, nearly three fifteen, she carefully descended the five well worn steps to the pavement and started to make her way down Queen Street towards the upper terminal of the Cliff Railway taking her down to Lynmouth and the Esplanade from where it was a short walk back to the Hotel; at the junction with Lee Road she stopped to cross over.

As she waited for a gap to appear in the afternoon traffic Elsie spotted the familiar figure of Suzanne making her way from the direction of the North Cliff path. She called and waved, successfully attracting her young friend's attention.

"Wait there, coming across, I am so pleased to see you" Elsie called above the intruding noise of a large delivery van changing gear to enable it to begin the steep descent into Lynmouth.

"It seems weeks since I saw you last, where have you been and what have you been up to?" After crossing to the

178

other side of the street she greeted Suzanne with a warm hug and a kiss on both cheeks. Before she had time to answer the question Elsie hurriedly continued.

"I have so much to tell you, I was on my way back down to the Hotel, but most certainly could do with an afternoon cup of something."

Again without waiting for a reply, she took Suzanne's arm, turned her around and started moving up the hill. Marshalled forward, Suzanne finally took the opportunity to speak.

"It is good to see you Elsie, perhaps our encounter is fortuitous, I too have questions which have been puzzling me for some time and I suspect you may be able to give me some answers."

Comfortably settled in the *Sir George Newnes Tea Rooms* with tea and buttered scones Suzanne looked around at the tasteful décor; most of the white linen covered tables were occupied with visitors and locals alike enjoying the pleasantries of a civilized afternoon break.

Elsie spoke, "This place is a gold mine; the owners have done a good job."

She stopped to acknowledge and exchange greetings with an elderly couple who were just leaving and were obviously acquainted with the hotelier.

"They only open five days in seven out of season, if it was me I wouldn't do that because I would want to maximize my profits. They recently won a National tea room award and look at the colour of those curtains!"

Suzanne listened for nearly ten minutes without reply as Elsie enthusiastically gave her thoughts on how the already very successful business could be improved without paying much attention to who may be listening, whether they wanted to or not. Eventually she was able to interrupt and stem the flow.

"Elsie Molland you are amazing, why is it your business mind never seems to stop working?" Lowering her voice she continued, "Elsie I need your advice. I need some information very quickly so I can put a stop to something prior to it getting out of hand and before people, including me, make total fools of themselves."

Before Suzanne could say more, a young waitress addressed them at the table asking if everything was in order and would they be requiring anything else? Having thanked her sweetly for the attention, the server was sent on her way with a professional dismissive wave of the hand by Elsie, who in the same movement stretched across the table and was now speaking in a much lower tone than previously.

"So my dear, do I detect an affair of the heart? Is there something I can help you with? I will do my best, you should know by now I always do. Tell me more!"

There was a pregnant pause as Suzanne searched her mind for the correct words to explain the situation she currently found herself in. After what seemed much longer than the ten seconds it really was, the silence indicated to Elsie perhaps Suzanne was struggling to express what she really wanted to say and came to her rescue by intervening.

"When we just met I was making my way down from my Solicitor's office in Queen Street having just made a decision hopefully I will not regret in the future."

Suzanne looked at her quizzically.

"It wasn't hard, I knew the time was coming, perhaps I should have done it several years ago, but then we would have never met. I don't think I have ever told you about my late husband, Richard, such a good man, although he died all those years ago it seems like only yesterday, I still miss him greatly. We had no children so perhaps that is why I enjoy your company. You are everything Richard and I would have hoped for in a daughter."

Elsie continued reminiscing about their married life together and how upon his retirement from the Royal Navy they had arrived in Lynmouth, purchasing and over time renovating the Hotel and Restaurant. Suzanne sat in silence, engrossed in what her mentor was saying.

"Oh yes, our partnership was made in heaven and then sadly, fifteen years ago, Richard passed away. It took a lot of convincing from some of my very good friends for me to continue with the business. I am so pleased I listened to them and did not give-up. It has provided a comfortable living and what has become a privileged position in our Community, but, as they say, all good things must come to end. After all those years of running the Hotel and Restaurant on my own, at seventy-one years of age I have decided to retire at the end of next year, sell the business and move away from Lynton and Lynmouth. I have a younger, unmarried, sister who lives near Hove in Sussex. I should be able to relax there and just put my feet up, but I am sure she will be able to find something to keep me occupied."

Suzanne sat in silence listening to what was being said before Elsie gasped and excitedly pointed to the antique clock that hung on the wall.

"My gosh, look at the time! I was meant to be back at the Restaurant ten minutes ago for a meeting with Cheffy to discuss the coming week's menus. I am so sorry my dear to have kept you, but I am pleased we met and you could be the first to hear of my future plans."

She pushed her chair back from the table to leave; Suzanne stood up and looked her in the eye.

"I am truly pleased to hear your news and you will have to tell me more when you know anything further."

As they reached the door to leave, Elsie turned.

"I am so sorry I went on a bit and didn't give you a chance to ask me about what you wanted to know."

With a resigned air, Suzanne replied.

"It doesn't really matter, it can wait."

Sensing the disappointment Elsie asked, "What are you doing tomorrow evening? We haven't had supper together for a while so shall we say six-thirty for seven at the Restaurant? That should give us ample opportunity to chat about almost anything you want. Give us plenty of time to talk."

The smile of relief spreading across Suzanne's face was enough to confirm the invitation for the older woman who, not waiting for further comment, quickly turned and hurriedly started to make her way down the hill, calling back as she went.

"Six-thirty tomorrow it is then, don't be late!"

*****

David closed the gate to the cottage behind him and started to walk down the hill following the footpath to the street where he had parked his car. Ever since leaving that morning his mind had been made-up. He would tell Suzanne how in the past life had been so cruel to him and now he would like to take her to meet the one person who once had been so special to him, having no doubt in his own mind whatsoever they would approve of his new found friend.

Near the bottom he glanced at his watch and quickened his step, David would have to hurry if he was to drive and make his late afternoon appointment in Minehead. Earlier in the day he had realised by leaving his Barnstaple office a little ahead of schedule a short detour would give him the opportunity of speaking face-to-face with Suzanne; telling her of the burden he carried and the hope perhaps she would help him lay it to rest.

The disappointment David felt on finding the young artist not home was profound, after first considering perhaps he should wait for her return, he wrote on a blank page torn from his pocket diary.

Must see you at the earliest opportunity, have tomorrow afternoon free. Not sure about cell phone

*reception so please can you call me on 01643 742849 and
if I am not there leave a message confirming you will be
home at around three. Sorry to have missed you today –
can't wait to see you again*
                      Take care, David

    Placing at eyelevel and ensuring it was firmly held in
place under the doorknocker, he turned and retreated down
the garden path.

    On reaching his parked car, David did not notice the
lone figure sitting in the driving seat of the blue Ford Focus
parked on the opposite side of the narrow street and who
appeared to be gathering a large pile of papers that had
fallen from the briefcase across her lap on to the floor and
front passenger seat.

    As he sped off to keep his afternoon appointment,
Mary Bowron paid little attention to the departing stranger
as she left her vehicle and crossed over to follow the
upward footpath leading past the property.

    On arriving at the closed gate Mary hesitated before
proceeding up the path towards the front of the cottage. As
she reached the door and lifted the old heavy brass knocker,
Mary ignored the note written only a few minutes
previously as it fluttered down and came to rest on the
ground. Each series of knocks was louder than the last as
Mary frustratingly failed to get a response from the house.

    "Suzanne Patterson where are you? I haven't driven
all this way not to see you. You cannot hope to understand
the past feelings I have had; nobody cares for you like me. I
have tried to make you understand, all I can do is wait and
return later. I have tried so hard and now the time is here
for us to share the love existing between us."

    Thinking aloud, as Mary turned on her heel to leave
the detached diary page caught her eye as the breeze lifted
it up and into a nearby garden shrub. She stooped, ready to
dispose of the loose piece of paper, a lone item of garbage

in the near perfect garden.

As she flattened and browsed the crumpled note Mary could not believe what she read. If this note was intended for Suzanne it was evident the woman she loved appeared to have a male admirer, someone who seemed to be competing with her for Suzanne's attention.

"You cannot do this, it was me who found and discovered you with your artistic talent, kindness and beauty. Suzanne Patterson I have sacrificed so much for you, but now I think the time has come for you to start thinking about repayment. Please, oh please, be here when I return this evening. I cannot leave this place without knowing that you care."

The note the former art teacher held was now tightly screwed up in her left hand. With a sigh she looked upwards as if seeking some heavenly guidance. Having decided on the course of action, still looking skywards Mary relaxed, opened her palms and stretched her hands before taking a deep breath and stepping forward to start the walk down the hill to the parked car.

*****

After Elsie had left her, before she returned home Suzanne had taken the opportunity to do some shopping in Queen Street at *Vincents*. She loved the old-fashioned food store where time seemed to have stood still. Every thing from the combined smells of freshly roasted coffee beans and linseed oil on the original wooden floor to the ornate ceiling plaster mouldings, all were from a time she was too young to have experienced. Cedric was from the third generation of the same family to be involved with the running of the business and seemed to know all his customers by name and their personal likes and dislikes. It was with a cheery late afternoon farewell he held the door open to send Suzanne on her way with two large carrier bags full of purchases from the store.

A little out of breathe, twenty minutes later she arrived back at her home. It was nearly five and she didn't want to be late for Elsie and dinner at the Hotel.

Putting her shopping on the ground Suzanne searched under the large rock adjacent to the front door where she normally hid a key when leaving the house. As she straightened-up to unlock the door Suzanne noticed the very crumpled note Mary had disdainfully dropped from her hand only an hour previously.

Suzanne found it strange for it to be there as normally she was so meticulous about keeping the pathway clear of rubbish and weeds alike. After entering the cottage she immediately unravelled the tight paper ball and found the note David had originally left on the front door. Without waiting to unpack the shopping she hurriedly made her way to the telephone in the kitchen, lifted the receiver and, hand shaking nervously, started to dial the number he had written down.

She could hear the ringing at the other end for what to her seemed an age. Expecting an answering service to respond inviting her to leave a message for David, Suzanne was surprised and taken aback to be addressed by a woman's voice.

"Hello, how may I help you?"

"I am so sorry I think I must have dialled the wrong number, I was looking for David Burge."

There was a few seconds pause

"No my dear, you have the right number. David lives here, but unfortunately he is away this afternoon working in Minehead and will not be back until later this evening. Can I take a message and may I ask who it is calling?"

Not knowing to whom she was speaking, Suzanne hesitated before replying.

"I am a friend of David's and my name is Suzanne. Can you tell him 'Yes' I will be available tomorrow afternoon at three o'clock and will be delighted to see him then."

"I will give him the message as soon as he gets home this evening. I am so sorry I didn't get your name, who is it?"

"He will know, I am sure, just tell him his friend from Lynmouth, Suzanne Patterson."

Without another word, the line went dead.

Chapter 20

Elsie was waiting in the lobby when Suzanne arrived at the Hotel, the warm hug and greeting was as enthusiastic as ever for her young friend.

"First we must eat! Cheffy tells me he has prepared something really special for us to dine on this evening and then we will retire to the Lounge to talk. Surprisingly for the time of year we have very few guests staying the night so we shouldn't be disturbed."

Suzanne smiled as her host offered to take her coat

"You know my dear; you really ought to be taking lessons to enable you to drive. If you're going to remain in Lyn when I have left, I think a car is essential for getting about; the isolation of the place while being a plus at times can also be a big disadvantage especially if you have no transport. With all your walking up and down the hills everyday you should be extremely fit. Once I was able to do it, but now at my age I certainly cannot."

As she removed her jacket and passed it to Elsie, Suzanne smiled again.

"Thank you. You know I don't think about it that much, especially during the summer months, although I must say very occasionally I consider it would be nice to be able to drive and it would be helpful in getting around the area with my work. Public transport does leave a lot to be desired."

It was Elsie's turn to smile as she led Suzanne through to the Hotel Restaurant and the proprietor's favourite corner table where the functioning of the whole dining room could be fully observed at all times.

They were well into their main course when Elsie, unable to contain her talk to everyday niceties, spoke.

"Your paintings have been selling extremely well recently, I think by the end of this month we will have sold seven and it will certainly be a very handsome cheque I will be giving you. If you have any more pictures finished and available it may be a good idea for you to drop them off."

"A couple at the framers should be ready at the end of next week. Currently I am completing a painting of St Mary's Church for the Vicar and then I have a couple living over in Bellington who want to commission me to paint their cottage. Being busy is one thing, but at times I think some sort of break is needed, I feel totally exhausted."

Elsie laughed aloud, the tone had now been set for the remainder of the meal and all talk centred on the whys and wherefores of Suzanne's business.

Settled in the comfort of the Hotel Lounge, it was the older woman who first broached the subject of Suzanne's request that they should talk.

"I have no idea about what you might be going to ask me, but whatever it is to be truthful despite our close working relationship you have told me very little about your background, family or friends. Perhaps a good place to start would be for you to tell me about your parents, siblings, friends…anything that will help me understand how such a talented young woman came to be living and working on her own in such a relatively isolated rural community?"

"But I didn't come for that" impatiently retorted Suzanne. "I didn't ask to speak with you so you could be bored with the disappointments, fears and failures of my own short life. I don't need support, my feelings don't matter and I came here to ask you because you are the one good friend I have made since arriving in Lyn. If you are unable to help then I must go elsewhere to find out. Nobody really cares, that has been the story of my whole life!"

Elsie could sense for no reason Suzanne appeared to be showing signs of stress and intervened in the face of the mounting tirade.

"Whoa! Slowdown my girl, I have no wish to pry into your affairs, but shame on me; I just feel I haven't taken the time or made proper effort to find out a little more

188

about you. As I told you yesterday, although it was a near perfect marriage we were never blessed with any children of our own and in a very short space of time you have become the daughter I never had. Please forgive me, I am not prying, but just want to get to know you better so ask me whatever you wish and I will try not to interrupt until you have finished."

A total silence followed. Eventually, after a deep breath Suzanne addressed Elsie.

"Well, just remember you asked."

Now sitting upright in her chair she started to give some detail surrounding her life.

"1972 was the year I was born in Oxford. My father worked at the University as for some time did my mother. Their marriage was not a happy one and my early days were spent with a succession of live-in nannies and later I was sent away to a girls' only boarding school in Dorset which has since closed, such was its success! In my absence my mother, who subsequently I have been told by then was an alcoholic, was sent away somewhere to enable her recovery from a mental breakdown. I haven't seen or heard from her since I went away to School, but I suspect my father had some form of contact in later years. For my part over fifteen years have passed since then and I have no idea of her whereabouts today.

My father then decided it was time to leave England and move to the South of France. I was just sixteen when he took me away from School, and the few friends I did have, to go with him to live in an isolated farmhouse.

I remember it was not too far from the French City of Montpellier. A few years after our arrival my father, who was called Henry, became sick. I am not a doctor, but besides having to look after the livestock I had to care for him alone without support due to being miles from anywhere and my inability to drive. Sadly all my efforts were to be in vain, after several months he gave up the fight and passed away quietly in his sleep. After hastily tidying his affairs to the best of my ability, I managed to make my way back to England, eventually finding myself in the beautiful City of Bath caring for a family's young children. Having been looked after for years by live-in nannies it wasn't hard to remember what to do with other people's children.

Whilst in Bath, and purely by chance, I ran into Mary Bowron, my former art teacher from the boarding school days at St Bernadette's, I think you know the rest. She had inherited the cottage here in Lyn and needed the property occupied rather than standing empty so here I am."

"…and the rest of your family, brothers or sisters? What about your Mother?"

The look on her face and the tone of Suzanne's reply made Elsie quickly realise perhaps it would have been better if the question had not been asked.

"I have no brothers, I have no sisters, I think that there may be a maiden aunt living somewhere in the Lake District, but we have never met so I am not certain there has been a great desire on either side. Perhaps we will one day, but as far as I am aware father never did have much contact with his sister."

Before Elsie could interrupt Suzanne continued.

"My mother is a different matter, although she had very little input regarding my upbringing, deep down I would still hope to get together once more, after all she is my mother. Father hardly mentioned her to me at all when I was growing-up and never after we had made the move across the Channel. It would be nice to meet-up again and if we do I know it will be hard. I have so few memories."

Lowering her voice and casting her eyes to the floor, Suzanne finished by sombrely adding "If I ever find out where my mother is, the question has to be whether she will want to meet me."

Elsie waited a moment before reaching across and

190

sympathetically patting her young friend's knee.

"You may think you are all alone in this world, but you have nothing to fear, the locals have certainly taken you to their hearts and so many here adore your personality and work and, if I may say so, especially the male population seems to adore your looks! It is surprising to me you have not already had suitors aplenty knocking at your front door."

Before Suzanne had the opportunity to make any comment about her observations, Elsie had sprung to her feet.

"Where has the coffee we ordered got to? Are they all asleep in the kitchen? So sorry to break into our conversation, but I think I will have to go and get things sorted."

As Elsie made her way towards the door she quickly turned.

"Now don't disappear this time as I won't be five minutes and I have a feeling we have much more to discuss."

The silent smile in reply did not reveal anything, but Suzanne thought "How very true."

Some minutes later she returned to the room complaining the young waitress had completely forgotten they were transferring into the lounge to finish the evening. Elsie repetitively asked why it was getting more difficult by the week to get good quality reliable staff. She placed the tray, complete with a large pot of freshly brewed coffee, on the table between them.

"Did you want anything else my dear? Perhaps you might like a liqueur?"

"No, thank you very much, just a black coffee, with no cream or sugar, will be just fine."

Her hostess poured two cups, placing one by Suzanne, before sitting again in the chair beside her guest.

Bending forward Suzanne once again took a deep

breath before breaking the silence.

"Elsie for all your observations about the friendships I have made since coming to Lyn, there is one person, besides yourself that is, who I have started to forge a closer relationship with."

Elsie sat back in her chair and raised an eyebrow as Suzanne continued.

"Surprisingly, I have been able to extract very little of his past, it is as if he has a reluctance to share and tell me more."

Elsie smiled. "'He... so what you are telling me is you have found yourself a boyfriend; if that is the case he is a very lucky man indeed. You must tell me more."

Suzanne was now blushing. Embarrassed, she now thought perhaps it had not been such a good idea to broach the subject of David.

There was a further pause before Elsie excitedly asked, "Well come on my dear, having started to tell me you now have a man friend you can't leave me up in the air. For goodness sake, what's his name? Might I know him? Does he live in Lynton or Lynmouth? You are a dark horse that is for sure."

Unable to look the older woman in the eye, Suzanne replied in a whisper.

"It's nothing really, for some time we have been seeing each other on a fairly irregular basis. There is nothing in it; we just enjoy each other's company." She looked up, "Nothing more than that I can assure you."

"So what if it isn't?" said Elsie with a wide grin spread across her face. She reached and lightly tapped Suzanne reassuringly on the arm.

"After all you are a very attractive young woman and a fair catch for the right man."

"But you see I know very little about him and it's as if he is holding back, as if there is something in his past he doesn't want me to know about."

Suzanne stopped as Elsie interrupted.

"Have you told him about your own past? One thing you have managed since your arrival in the area is to create an aura of mystery around yourself, not many people have wanted to know about your private affairs, perhaps with the fear if they asked too many questions you would leave just as suddenly as you had arrived."

"I know what you are saying" Suzanne replied. "The locals have been so good to me since I got here, you especially, but things have happened in my past I would not care to discuss with anyone."

Once more there was a silence, broken by a now less exuberant Elsie.

"Sorry, I did not mean to upset you and pry into your affairs. Let things between us be the way they are and you can tell nosey old farts like me to mind their own business!"

It was Suzanne's turn to smile.

"I would never ever do that; you have been so kind to me."

Suzanne cast her eyes downwards with an air of disappointment in her voice.

"Maybe one day, when the time is right, I will be able to share my muddled life with you and the world."

"Well don't let us spoil our evening by being so melancholy; tell me more about 'Him'!"

Hands resting in her lap, Suzanne leant back.

"You told me once before you knew of, to use your word, 'Him'. He doesn't live in Lynmouth or Lynton though, his work means he travels around, but is often here. I think he lives with his widowed mother over near Blackmoor Gate."

"Do you mean David?" Elsie interjected.

With a look of blank amazement Suzanne's jaw dropped.

"And by the look on your face can I take the answer to the question is 'Yes'? Of course I know the name David

193

Burge, as do most residents of our Community."

"Yes, it is" Suzanne stuttered. "I first met him shortly after arriving here, he seemed so charming. Our friendship has since grown, especially over recent weeks. He has even spent one night sleeping on my sofa after he had too much to drink and I don't think it would have been wise for him to drive home." Defensively adding, "Whatever you may think, nothing happened between us and he acted as a perfect gentleman!"

Elsie sat listening attentively, not interrupting and allowed Suzanne to continue in full flow.

"We have walked, talked and dined-out together. On one occasion he took me to the theatre in Exeter; charming and as I said earlier always the perfect gentleman."

"I wholeheartedly agree, a lovely man, but excuse me for asking, have you any feeling for him? I would hate for either of you to be hurt by any misunderstandings."

Suzanne gave her elder a puzzled look, to her it seemed a strange thing for Elsie to be asking, having only just told her about the fledgling relationship.

"Yes, in a relative short space of time I have become very fond of David and if my feminine intuition is to be trusted I think our feelings are mutual."

"Good I am pleased to hear it, as I think most of the population of Lyn will be."

Once again Suzanne was puzzled.

"Actually we are getting together again tomorrow afternoon; David said there is somebody he would like me to meet. First I thought it may be a member of his family, but now somehow I don't think it is."

There was a short pause before Suzanne continued.

"I must confess that was one of the reasons I accepted your kind invitation to dinner this evening hoping you may know David and perhaps be able to throw a little more light on his background for me. I just have a feeling there is something he's not telling me about himself. If you know anything Elsie please tell me, good or bad, I need to know."

"My dear, before I start telling you what I and most of the locals know already, may I pour you another cup of coffee?"

Waiting with great expectation to hear what Elsie was about to reveal, Susan declined the offer.

She started in a slow and deliberate tone.

"First and foremost I must assure you all I know and am going to tell you about David Burge is positive. He is a good, kind and a quiet man."

A visible look of relief spread across Suzanne's face.

"That you have probably already found out for yourself, rather like what I worked out some weeks ago. I have been around long enough in this world to recognize signs of another person taking your attention."

Elsie stopped, Suzanne waited for more.

"What you are probably not aware of is the terrible and tragic happenings that occurred in his life eighteen months or so before you arrived in Lynmouth. David was recently married to a young Primary School teacher who taught at the local School, Morag was a stunner in every sense of the word, a Scottish lass who everybody loved. Newly qualified she may have been, but everybody adored her, the school kids, their parents and everybody from our Community where she seemed to make herself involved with every local group one can think of, you would have loved her.

Six foot David Burge, built like Adonis, and this bubbly, petite, green eyed, dark haired girl, for that is all she was really, seemed to be an unlikely match, but David worshiped the ground Morag walked on. Outside of School hours rarely were they found to be far from each other. Soon they were engaged and nobody was surprised when six months later they were man and wife. David had been born and grown up in the area as an only child, his father died in a farm accident when David was five years old. Both he and his widowed mother are very popular and known to everyone in Lyn. You can imagine the populous delight felt when the newly weds decided to settle down in the area, buying a property in the next village to his mother's cottage and less than a twenty minute drive into Lyn."

Suzanne sat still and upright, listening attentively to every word Elsie had to say.

"Everybody idolized the girl and everything seemed to be going so well for the couple until that fateful day…"

Elsie stopped what she was saying and waited for some sort of a response. None was forthcoming from Suzanne so she asked "He hasn't told you, has he?"

She didn't answer, but gently shook her head to indicate this was all news to her, eventually inviting Elsie to continue.

"Please go on, I need to know."

"It was a windy and dark winter's evening, it had been raining hard all day. She was on the way home after a late finish in School, to say driving conditions were not at their best would be an understatement, and it was at the bottom of Trentishoe Hill the other driver hit her car head-on. He should never have been driving in those conditions at his age."

Elsie stopped.

"Please continue. I need to know the full story."

"Very well my dear, but please don't say I didn't warn you. Morag's car left the road and crashed though the worn picket fence, plunging a great distance down the wooded ravine, only coming to a stop when it reached the swollen river at the bottom. The other driver was totally unscathed barring a few bruises and after a night's observation in hospital he returned home the next day."

"And?"

Elsie took a deep breath.

"Unfortunately the newly wed schoolteacher was not so lucky. She was seriously injured and when eventually the ambulance crew and police were able to get her away from the car and back up to road level there wasn't much they could do for her. By the time they reached the hospital she had succumbed to her horrific injuries and passed away."

Suzanne was visibly shocked by what she had just heard and with tears in her eyes quietly asked "What about David? He must have been devastated."

"Of course he was, David had been away working and when the news reached him in Taunton he rushed back to be at Morag's side. Unfortunately he didn't make it back to Barnstaple in time.

Tears were now visibly running down Suzanne's face.

"Perhaps what people found so sad was the news the couple had not then shared with their friends or families. Morag was nearly three months pregnant and the couple had been expecting their first child."

"That is terrible, I had no idea, what can I say? I feel so humble, poor man."

Chapter 21

It was after midnight when she finally left the Hotel. Declining the offer of a bed for the night, Suzanne told her well-meaning hostess the news about David had initially shaken her, but still managed to convince Elsie she was more than capable, even at that time of night, of walking the relative short distance home.

"After all it is a cloudless and moonlit night and the night air will be good opportunity to clear my mind."

Making her way along the empty street and past darkened shop windows, Suzanne found her mind was awash with thoughts of David. The information Elsie at first had been reluctant to part with certainly went a long to explain his reserved behaviour and helped to answer some of the questions Suzanne had been longing to ask him.

"Poor David, he obviously has found it hard to live with the sad memories of his past, I will have to tread very carefully if I am not to add to his misery. Somehow fate has brought us together, I will try to understand and help him, but it doesn't alter anything and I know what my own feelings are telling me," Suzanne said to herself aloud.

As she turned off the roadway to climb the steep incline towards her home she shuddered as a cold gasp of air brushed across her face. The breeze seemed to make her steps more intense, hurrying as she began the steep path upwards.

Reaching the front gate of the cottage she couldn't help noting the light burning in a downstairs window. Suzanne was puzzled, it had still been daylight when she had left the premises so there would have been no need to have the sitting room light on and what was more puzzling, the curtains covering the window was closed shut. Even if she had left a light burning there was no way her curtain would have been drawn. Looking at her watch, it was 12.34 am.

Suzanne reached and tried the handle and to her

surprise found the door firmly shut. Like many of the trusting locals, often she did not lock the door when being around Lyn; such is the nature of the place. It was one of the few things Elsie always criticised her about.

Trying once more, just to satisfy it wasn't just a case of it having stuck, Suzanne reached under the stone to find the spare key. Rummaging without success in the dark she stopped, 'Yes' Suzanne told herself she was not mistaken, there was soft classical music playing within the house. It was probably coming from one of her CD collection, instantly recognizing a favourite piece by Brahms.

Suzanne tried the door once more to no avail so decided to knock hard three times.

The music stopped and was followed by the sound of someone crossing the room. Suzanne thought it odd as the bolts at the top and bottom of the door were slid back; with the lock closed it was something she never bothered with when alone in the house. Finally it was opened by the figure of a woman dressed only in Suzanne's bathrobe.

There was a moment of silence between them before a shocked Suzanne stepped into the house. The robed figure shut the door firmly behind her and returned the door bolts to their closed position before speaking.

"How nice to see you again my darling, it seems such a long time since we have spoken. Are you well? I have missed you so much."

Moving forward as she spoke, both arms came up in an affectionate embrace around Suzanne's slim shoulders.

After the initial shock of the unexpected greeting she pulled herself away from the intruder and managed to stammer.

"What are you doing Mary? I didn't expect to find you here. How did you manage to get in? You have no right to think you are just able to walk in here like this."

A smile spread across the older woman's face.

"That is hardly the way to greet your greatest admirer, but to answer your question, I thought I might at

199

least have had the courtesy of a reply to my earlier letter. It was rude of you not to have even acknowledged and that isn't the sort of manners you were taught at St Bernadette's!"

Ignoring the reference to their former School, Suzanne angrily replied.

"Perhaps I had no wish to; I understood well enough what you were trying to say!"

Mary remained calm.

"Please, take off your jacket, sit down on the sofa and just let me finish."

Having overcome the initial shock of finding the former art mistress as an uninvited guest in her home, throwing her jacket on to an upright chair, Suzanne crossed the room to the sofa and sat down, straight faced, arms folded and with a visible sign of indignation.

"Well at this time of the night I hope your reason for being here is a good one. I am tired and had some difficult news to deal with this evening. I am exhausted and I want to go to bed."

"And so shall you my darling, but first the answers to your questions. In recent weeks I have repeatedly tried to reach you, contact by telephone is so impersonal and you don't even respond when I write you a letter."

There was no immediate answer from Suzanne.

"Did you even read what had been written to you? I think my feelings were made pretty clear. Don't you understand?"

As the older woman moved to join her on the sofa Suzanne hesitatingly began to speak.

"It is a bit of a shock returning home late at night after an evening of dining-out with a close friend to find a light left on inside the cottage because it is not something I am given to doing."

Mary smiled.

"But then to find oneself locked out of one's own home and next to be greeted by a person who I was least expecting to see dressed in my bathrobe! Please tell me why I shouldn't be more than a little surprised and shocked? I am sorry, but I think you owe me more than a letter by way of explanation for your behaviour."

"My sincere apologies; I hope you had a very pleasant time this evening, spoiling it was the farthest thing from my mind. Was the company good?" Quickly adding, "You didn't tell me you had a boyfriend."

A comment Mary knowingly guessed would invite a response from Suzanne.

"Although it is none of your business, for your information I dined this evening with someone who you maybe acquainted with, the proprietor of the *Lorna Doone Hotel and Restaurant*, my good friend and mentor since I have lived and worked in Lynmouth, Mrs Elsie Molland."

A look of relief seemed to spread across the former art teacher's face.

"I wasn't trying to pry my dear" she answered defensively, "Just curious, wondering if you were presently in any meaningful relationship, male or otherwise. Yes, I once met her some time ago and no, I don't think the lady is your sort, too old and certainly not my Suzanne's type."

As she stretched forward to place her left hand softly on the younger woman's knee the bathrobe briefly dropped open revealing Mary's bare, well formed but still firm breasts, before she drew the robe together again with her free hand.

Suzanne quickly pulled back while at the same time removing Mary's hand from her leg.

"I was surprised, but also pleased to find the front door key to the cottage, the one I retained to the property doesn't seem to work any longer."

"No, it wouldn't, David kindly changed it for me a couple of weeks ago when the old one broke."

Not reacting to the mention of a male name she failed to recognise, Mary made a quick mental note to return to the subject later.

"I have been trying so hard to see you for several days now. For the past couple I have been staying at a Guest House just outside of Ilfracombe. When I repeatedly didn't find you at home, and after climbing that damn steep hill for the third time today, I decided more direct action was needed so I decided to invite myself in and wait until you finally returned however long it might take. Leaving the key under the stone just made it easy for me. When I decided to help myself to a shower and freshen-up I thought it best to put the bolts across on the front door, after all I didn't want any stranger walking in on me, did I?"

"Well now you are here I suppose you had better stay the night. I am sorry Mary, but for both our sakes I don't want you here any longer than need be, I would like you to leave first thing in the morning. You can sleep here in the lounge as I have it on good authority the sofa is quite comfortable to sleep on."

Hanging her head, Mary ignored Suzanne's ultimatum and started to speak what appeared to be a well prepared reply, having been ready and prepared for this possible situation.

"How old are you my dear? I remember the year you first arrived at St Bernadette's; you must now be nearly the same age as I was then. I had just returned to work following the birth of Philip. Tony is some years older than me and I married him at eighteen when I found myself pregnant. After the birth of Rupert, Ian followed two years later and then came Philip. Being a mother with three children under ten years old is not a fun thing, believe you me."

There was a slight pause.

"I have always appreciated things of great beauty, call it my artistic eye of vision if you will, but then my world changed when you arrived at the School. I don't know if it was your natural attractiveness that first drew my attention to you. In truth I think not. Your pure and innocent beauty set something alight within me; here was something I longed for. My desire became an obsession and soon I was dreaming of nothing else, it was a blissful mirage. It was like no other feeling I had experienced before. You can imagine my joy when the opportunity was presented to me on a plate and I was able to invite you into my home. Tony thought you were great, he had nothing but a fatherly admiration for you and all three boys adored you, but nobody loved and nobody lustfully desired you like me."

"You are sick! I have heard enough and think perhaps now is the time I should be getting some sleep. You will find any blankets you may need in the cupboard over there under the stairs. Hopefully by the time you leave in the morning you will have come to your senses!"

"I left my clothes in your bedroom and my overnight bag is in there too."

Suzanne stood-up and made her way towards the staircase.

"That's fine, I will leave everything on the landing outside my room; you can put your clothes over the back of a chair."

As she climbed the stairs Suzanne turned and saw Mary was still sitting on the sofa, bent over with head in hands. Putting everything belonging to Mary outside the bedroom, Suzanne winced as she heard the loud uncontrolled sobs of her former teacher reaching up to her.

"Poor Mary" Suzanne thought, "How sad," firmly shutting the bedroom door behind her.

*****

She didn't know how long she had been asleep, but to her it didn't seem very long. Suzanne's bedside clock showed 3.34 and it seemed an eternity since last making a sideways glance at the timepiece set on the small table alongside her bed, but instead it told her in reality only eight minutes had elapsed.

Initially it hadn't taken her long once she had got

under the cover to fall into a deep sleep, but now found that she was wide awake. Her mind was a swirl with thoughts of meeting David later that afternoon and learning what was so important to him. What a shock the news had been Elsie had given about his tragic past. Amongst it all Suzanne tried to put from her mind what was presently asleep on the sofa in her own living room, a woman who seemed intent on what?

Mary was clearly had some infatuation with her, "But why?" Suzanne asked herself, at no time had she encouraged her former art teacher, who was surely now nearer forty than thirty. Suzanne shuddered at the thought of any physical relationship with the older woman, but could not help feeling anything but sympathy for Mary.

Suzanne turned over in her mind the question of how many other young women, both before and after St Bernadette's, had also been subjected to Mary's unwanted attention, they had probably been driven to similar despair by her controlling desires. She closed her eyes and in a supreme effort to regain the comfort of sleep pulled the duvet up and around her head.

The landing light being switched on and the soft bare foot steps moving up the staircase she did not see or hear and soon the light coming from under her bedroom door was extinguished.

Suzanne was drifting in and out of sleep and did not hear the handle gently turn, the door open eighteen inches and then silently be closed by the shadowy figure now standing close to the foot of her bed.

She was awoken from the sleepy stupor by the familiar voice of Mary Bowron whispering.

"Wakeup Suzanne, wakeup, we have to talk. I need to show you have nothing to fear and I don't think you understand just…"

Before Mary could finish the sentence Suzanne sat up and swiftly turned the bedside light on.

"Go away! Go now!" she yelled. "Don't you

understand I have moved on with my life and any feelings I may have had for you in the past were as my teacher, mentor and friend. I have never had any physical attraction towards you so please, please, go away."

Suzanne cried, burying her head deep into the pillow.

Mary moved to the side of the bed and let the bathrobe covering her body fall to the ground. Lifting the duvet to one side, she let her naked figure slide into bed behind the trembling body of Suzanne, now in a foetal position, ready to protect herself from the nightmare appearing to unfold. Reaching and turning the light off, Mary lay down and felt body warmth emitting through the thin nightdress as she pulled herself nearer to Suzanne.

Lying close together in the darkness of the bedroom, it was the intruder who in a hushed tone spoke first.

"So my dearest what is it you fear the most? I am aware you have many secrets from your past you have chosen not to talk about, but now I am offering all of myself so you will be able to unburden your feelings. I have no idea what ever happened after you left St Bernadette's, but perhaps you will now start to share your past, present and future with me."

As Mary tried to put a hand of reassurance on Suzanne's back she felt the muscles of her younger bed companion tighten between the shoulder blades.

"Relax, you have nothing to fear. I have nothing but love and admiration for you"

Suzanne was now crying into her pillow. She could feel her nightdress slowly being lifted from the back and she could feel Mary's soft touch caressing her left breast.

"Your body is so beautiful" she heard as the older woman bent and kissed the small of her back.

"Please, oh please Mary, go away and leave me alone", Suzanne repeatedly pleaded.

"Not now my darling, never, I have waited so many years for this opportunity. Suzanne you don't understand, I love you."

The last three words of the sentence were still reverberating in the ears as she felt her nightdress lightly being lifted above her head.

Now rolled on to her back, Suzanne tried to speak and cry out, but with the shock of the situation no sound came out from her mouth. When asked about it afterwards Suzanne told of feeling a hand slide between her legs and despite repeated efforts to pull away being kissed all over her body.

The last thing she remembered about the awful night was both of them lying completely naked on the bed with Mary continually kissing her passionately on the lips. The heavier woman was laid across the top holding her wrists to prevent any interference, forcibly thrusting her leg between the younger woman's firm white thighs.

*****

By the time she awoke sunlight was peaking through the gap in the bedroom curtains. Suzanne turned, stretched out an arm and discovered with immense relief she was now the sole occupant of the bed while the bedroom door was slightly ajar. Gathering the cover about her body, Suzanne sat up and looked around the room; the nightdress lay discarded in one corner and the bathrobe Mary had worn lay in a crumpled heap by the side of the bed. The clock read 7.28 am.

Gathering her thoughts, Suzanne quickly dressed and went to the top of the stairs. Ashamed of the previous night's events, she had the immediate feeling head-on was only way to confront the distress and nausea she was experiencing.

"Mary, Mary, where are you?" There was no reply, once more she called out. "Mary, where are you?" Again, to no avail.

Suzanne checked the rest of the cottage, the front door was open, but there was no sign of the uninvited guest. After checking the garden was clear she closed the door.

Returning to the lounge, Suzanne's attention was drawn to the neatly folded blanket, sitting where Mary had left it in the middle of the sofa and on the top of which she noticed what appeared to be hastily written note.

My Dearest Suzanne,
I am truly so sorry to have had to leave before you were awake. After last night when my feelings were returned in such a loving and passionate manner, I am now certain our destiny is a joint one and the future is to be shared. Unfortunately I have to be in Birmingham for a lunchtime meeting, after which I have to journey onwards to Edinburgh regarding my work. Here is the address of where I am now living in Bath; you will be able to contact me there, failing which when I return south next week I will be in touch.

Take care my dearest
Mary

Flat 4a
139 Swinbrook Road
Lower Weston
Bath
    P.S. Should you need it my new cell phone
        number is 0752197274

Suzanne read the incredulous note with disgust. Whatever happened between them the previous night could not be allowed to happen again, ever! It was an easy decision; the time had come to cut loose from Mary Bowron, even if it meant giving up the cottage and moving away from Lyn.

Chapter 22

The weathered steeple of the tiny church of St Peter reached towards the darkening evening sky. A place of worship had stood on this isolated spot since Saxon times and this was reflected in parts of the old stonework, but the pyramid sitting astride the stumpy tower was attributable to an unnamed early Victorian entrepreneur. In the harsh present-day climate of the Diocesan Accountant's strictly controlled programme of expenditure it was only occasionally used, but the vicar of the nearby village parish insisted on keeping the interior available for prayer. Visitors came from far and near to visit the microscopic church which once served the long-gone cliff top settlement that in winter had faced the angry sea and during the summer months basked in the warmth and glow of spectacular evening sunsets.

As outside fading skies heralded the end of another autumn day the oil lamp burning in the chancel seemed to shine brighter. At the far end of the nave the font stood alone in the gathering gloom as if charged by the Lords of Time to act as a guardian to this ancient place of gathering.

Inland, the good people of Bellington were preparing themselves for the start of the dark winter months and long seasonal storms which stirred with frenzy the waters of the Atlantic Ocean and pounded the rocks far below.

Twinkling in the shadows of the past day, across the bay lights were beginning to show in the fishermen's cottages surrounding the small harbour. Night-time was fast approaching when the outsider came.

Finding the door to the building unlocked the lone stranger stepped briefly into the gloom of the interior. Dressed in a long dark coat to protect from the cold, the figure soon re-emerged. Following the pathway around, the shadowy outline stopped below the stained glass west window and stared towards the sea before eventually moving on and taking the trail leading away from the small building. Some steps further, hidden amongst the cliff top rocks, lay an outcrop of sandy soil and the hidden graveyard which many an unknowing visitor failed to discover.

At the rear of the old burial site, the lone person stopped in front of an area of freshly dug ground. From this isolated spot the accompanying headstone had an unobstructed view of the ocean and the daily setting of the sun.

Alongside the newly created mound the stranger stood in silence, sharing with the entombed sounds of the sea crashing into the rocky shoreline below.

The head dropped and, as in previous visits to this final resting place, whispered a few words. The lone figure then turned and moved quickly back to the track and past the church, before reaching the worn footpath which for nearly a quarter of a mile twisted and turned through the scrub and undergrowth to finally reach the wicket gate that lead on to the narrow lane and a waiting car.

Across the bay in the advancing darkness the lights around the harbour seemed to grow brighter. In nearby Bellingtron the landlord of *The Duck* prepared to receive his first customer of the evening while the flame in the chancel lamp continued to endlessly burn. In the tiny graveyard below the damp and recently disturbed earth lay the unmarked coffin. Above, bearing witness was a simple tombstone.

Morag Burge   1971-1994
Love bears all things
Believes all things Endures all things
Love never dies

*****

It was nearly lunchtime before Suzanne finally gathered her thoughts; she had changed her clothes and showered, trying to convince herself a symbolic thorough cleansing of the body was the answer. While seated and still pondering what course of action she should now take against the uninvited advances of her former art teacher Suzanne managed to eat a single slice of toast and drink a mug of black coffee.

Finally, shortly before midday, as many times before in her life, she returned to the canvas. Sitting in front of her easel Suzanne tried with some success to eradicate any thoughts of the previous night. The unfinished picture, by her own very high standard was not the best she had painted. It showed the narrow streets leading down to Lynmouth's tiny harbour, but Suzanne knew such views were always guaranteed to sell to tourists and visitors.

Working in the conservatory at the rear of the cottage, Suzanne did not hear the heavy knock at the front door and it was only the sound of David's deep voice that interrupted her. "Suzanne, Suzanne, are you home?"
He opened the door further and called again.

"Sorry I am a little early, I was free and I couldn't wait to see you. Are you at home? I…" Opening the door of the conservatory he stopped in embarrassment.

"I'm so sorry to barge-in, I just wanted to check that you were OK. It was so rude of me just to enter your home uninvited."

With a smile spread across her face, Suzanne leapt to her feet and flung her arms around David in a warm embrace.

"Even if you did give me a shock, I am so pleased to see you, I didn't even hear anyone come into the house," she said with an air of relief.

Still clinging tightly to her visitor Suzanne continued. "Oh David you don't know how relieved I am to see you."

He waited a few seconds before unravelling the arms

tightly wound around his neck and quizzically looked into her eyes.

"Well now Miss Patterson what might all this be about? To enter uninvited into a friend's house is one thing, but then to be so warmly greeted is another, what's the problem? Have you forgotten the arrangement we made for this afternoon? There was someone I wanted you to meet, but if you are working right now, sad though it may be, I will understand."

David held on tightly to Suzanne's fingertips, her arms sitting loosely at her side, head bowed looking at the ground, she spoke softly to David.

"I am so sorry; I did forget about today and I had been so looking forward to it."

"It's OK, I am no stranger to disappointment, don't worry, I understand."

"That's just it David, you don't understand, nobody understands!"

Tears now flowing down her face, Suzanne took a step backwards before speaking again.

"Can I talk to you, tell you what has happened and tell you why I have decided to leave this house and Lynmouth for ever, but if I do first you must promise never to tell anyone about it."

"Suzanne you have my word; rest assured, whatever your secret it is safe with me."

As she wiped the tears away with the back of her hand, half a smile returned to her face.

"Go and make yourself comfortable in the lounge and I will make you a cup of something. Would you like tea, coffee or perhaps something a little stronger? I think you may need it after what I have to tell you!"

"Coffee will do, thank you. It is only two thirty and I think I should be totally clear-headed if you are still up for it?"

Returning from the kitchen Suzanne once more found David facing the stone fireplace and the picture hanging above.

"Are you ever going to tell me where exactly this was painted? I really do find it fascinating. All you told me was that it happened to be in France and wasn't local."

He turned and took both the steaming mugs and placed them on the side table next to the sofa,

"If it isn't Exmoor as I first thought where exactly did you paint the picture? Is it just a place from your imagination?"

Now seated by his side, David was more than a little taken back by Suzanne's answer

"As I told you, the painting is from somewhere in the South of France, a place that holds many memories for me, not all of them good." With a sad vacant look in her eyes, adding "I lived there with my father for a short while, when he passed away I returned to England, it was a very hard time for me."

"I had no idea you had lived in France and I am very sorry about your father; you have never talked of him before and whilst having no wish to upset you, how old were you when he died? Was it recently?"

Choosing not to answer either of the questions, shaking her head and with a forced half smile Suzanne looked-up.

"Don't worry it's all in the past and long forgotten, but I promise one day I will tell you everything, perhaps one day we will be able to visit the place where the picture was actually painted as it is very close to where my father is buried."

"I would like that" David answered gently, "Yes, I would like that very much."

A sombre air descended on the room and was broken only by Suzanne's cheerful interruption.

"Let us forget pictures from the past for now. The afternoon is moving on quickly and you told me there was someone who you wanted me to meet, if you are still keen you had better hurry and drink up your coffee!"

Leaning across David quickly kissed her on the lips and standing-up reached down his hand to pull her from the sofa.

"And so you shall my woman of unanswered questions, beautiful and mysterious, no wonder I have fallen in love with you, I am sure she will approve." Adding before Suzanne could make any further comment, "You had better bring something warm to wear because although the sun is shining I think you will need it where we are going."

He turned and walked out of the room, stopping before leaving through the front door.

"Come on slow coach, we shouldn't be late!"

Grabbing her worn denim jacket from the hallstand Suzanne followed. Having no wish for any further surprises to be waiting on her return to the cottage, she locked the door firmly behind her. Briefly her thoughts once more turned to the unpleasant happenings of the previous night, an opportunity had been missed; David had to be told of her persistent and unwanted suitor.

*****

Turning from the main road, David drove the car slowly along the country lane towards the small village. Bellington had changed very little over the years; following the long overdue retirement of Agnes Newman, affectionately known to the local population as "Auntie Aggie" it had recently lost its tiny store and Post Office. The eighty-four year old spinster had been irreplaceable as everyone declined the opportunity to run the small business as it was commonly known to have struggled to balance its books for decades.

Like many others in Bellington, the property had since been converted into holiday accommodation consisting of four small apartments which helped cater for the thousands of visitors which poured into the area year-round.

Suzanne and David spoke very little on the twenty-minute car journey from Lynmouth, but as they passed the village pub he commented about the high standard of food served at *The Duck*.

"We should stop there on the way back and eat, the meals are superb and I have never been disappointed. The landlord's wife is responsible for the menu and its preparation and most of the ingredients are local, fresh and even better, home cooked. What do you think?"

"I would like that very much" Suzanne replied, "It will give us more time to talk."

David smiled, "A perfect end to a perfect day!"

She did not reply, but the word "Hopefully!" did pass through her mind.

"It's not far now, left at the hidden turning just up the road here and then ten minutes or so along a very narrow lane where there are very few passing places so I always hope I don't meet anything coming the other way!"

For the next half a mile silence returned, at the turning it was David who spoke.

"Relax, you look so worried. You have hardly said a word since we left the cottage," reassuringly adding "You have nothing to worry about, we are here together."

"David, the fact that 'We are here together' is great, but to say I have nothing to worry about is just not true."

Turning her head to look outwards at the passing tall Devon hedgerows she whispered.

"When all is said and done all you have to remember is that I love you and all I want is for us to spend the rest of our lives together."

Before David could answer or comment on Suzanne's words he had to bring the car to an abrupt halt as a large advancing farm tractor blocked their way ahead. After hastily putting the car into reverse gear, the safe haven of a field gateway was quickly found before the tractor rumbled by with the cheery rural figure of the driver gratefully acknowledging David's efforts in letting him pass.

Continuing along the narrow lane no additional words were exchanged and no further traffic in either direction had to be coped with until they finally pulled up on to the grass verge by the wicket gate.

Slowly, hand-in-hand they walked in silence up the winding pathway to the weathered church. David pushed upon the heavy old wooden door which swung slowly open and led Suzanne through into the cool shadows of the interior. He took her to a worn oak pew at the rear of the tiny church and sat down at Suzanne's side.

"I have brought you here as I want to tell you things and there is somebody I would like you to meet, somebody who..."

Suzanne affectionately squeezing his hand tight interrupted David.

"You don't have to do this to yourself, I am aware, I know."

He didn't hear the words coming from her mouth as he gently put a finger across Suzanne's lips to indicate now was the moment for him to speak and this was not the time for her to be talking.

"What I have not told you before, perhaps because a fear of rejection haunts me, is a secret from my past. Silly you may think it is, but as we have begun to see more and more of each other, it has become harder and harder for me to pluck up the courage to tell you. I should have explained it all a time long ago when we first got together at those cliff-top meetings."

He stopped and took a deep breath before continuing; David took both her hands in his and with tears welling in his eyes looked straight at her.

"You see, I was married to a person who at the time was the most wonderful woman in the world and then she had to leave me. She could never be replaced and I thought it was the end of the world."

Looking at him with tears now trickling down his face, Suzanne spoke in a soft, but deliberate tone.

"I know about it David, there is no need to upset yourself. I know all about the tragic accident, it wasn't her fault she was taken from you."

"How do you know?" was his surprised answer, "Perhaps I should have, but I haven't shared my secret with you before now. How do you know?"

"Elsie, Elsie Molland made me promise not to tell you, she was sure you would tell me in your own good time. Elsie was just worried about my feelings, saying in the long run I would be the one to suffer and did not want me to get hurt. She was only looking after my interests and I was only respecting her wishes by not discussing it with you."

With tears still running down his cheeks, David gave a laugh and threw both his arms around her.

"Oh if only you knew, if only you knew!"

He squeezed her again, before releasing her from his firm grip and sitting back on the church pew.

Suzanne reached across and wiped David's now smiling face.

"At the time you stepped into my life I couldn't believe it. Here was such a kind, thoughtful, talented and stunningly beautiful creature. I had never as much as looked at another woman since my wife's unfortunate accident, but then you appeared, it was as if you had been heaven sent."

"I have been called many things in my life," said Suzanne with a smile, "But 'Heaven sent'? I hardly think so!"

Standing up he held out his hand.

"Come on, we have come this far and she has been waiting to meet you for some time, I think the time has arrived for you two to be introduced."

Suzanne stood and at the same time as giving her a kiss lightly on the cheek, David bent over and whispered a big "Thank you!" in her right ear.

Passing along the narrow pathway towards the hidden cemetery, a light wind blowing inwards off the sea forced Suzanne to pull her open jacket together and as they walked on without a word being exchanged between them David put an arm around her shoulders and drew her closer into his side.

Standing at the foot of the grave in silence it was Suzanne who spoke first.

"Morag, what a lovely name, I have been told she was very pretty. The pair of you must have made such a handsome couple."

He did not answer, just dropping her hand gently to the side before resting his own in front of him and focusing on his late wife's headstone.

"This is Suzanne, I have told you about her before" he said, "She is a wonderful person and I think you should know I love her. If you were still with us I am sure you would agree she really is a very special person," gently adding, "As you were my dear before you were so cruelly taken."

With moist eyes, Suzanne turned and quietly slipped away from the ancient burial ground. Standing on the cliff edge, she looked outwards to sea where the afternoon sun, having broken through the clouds was now glittering on far off wave-tops. Her thoughts were with David, he really had wanted to bring her to Morag's secluded last resting place, finally summing up the courage to tell Suzanne of his former wife. How it must have hurt and been so painful for him, but perhaps now he would be reconciled with the past.

All Suzanne knew was her own feelings had become more than just those of another human being caring for another who, like her, had already suffered so much in life. She was aware of her deep emotions and a growing desire to spend more of her life with him.

For the first time Suzanne realised she was experiencing falling in love with another and prayed he felt the same way about her.

A firm hand on her shoulder and the soft tones of David's voice brought her back to reality.

"Why are you crying?"

She turned and threw herself into David's arms.

"I am so sorry, but why did you have to bring me here? You obviously loved her so much, it must have been so painful...we should go!"

"Come and sit over here and let me explain, but first you must dry those tears away, now is not the time to be sad."

"But you loved..."

"No 'buts', I know what you are going to say and 'yes' I did love her very much; come on, sit over here by my side" David said, touching the large rock to which he had moved.

"If the wind is too much, you can cuddle up to keep warm."

Suzanne moved across to the boulder, sitting herself close to his side and sought the comfort of David's arm around her shoulders as they sat looking far out to sea at the horizon.

After nearly thirty minutes of silence and being close

together, his thoughts were beginning to tell David perhaps now was time he should be telling Suzanne about the final piece of the jigsaw, but was startled from wrestling with the dilemma by his companion suddenly leaping to her feet and declaring she was tired, cold and hungry and the hospitality of *The Duck* at Bellington seemed a good idea.

Moving back to the pathway leading from the church, Suzanne tauntingly called to back to David.

"Come on slow-coach, I'll race you to the car, you will never catch me!"

"We will have to see about that!" David mockingly replied as he got to his feet with a smile on his face.

Chapter 23

At that time of the early evening, with the exception of Stuart Taylor, a local farm labourer and Robin Devin, whom nobody was ever sure what the normally well dressed gentleman in his late 60's did, or ever did, for a living, the place was empty. To observers in the know, he always seemed to be propping up the pub's bar ready to share his thoughts with anyone who cared to listen, especially if his next pint of beer was at their expense.

Normal courteous greetings were exchanged all-round when David and Suzanne entered and made their way to the worn pine table and chairs placed in the far corner of the oak beamed room where the mullioned window afforded a distant view of the ocean.

Returning to the bar David was recognised by the Landlord who, after taking the order for two soft drinks, recommended if he and his lady companion were thinking of also having food they should consider trying some of his wife's homemade, freshly baked today, chicken and mushroom pie, served with baby new potatoes and fresh vegetables grown in his own garden, "Its delicious!"

Not waiting for an answer he continued.

"Where have you been David? You haven't been here for a long while and you were always calling in."

Realizing immediately the awkwardness of the question he quickly added "I don't think we have seen you since...such a tragic...we were all so sorry..."

The Publican was interrupted.

"Don't worry, all that is in the past and it's time to move on."

Looking across at the lone figure of Suzanne sitting at the table wistfully looking out of the window, the man behind the bar replied.

"For your sake I truly hope so."

Clutching the glasses David turned.

"Thank you for your kind thoughts," with a smile

adding "And make it two servings of the chicken and mushroom pie please."

The food served was not a disappointment and lived-up to the superlatives being offered by the cook's husband. It wasn't until their plates had been cleared away and the glasses re-charged that Suzanne tried to broach the subject which was tearing her apart inside.

"David, you know so very little about my past and you are so gentle and kind. There are many things you should be aware of if we are to let our relationship grow. You have undoubtedly been hurt beyond all measure with events that have happened in your past; Morag was your life and is obviously still very much so."

She paused and reached across the table to put her hand gently on his.

"Do not get me wrong, whatever you may think, I understand, but all I want is to be part of your life. I believe my feelings for you are reciprocated, you are such a good person and I have to keep questioning myself about what I am doing; there is so much you don't know and I am frightened for you. Watching at the church this afternoon I decided you must be told everything, we must talk."

Shifting uneasily on his chair, David leant forward, placed both his hands on top of hers and with a smile looked straight at her.

"And what deep secrets are you hiding Miss Blue Eyes? I am sure you will find it very hard to shock me. If this is to be confession time let me ask the first question. You have never told me properly what brought you to Lyn in the first place?"

"I am an artist and it suited me so when the opportunity presented itself I came."

"I know the cottage where you live once belonged to a local old-timer and when he passed-away some distant relative of his inherited it. The next thing folks knew was the house had been occupied by some gorgeous painter who everyone in Lynton and Lynmouth seems to love. It was my lucky day when out alone walking the cliffs I run into this beautiful newcomer to our Community who everyone seemed to know about except me!"

Suzanne laughed nervously.

"Oh come on David, you are making me blush and it didn't really happen like that."

"Tell me more then, don't leave me guessing."

"I lived in Oxford with my mother and father and was an only child. I remember it as if it was yesterday. My mother was highly strung and seemed, amongst other things, to have a problem with drink so home was not a happy place. At the age of eleven I was sent away to a girls' boarding school. My father made all the arrangements as by this time my mother was suffering from what I now believe was a mental illness. Father tried to explain it all to me, but at such a young age I don't think I fully understood what was going on. One day I returned from School and she just wasn't there. As I understand it now, I think my father probably had her institutionalised, but I haven't seen or heard from my mother since those times and I was discouraged from talking about her or even mentioning her name to my father.

Do I have any regrets? I would be the first to admit although she was not a particularly good mother, there was a lack of effort on my part following it all up; I just put my head in the sand and hoped it was all a bad dream."

He affectionately squeezed Suzanne's hand.

"That is terrible, you poor thing. What eventually happened to your mother? Where is she now?"

With tears welling in her eyes she whispered.

"This is the awful thing David, I have no idea. Through no fault of our own we completely lost touch,"

A pause followed before she continued.

"There is more, shall I continue?"

David nodded agreement before he spoke.

"But only if you want to do so."

"I do" Suzanne replied.

"When I was just sixteen my father decided he would give up his academic position at Oxford University and both he and I should move to an isolated part of southern France. At St Bernadette's my love for art and the ability to paint and draw better than most of the pupils was brought to the fore and under the close guidance of the School's art mistress, my artistic ability was allowed to grow and blossom. Father thought his living off the land in secluded rural France was the way he wanted to spend the rest of his life, with no real consideration for any aspirations his young daughter might have. She could cook, clean and assist him with his efforts to develop the farm and if she did have any time left over in her day then she could indulge herself with painting the scenery and landscapes."

He chuckled.

"Most people I know would give anything for a more sedate and less pressurised life style. It sounds idyllic!"

"Well, I suppose it was really, at the time to a naïve sixteen year old it seemed a great adventure. To begin with everything worked well, then I suppose it all started to go wrong with the arrival of a young French couple who my father met in a local bar, they were something else."

Suzanne paused to gather her thoughts before continuing.

"Sadly, six months after their arrival father died, it was all very sudden."

Now oblivious of her companion she seemed not to hear David ask the questions.

"Was he ill for very long? Did he pass away in hospital?"

"Father was buried on his land close to the farmhouse which had become our home and a whole world away from his beloved Oxford."

"I had no idea, I am so sorry. When did you return to England? It must have been a very unsettling time for you."

Standing up Suzanne held out a hand and took a step towards the door. Taking his hand into hers she answered.

"Oh, it was a time in my life I would rather forget, but I don't think it is a subject we should continue talking about here in the pub. There is so much more to tell, including a very delicate situation I am currently facing. If you are not tied to time let us go back to my place; it's a little more comfortable and we are not likely to be overheard."

The two customers standing at the bar when David and Suzanne entered had been joined by an unidentified third and a trio of heads turned in unison to admire the trim figure and backside of the attractive young woman leading her man by the hand out of *The Duck* and into the car park.

*****

Driving back into Lynmouth the subject of conversation was just about everything except Suzanne's life before her arriving to live in the small North Devon Community, but once settled and seated together on the sofa in her lounge it did not take long before she picked up from where they had left off after the meal at the pub.

"I eventually made my way back to England as there isn't much one can do about living in isolation in a foreign land. I had no inclination to continue with trying to make the farm work, besides, and I never did tell my father this before he passed away, I was already very homesick to be back in this Country. As I told you earlier, to begin with at the time it all seemed a big adventure and it made me very happy just to see how relaxed and focused father was over the whole thing."

"So what happened next? Where did you go once you got back here?" asked David, eagerly awaiting Suzanne's reply.

"I arrived in London and stayed there for a short while before I moved west to Bath in Somerset."

"Why there?"

"I was lucky enough to get a position with a very nice couple working as a live-in nanny looking after their kids. It was a very steep learning curve as it was the first time in my life when I had had to support myself." Suzanne smiled, "I suppose it should have been easy really, all I had to do was remember my early days of being brought-up in Oxford and all those wonderful young ladies employed by my parents to look after me. The nice part about the job was it allowed me time to get back to my painting as I had left all of my previous artwork behind at the farmhouse."

She glanced towards the picture hanging over the fireplace.

"All except one that is."

David slowly followed her eyes.

"Can I presume this is the picture to which you are referring?"

He rose from the sofa to closely study the painting.

"It is very detailed... you never did tell me where it is...is it just somewhere from your imagination or is it a real place? It is full of contrasts...the surrounding hills look so grey and daunting and yet the areas of blue caught in the setting sunlight seem to add living colour to..."

"It's lavender, it grows freely with great abundance in the area, during the summer months all the surrounding hill tops are covered and the scent has to be experienced; it's awesome!"

David turned to face Suzanne.

"So what you are telling me is that this is a real place and not somewhere conjured up out of your mind?"

"Sure enough David it's real, this is where I used to live. The painting is looking down the valley in the direction of Montpellier. If you look closely, away to the right you can see the farmhouse with its outbuildings; it is a place I have mixed feelings about," slowly adding, "Father is buried there."

David returned to the sofa, kissing her lightly on the cheek as he passed.

"You are so clever; the picture like you is so beautiful."

"There you go again, please will you stop it. Making me blush all the time is not acceptable, the painting is not that good."

"You get embarrassed too easily - even when we are alone. I am only telling you the truth. The picture obviously means a lot as after all it is part of your life. Perhaps one day we should go and visit the area and then, but only if you should want, we could go and find your father's last resting place and let him know his pretty daughter is alive and well. It would be a journey into your past, evoking good memories of earlier days."

Suzanne reached and clasped his hands, placing them gently on her lap.

"David thank you so much for your kind words. Yes, the painting does mean a lot to me and is why, although I left a tremendous amount behind, I managed to find room in my returning luggage for the rolled canvas."

She paused.

"As regards returning to France to visit father's gravesite I don't think so, not yet anyway, the whole place holds too many memories and as in life not all of them are good. Perhaps one day I will take you there, it is all so pretty, but I am not ready to return yet…perhaps one day."

As her voice tailed off David realised this was not the time to pursue the matter further as it was clear to him Suzanne was still harbouring feelings about the time spent during her life away in France.

"So there you were living in Bath, which doesn't explain how you ended up here on the Devon coast making your living as an artist and a pretty successful one too if I may say so."

"Coincidence or fate? Call it what you will, but a chance meeting one day in the middle of Bath was all it took."

"With who, anyone I might know?"

"I doubt if you do, it was my former art teacher from St Bernadette's, Mary Bowron. Her family used to live close to the School, which was not very far from Bournemouth, but they moved their home when her husband was transferred to his employer's Bristol offices."

"...and? Still a long way from Lynton."

"Don't be so impatient David. Let me finish in my own good time as I might find this part difficult. Please try and understand what I am about to tell you is hard for me to explain, but please, please believe me none of this is of my own making."

Suzanne finished what she was saying and sat back on the sofa hoping the words had come out in the right way. She was praying to herself their newfound love would have opportunity to flourish and what she was about to say would not prove repulsive to him.

David sat in silence, observing the concerned look appearing on her face.

"It has subsequently become very clear to me, while still a pupil at the School Mary developed an unexplained infatuation with me. I began to realise in more recent times this close attention was more than an interest in my artistic abilities, looking back, undoubtedly there were sexual undertones in her intentions. Call me naïve if you will, but in all my previous contact prior to our chance re-acquainting in the middle of a busy Bath thoroughfare, with the exception of my discovery of an erotic painting she had completed without my knowledge or consent, I was never conscious of the woman's attraction to me."

David, arms now folded, sat back listening, concerned as to where this story was leading.

"You spoke earlier of a distant relative inheriting this cottage, well the relative was Mary Bowron and it was she who encouraged me to leave my Bath family and relocate to Lynmouth. Blinded by the opportunity to make a full time living from my artwork I readily accepted her offer to move in here. In hindsight, it was clearly self-interest to be able to isolate me and get her wishes and, if I had been in any doubt, correspondence I have received from the woman in recent weeks clearly shows she is determined to force her attentions and sexuality on to me. It appears some time ago husband, Tony, discovered her appetite for younger women and I do not believe I was the first by a long way.

I have long repaid any money she lent me to get my business off the ground and all matters relating to the property are, at Tony's insistence, dealt with by a solicitor with an office in Bath, unlike the months after I first moved in here. There are now no regular visits which suits me fine, although at first I did miss not seeing their three children."

"So what are you going to do about it? You seem to have an adequate business arrangement with the owner of the *Lorna Doone Hotel* and if all matters relating to the upkeep and rent of this place are handled by a third party, I fail to see where the problem lies. Just forget her, she sounds evil!"

"I wish it was as easy as that" Suzanne replied, "It was clear from the first letter I received, Mary is blinkered in thinking I have the same feelings for her which just isn't true."

David raised his eyebrows.

"So what are you trying to tell me? Are you saying that because of some lesbian weirdo who happens to think the same way as I do that you are a personable, gorgeous, sweet and talented young lady I have to share you? Come on, all you have to do is tell the stupid woman to piss-off once and for all, if you can't do it I gladly will!"

Shocked by his anger, Suzanne burst into a flood of tears.

"Don't get mad at me David, it's not my fault and I certainly did not ask for Mary Bowron's close attention, please, all I am asking for is your understanding."

Quickly realizing he had over-stepped the mark, David moved swiftly to put his arm around her shoulders. Sobbing, with tears running down her cheeks, she turned her face into his chest.

"Sorry, I didn't mean to upset you that was totally

unfair and uncalled for, please forgive me."

She lifted her head to speak.

"You have nothing to be sorry for, I am the one who should be asking forgiveness. The whole situation has become out of hand and I can't take any more of it and a hard decision has to be made, one I have yet to share with anyone."

Taking his arm from around Suzanne's shoulders, he gently wiped the tears from her face.

"And what might that be? Before you say anything just remember I love you and don't make any decisions in haste you might later live to regret, promise?"

"Let me finish David, there is more; I can see only one solution to the problem." She paused to catch breath. "Yesterday I was away from the house for most of the day and evening. I had supper with Elsie at the Hotel and when I returned to the cottage lights were on inside the house. The front door was locked, something I rarely do, and when it was opened you can imagine my surprise to find Mary standing there dressed only in my bathrobe. I was not only shocked, but also very angry. As is her way; she seemed to explain the whole incident away with ease, begging to be allowed to stay the night at my place. It appeared she had been drinking, so with the strict proviso Mary left early the next morning, I reluctantly agreed, first giving her blankets so she could sleep here on the sofa, I left the room and went upstairs to my bed. I soon fell asleep, only to be disturbed in the early hours by Mary Bowron creeping into my darkened room. She lifted the bedclothes, removed the bathrobe she was wearing and slid naked into the bed beside me."

Suzanne stopped; nothing was said between them for what seemed an eternity, before she continued.

"Is there any need for me to go on? The experience was terrible and I'm ashamed of myself. I could have rejected her advances, but I was so frightened. I did nothing to encourage her, but I did so little to discourage. I just let

229

Mary have her own way."

There was another pause.

"Eventually, I must have dropped off to sleep, because when I awoke it was daylight and she was gone, leaving a note downstairs saying she would be away for a couple of weeks, but would return soon to enable us to continue our beautiful relationship."

David listened in silence.

"You must understand, I have done nothing to deserve this and any respect I may have had for the woman has gone. She has taken full advantage of my situation and I have to break the hold Mary seems to think she has over me."

"So what are you going to do about it?"

Suzanne started to answer the question slowly.

"Before you arrived here today I made a decision…it was a very painful one to make. As she has been so good to me, I really wanted Elsie Molland to be the first person I told, she will be very disappointed."

"I am sure whatever the decision may be it will be the right one. It is unbelievable a so-called friend who has known you since childhood could take such advantage of you. I am dumbfounded. You claim you were very naïve, I would call it very vulnerable, but have no fear, I love you like no other and always will. "

With tearful eyes, Suzanne reached forward and threw her arms around David.

"And I love you so much too!"

Drawing back, she asked "But aren't you going to ask about what I have decided?"

"No, because I am sure you will tell me after speaking to your good friend from the Hotel. I am sure it is all good, anything to rid yourself of the awful woman."

There was a pause before Suzanne replied.

"I am afraid it is not all good news and I am sure you will not like what I am about to tell you."

"Which is?"

"I have decided the time has come to leave this house and move to somewhere Mary will be unable to discover. To leave Lyn, find a place to settle and continue with my painting is the only way out for me. I will be gone from here within a few days."

David looked at her in amazement.

"The local people think so much of you. Whatever your reason may be, to decide overnight to uproot yourself and move is crazy; if you do move what about us?"

Suzanne said nothing instead, moving from the sofa, she went through to the kitchen only to return to the lounge a few minutes later carrying two mugs of coffee. She was taken by surprise when David leapt to his feet, kissed her firmly on the lips and broke the period of silence between them.

"I'm afraid the coffee will have to wait, don't do anything until I have spoken to you sometime tomorrow, perhaps there is another way!"

He moved rapidly towards the front door, talking in haste as he went.

"Just remember Suzanne Patterson I love you, if you think I am going to let you go that easily you are mistaken; rest assured together we are going to solve this problem once and for all!"

As the door slammed noisily behind him, she stood, still holding the two mugs, in a shocked silence before returning to the kitchen, whispering to herself as she went.

"And oh how I love you too David Burge."

Chapter 24

After a restless night chasing thoughts around in her head about what the future may hold away from the security of the friendly Community, Suzanne faced the morning with a new sense of resolve. Although she had no great desire to move on, the thought of being able to live the rest of her life without the constant threat of intrusion and unwanted close attention from her former art mistress was more than a little appealing. The question still remained though of what she should do about her deepening relationship with David?

Telling Elsie Molland about the decision to leave Lynmouth was something she was not looking forward to, but Suzanne knew the sooner she did the easier it would be and not to at all would be a mistake.

As she walked down the hill towards the *Lorna Doone Hotel*, the question of where she might go was uppermost in her mind. Time was of the essence if she did not want to see Mary again and give her an opportunity to try and persuade Suzanne to stay.

Immediately recognized, upon entering the lobby she was cordially greeted by a middle-aged receptionist.

"I am very sorry Suzanne, but Mrs Molland is not going to be back before later this afternoon. Is there a message I can give to her when she returns?"

Disappointed at being thwarted in the attempt to share her life changing problems, without answering Suzanne turned to walk-away, but then stopped and with an air of resignation looked at the lady behind the desk.

"Perhaps there is, please can you make Elsie aware I was in this morning. Say I came in to inform her sadly it's all over and I will get in touch as soon as possible about the paintings, for the time being she had better just look after them for me."

Not waiting for a response, she moved quickly through the door of the Hotel and out onto the street.

After riding the Railway to the upper reaches of Lynton, she started to walk the footpath away from habitation and along the cliff tops. It was a cloudy day, there was a little breeze, but the temperature was quite warm; Suzanne felt although a couple of pictures needed urgent completion there were a number of things she should be addressing first. Having decided to leave Lynmouth her ability to answer the question when asked of where she was going seemed the most important. She would have to write immediately to the solicitor in Bath regarding vacating the property, inform the Utility Companies that she was moving out besides letting the few friends made since her arrival she was going and, most important of all, write a formal letter to Mary Bowron...and then there was David?

Suzanne wanted time to clear her mind to put things into an order and needed to be alone with her thoughts in the place that had been so inspirational during recent months. Looking at her watch, it was still before midday, she would still have plenty of time to call into the Hotel on her way back to the cottage.

Now slightly out of breath from the pace she had been walking, Suzanne muttered to herself.

"Damn you Elsie, why couldn't you have been there this morning? Your advice is always so good and I'm sure your thoughts and suggestions would have been helpful. I just pray we are able to talk before the day is out."

Suzanne left the worn main cliff top path behind and started to follow the nearly undistinguishable downward track to her favourite spot hidden away amongst the rugged boulders.

Alone, and as many times before, deep in thought she looked out on a dead calm sea. The whole place was so quiet that even the normally ever present noisy and squawking seabirds seemed absent; it was as if the whole world was allowing Suzanne time to think alone.

Sitting on an exposed rock, she lent back to rest herself on the bank behind; her mind was a blank and any

233

ideas on where she might go in the future just seemed not to have any desire to start forming.

Suzanne felt so tired; the events of the previous forty eight hours had taken their toll on her mind and body. Reflections from the distant ocean started to appear as the clouds slowly started to part and the afternoon sun finally began to make an appearance. As she half closed her eyes to protect them from the bright sea images, Suzanne did not fight the feeling of drowsiness beginning to encompass her, but instead moved to a nearby grassy outcrop and rested her head upon the soft ground. Soon she was in a deep sleep.

The sun had moved westwards by the time she awoke to find herself lying under a warm bright sky. Quickly glancing at her watch, Suzanne soon realised she had been asleep for nearly three hours and, if she was to stop on her way back to try and speak to Elsie, it was time to be leaving the secluded cliff-top haven. Suzanne sat-up and stretched her arms.

A voice from somewhere behind suddenly asked. "And how long have you been here asleep? You looked so pretty I really didn't want to disturb you."

Startled, Suzanne quickly turned. Sitting cross-legged on a rock above her and some twenty yards away she saw a smiling familiar figure.

"David Burge, how dare you frighten me like that? For your information I have just arrived and was only taking a quick break to rest my eyes!"

He laughed heartily.

"A likely story indeed, you will have to do better than that! Having first gone to the cottage, I called into the Hotel, and then looked for you all over. I have been sitting here having to watch you sleep for over an hour knowing if I waited long enough you should awake. I could have woken you earlier, but then you would have probably looked at the time and claimed there was a need for you to be elsewhere and I certainly didn't want that."

David scrambled down the uneven ground and sat

himself on the grass beside her.

"I didn't want to admit I had been asleep for so long, it is not usual, having a nap in the middle of the day is just not me. The problem is being so tired, stressed and the need for some time alone to be able to think; life seems to have become so complicated."

He lent across and kissed her lightly on the cheek.

"Don't worry; I can understand the dilemma you face. The question is if it wasn't for this so called friend of yours would you really have wanted to move away from Lyn? Be totally honest with yourself, could you wish to be anywhere better and if so where might it be? Have you been able to make any firm plans for the future since we spoke last?"

As David looked at her with pleading eyes, there was no immediate reply.

"Well?"

"Of course, I have no desire to leave, but my life has become impossible with the situation I now find myself in, living in a house she actually owns has made the whole thing totally unworkable. Even if I was able to find another suitable property to rent, I would still feel very insecure in the knowledge she was still out there somewhere and could attempt to re-enter my life at any time," adding, as she looked down at the ground, "It's so unfair David, I just want to be near you, but unless something drastically changes, presently I know that is near impossible."

With his reply her head turned sharply towards him.

"But it isn't Suzanne, there is a way and that is what I wanted to come and tell you, but you were so hard to find. Do you want to hear? You will have to let me finish and not interrupt, I hope you like the solution I am about to suggest."

With an inquisitive look upon her face Suzanne took both hands and placed them between hers'.

"What are you waiting for? I just can't wait to hear the answer."

Picking his words carefully, David started slowly.

"You don't have to agree right-now, but tomorrow I would like you to meet my mother. She is a quiet but determined lady, sweet, and very independent, I am sure you will like her as soon as you meet. My mother was very fond of Morag, but I am positive you two will also hit it off immediately."

"Of course I will agree to meet her!" Suzanne exclaimed, "I am sure the mother who has such a special son will be something special too."

She returned his earlier action by kissing David on the cheek.

Replying, he pulled back.

"Just a minute! You promised a minute ago to let me finish what I had to say and you wouldn't interrupt me!"

"Sorry, I thought you knew me well enough by now, carry on, I will not speak again until you have finished, I promise."

"Well, let me start by asking one simple question. Do you really want to move away from the Lyn area?"

The answer was returned very quickly and could not have been more definite.

"No, of course not, I thought I had made that quite plain to you."

Realising her reply had been a little abrupt, Suzanne took his hand.

"I am sorry, that sounded rather rude, believe me when I say it wasn't meant to be, but it appears there is no choice. Even if I didn't have the problem of Mary's close attention, there is the question of finding a place to enable me to have a roof over my head, the cost of renting in Lynton or Lynmouth is still well beyond my means. Don't you think I want to stay? Besides it will be very hard for me when there is perhaps hundreds of miles between us."

"But that is what I came to tell you; there is a way you can move out of the cottage, keep working in Lynmouth and not have to live there or Lynton. If you will agree the answer is so simple."

There was a pause as what David had just said took time to register, before an inquisitive but smiling Suzanne turned to him.

"And what might the solution be, I am so exhausted by just trying to think of one?"

"It is quite simple really, you can move in to live with us; you can have your own room and there is space enough to enable you to set-up a studio in our outbuildings at the rear. To begin with getting to and from Lyn may be a bit of a problem, but not insurmountable as to begin with I am positive we can all ensure you get a lift whenever needed. I can then teach you how to drive and once you have passed your test we can get you a small second hand car. Mother says of course there will be no charge for rent and…"

"Hold on a moment!" Suzanne exclaimed.

"Don't get ahead of yourself here, if I hear you correctly, what you are saying is that I should move from the cottage in Lynmouth to Blackmoor Gate and live with you and your mother? Once there, even if I do have a degree of independence, do you really think it would work? Truthfully, what does your mother think about the whole idea?"

"When I told her about the situation you found yourself in, it was mother's suggestion you move-in with us and that you could stay as long as you wanted."

"But we have never met" Suzanne replied, "She knows nothing about me; we may not get on well together."

"I have told her all about you. After Morag died mother always felt no girl would again be good enough for her son, but with you she knows it's different."

"What have you been telling her about me?" Suzanne chuckled, "I would hate to disappoint her!"

It was David's turn to smile.

"I don't think for one moment you will because…because…you Miss Patterson are out of this world."

"Please don't mock me! If I do agree your mother must charge me board and lodging plus extra for any additional space I may use for a studio." Adding firmly, "It is certainly non-negotiable!"

"We will have to see about that, but are you saying 'Yes' to my offer?"

"When do I get to meet your mother? If we do agree to go ahead with this arrangement when do you have planned I move in? What you must remember is I only have a couple of weeks before Mary is likely to showup at the cottage again and if I do decide to move how am I going to get my belongings over there? I haven't a lot of my own furniture and my wardrobe is not extensive, but my work materials would more than fill your car twice over. There are so many questions!"

"In answer to the first one, what are you doing right now? We could go there straightaway."

"Sorry David, that's just not possible. I have to let Elsie Molland know about my future plans, I think it is only fair and if in the end should I decide to leave the area altogether she should be one of the first to know. I was going to call-in and see Elsie on my way back; I was told she should be there at around five."

"I fully understand, don't worry, what say you if I walk with you now to the Hotel, leave you there, and return to the cottage to pick you up at seven thirty to take you over to my place so you two may get acquainted."

"Sounds like a plan to me" said Suzanne getting to her feet.

"Come on, I still have a lot to accomplish if this is to work, I just hope I won't be a disappointment to your mother."

Suzanne had started to climb towards the cliff-top path, as David followed behind he was heard to call "Have no fear…you won't be!"

*****

238

Elsie Molland listened attentively to what Suzanne had to tell her.

"I was always suspicious of that woman and was almost inclined to tell you about my feelings – she was not to be trusted."

"It would have been very wrong of me to have had such thoughts, after all she was very supportive of me in the past and in a way I am very sad about the way things have turned out."

Elsie grunted her disapproval.

"Do not be mistaken, all her apparent generosity was a means to an end. It was all in self-interest; the woman has taken advantage of you and she should be ashamed of herself."

"Don't be too harsh on Mary. Perhaps I shouldn't have told you and just upped and left the area once and for all to a place where no one could trace me."

"Without saying goodbye or giving me any reason why you had left? Having come to believe our friendship was more than a straight forward business relationship I would have been very disappointed in you."

A hush descended upon the living room of Elsie's relatively small but very tasteful living quarters set amongst the eaves of the old Hotel. It was Suzanne who broke the silence.

"But that isn't all that I came to talk about, you see maybe I have found a way to stay in Lyn without her involvement. Hopefully, by tomorrow I will have it all sorted and be free of any worries, able to resume my work without the dark cloud of Mary Bowron hanging over me; Elsie I am so excited!"

The older woman smiled.

"Well, that's a relief, now I hope you are going to tell me what those plans may be?"

"If you are still happy with our arrangement, there will be no need for any dramatic change," with a cheeky smile, quickly adding, "If everything works out as hoped the new working environment will be more than acceptable too."

"I am all ears so tell me, I can't wait to hear."

"Later this evening David is taking me to meet his mother and if she agrees, which he assures me she will, the suggestion is I move-in with them. David tells me there is also room in the adjacent outbuildings for me to set-up studio space to work and the question of me getting to and from town when needed will be solved by purchasing a small second-hand car and him teaching me how to drive. I will have no need whatsoever to deal with Mary again. She will be out of my life forever."

Elsie Molland raised her eyebrows.

"And what else will the boy be teaching you? Being selfish, I realise any such deal you make would be advantageous for me also and I know in a short space of time you two have become close friends, but Suzanne please be careful, I would not wish for you to be let down yet again."

"I am a grown woman Elsie, naïve at times maybe, but I am now old enough to make my own decisions in life."

With more than a hint of annoyance in the voice, Suzanne continued.

"I thought you would have been more than a little pleased about what I have just had to tell. You have no idea as to what I have endured in past weeks with the threat of that woman hanging over me!"

"Calm down Suzanne, all I am trying to do is think of what is best for you."

"I'm so sorry to sound cross, it was very rude of me, but you don't understand, the more time that I spend with David the more certain I am he is special and the one for me. The thought we will be living under one roof and especially under the circumstances I currently find myself in, it is just an offer that I will find very hard to better."

"Oh, I see, you have already made up your mind to

240

accept?"

"Yes, I think so, if his mother agrees."

"Probably David has already discussed the matter with his mother and she knows your feelings about each other are shared, no doubt it will happen."

"So I would move with your blessing?"

"Of course, if that is what you want, anyway you seem to have made up your mind, whatever my thoughts may be on the matter."

"Please do not be cross Elsie, it is as if…"

"You do know about David's former wife and her awfully sad accident? I think I may have already told you."

Sounding a little intimidated by the question Suzanne answered.

"Yes, you have already told me about the accident…and so has David, only the other day he took me to visit her gravesite. He has told me all about her, including the tragic event which took her away from him."

"Good, I am pleased he has told you everything. David's mother was extremely fond of the girl…so, of course, you do know Morag was pregnant when it happened…. sadly the baby died with her?"

*****

It was clear from the outset that Rebecca Burge had been well prepared by David. His mother seemed very well informed about her, but Suzanne wasn't quite sure just how much she knew about Mary Bowron's unwanted part in the need for her son's female friend to be seeking an alternative place to live.

"David was quite right – you are indeed a very attractive young lady and from what I have seen and heard very talented also."

With a smile she offered her right hand in greeting.

"At last, I am so very pleased to meet you, I have heard so much good and now I finally get to see the woman David never stops talking about."

241

Warmly shaking the outstretched hand, Suzanne blushed.

"I am also very pleased to meet you Mrs Burge, I hope he hasn't told you too much about all my bad habits!"

"Have no fear Suzanne, he has been the perfect gentleman, but if you are to live with us the first thing you can do is drop the 'Mrs Burge' – it's Rebecca or Becky for short; so welcome to Blackmoor Gate. I will show you around the house and your bedroom which will enable you to decide if you wish to stay here with us and if so I understand from David you would also like some space to create a studio for your work so shall we start there by looking out at the back to see if any of the empty buildings are suitable? We can all sit down and discuss later over a cup of tea, but David has also said you would like to be able to move out of your cottage as soon as possible?"

A frown appeared on Suzanne's face.

"Yes, if that it is alright with you, will it be a problem?"

"Of course not my dear, if everything is to your liking you can even move here tonight!"

Relieved, she quickly answered.

"I don't think that soon will really be necessary, but thank you very much all the same."

David returned Suzanne to Lynmouth shortly before eleven. He dropped her near the bottom of the incline to the cottage with a kiss and a warm embrace. Suzanne had told him if they were going to move her out in the next forty-eight hours she needed time alone to clear both her mind and the cottage. He hadn't questioned her, but just accepted this was going to be a difficult few days.

Secure behind a locked door and the warmth of her own bed, Suzanne couldn't help thinking how well the evening had gone. On the positive side, Becky seemed so kind and understanding; the living accommodation she had been offered free of any rent, although in good natured discussion Suzanne had argued it was a matter for future conversation and the same went for the generous offer regarding the proposed studio.

On the down side, being a little distance from Town would initially cause her a little inconvenience, but as David kept suggesting, she would just have to get herself a car and learn to drive. In all senses the new arrangement appeared to be heaven sent.

As she started to plan what had to be achieved within the next two days there was only one thing which kept bothering her.

David had been most open to her about his earlier marriage, but surprisingly it had not been a subject of conversation the evening the three of them had sat around drinking tea in his mother's lounge. He had taken her to the cliff-top cemetery of his own volition, but at no time did David mention Morag having been pregnant at the time of her death. It was something that was still niggling Suzanne as she fell into deep sleep.

Chapter 25

Hollerday Hill dominating the western side of Lynton and Lynmouth rises to 800 feet above sea level and gives spectacular views across the Bristol Channel and Exmoor, while the surrounding heath and woodlands offer excellent habitat to many fascinating species of wildlife.

Astride the hill, Hollerday House was built in the 1890's as the grand residence of publisher Sir George Newnes and is where he died during the summer of 1910. Following his death the buildings and land were offered for sale.

The House boasted *21 bedrooms, 3 bathrooms, spacious lounge, hall in oak, four receptions, a billiard room, offices, stables, motor garage, croquet lawns, gravel tennis courts and a bowling green, as well as 40 acres of Hollerday Hill.*

In July 1911, *The Times* of London unsuccessfully advertised it for sale at £13,000 so the property remained closed, empty and boarded-up. On August 4th, 1913, the same daily newspaper's headline read *Devon Mansion Destroyed by Fire – Supposed Suffragist Outrage.* It was later said by the residents of Lynton and Lynmouth, prior to flames being seen to pour out of the house, a series of explosions were heard.

The firemen arrived, but the pump bringing water to the house was not working and the water they tried to get from the village had no pressure so the crew were left with no alternative but to let the building burn. After, it was generally accepted the fire had been the work of arsonists, but until this day rumours abound, from suffragettes to the need for some person, or persons, to make money through an insurance claim, nobody can be truly certain.

Today, excepting the breath-taking views, very little remains where the splendid house once stood, but those following the main path from beside the Town Hall tread the driveway to Hollerday House.

At the time the events of nearly 100 years ago caused much controversial community discussion, but, unknown to the present-day majority, history had now reached the point of repeating itself.

*****

The following day Suzanne posted an envelope to the Bath solicitor containing the cottage key, with it went a letter giving notice she would be moving-out with immediate effect.

Earlier they had a copy of the front door key cut at *Andy King's Ironmongery* in Lynton; the intention was on leaving the cottage for the final time to place the duplicate back through the letterbox as she had no wish to see or meet her former art mistress ever again.

The letter to the lawyer had not included her new address or any information about where she might be directly contacted in the future. David thought the duplicate key was insurance after Suzanne had insisted if she was to move-out immediately permission for legitimate access would have to be granted at the same time as the notice of her leaving.

David said the key would enable her to return to collect any item that in the rush to leave had been left behind, remembering Mary would be away for at least another week.

Despite Suzanne's earlier protestations that it was extremely unlikely anything would be forgotten, in the morning the first thing she did was to give the key to him for copying.

It had been agreed the previous evening Suzanne should move to Blackmoor Gate immediately, but she had insisted on spending her last night at the cottage alone. She had risen early and was well into the job in hand when shortly after eight David arrived.

First checking Suzanne was fine after being alone overnight in the cottage and making his case for the duplicate key, David declined the offer of breakfast citing he had already eaten.

"I will leave it to be cut at the ironmongers, but then I have to be in Barnstaple by 10 a.m. for a meeting.
I am going to be hard pressed to make it, but promise to be back here before six o'clock so you will have time to post the letter with the key to the solicitor."

"That sounds just great as most of the furniture came with the cottage so packing will be straight forward enough. There is more of my working material than anything else."

"It will probably all go in two trips, three at the most." As she passed the front door key to him, he gently squeezed her hand.

"I would love to stay and help you, but if I'm not careful I will be late."

David leant forward and kissed her firmly on the lips before turning and quickly exiting.

Suzanne called after him.

"Don't be late, I can't wait and just remember I love you."

As he ran down the garden path and out of the gate she heard him call back to her, "And I love you too Miss Patterson!"

With a smile, sigh and shrug of the shoulders, Suzanne returned to the task of sorting and packing the few worldly goods she had managed to gather around her during the time she was living at the cottage.

She planned to let Elsie know tomorrow or the next day what had been decided and Suzanne could let Mary's lawyer deal with any outstanding invoices if she advised the Utility Companies where to send their final accounts. He could just deduct the amounts from the rent money for the coming month which he would have received only a few days ago. Suzanne could not think of any, but if other outstanding bills were received she had asked the lawyer to forward them c/o *The Lorna Doone Hotel* marked for her attention. Elsie wouldn't mind and certainly wouldn't let on to anyone she had knowledge of where Suzanne might now be living.

By lunchtime she had made enough progress to enable her to take a break from packing duties; a couple more hours of work and she would be ready for David's return. Suzanne had already written the letter for the solicitor and the large addressed envelope lay on the kitchen table.

Shortly after three the job was complete and most of her worldly possessions lay stacked in the middle of the lounge waiting for David to come back. Having given the matter much consideration, Suzanne had one task left to complete before finally leaving.

Deep in thought at what she was going to say, she sat at the kitchen table. Taking paper from her leather writing case, Suzanne began to write. The first six attempts finished as screwed-up paper balls on the floor, but at the end of the seventh she sat back, relaxed, and read her effort aloud.

Dear Mary,

Having already made the necessary arrangements, I am today vacating the cottage for good. Your solicitor has been sent the key to the premises, as we are both aware, you already had free access, but the key in your possession no longer works as for my own safety I once more had the lock changed. There never was a key to the door at the rear and as I didn't have need to use it security was achieved by just keeping the interior bolts in place.

On the mat you will find a duplicate key posted back though the letter-box when I finally secured the building.

I sincerely want to thank you for all your kindness in giving me so many chances to succeed. From my early days at St Bernadette's until the opportunity you gave me to move to Lynmouth, you were terrific.

You undoubtedly taught me everything I know and it makes me very sad that I am unable to repay you in the way you would wish. My true love is for a passionate man full of kindness and integrity who has already suffered much disappointment and sadness in his life. I believe he loves me and hope in the future our lives will follow a shared path.

You must understand what happened between us was totally of your own making, call me naïve if you will, but at no time did you arouse feelings in me as this man does.

I have purposely left you without my new address or telephone number. The solicitor will be aware of how I may be contacted if he so desires, but I have expressed a wish to him that he does not share the information with anyone else. I am moving away from Lyn so I ask please, please, do not make any effort to make contact with me.

Again, thank you from the bottom of my heart for the opportunities in life you have given me and I am so sorry I was unable to repay as you desired.

With my best wishes for the future, God Bless and goodbye.

Suzanne

Satisfied with her efforts, she folded and placed the undated note into a separate envelope on which she wrote in large letters *Addressee Only*. With relief Suzanne sealed it shut and placed with the key and the earlier letter she had written to the solicitor into the larger envelope.

It was with an air of new found confidence Suzanne immediately headed down the hill to the Post Office clutching the package destined for Bath.

*****

Suzanne returned to the cottage shortly before David's arrival.

"I'm afraid I will be unable to cook supper for you as everything has been packed to go and the shelves in the pantry have been cleared. On our travels we will have to find a place to eat, this time the treat will be on me."

"There will be no need for us to worry about food this evening as my mother has already said as soon as we complete the move she will have our supper ready. Having no idea of your culinary preferences hopefully I told her the right thing when she asked me if lasagne was to your liking."

"It most certainly is" Suzanne replied.

"With a home-made crumble made with apples out of our own orchard to follow."

"It all sounds very delicious, I can't wait, but how many trips do you think it will take to finish?"

"Probably two" said David reaching for a large and heavy box full of artist materials and making for the door.

Within an hour, having dropped a load at her new home, the couple returned to the cottage. They managed to squeeze the final items into David's car, before she carried-out a cursory check both upstairs and downstairs to ensure nothing which mattered to her remained; once Suzanne walked away from the cottage she had no wish to return. As far as she was concerned this was just another of those unhappy events that had happened in her life which was now done and past.

Suzanne hesitated before she finally turned the lock and heard the tumbler fall into place. Removing the key she held it tightly in her hand before her mind was refocused by David calling her name as he stood at the gateway to the garden.

"Suzanne! Suzanne hurry-up or we will be late for mother's meal; don't be such a slow-coach!"

Surreptitiously she dropped the key back though the letter-box, with a hint of tears in the eyes, turned her back on the former home and hurried down the garden path to join David at the gate.

Suzanne reached-up and kissed him on the cheek with a simple "Thank you" and as they started to walk down the steep incline towards the parked car she gently slipped her arm through his. No words passed between them as if both realised this was a new beginning for everyone.

Rebecca Burge was very welcoming; the meal she prepared for the couple was ready and waiting for them when they arrived.

"Leave it all in the car and you can finish the unpacking when you have eaten. As with the rest of the items you delivered earlier, anything you don't want to keep in your room just leave in the hallway and we can either find somewhere to store in the house or move it out to the building you are going to use at the rear."

Mrs Burge chose not to dine with the couple, when told they were unsure of what time the moving would be complete, she had decided to eat earlier in the evening. His mother, as some mother hen fussing around her brood, chose to pamper her son and his attractive and very personable girl friend as they heartily ate all the food put before them. Rebecca Burge was already totally consumed by her new lodger and could not help thinking back to the past when he had first brought an equally attractive woman to the table; she had not seen David so animated since those times.

Although Suzanne had insisted on helping clear the dishes his mother declined the offer saying it was better if David assisted Suzanne to get the rest of the things from the car and stowed them away in her room.

She was hiding behind the bedroom door when the last item was carried up the stairs and as David entered the room Suzanne pushed it shut with her heel and from behind flung her arms around his neck. As he turned to confront her she took his face into both her hands and kissed him firmly on the lips.

"You must be bored by the number of times I have told you already today, but I do love you!'"

Letting the item he was carrying in his right hand slide to the floor David took Suzanne firmly in his arms, he could feel the warmth of her tiny body radiating through both their clothing.

"Bored? Me? Never!"

After a few moments Suzanne drew back.

"David, you really will have to learn how to control yourself" adding with a smile, "We are living under the same roof as your mother and remember her bedroom is between ours just to make sure we behave ourselves."

"But she will have no objections; we are grown adults you know!"

Mockingly she answered.

"So let us start as we intend to go on by acting…"

Suzanne stopped in mid-sentence as she looked down at the painting David had been carrying and now lay on the carpet beside him.

"Please would you hang the picture over the bed, it is rather special to me and is the last thing that I would want damaged."

As David looked down he saw the painting that had been hanging over the fireplace in the cottage. He reached to pick it up.

"You never did finish telling me exactly why you painted this?"

Before Suzanne had the opportunity to answer him there was a timely shout from the foot of the stairs.

"David, could you come down and give me a hand, I am trying to make some room for Suzanne out at the back and need some help in lifting some of the heavier stuff."

"I'll be right there mother." he quickly called back.

Turning to Suzanne he asked "Well what is it about this place? It obviously means a lot to you."

Looking at the picture now propped-up by the pillow on the bed, Suzanne did not answer him directly.

"Your mother needs some help, go down and give her a hand, I am very tired and once this is done I might just call it a day. Please say goodnight to your mother for me and thank her once again for all her kindness, it really has been appreciated."

Sensing he was being dismissed, David kissed her lightly on the cheek as he passed on his way to the bedroom door.

"I'll say goodnight then; I will probably have left for work by the time you are about in the morning so see you tomorrow evening, sleep well."

"You too David."

As the door closed behind him her soft voice added "I will explain more about the painting another day, you are so right in saying it is very special to me, but don't worry about it."

There was no further response and the door finally shut tight.

*****

The new arrangements were working well and Suzanne was more than happy with her new place to live; Rebecca Burge had been so kind to her, it was as if her new lodger was the daughter she had never been able to have after her husband's unexpected death all those years ago.

Nearly three weeks had passed since the move from the cottage and at the Hotel Elsie Molland was just so pleased Suzanne had found a new home so close to Lynmouth and their prospering business relationship was able to continue. She learnt of the move four days after the event, but now fully understanding the circumstances for the change was more than happy to go along with the arrangement Suzanne had requested of her regarding receipt of mail from the solicitor.

Elsie noted to-date she had only received one letter with a Bath postmark; Suzanne had told her at the time it was only a note acknowledging receipt of her intention to quit and safe receipt of the key to the cottage. Consequently the Proprietor told herself to be very wary of any future handwritten envelopes which might arrive at the Hotel addressed to her young friend.

It was Wednesday, earlier that morning Rebecca had dropped Suzanne in Lynmouth as she wanted to leave two finished paintings for Elsie; one was a commission and the other intended for open sale at the Hotel. Suzanne asked David's mother not to wait for her as she would use the twice daily public transport to get back home.

Elsie Molland was pleased to see her and over morning coffee said, to the best of her informed knowledge, Mary Bowron had not been seen back in Lyn since Suzanne's departure from the cottage.

"I have one very interesting piece of news though; you will never guess what it is."

Suzanne, with a puzzled frown on her face, looked at her friend.

"Go on, surprise me and don't be such a tease."

"The cottage already has a *For Sale* notice outside; she has it listed at five hundred and forty thousand!" Elsie incredulously blurted.

"What! Are you sure and how do you know?"

"The sign outside the place doesn't lie and having heard the rumour it was on the market I took a stroll up the hill to see for myself."

"Can you be sure about the asking price? It seems rather high."

"That was the easy part, the name of the Estate Agent on the board is one Donald Tremlett from Lynton who is a good friend of mine and dines here often. A quick visit to his office resulted in him telling me the price, although he did say the vendor would probably settle for a lot less as she appears to be desperate to get rid of it. Apparently, to-date all the paper work has been handled through a solicitor in Bath, I suspect it is the same firm you dealt with and Donald told me he has yet to meet Mary Bowron herself."

"You are quite right, I would never have guessed. Perhaps that woman's shadow is about to disappear from my life forever."

The uneventful journey back through the narrow country lanes was on a near empty bus and Suzanne arrived back at Blackmoor Gate shortly after three thirty.

The cheery bus driver stopped directly outside the

253

house to allow her, together with a heavily laden bag full of shopping, to alight. As nobody appeared home, she used the key Becky had given her to allow access to the house, leaving the bag at the bottom of the stairs she immediately headed for the privacy of her room.

Suzanne was feeling exhausted, all the activity of recent weeks was beginning to catch up with her and with no one around to disturb her she considered it was the perfect time to take an undisturbed afternoon nap before the return of the other occupants.

*****

She was woken by someone knocking gently on the bedroom door.

"Suzanne is everything ok?"

Coming to her senses she did not respond immediately.

"Are you awake? Mother says you have not made a sound for ages."

The door opened slightly.

"Are you there?"

"I am sorry David, come in," adding as she swung her legs down from the bed, "Don't worry, I am fully dressed, I just lay down when I got in and immediately fell fast sleep."

After rubbing her eyes clear she saw the smiling figure of David filling the open doorway.

"Wakey, wakey! My mother sent me to find you. Seeing the shopping unattended at the bottom of the stairs when she came back three hours ago she guessed correctly you were hiding up here. I have also been home for nearly two!"

"I am sorry, but I am just so exhausted; what time is it anyway?"

"Nearly seven-fifteen."

"Oh no, that's terrible!"

"Mother said not to worry, supper hasn't been cooked

yet. We'll eat at around eight if that's alright with you?"

"Of course it is…how embarrassing…now I have to hurry and tidy myself, I must look like a wreck."

"You look fine."

Advancing into the room and sitting himself on the bed beside her, David continued speaking with a cautious air.

"Suzanne, I have something to ask you, if you think I'm out of order just stop me and I will forget the conversation ever took place."

"Well, what is it?" adding with a smile, "It seems today is the day when everyone wants to surprise me!"

There was a pause as David gathered his breath.

"Have you anything planned for the coming weekend? Let's say the day after tomorrow until Monday evening."

"Paintings I would like to finish, but nothing in particular. Why, may I ask?"

"Would you consider spending time away together…not too far…we don't have to spend a lot of time travelling…just down the coast in North Cornwall."

Suzanne looked at him quizzically.

"It would be very restful for you to get away for a few days, by your own admission you are exhausted."

Before she had time to respond he quickly moved on.

"A friend I work with owns a small two bedroom holiday cottage across the estuary from Padstow. Normally he has it let year round to tourists, but it's unexpectedly empty for a few days and he said I am welcome to have use of it, free of any charge, this weekend. I have been there before; it is isolated and very basic, but just the ideal spot for a quiet few days, just me and you. I didn't want to ask and embarrass you in front of my mother just in case you said what a ridiculous idea it was."

There was an awkward silence.

"Perhaps you need a little more time to think about it, don't worry I understand and I'm sorry I put you on the spot; just forget I ever mentioned it."

David raised his bowed head to be greeted by Suzanne's beaming smile.

"I don't consider there can be any other answer…two bedrooms you said…isolated…next to the sea…just us two…I am female so I need to know…"

A worried look had spread across David's face.

"Please tell me, what else do you have to know?"

There was another elongated pause before Suzanne burst into laughter and flung her arms around his neck.

"Just let me know when to start packing please."

Their joyous frivolity was interrupted by a loud call from the kitchen area below.

"Are you two coming down soon? Supper is nearly on the table."

"Off you go and explain to your mother I need to freshen-up and I will be there in a couple of minutes…and don't forget I love you."

David was chuckling to himself as he quickly moved to leave the room.

"Oh, I'm pleased to say mother is also already well aware of that too!"

Chapter 26

"An old Cornish proverb says *There are more Saints in Cornwall than there are in heaven.* Did you know that?" David asked as he manoeuvred the car through Barnstaple and out on to the busy A39.

"The traffic can be quite horrific here in July and August – especially at weekends."

He glanced across at his passenger who was taking-in everything as she looked through the window at the passing countryside. Realizing that Suzanne was not paying him too much attention, David just continued with his factual presentation.

"Cornwall has the most southerly point in mainland Britain with The Lizard, it can also boast the most westerly point in England and that's Lands End."

Still not getting any response David added "According to legend King Arthur was born at Tintagel Castle on the North Cornish coast. Perhaps we could make time to visit the spot as it's not very far from where we will be staying or we could make a trip down the coast to St Ives. As an artist I am sure you would find the place very interesting."

Suzanne stopped viewing the passing scenery, turned towards the driver of the car, leant across and kissed him.

"Here, steady-on, don't distract me I don't want the car with both of us inside over in the ditch!"

Suzanne laughed.

"Sorry, but I think you are terrific. First I am treated to a history lesson about Cornwall where I have never visited in my life and the next ..."

"You were listening and paying attention to what I was saying?"

"Without exception, I always listen to every word you have to say, but I thought you already knew that. Secondly, you then start to tell me about places you think we ought to visit; you are so enthusiastic about everything, but honestly David I agreed to come away with you this weekend for a restful break so that we could be alone together. If what you have been telling me is true about the place you are taking me just let's try to be us."

Suzanne smiled as she reached across and placed her hand over his.

"But truthfully I do love your boyish enthusiasm!"

"Sorry, I can be so boring without really being aware of it; I'll just shut up and let you enjoy the scenery. After Bideford it's about fifty miles, say an hour longer. Still on the A39, just before Wadebridge, we have to make a right turn and head towards Port Isaac."

David reached and turned the car radio to the soft sounds of a classical music channel while Suzanne lent back in the passenger seat and closed her eyes.

"Not that I have any complaints about listening to your dulcet tones you understand," eyes still closed, impishly adding, "But the music is so soothing!"

They had left Blackmoor Gate shortly after lunch. Before driving away from the house Rebecca Burge had not said anything to David about her own feelings, but she felt perhaps he was at last beginning to emerge from the shadows of the tragedy experienced over three years ago. She had not seen her son so buoyant and full of zest since the death of Morag, indeed since that time until now there had been no other girl in his life and then, as if from nowhere, the captivating Suzanne had appeared. The one worry lingering inside Rebecca was that David would be drawn into a deep and meaningful relationship with this girl only to be once more hurt and devastated. She had to keep telling herself there was nothing wrong when a mother worried, especially when her only son had previously suffered so much. Yes, Suzanne was different, but it was only right she should want the best for her boy.

She welcomed it when David had told her the pair of them planned to go away together for the week-end. On more than one occasion she had tried to question her son about Suzanne's background, where was his friend born, what about her family, parents, brothers and sisters?

Rebecca had a little understanding of her recent past, but was left with the impression there was a lot Suzanne did not want to talk about. David appeared to have no answer to the questions either, but repeatedly told his mother not to worry and he was sure in due course all would be revealed.

She wished the departing couple a good few days away, but warned them the present fine weather may not hold as the forecast was for heavy storms moving in from the west. As she watched the car disappear from view, she could not help hoping the coming weekend might just reveal some answers to a few of the mysteries which seemed to surround the new love in her son's life.

Having made a short refreshment stop enroute, two hours after leaving home and half-a-mile from the river crossing at Wadebridge, David slowed down to take the turning right off of the main road, the signpost read *B3314* and pointed towards the old fishing village of *Port Isaac* four miles away.

For thirty minutes Suzanne had been in a deep sleep, surprisingly for a Friday evening the road traffic was light, but the slowing, stopping and turning on to the secondary road seemed to disturb her.

Waking abruptly and quickly looking around whilst rubbing her eyes Suzanne asked "How long have I been asleep? It seems like ages, why didn't you wake me?"

"I didn't like to, you looked so at peace with the world and besides there was no need."

"Where exactly are we? How much further before we get there? I can't wait to see the place. Are we far from the sea? Is this really happening?"

David smiled.

"Questions, questions and still more questions, you will just have to wait, in only ten more minutes you will be able to judge for yourself and yes, believe you me it's certainly happening."

Looking to find a hidden break in the hedges, trees and undergrowth lining both sides of the narrow road, David suddenly took a sharp left from the paved highway and started to drive the vehicle along a well worn and bumpy track. Unfastening a padlocked farm gate, he continued to take the car on a twisty downwards course until finally coming to a stop.

Suzanne could not believe her eyes, spread out in front of her was a sandy cove and in the fading evening light she could see the open ocean beyond; to her left trees and carved into the rocks steps that led up to what appeared to be a small fisherman's cottage. On the facing side of the small valley was unkempt woodland which as she looked upwards seemed to disappear into the encroaching darkness. The sound of tumbling water indicated the close proximity of a rocky stream on its downwards route to the nearby shoreline.

"Well, what do you think?"

"It's beautiful; I can't wait for daylight to explore!"

"Let's get our bags out of the car and go up to the house, its going to be dark soon and I don't want you slipping on the steps, even when the weather is hot and dry because of the location they tend to be slippery. We are truly off the beaten track here, the only people one tends to see are ramblers following the coastal footpath, but they cause little or no problem for my friend who owns the property."

Once David had unlocked the door, they carried their bags and what little food they had brought with them into the cottage. Equipped to provide holidaymakers with all their basic needs, his friend had told him to use as his own and leave everything to be cleaned by the local who was employed to keep the place in order for the next user.

It didn't take Suzanne very long to establish the property consisted of only two rooms up and two down. There were two bedrooms on the first floor, whilst the ground floor consisted of a living room and kitchen off of which led a small bathroom. She thought how right David had been when he had told her the accommodation was neat, clean, but very basic.

"So what do you think? Will you be able to last three nights here? I know it isn't the Ritz, but I am sure you will like it when you have had opportunity to explore in daylight."

"I love it David and I'm already sure we are going to have a great few days, but as you could see by my behaviour in the car, I am absolutely shattered and even though it is only nine-thirty I am going to have to say goodnight. I am so sorry, but want to be about bright and early in the morning."

"Which bedroom do you want to use, front or back? I'll take which ever one you don't if that's alright with you?"

"If you are sure that's what you want," Suzanne replied hesitantly, "Just remember no one is here to stop you doing whatever you wish – it's only me and you."

"I know, but that's the way I want it for now, please understand."

Suzanne kissed him firmly on the lips.

"Believe me when I say I do…..but please will you carry my bag upstairs while I have first use of the bathroom."

*****

There was an eerie glow in the night sky. The storm which had been gathering for most of the previous day was yet to break, but the small church sitting at the cliff top was silhouetted against the dark background, while across the bay very few lights showed around the small harbour. The steep hills surrounding the seaside community were in total darkness except for the flickering light dancing between the tall trees which increased with intensity within a very short period of time. The unfolding events were barely visible to those living below in Lynmouth and totally invisible to others above in Lynton, only the interred in the church's ancient cemetery had a clear view of what was unfolding above the village across the bay.

The following lunchtime, with the exception of Phillip Devine, the bar at *The Duck* was empty. There was very little conversation taking place between customer and barman until the arrival of Stuart Taylor and two of his friends.

"Good morning Phil" he said addressing the figure that stood there drinking, whilst one of his companions ordered three pints of best bittier from the person behind the bar.

"They say it was quite a spectacular show in Lyn last night; did you see anything of it? Quite a fire and in the end there was nothing they could do to save much of the building. The local lads had their work cut-out and by the time the crew had arrived from Barnstaple it was too far gone, it appears they let it burn-out and just ensured the flames didn't spread on to the wooded hill side. By the look of the sky outside I think we are about due for some heavy rain, but last night if the fire had taken hold of the trees and undergrowth it would have been some blaze because presently everything is so tinder-dry up there – the whole hillside would have gone up in smoke."

Phillip Devine listened closely.

"I know nothing about what you are telling me, are you saying there was a big fire in Lynmouth last night? Whereabouts, what time, anyone hurt?"

Stuart Taylor paused to accept the freshly pulled pint from his friend and took a swig through the froth on the top of the glass, before placing it back on the bar.

"Hhmm, the first mouthful of the day always tastes so good!"

He pointed at the second of the two lads who had entered *The Duck* with him.

"You'd better ask Jim here, he lives there and this morning it was all people were talking about."

Sitting himself on a vacant stool, lifetime Lynton resident, Jim Furlow took centre stage.

"They said it started in the early hours and it was a cottage on the path which leads up the hill from Lynmouth. By the time the crew got down from Lynton the whole place was ablaze, the fire had got a hold of the roof by then. I gather there was a bit of a problem with the water because of no hydrants being available so they had to pump it up from the river. As is procedure, a fire engine with its crew also turned-out from Barnstaple, but by the time the help arrived it was too late to save most of the building so they decided to contain the fire to make sure the whole thing didn't spread. As Stu has already said, it could have turned into something quite ugly."

Jim turned as the listening pub landlord, together with his wife, emerged from the direction of the kitchen area.

"Which property was it? There aren't many up that way."

It was the turn of Stuart Taylor's second friend to speak.

"As I understand, the cottage near the top of the pathway, it used to be old Mike Edwards' place, but he died some time ago; until recently a young woman was living there alone. I think she was a painter or something, a good friend of the guy David Burge who lives with his mother out at Blackmoor Gate."

"I think I know who you mean, the couple were only in here recently, I can remember Phil and Stu admiring her rather attractive ass when she left!" said the chuckling landlord.

"And I suspect you were looking at it too!" said his buxom wife smiling, amid all-round laughter, feigning to clip him around the ear.

Stuart Taylor continued.

"The place was empty and had a *For Sale* sign outside, but the police have taped-off access to the footpath and I have heard they are blaming kids or maybe some tramp for breaking-in and starting it. In this day and age you can't leave an isolated place like that unattended even for a short period of time. Before last night some windows had already been broken and boarded-up, but whoever it was appears to have been well clear before the fire really took hold. They say nobody saw or heard anything suspicious beforehand."

After a while and with no more relevant local gossip on offer, the landlord and his wife returned to their food duties in the kitchen, leaving his barman and four customers engaged in idle conversation, while outside the first heavy drops of rain began to fall.

*****

Suzanne rose early the next morning. Having been awake most of the night, unable to sleep she could not fathom the reason, whether it was the strange bed, the thought of being alone in the house with David or just the unpleasant sticky heat, maybe a combination of reasons, but the humid weather under a heavy sky was certainly not as they had planned; at least as yet it wasn't raining.

It was nearly eight before David went down to use the shower, she had already found her way to the beach and through the narrow window he could see her sitting in the middle of the sandy cove on a large rock looking away and far out to sea.

By the time Suzanne returned to the cottage there was a pleasant aroma of fresh coffee throughout.

"Oh, you're back!" called David from his bedroom, "I'm getting dressed and will be right down. There's some just brewed coffee in the pot, but I am afraid we didn't bring much else, milk, bread, bacon and some eggs is about it. I think there is also an opened packet of cereal left behind by a previous occupant; I don't know how fresh it is though."

Still tucking his shirt into the top of his jeans, David clattered down the narrow stairway and reaching across kissed Suzanne firmly on the lips.

"Good morning my gorgeous creature, you were up and about early this morning."

"I was awake most of the night unable to sleep. When it got light I decided to go and explore and sat alone for a while on the beach," adding with a smile, "Hearing the snoring sounds coming from your room I didn't think you would thank me for disturbing you."

"Why not? I would have joined you, besides, I thought we were planning to do everything together this weekend," he said with an air of disappointment.

"Well, what is the order of the day?" asked Suzanne, "With the weather threatening I am not too sure I want to spend it on the beach."

"I agree, shall we visit Tintagel, it is so romantic? Did you know the twelfth century castle is a very strong claimant to the title of King Arthur's *Camelot*?"

"Actually that is something I did know" she replied squeezing his arm affectionately, "You can be my own knight in shining armour; I think it sounds a great idea."

"We can then drive back to Camelford; I know of a charming little place to get some lunch. After we could move on through Wadebridge to Padstow and go across the estuary on the ferry to Rock for supper and finally back here for a nightcap!"

Suzanne leapt to her feet.

"Well come on Sir Lancelot let's get going, what are we waiting for?"

First driving along the coast to Port Isaac, they found the old part of the village to be a jumble of fishermen's cottages squeezed into a steep coombe which ran down to the small harbour where the buildings still in existence seemed to have retained much of their charm and curiosity. Looking around Suzanne immediately declared in her opinion it was an artist's paradise and expressed a wish they return some time in the not to distant future to explore further the lobster pot strewn harbour, the narrow streets and numerous dark alleyways. As he drove away towards neighbouring Port Gaverne the comment was, "If it is subject matter you are looking for just wait until you have seen Tintagel."

Indeed, Suzanne was not to be disappointed, having her breath taken away by the sight of the castle's majestic remains standing alone on a wild headland, part of which had been severed from the mainland through years of weathering.

As they happily walked arm in arm across the open ground back towards the parked car, it would have been very clear to any passing stranger here was a young couple very much in love.

As David left the car park behind and started to negotiate the incoming tourist traffic making its way along the narrow road he explained, *"The Mason's Arms* in the Market Square at Camelford next stop – it's nearly twelve and time for some lunch!"

"Drive-on Lancelot!" a smiling Suzanne retorted.

As planned, Saturday afternoon was spent on the Camel Estuary in the old fashioned town of Padstow. It certainly had been a very busy port until the mid-nineteenth century when silting occurred which produced the Doom Bar preventing larger ships from using the harbour.

David and Suzanne walked the streets, looking in the small shop windows, and spent time visiting the sixteenth century Raleigh Court House where he explained Sir Walter Raleigh had had his headquarters when Warden of Cornwall.

Suzanne tried to show some enthusiasm for David's undoubted passion for the area's rich history, holding on to his hand she was eventually guided towards the steps leading down from the top of the harbour wall.

"Come on, there is nothing to be frightened of"; David clasped Suzanne firmly as he helped her on to the tiny ferryboat which was rising and falling on the slight swell. No sooner had a short rotund man, complete with a mariner's beard, collected theirs' and the six fellow passengers' fares than the small craft cast off and the crew of two had the boat heading into the deeper waters of the River Camel.

Once across on the opposite bank, David led Suzanne away from the visible buildings of the village and along the deserted shoreline.

"There's some time to spare before we have to make our way to the restaurant, I have made our reservation for seven o'clock; let's walk. We shouldn't miss the opportunity as I am afraid there is a storm on the way and the last thing I want is for you to get soaking wet."

Beneath the cloudy sky they started to move along the sandy beach.

"Sun or no sun, David this is so beautiful, thank you for suggesting we spend the weekend doing this."

"I assure you the pleasure is all mine" he said, "As long as the rain holds off shall we walk to St Endoc Church and back?"

Suzanne stopped to remove the sandals she was wearing,

"I'll go anywhere with you, but you will have to catch me first!" and with a laugh she ran-off along the sand, leaving David fumbling to untie his own laces

"Come on David, you will have to do better than that if you really want to catch me!"

Having reached the old weathered building set amongst the sand dunes, David and Suzanne had little time to spare and could offer no more than a cursory glance into its interior. It was clear if they were to make it to the restaurant on-time their return along the shoreline would have to be at a faster pace than the outward stretch.

Back in Rock, it was an out of breath couple who arrived at the entrance to *L'Estaurie* restaurant.

"David, I can't go in here, I am not dressed properly, my…"

"Nonsense, as always you look gorgeous - you are fine. You told me a while ago you liked French cuisine, well this is the best so just relax and enjoy yourself."

It was sometime before nine when the pair made their way back to the river's edge to board the last ferry of the day back across the flowing Camel.

"Thank you so much David that was a fantastic meal and the ambiance was terrific, it was so relaxing," adding with a smile, "So Continental – so French!"

As they waited with eleven other passengers for the small craft to arrive on its short journey from Padstow, a muffled groan went up from the assembled group as the first large spots of the long threatened rain were felt.

By the time the harbour steps were being climbed in the gathering gloom, the disembarking passengers were huddling closer together.

Earlier, David had parked the car close by in the former railway station, now the fish market yard, and there was unfettered laughter from the pair as they ran quickly for its shelter.

While driving back to the cottage the shower-like rain turned into a torrential downpour and ascending the steps to the front door David and Suzanne were both drenched.

"You will have to excuse me David, but I will certainly need to change and put on some dry clothes."

"Me too, listen to that rain, I think we may have dodged a bullet in Rock. The food wouldn't have tasted nearly as good if we had to eat it like this.'' he jokingly said.

Suzanne smiled as she made her way up the stairs and shut the door to the bedroom behind her.

An hour later she had not reappeared, having changed his own clothes, David decided perhaps closer investigation was warranted. Going up to her room, he put his ear close to the door and hearing no movement from within he quietly opened to find Suzanne curled on the bed in a deep sleep.

Gently closing the door behind him, David smiled and went across the passageway to his own room. A distant roll of thunder indicated perhaps the weather would have the final say on the plans for the next day. He undressed and climbed into bed, amid thoughts of how wonderful it had been to have been given the opportunity of spending the whole day with Suzanne, soon he too was in a deep sleep.

The storm must have been directly overhead when an incredible clap of thunder had woken him. He reached for the bedside light, but to no avail, the adverse weather seemed to have taken the power supply out. David just lay back on his pillow thinking he should not worry as it would all probably pass before daybreak when, hopefully, the sun would shine again.

Again, the room was lit by a flash of lightning, closely followed by another deep roll of thunder. He closed his eyes and turned as if to attempt sleep, but as he did so was aware of his bedroom door squeaking at it appeared to be slowly opened.

"David, David are you awake?" Suzanne's whispering voice called.

He turned and sat upright in the bed.

"David I am so sorry, but I cannot sleep…I hate this weather at the best of times…it frightens me…and now the electricity has gone off!"

"Suzanne, there's nothing at all to be frightened of, it's just a storm and it will all be gone by the morning, don't worry about it just go back to bed."

He looked on as a further flash of light illuminated

the doorway showing, dressed only in a flimsy nightdress, a rather pathetic looking Suzanne.

Reluctantly she turned as if to make her way back

"Goodnight, if you are able, sleep well. I am frightened, and know it's going to be hard for me to get any rest."

"Suzanne, please wait a minute, just come here."

She turned around to see David pulling the bedclothes alongside him to one side and patting the mattress.

Suzanne needed no second invitation and crossed the floor to slip under the covers. As the storm continued to rage, she could feel his body warmth close-by as he stretched out to place his arm tightly around her shoulders.

No conversation passed between them as they moved closer together and Suzanne could feel the excitement within David's body rising.

Chapter 27

The start of the next day was so different, the sun was streaming through the window and as the couple lay in bed together looking at the near cloudless sky it was Suzanne who broke the loving silence.

"Come on David, it's time we were out and about enjoying the beautiful day, such a contrast to yesterday."

David grunted disapprovingly as he pulled the sheet over his head, Suzanne saw her opportunity. Throwing the bedclothes from her naked body and grabbing the nightdress on the floor she made a dash towards the door.

While sitting on the end of the bed before dressing, David could hear her childlike laughter coming from the shower below and once dressed and fed they spent the rest of the morning exploring the area surrounding the secluded sandy cove.

At around midday, another couple with two leashed dogs had passed along the coastal footpath, they had interrupted their little game of skimming flat pebbles off of the water taking time to wave back and as the walkers disappeared into the distance David and Suzanne were once more left to enjoy the solitude and each others company.

A snack lunch was followed by a trip down the coast towards Newquay, the original plan had been for her to see artistic St Ives, but having spent so much time visiting the historic Tolgus Tin Mine and the bird sanctuary in Hayle they made the decision to return to Newquay for supper before wending the way back to their retreat. After watching the sunset together on the beach, it came as no surprise to Suzanne that David welcomed her once more to share his bed.

Monday's weather came as more of the same and in the early afternoon they locked the cottage door for the final time to begin their journey back to Blackmoor Gate.

David's chosen route purposely gave the opportunity for them to visit several places of interest Suzanne had expressed a wish to see on the way home. Coombe Valley and then Hartland, which proved to be a convenient stopping place to explore the coast at Hartland Point. By the time Clovelly was reached both of them claimed to be starving and walking half-way down the steep and narrow cobbled street they decided to stop and dine at *The New Inn Hotel*.

After the meal, the sun was beginning to disappear as David and Suzanne continued their walk downwards towards the seafront.

"Again David, thank you so much, that was a splendid meal; when we get home you must let me know how much I owe you for the weekend."

"What are you talking about? Nothing, the complete weekend was my treat!"

"You know by now I am a very independent individual and I hate being a kept woman," she slipped her arm through his, "Please."

He did not reply, but kept on walking, eventually leading her to the wall at the end of the harbour.

"Just forget it, you know I love you and the past few days have been so good for me too."

As they sat together, legs hanging loosely over the side of the harbour wall, David continued, "Perhaps, one day we will be together permanently; I would like that."

Without taking her eyes off the distant horizon and the sinking sun, Suzanne quietly answered.

"Perhaps, one day."

The rest of the journey back to Blackmoor Gate was uneventful, soon after the car left Clovelly she had fallen asleep and it was just before eleven when Suzanne was woken by David telling her they had arrived home.

Discussion had taken place before the return regarding their future sleeping arrangements and both agreed with deference for Rebecca, for the time being at least, it would be better if things were handled with caution and the status quo of separate bedrooms continued.

"As I need to be up early in the morning for work it's off to bed for me as soon as possible," David said as he entered the kitchen and reached across the table to read the handwritten note.

As Suzanne entered he spoke.

"Mother apologises for not waiting-up for us to come in, but was so tired she couldn't wait any longer and had to go on to bed. The other thing was she took a phone call for you on Sunday from Elsie Molland. Mother told her we wouldn't be back until late this evening, but Elsie asked if you could contact her at the Hotel first thing on Tuesday morning; Mother says it sounded quite urgent."

Suzanne looked puzzled.

"I wonder what that might be about; I thought everything was up-to-date between us."

"Don't worry about it now, it's past your bedtime," David said, "If you are up early enough, on my way I will drop you there."

*****

The next morning Elsie Molland was surprised to see Suzanne at the Hotel so early.

"I hear you were away with David, did you have a nice weekend?"

"Very, thank you. The weather wasn't so good on Saturday, but Sunday and Monday were beautiful. We didn't get back until Monday evening. Sorry I didn't call you then, but it was late and his mother seemed to think you wanted to talk urgently, so here I am. David dropped me off on his way to work."

Elsie hesitated before answering.

"Go on into the Hotel lounge, we can talk there, just give me a minute to check what's going on in the kitchen. We didn't have many in last night, but tonight we have a large reception function being given by the Chamber of Commerce so I'll let the staff know where they can find me if they require help; won't be a moment."

Ten minutes later the Hotel owner returned and

seated together in the farthest corner of the room, she started the conversation with Suzanne.

"You obviously haven't heard what happened in Lyn on Saturday night?"

"No, why should I? As you know I was with David until Monday evening. It must have been very important for you to have called me."

"Well, given the circumstances of you having to leave the cottage, the first part wasn't so important and I wouldn't have blamed you for thinking it was for the best when I tell you the building was totally destroyed by a fire on Saturday night. As you are already aware, the place was put on the market shortly after you moved-out and it did not take long for it to develop an air of neglect, rather like it did when the old man died who lived there before you. Broken windows, overgrown garden, it was certainly a lot different in your time."

"How very sad, I enjoyed living there. What was the cause of the fire and how much damage was done?"

"Because of the blaze's ferocity, the fire people couldn't easily get inside the building to extinguish the flames so they let it burn under control at the same time as making sure it did not extend on to the hillside; there is a lot of dead wood lying around up there. At first they believed a vandal or maybe even a tramp was responsible for starting it, but whoever the building was left gutted."

"That is just so awful, I was so happy at the cottage and if things had turned-out differently I would have been quite content to have continued living there."

"There is more, shall I continue? Would you like some coffee, perhaps something a little stronger, to drink?"

Suzanne forced a smile, "No coffee and certainly no alcohol at this time of the morning, what are you trying to do make me drunk?"

"You may change your mind when you have listened to what more I have to say."

Elsie continued.

"Sunday lunchtime is normally very busy in the Restaurant and two days ago was no exception, but that day we were also asked to deliver half-a-dozen packed lunches up to the Fire Hall for some of the crew who had stayed on-site at the cottage throughout the night and were only just about to finish-up their duty roster. The Hotel duly obliged and, as the rest of my staff were busy, I offered to be the one to drive up to Lynton and drop them off at the station."

"That isn't so abnormal is it? Why are you being so secretive?"

"Don't be so impatient, just let me finish. On arriving at the fire station the crew had not yet returned and so I left the food and drink with the one man there, Chris Bater - he's been around Lyn's fire service for years and I know him well. As I went to return to my car he called me back and began to talk of the most terrible thing. Earlier that morning and following a torrential terrible downpour which started around 5 a.m., the guys were checking through the building for any remaining smouldering hotspots when they came across the charred remains of a body."

Suzanne gasped.

"The police were immediately called to the scene and the whole place was sealed off including the footpath up the hill which had been closed following the discovery of the fire. Lyn has been crawling with police since then, all trying to trace any missing person. That is why it was so imperative that I spoke to you before they did."

A puzzled look appeared on Suzanne's face.

"Why should it concern me? I wasn't here and I no longer live there. I was miles away with David, what can I possibly tell the police that might be a help with their enquiries?"

"Calm down young lady, there is more to tell."

She reached across and took Suzanne's hand.

"The charred corpse was removed to Barnstaple where they took it to the hospital for identification purposes. On Monday morning I heard that the victim was thought to have been female and Caucasian; further forensic testing and enquiries were on-going. A rumour took no time at all circulate that it was your body which had been found at the cottage, something I immediately did my very best to squash!"

Elsie paused.

"But being such a small and close knit community and knowing what I do about the situation, to my mind what has a lot more credence and is much more likely…"

"And what might that be?" said Suzanne abruptly interrupting.

"On Saturday morning, around coffee time, I was working on the front desk and having just checked-out two overnight guests, I looked-up and was surprised to come face to face with the awful woman who you had been renting the cottage from."

"Mary, Mary Bowron?"

"She started to demand I tell her where you were living, of course, having been told of your experiences I wasn't going to tell her anything, just saying I believed you were presently away on holiday with a man friend. The more I refused to help her the angrier she got, at one stage waving what appeared to be a handwritten letter under my nose and saying you had written it, probably with my help, accusing me and everyone else of poisoning your mind.

Such was the commotion she was making if the events had not turned-out as they did one might have said they were bordering on the farcical. The woman was acting uncontrollably like a lunatic and this went on in-front of everyone for about fifteen minutes. I tried to keep calm and not to start telling her exactly what I was thinking, but Cheffy heard the disturbance from the kitchen and came through to investigate what the noise was all about. In the end he firmly guided her by the arm through the front door and she was still ranting and raving as she disappeared from his view down the street."

"Wow, I'm so very sorry, when Mary started to cause

the trouble you should have called the police."

"I had no wish to make her any more trouble, but maybe I should have, at least Mary Bowron would still be alive today."

"What do you mean by 'Alive today'?"

"Suzanne, what I am trying to say is the rumour doing the rounds relates to the body recovered from the cottage. People are now saying it's that of your former art mistress, Mary Bowron, but only further forensic tests will prove or disprove otherwise."

*****

Suzanne found the following two weeks very hard. There had been the interview with the police; following the news Elsie Molland had first given her, it was confirmed within a few days the body recovered from the burnt-out cottage was that of her former art mistress. They made contact with Suzanne through the Hotel owner and had only been too pleased to meet her at Blackmoor Gate. Rebecca Burge discreetly decided not to be around the afternoon a woman CID officer from Barnstaple called at the house to talk to Suzanne.

Their informal chat in the drawing room over a cup of tea had been deceptively low key and Suzanne felt she answered all questions to the police officer's satisfaction. She was very relieved there was no embarrassing questions asked surrounding Mary's sexuality and therefore did not have to give-up any answers which may at a later date be construed to have been misleading. The plain clothes policewoman seemed more than satisfied that Mary's interest in Suzanne was purely for plutonic and professional reasons.

"So why Miss Patterson did you actually decide to move from Lynmouth and live in this village?" she asked.

"Although it is some miles out of Lyn, Blackmoor Gate is where my boyfriend lived and I just wanted to be able to spend more time with him. When David asked if I would like to move in here with him and his mother it was a no-brainer and an offer I just couldn't refuse" answered Suzanne, hoping that she wouldn't be pushed any further on the subject.

"You are very pretty" the police officer replied, "I know a little about the background of David Burge, it was very sad for him when his wife was killed in the road accident, it is good to know things have finally turned around for him. I have also been told he is a very sensitive, thoughtful and physically very attractive person" smiling she added, "You two are very lucky to have met and I wish you well for the future."

Blushing, Suzanne replied "Thank you very much."

After asking a few more routine questions and declining the offer of more tea, the CID office stood to leave.

"Well, unless you can think of anything else which may be helpful I think that will be all I need, but if by any chance you think of something we should know please do not hesitate to contact us; here is my card."

Showing the visitor to the front door she nonchalantly asked.

"Are they positive it was Mary Bowron and if so what was she doing visiting the cottage? It had already been put up for sale."

"Well you may ask, but they are sure the body is that of Mrs Bowron. Has she not been estranged from her husband for some time?"

Suzanne nodded her agreement allowing the police woman to continue.

"Why she should be there at this time your guess is as good as mine. The theory is having visited the house earlier on Saturday she went back with a load of booze and by the time it came to leave Mary Bowron was quite drunk and unable to drive, the local police found her vehicle parked-up in Lynmouth on the Tuesday. There was no electricity supply to the cottage as it had been disconnected so when it

278

got dark we can only presume she either found some candles or lit a fire in the grate – who knows? After the incident, the investigating officers found evidence of at least four wine bottles about the place so the current thinking is she probably drunk herself into a deep sleep and the candles or whatever was responsible for the rest. They are hoping to finally release the body to her family within the next few days."

There was silence between the two women before the visitor thanked her for the help and with a firm handshake bade farewell, leaving Suzanne standing on the doorstep still harbouring thoughts of the former art mistress.

Over the following days, despite David's many attempts to reassure her she was blameless in the death, Suzanne could not help feeling a sense of guilt and that perhaps she could have done more to help her former mentor understand her own feelings.

Doubts of past happenings in her life also began to surface in Suzanne's mind and the self-question arose of her own culpability. As then, could or should she have done more to prevent the tragic events?

Now autumn was upon them and Suzanne spent much of her time away from the house walking the coastal cliff-top paths around Lyn. At the end of each day David would invariably collect Suzanne and return with her to Blackmoor Gate, but she was always deep in thought and following their evening meal would often disappear alone to her room for the rest of the evening leaving Rebecca Burge and her son alone downstairs.

Mother repeatedly tried to reassure David that whatever the circumstances, with the death of Mary Bowron, Suzanne had experienced a great loss.

"Didn't you say that the woman was originally the support and inspiration for Suzanne to get into her art work?"

"Yes, I did and of which I am well aware, but it doesn't mean she wouldn't have made it on her own.

Suzanne really has natural talent, people just love her work and personality and she is so pretty, people worship her."

Rebecca Burge smiled.

"As you do, don't deny it. Just be patient, I am sure after a few weeks Mary Bowron will be a forgotten figure from the past so don't jeopardize the relationship because of things you may not understand."

"Mother, as always, you are right, but I am sure there is something more. Suzanne has been acting so differently since we returned from our weekend away and it's as if there is something else on her mind besides the fire. I just have no idea what it might be."

His mother moved to leave the room.

"David, just listen to me, I would gladly have a motherly conversation with Suzanne to find out what is worrying her, but at this time I don't think there is anything to gain so just take my advice and be patient. The last thing I want to see is either of you ending up hurt."

It was nearly six weeks after the advice from his mother; a Friday and for the previous ten days the weather had been exceptional. David was pleased Suzanne had agreed to his suggestion that if she was going to be in or around Lyn in the afternoon he would finish work early and they should meet in the spot above the sea where they had first met, affectionately known to them since then as 'Our place.'

His thoughts were of a quiet time alone together, walking, talking and generally once more just being themselves might help him have a little more understanding of what at present seemed to be bothering her.

As he wend his way downwards from the well worn path, David shielded his eyes to protect them from the sun's reflections as it made its way towards the sea and the waiting horizon. David was a little earlier than expected, but when taking the final descent towards the lonely figure sitting on the large rocky outcrop the sound of disturbed tumbling loose stones forced Suzanne to turn her head around towards him.

"Oh hello, you're here earlier than I expected."

Greeting her with a light kiss on the cheek, David slid on to the rock and sat down beside her.

"I know, but there was very little traffic on the road from Barnstaple. Anyway, how are feeling? I left early this morning so what have you been up to today?"

Without taking her eyes from the ocean, Suzanne replied.

"I'm fine, but I am so confused and now don't know what to do."

Before David could respond, she continued.

"This morning your mother went shopping and dropped me in Lynmouth where I had a couple of completed paintings to deliver; the first being a commission which I left to be collected at the Tourist Centre; the second I was going to leave for display at the Hotel.

Elsie wasn't there when first I arrived, but as I was about to leave she appears and says a letter had arrived in the post today addressed to me."

Suzanne reached into her canvas shoulder bag and withdrew a white envelope, pausing before passing it over to David.

"Please read, at present it's what I have no need for, but I do think I am obliged."

Looking at the outside of the envelope and turning it slowly around in his hand, David's reply was simple and quiet.

"It's from a Solicitor."

Chapter 28

The taxi had dropped the lone figure directly outside the large wrought iron gates; it was a cold and wet morning. As the transport had driven away into Pitcombe Lane its solitary passenger made their way through the grandiose entrance of the Victorian Cemetery. Damp fallen leaves deadened the sound of footsteps as they followed the paved driveway past the old mortuary chapel.

In a distant corner of an open space a small group of people stood around a hole in the ground while at the side of the narrow roadway stood a variety of waiting vehicles, including an empty black hearse. Watching and hidden from the mourners by the spreading branches of a worn and weathered tree it was clear the interment had been missed. After a closing prayer from the minister and a few whispered parting words, the group started to move away from the open grave towards their waiting cars to drive past the hidden observer.

When she thought she was alone, Suzanne stepped out, past the headstones of previously long departed souls, across the long unkempt grass and although it had now finally stopped raining, the depressed feeling of overgrown neglect was not helped by the incessant sound of dripping from the leaves of surrounding trees.

Suzanne stopped at the mound of earth soon to cover the wooden coffin lying at the bottom of the dark hole before her. Shortly a member of the cemetery staff would arrive to replace the soil into the ground and the contents of the casket would be lost forever.

First checking she was alone, Suzanne stood at the foot of the open grave and lowered her head and spoke in a hushed tone.

"Hello Mary, I've come to say goodbye. I have much to thank you for and which I will always be truly grateful. What you must understand was I could never ever return your love for me in the way you desired and for that you must forgive me. You were still very dear to me in a very special way, without your guidance and support I would not be the person I am today."

A lone tear trickled down her cheek.

'I am so sorry, I have given my heart to another, but deep down there will always be a special place for you."

She stood alone in silence not hearing the muffled footsteps approaching through the grass behind and was surprised by an arm being gently placed around her shoulders.

"Please do not cry Suzanne."

Startled she turned and came face to face with the husband of the late Mary Bowron.

"I am so pleased you are here", he said as the couple warmly embraced. "It is a pity you couldn't make it to the church service."

"I wanted to see the boys again, but it was all I could do to make it this far; I had hoped they would be here too."

Wiping her eyes, Suzanne managed a brief smile for Tony Bowron.

"I bet they are quite young men by now. Anyway, I should be going, I have a train to catch and would hate to miss it."

She moved as if to walk away. First Tony stepped aside to let her pass, but then reached out to restrain her lightly on the arm.

"Please wait Suzanne; I have much to tell you. Not knowing where you were now living after your move I asked our solicitor to try and make contact with you as he indicated his office was in possession of a forwarding address and that is why last week you should have received a letter with details of today's church service and internment. I won't keep you long, but it is imperative we talk today. Once we have spoken, if you so wish there will no need for us to communicate with one another ever again."

She found it hard to explain, but Suzanne was frightened.

"I am sorry, but I have a train to catch; I had to spend last night in Bath at a Bed and Breakfast." Looking at her watch she started to hurry away. "If I miss this one I will have to wait until early tomorrow morning as there are very few connecting services."

In the rain, which once again was again beginning to fall quite heavily, Tony hurried to keep up with her.

"Suzanne wait, listen to me. How are you going to get all the way down to the railway station in this weather? You will be soaking wet by the time you get on to the train."

"I'll just walk down the hill into the City and take a bus, I'll be fine."

Her pursuer caught up and held Suzanne back, catching her by the arm.

"Tony, I have nothing to say, will you please let me go; you are going to make me late."

Out of the corner of his eye he could see a rather burly male cemetery worker arriving at the gravesite to complete his day's work paying the couple close attention. The last thing Tony Bowron wanted was to be reprimanded for harassing an attractive woman in the cemetery the same day his wife's remains had been buried there.

He immediately let her arm go free, but seeing this as his last opportunity managed to speak as she turned to go.

"Suzanne let me drive you to the railway station, it is the least I can do."

Suzanne had reached the paved roadway and was heading in the direction of the cemetery's imposing gates. Tony had hardly moved from the spot when in desperation he suddenly called after her.

"Don't you want to know what happened to your mother all those years ago? I have the details and if you will give me the opportunity will share them with you."

Reaching into the inside pocket of his long dark

overcoat he withdrew a crumpled envelope and waved it in the air.

"This is all I want to tell you about."

Suzanne stopped in her tracks and slowly turned to face Tony Bowron who was now hurrying his way towards her.

She slowly and deliberately asked the question.

"Did you just mention my mother?"

"I did indeed; when you were young did she not live in Oxford?"

"I don't think I have ever talked much about either of my parents to anyone – certainly not my mother. When I was at boarding school the nuns and teachers must have known a little, but I have never been sure how much."

Out of breath, he caught up with her.

"Well, I suggest you take advantage of my offer and let me drive you to the railway station which will allow me to give you the information I have in my possession," adding with a smile, "Besides, you will find it a lot drier than walking in this rain!"

A pensive look crossed Suzanne's face.

"Oh come on, don't be so stubborn; you have nothing to fear from me. My car is parked out on the lane just outside the front gates."

Without speaking a word, in dutiful fashion she began following Tony back through the entrance, silently wondering to herself what news she was about to learn about the fate of her own mother.

*****

As they drove down the hill into Bath, the normally outstanding view of the City was obscured by the inclement weather. At first the conversation between the pair had been limited, but as soon as they had been seated in his car she had taken the time to express her condolences for Mary's death.

285

"As you already know we had not been together for over a year. To begin with I found it very hard, but as the time moved on I began to realize our marriage was over. I managed to come to terms with the situation, even with the thought that maybe all the time we had been happily married was a sham and she had been living a lie."

"I am so sorry, but of course you did know about Mary's physical attraction towards me? I found it so difficult to deal with, especially after all the past help she had given me."

"After our break-up the hardest thing of all to cope with was Mary's attitude towards our children. At first she wanted nothing to do with the boys, all three were supportive to their father and after a while they found it very hard to even meet with her."

"That is so sad, Mary always gave the impression they were so important to her."

"Earlier today they went to the church service, but thought better of attending and refused to be present at the internment."

Tony paused in thought before continuing,

"In fact most of the people you saw there today were my friends or family, both Mary's parents died last year, but I did notice an elderly uncle and aunt came that as far as I know she hadn't seen for years."

There was silence between them until Suzanne spoke as the car went past Prior Park School and started to descend Ralph Allen Drive.

"More importantly, under the circumstances, how are they doing?"

"The boys are fine, all rapidly becoming young men. All are living at home with me and will be very annoyed when I tell them I have been with you today. I am sure they will be quite jealous."

Suzanne smiled.

"I would very much have liked to have met them, perhaps another day. What about you? All this business must have come as a bit of a shock?"

"To say it didn't would be untruthful. The intimacy Mary craved for with you was one thing, but over the years how many more unknown relationships were there? The news of her death did come as a surprise. The circumstances appear more than a little questionable, but to quote the police it was 'An unfortunate accident.' What I have since learnt from the solicitor, the same one who made contact with you, is that in the weeks before her death she seemed to be acting in a very strange and irrational way."

Eyes fixed on the road ahead, Suzanne muttered, "Probably because of me, I was the one to blame for your wife's death."

Tony Bowron did not react.

"The worst part about the whole affair was the waiting. The hospital would not release Mary's remains for over five weeks. We all wanted to bring closure, but until all the forensic tests and reports had been completed nothing could happen and the boys found that part of it particularly hard."

Silence followed and no further conversation passed between them until the car was forced to pause by traffic lights at the Churchill Bridge.

"So, Tony you said you had something to tell me about my mother?"

As the car began to move with the flow, hesitantly at first, he began to tell Suzanne the information she had been waiting for.

"Immediately after her death I went to Mary's flat in Locksrook Road. Our lawyer arranged matters with her former landlord so I could have easy access; the plan was to check for any personal items I might wish to retain for the boys – jewellery, mementos, photographs; you know the sort of thing. Mary had very few close relatives and when contacted every indication was they were far from interested in getting involved.

When I first entered the ground floor apartment, it immediately struck me how she must have been living as the comforts we had had in our family homes seemed to be missing. Living and bedroom, small kitchen and a bathroom, it was clean, but very basic and the furniture looked worn and tired. There were indicators about the place she must still have been earning some money from teaching, but, bearing in mind my original intention for going there, I was struck by so few photographs being on display. There were only three in total, two in the bedroom and a large framed portrait on the drawing room mantle piece."

Tony Bowron paused.

"The three pictures were of you and all of them looked as if they had been taken some time ago."

Suzanne sighed.

"It figures."

"Only when I went to the sideboard did I find other photographs, mainly of the three children growing-up, all jumbled tightly into one drawer as if discarded and forgotten. The other drawer was full of personal papers, bills, bank statements and such like. There was also this odd bundle of letters held together with an elastic band, probably a couple of dozen or so, but nothing of particular interest to me excepting the last one.

It was a lengthy handwritten letter addressed to Mary from a Sister Veronica Phillips who, if my memory serves me correctly, was in-charge when St. Bernadette's School finally closed its doors. I will give you the letter when we arrive at the Station, it is here in my coat pocket and you can do what you will with once you have read it.

I took very little else from the flat, but I did take all the photographs of you away with me, feeling the fewer questions people were able to ask about Mary's relationships the easier it would be. The lawyer has your contact address so I will arrange for them to be forwarded to you as soon as possible."

"…and the letter from Sister Veronica? What did it say?"

Suzanne waited for what to her seemed an eternity. She guessed from his earlier insistence they should talk what Tony had to say next was likely to be stunning and probably have further repercussions. As they pulled into a car parking space in front of their destination, Tony Bowron started to tell her about the letter's message.

"It was postmarked from somewhere up North, Durham I think, and the date showed me that it had been posted over four years ago. The content seemed to indicate shortly before her writing, Sister Veronica had been contacted by the Police who were trying to trace a former St Bernadette pupil and in one last desperate attempt to do so they were contacting the former Head in the hope that over the passing years she had maintained contact with the person they were trying to trace. The letter named Suzanne Patterson as the person who the Police were trying to find."

Suzanne, mind racing, let out a stifled gasp.

"Did she say anything in the letter about what they wanted to know?"

"Quite a lot really, it appears up until about five years ago there was some form of Mental Institution in South Wales, exactly where I am not sure, but it doesn't really matter as the place, like many of its type before it, was scheduled for closure.

At the time of which the letter speaks, the number of inmates had been greatly reduced to enable the shut-down to go as smoothly as possible. One of the remaining few was a woman; in her mid-fifties would be my guess. The letter does not include full details of what the woman spoke of in her more lucid moments, but she repeatedly claimed that she had once mothered a daughter with an attractive German student and the child had been taken away from her, by whom nobody seems certain. What the woman was adamant about until the end was all those responsible for holding her against her will should be careful because when the daughter arrived to take her mother home it would be time for all of them to pay the price for having made her suffer for so long. You can read the full details at your convenience later," he said as he reached into his coat pocket and withdrew a crumpled envelope.

"It seems the woman's name was Elaine Patterson,"

Tony paused waiting for her reaction and when none was forthcoming continued.

"Unfortunately, at the time the Doctors and Staff thought because of the medicinal cocktail being administered she couldn't be helped and it was just a drug induced figment of her imagination talking."

"So what happened to the poor woman?" Suzanne expectantly asked.

"You must make-up your own mind, but from the letter and what I can read between the lines is that her claims were totally ignored which only had the effect of pushing her further over the edge. One morning, two weeks before the place was to be finally closed, she was found dead in her bed. 'Death by natural causes' was the official version of events, but after all she had suffered alone I think mind and body just gave-up."

Suzanne spoke in a hushed tone.

"What you are telling me means that Mary must have known the whereabouts of my mother and that she probably was still alive, but never thought it important enough to tell me about it."

"The matter would have probably rested there, but an alert administrator who heard about the goings on started to investigate further and when he or she began to ask a few more questions they must have got as far as tracing the trail back to the School before it went cold. I should add there is no mention in the letter of where your mother was buried or where her ashes may have been scattered."

Finally accepting the envelope Tony had offered to her, Suzanne gazed upwards to the clock face hanging above the entrance to the building.

"Look at the time! I don't wish to be rude, but unless I start to make a move the train will be leaving without me."

She leant across and kissed him lightly on the cheek and started to leave the car.

"Thank you for the ride, I am so pleased not to have to travel in soaking wet clothing."

There were tears in Suzanne eyes as she placed the envelope in her bag and finally left the car.

"I don't know what else to say, once I have had the opportunity to digest what you have just given me, perhaps one day I will have the courage to get in touch again."

With the dawning realization that this may be the final time she had contact with a member of the Bowron family she sighed.

"Thank you so much for coming today to say goodbye to Mary, I really appreciated you taking the trouble."

"It was a struggle, but you were more than welcome, give my regards to the boys, look after yourself and please don't think too harshly of Mary; she wasn't all bad really, just believe me."

Hitching her shoulder bag high, Suzanne turned on her heel and walked briskly across the car park towards the Station. Passing through the main entrance she briefly glanced back at Tony still sitting motionless in the front seat of his car.

*****

The train was fifteen minutes late arriving in Taunton. Suzanne was surprised to be met at the Station by Becky rather than her son.

"David is very apologetic he isn't here to meet you. Only yesterday he was told he had to be in Plymouth today, something to do with his work so I offered to drive here this evening and meet the train."

"That was kind of you, I am very grateful, otherwise goodness knows what my taxi fare home would have been!"

"There is one good thing to tell you, before he left this morning David told me he plans to take the whole day off tomorrow as he is owed a lot of time in-lieu of the long hours worked over recent weeks. Also, I am going shopping with a friend in Exeter so you will be able to have the complete day alone together," she said smiling.

Suzanne returned the smile, but did not verbally respond; the whole journey back to Blackmoor Gate was a complete series of pleasantries, there was no reference by either of them to Suzanne's night away or the events that had occurred earlier in the day and there was still no sign of David when they arrived. Explaining she was very tired, shortly before nine Suzanne wished Rebecca goodnight and made her way-up to bed.

Before the train pulled into Taunton station, she had read the letter which Tony had given her several times and now just wanted time alone to consider its content. Whatever Suzanne had in her mind as she went up the stairs in the end really didn't matter because once in bed the tiredness took over and soon she was asleep.

Early the next morning, she made her way downstairs in dressing gown and slippers and as there was no sign of Rebecca, Suzanne assumed she had already left for her shopping day in Exeter. David's car was now parked in the driveway, but there was no obvious sign of his presence either. As she filled the kettle at the kitchen sink the sound of a hearty chuckle, followed by a pair of strong arms being wrapped around her and finally a kiss to the nape of her neck announced his presence in the room.

"Good Morning!"

"David stop it, you frightened me and don't be so rough, I am very fragile you know," she turned to face her aggressor, "So I suppose you want a cup of tea?"

"And don't I get a proper kiss?"

"You can jolly well wait. Your mother is out for the rest of the day so you can learn to control your feelings."

David mockingly frowned back at Suzanne, sitting himself down at the kitchen table he asked.

"Sorry I wasn't at the station to meet you yesterday, but I didn't get back from Plymouth until late last night and by then I suspect you were fast asleep. How did yesterday work out for you? I think you were very brave to go alone and you know I would have gladly come with you if able."

"It was fine, but in the end I only went to the interment at the cemetery as I couldn't face going to the church service not knowing who I might meet there."

Suzanne placed two mugs of tea on the table and sat down opposite David.

"I have so much to tell you, I am just glad your mother is not here to listen."

"Me too, I just hope you believe what I have to say, but you go first."

Suzanne told David about the content of the letter Tony Bowron had outlined so well before passing it to her as she left Bath.

"There are certain parts I still have difficulty understanding, probably never will, but what is so sad is that Mary had known my mother was still alive and did nothing to enable us to get back together."

She stopped and placed her hand over his.

"But that is now all in the past; I'm so sorry, in recent weeks I must have been awful to know. The other matter I wanted to tell you about relates to the future of…"

In a childlike manner David cut her off mid-sentence.

"My turn now. The reason for me having to be in Plymouth yesterday was a job interview, which seemed to take most of the day, but was worth it in the end. I have been offered a new position at work, it means a big promotion," he grinned as he added, "Together with a much improved salary."

"I am so pleased for you and once again just love your enthusiasm."

"There is a downside though."

Suzanne looked puzzled and withdrew her hand.

"Unfortunately the job will entail me having to move from here to live in Plymouth. I haven't yet had the opportunity to tell mother, she will be very disappointed."

"Don't worry, I will still be around to look after her, it is the least I can do."

"I hope not!" replied David abruptly.

Suzanne's mouth dropped at the brusque manner of the reply to her offer. Before she could rebuke David for his attitude, lovingly he gently placed both his hands across the table on top of hers'.

"You know I love you very much and now want you to come and live with me," there was a short pause before he continued "Suzanne, I want you to be my wife. Please will you marry me?"

Another few moments of anxious silence followed as he waited for the reply, before Suzanne rose from her chair and quickly moved around the table to fling her arms around David's neck.

"Yes! Yes! Yes, of course I will and can't wait to be your wife so we can be together always!"

She stopped and screwed her face-up before breaking into a beaming smile.

"It's just as well you asked me now."

A questioning look appeared on his face.

"I was trying to tell you earlier, but your enthusiasm got in the way; I can't think of anyone to be a better daddy to my children, you see David I'm pregnant."

Chapter 29

The tiring two hundred mile road journey from Paris was followed by an overnight stop in Lyon, but now the urban sprawl of the French City was giving way to the vineyards of the Rhone Valley. To compensate for the rigours of the previous twenty-four hours it was agreed the next day's travelling would be shorter and curtailed at Valence. The chosen route would then take them through Vienne and the prime grape growing area of the region where vineyards seem to stretch as far as the eye can see.

Nearing the targeted goal, with the third person now fast asleep in the back of the car, the two of them happily agreed there was no need for rush. Circumstances were such it seemed a good idea for them to continue south for another sixty miles to Nimes, allowing the whole of the next day for rest and exploration of the historic City before setting off towards their ultimate destination.

*****

The wedding had been a very quiet affair. David, Suzanne, his mother and Elsie Molland were the only people present at Barnstaple Registry Office. Everyone who knew the couple gleefully received the news they were to wed, including Rebecca Burge who was so pleased her son had finally been able to overcome the tragedy surrounding the death of Morag and even more ecstatic when given the news that, god willing, she would shortly become a grandmother.

After the brief ceremony the four had returned to Lynmouth where Elsie insisted laying-on a celebratory party for them and a small group of their close friends all at her expense.

The newly weds left their small group of guests at the *Lorna Doone Hotel* shortly before six in the evening. David had made arrangements for them to revisit his friend's cottage near Padstow where they would spend a few days together before his return to work and their continuing to make final arrangements for the move.

In the early hours of the next morning unlike David lying beside her Suzanne was unable to sleep. She was again being haunted by those dormant thoughts of the past that unexplainably seemed to have been reawakened since making the commitment to David.

Following the fatal fire at the cottage, the later discovery the former teacher had been withholding information regarding her mother and, despite her protestations, Mary Bowron's close physical attention had all proved very stressful for her.

What troubled Suzanne the most was the demise of her father. In the past she always managed to shut the unfortunate events of his last days from her mind, but had long come to accept she had been the one ultimately responsible for his death. It was a secret she now regretted not having shared with David before their marriage and soon the situation was to be further complicated with the birth; Suzanne's mind was in turmoil asking what was the best thing for everybody.

Unable to sleep, as the first signs of daylight reached between the open curtains Suzanne slipped silently from the bed, quietly crept from the room and made her way downstairs to the kitchen, where through the window the sun was rising on a clear morning. Taking the warm fleece hanging behind the kitchen door, Suzanne was still surprised by the cool daybreak air on her face as she walked towards the edge of the small beach before sitting herself down and huddling into a sandy crevice between two large shoreline rocks.

The sound of the incoming tide running up the beach and the rhythmic tumbling water from the freshwater stream running down to meet the ocean had a calming effect upon Suzanne's mind as she lay her head down on the soft sand and earlier bad thoughts seemed to evaporate with the serenity of the surrounding environment.

Curled-up with feet tucked away for warmth, she was soon fast asleep on the beach.

Suzanne did not know how long she had been there, but from afar a voice seemed to be talking as she slept.

"Well, at last I've found you, what are you doing here?" The voice chuckled, "A fine way to spend your wedding night! Are you coming back to the house or do you intend to spend the rest of the day asleep on the beach? Truthfully I don't think it would be good for the baby, you will both catch a death of cold."

Suzanne opened her eyes to find David kneeling beside her; she focused and sat upright before speaking.

"Sorry, I couldn't sleep and felt by coming out here it might help to clear the head, my mind is overflowing with so much."

David leant across and kissed her on the cheek.

"So you leave your new husband alone in bed on his wedding night, I think that is..." he was interrupted.

"I hardly think that's fair, please don't go on, I just wanted to be alone with my thoughts."

As he helped her to her feet David was smiling, but never the less was puzzled to have found his new bride asleep on the secluded beach.

His arm around her shoulders, they silently made their way back to the cottage where, seated in the kitchen with two mugs of tea between them, David again asked the question.

"If you couldn't sleep why didn't you wake me to talk, especially if there was something particular bothering you?"

"I didn't want to disturb you and after all the excitement of yesterday's wedding I didn't think it would be really fair."

"For goodness sake Suzanne I am your husband, don't married couples normally share everything, good or bad? I am aware more than most people of the problems you have had to face over the past year and consider I have been fully supportive," there was a pause, "Unless you share your concerns with me I can do nothing about them. Is it the move, the wedding or perhaps the thought of becoming a mother in less than five months time?"

"I assure you it's none of those things!"

"Was it the fire, that woman's death, news of your mother? Just tell me so that I can help, please."

First taking a mouthful from the mug in front of her, Suzanne slowly and calmly replied.

"David, it is true all the things you mention have been to a lesser or greater degree some worry to me over recent months. The most concerning was the news surrounding my mother, certainly the most exciting was you were going to be the father of my first child and we agreed to spend the rest of our lives together as man and wife. You must understand, I love you very much, but recently I have been living under so many dark clouds that hopefully are now just beginning to clear. Your mother has been fantastic, I can't thank her enough for the help she has given me, likewise Elsie Molland, people have just been incredible and I don't know what I would have done without everybody's support, most of all you."

She leant across the table and kissed him firmly on the lips.

As Suzanne returned to her seat, he looked pensively across the table at her.

"And I love you too with all my heart and I would do anything for you so why oh why wouldn't you share the thoughts bothering you last night?"

"You turned over and went to sleep directly after we had made love."

"I have no wish to argue with you, but that is absolute rubbish," retorted David.

Suzanne cast her eyes downwards and there was a full sixty seconds where neither of them spoke before, with tears in her eyes, she looked across at her husband.

"You are quite right, recent events have been

extremely stressful for me and all I can say is I am so thankful to you for your support, love and most of all friendship. What I am about to tell you should have been said months ago and long before you would have been able to say a devious woman cornered you, believe me when I say that scenario is simply not true."

David held his breath to hear what his new wife was about to tell him, Suzanne rose and went around the table, as she spoke holding out a hand to lead him.

"Come with me David, I am going to tell you everything, after which I pray you will not allow anything to be any different between us," adding as she patted her stomach "If only for her sake. Oh and before you ask, I just know it's going to be a girl; call it woman's intuition if you like!"

David offered no words, but only a quick nervous smile in return.

"Let us go upstairs, I'm cold and think I am going to need more than a little cuddle to get through what I am about to tell you."

Suzanne led David through the kitchen door and upwards towards the bedroom.

*****

After having taken most of the preceding week on the road, the day spent in and around the capital of the Gard department was one of total relaxation. Nimes, rich in history dating back to the Roman Empire, is a popular tourist destination and without doubt they had found the old Amphitheatre the most impressive feature of the City's centre, but the ambiance surrounding the near-by Jardins de la Fontaine certainly took some beating. From there he had insisted on climbing the adjacent hill which is said to be the highest point in Nimes It was crowned with a Roman Tower dating back to 16 BC and on reaching the garden at the summit he had sought shade from the hot afternoon sun.

The following day they checked out of the downtown

Empire Hotel shortly after breakfast and soon found themselves leaving the outskirts of the City on the final leg of the promised pilgrimage.

*****

The first full day of marriage had not been easy for Suzanne, but he had made it so much easier for her than she could have ever have hoped for. Lying there in bed, crying uncontrollably, David had held on to her tightly as she tried to explain everything about the circumstances leading up to the death of Henry Patterson and her subsequent return to England.

David listened intently, on occasions soothingly stroking her back and neck, only when Suzanne had completely finished telling the sorrowful tale did he talk. To her amazement he just comforted her and offered Suzanne warm condolences about the tragic accident, telling her that was all in the past and however could he hold Suzanne responsible for happenings far beyond her control and it was now his responsibility to ensure she never had to suffer such horrors again.

The only response offered was one of loving gratitude, a promise she would be an exemplary mother for their children and an assurance there was nothing else from her past he should be aware of.

David simply took Suzanne into his arms and whispered in her ear.

"Our secret until the day we die, but I still can't believe you couldn't trust…"

He was cut off in mid-sentence as Suzanne pushed him onto his back enabling her to forcibly kiss him long and hard on the lips.

*****

How life had changed since that time, eyes shut and ignoring the passing french countryside, Suzanne layback in the passenger seat as David drove westwards towards the expected mind confrontations with the past.

The move to a new home in Plymouth and a new beginning had been hastily completed shortly before the birth of their first child; Suzanne had been intuitively correct it was a girl. There had been very little discussion on names for their daughter as both parents were soon agreed that Emily Rachel was fitting for their little bundle of joy.

Close contact had been maintained with the owner of the Hotel and Elsie Molland was pleased to be able to continue with the previous business arrangement.

After Suzanne's unburdening to him about the earlier sad events of her life there was never again any mention of the past, but after the birth of their daughter David was only too aware something else was causing Suzanne concern. Often he would observe her just sitting at her work, eyes fixed and staring at a blank canvas, her mind appeared to be elsewhere. David was worried, she was undoubtedly an exemplary mother to Emily, but thoughts of Suzanne's own mother and what eventually happened to her had started to enter his mind.

Returning home one evening from work David found his wife sitting in silence staring at the painting he had first observed hanging in the cottage and which seemed to take pride of place wherever Suzanne went.

Entering the room, from behind her he spoke "Although I have asked many times, you never have told me exactly where and why this was painted, the picture seems to have had some hold over you, perhaps now is the time to share your thoughts and tell me?"

Without taking her eyes from the landscape, Suzanne started to reply.

"This is where I lived in France with my father and this is where he is buried, the circumstances I have already explained and which you have been so good never to have mentioned since."

She turned to face him.

"But recently I have been thinking hard, Emily will never meet either of my parents which I think is very sad and, in truth, it is entirely my fault. I have to bring proper closure, if only for Emily's sake, I need your help."

Taking his time, he didn't answer immediately.

"You know I would do anything for my wife and daughter, what is it you want of me? Just ask."

"It is very simple really, I don't know if you will agree, you may think it too risky, but having thought about it after all these years I hardly think so."

He was puzzled and did not reply.

"David, next year Emily will be two and old enough to travel so what I think we should do is take a summer holiday in France. We can travel by car and take our time driving south, but at the end of our journey I would like to end up here."

Suzanne swiftly turned and pointed at the picture on the wall.

"If it is possible, I would like to visit my father's final resting place and take the time to tell him about his new granddaughter."

*****

The journey had been uneventful. They had stopped briefly in Alés before taking a longer break when reaching Anduze for Emily who much to her parents delight had long mastered the challenge of taking her first unassisted steps. There they had a picnic lunch sitting on the banks of the river Gard.

It was late afternoon by the time they reached Florac. Only twelve miles from the intended final destination, David happily parked the car in shadow offered by trees surrounding the large Square situated in the middle of the small town.

"You two had better wait here in the cool while I try and find a phone to see if I am able to book us some accommodation for the night."

302

Leaving to cross the open space, he made his way towards an illuminated *Bar* sign and the near certainty he would find a public telephone available there Meanwhile the first twinges of uncertainty about whether it was the right thing they were attempting to do had started to infiltrate Suzanne's mind.

When David returned he found the car unattended, but looking around his wife and daughter were soon spotted some yards away seated on a wooden bench next to the ornate water fountain in the opposite corner of the Square.

Emily noted his reappearance immediately and as he approached threw out her arms to be pulled up, which he duly obliged her with.

"The buildings are as I remember, nothing seems to have changed," Suzanne said, "They used to hold the weekly market right here in the Square, probably still do, but somehow it doesn't feel the same."

As he bounced a giggling Emily around in his arms, Suzanne continued.

"You know David, perhaps it wasn't such a good idea to come back after all these years, call it my silly intuition again, call it what you will, but I just have the feeling all is not going to turn-out as it should."

"What do you want Suzanne? I can understand if you are finding this part of our holiday hard, resurrecting memories long past and forgotten is never easy, but remember originally it was your idea and one I was quite happy to go long with just to please you. We can leave here immediately and never ever return if that is what you want?"

"Something tells me I must go on, but goodness knows what lies ahead in the next twenty-four hours."

She took Emily, affectionately squeezing her before kissing on the forehead, and looked her husband straight in the eye.

"I'm just being silly, getting cold feet, having come this far I must have the power of my convictions; if we turn back now we will never return."

"That's my girl, the Suzanne I married, I love you both so very much!"

Mother and daughter returned his warm smile.

"So, how did you do finding us somewhere to sleep tonight? I hope you were successful, this little angel of ours is very tired and I don't want her late to bed again, so far with all the travelling she has been marvellous. I don't want her to be grumpy tomorrow; even happy children have their limits."

"We said yesterday, if it was at all possible the ideal situation would be to reach Pont de Monvert by the end of today. It is a small place, only three hundred or so people live there; only two establishments offer overnight B and B and, surprisingly for this time of the year, one of those is closed for renovation while the other, aptly called *Auberge du Tarn*, has a room available. I don't know what it is like, but I took the risk and booked us in for the night. I spoke to the owner's wife on the telephone, she was very pleasant, and I explained where we were calling from and she said it would take us less than thirty minutes to get there - I have the address."

Without responding, Suzanne scooped Emily up into her arms and defiantly started to make her way across the Square and back to the car.

Chapter 30

Pont de Monvert is situated in the centre of the Cevennes. The small community sits on the southern slopes of Mont Lozere where over recent decades in the high valleys the population has been ever decreasing. Protestant chapels, Catholic churches, old memories of the dreadful 17th century religious conflicts and reminders of the violent and bloody period of the Camisards all abound here.

Thoughts of deep valleys and winding rivers were far from Suzanne's mind as they approached along the winding road towards the tower standing beside the ancient bridge which would take them across the rapid flowing river to their overnight stop.

There were several narrow streets running tantalisingly up the hill and away from the main thoroughfare, but situated on the side of the highway and backing on to the river, with two worn metal tables plus chairs standing outside coupled with a weathered swinging, wooden sign hanging from the building proclaiming *Auberge du Tarn,* it had not been hard to find.

David pulled off the road and onto the small patch of gravel in front of the inn, while Suzanne apprehensively looked out of the window, as memories slowly re-ignited in her head.

The mind was quickly focused to the present as the car coming to a grinding halt disturbed Emily who had fallen asleep on the back seat shortly after leaving Florac.

Suzanne moved to tend the youngster whilst David, realizing the sooner they got the over-tired child to bed the better it would be for all of them, made for the entrance to find the Proprietor. Cuddling to the chest, Suzanne comforted her daughter, gently rocking side to side and softly humming a familiar lullaby in her ear; Emily in her mother's arms was soon once more fast asleep.

Full of his boyish enthusiasm David soon reappeared. "It is all very antiquated, but at least our bedroom looks OK, I checked the sheets and they looked clean enough. The owner's wife, a Madame Dubois, has put a small camp bed in the room for Emily as I asked, but you know what your daughter is like, she will want to spend the night sleeping between us."

Suzanne smiled.

"Can you blame her? After all she's only two!"

"Madame also said Monsieur Dubois would not be around until later, but in the meantime if there was anything else we needed just to let her know."

David removed two holdalls from the heavily laden rear of the car.

"Follow me, I'll carry our overnight cases up, you take Emily" and once more strode off towards the entrance where he waited for his wife to catch-up.

There was no sign of life as the three of them ascended the narrow twisting staircase, bare wood and each step worn down by the countless feet of others who over the years had made the short journey up to the rooms on the first floor.

Suzanne placed her sleeping daughter on to the tiny bed before she stopped and surveyed the room; in her experience the furniture and décor were typical of that found in any rural auberge. Passing through the unoccupied ground floor room she had noticed the arranged tables and chairs and in the corner there appeared to be a fully stocked drinks bar. Suzanne hoped any excessive late noise from the *Auberge du Tarn* clientele would not be a disturbance to their overnight rest which, not to mention Emily, David and her were desperately in need of.

As indicated, Suzanne found their room unpretentious, basic, but scrupulously clean and totally suitable for their chambre et petit-dejeuner.

She carefully covered Emily with a soft blanket and for the time being left the youngster asleep; to wake her now seemed so unfair.

As Suzanne started to unpack their overnight

bags David was standing looking out of the room's only window at the fast flowing torrent below, the foundations of the auberge and all the adjacent buildings along the river bank seemed to reach down well below the surface. In the fading evening light the water tumbling over the boulders seemed very peaceful, whilst on the bank beyond, dark wooded slopes added a sinister air to the tranquillity.

"When you have stopped viewing the countryside perhaps you might like to be more helpful; in a while Emily will be awake and will be very upset."

David stepped back from the window, at the same time giving his wife an inquisitive look.

"I need you to go down to the car as soon as possible because her beloved teddy bear, the one she always cuddles herself to sleep with, unfortunately in our haste was left on the back seat. You know what will happen if she wakes and doesn't find it with her."

David stepped forward and kissed as they passed, "Your wish is my command!" adding as the door closed behind him, "Anything for a peaceful night's sleep."

Within a few minutes David returned to find Suzanne, having completed the little unpacking they had, sitting with her legs up on the bed, Emily was still fast asleep.

"No sign of Madame Dubois, only two locals drinking at the bar and didn't bump into any other guests, all very quiet," he said handing over Emily's comforter.

"I helped myself to an old newspaper sitting on the small table in the hallway."

David held up a well read copy of *Journal de Mendes* to show her.

"Over a month old, but it appears to be a copy of the area's weekly newspaper; whatever, you know how little French I understand so it's not much use to me."

He threw the old newspaper on to her lap.

"News is out of date, but I thought you may be interested for old times' sake."

307

She picked it up.

Soon Suzanne was engrossed in reading the front page. She just lowered the paper from her face and smiled as David announced, having discovered the whereabouts of the bathroom, he was about to take a shower. Thankful for a still sleeping Emily, Suzanne continued scanning the worn columns of French newsprint.

Having no wish to disturb his young daughter or any fellow guests while in the shower, David showed restraint with his normal disharmonious vocal efforts, but it was still a full thirty minutes before he returned to the bedroom with a towel wrapped around his middle. The scene that greeted him was totally unexpected.

Emily, by then clutching the soft toy he had earlier recovered from the car, had not moved and was still soundly asleep on her bed, but it was Suzanne that caused his concern.

Crumpled pages of *Journal de Mende* lay scattered over the bed and across the floor while Suzanne still remained seated as when he had left, supported by the pillows behind her, bolt upright and staring ahead with a look of bewilderment across her face.

Realizing there was something seriously wrong David rushed to her side.

"What is it my dear? What's wrong? You look as if you have just seen a ghost!"

At first she did not reply, but without altering her pose eventually whispered.

"My God David if what I have just read is true it alters everything."

*****

Emily slept through and did not wake before sunrise. Once Suzanne had explained to David the significance of what she had read in the old newspaper, it did not take long before the couple were also fast asleep in one another's arms.

308

In the morning she was the first to awake, it was still not daylight and looking at her watch Suzanne saw it was just before 5.15. Lying in the darkened room she considered the implications of the information the old weekly had offered her.

"If only there was a way to check its validity."

Churning the thought around in her mind, by the time her husband was awake a seed of an idea had started to grow.

"Good morning my dear, how are you today?" he put his arm around her bare shoulders and asked, "Are you still concerned about what you told me last night? You can't be sure so if I were you I would just try and forget it, it is all in the long past."

She turned and kissed him.

"Good morning!"

There was a pause before, not believing the words coming so easily from her mouth, Suzanne continued.

"But that's just it David, you are not me. Don't worry though, I was just being paranoiac and the story probably had no connection to the past whatsoever."

Knowing she was lying and being deceitful to her husband Suzanne hated herself, but this was a once and only opportunity. Having lived with the situation for most of her adult life, if at all possible, she wanted to bring it to a satisfactory conclusion without David or anyone else's interference.

A waking Emily interrupted their thoughts. Hearing the sound of her daughter starting to cry, Suzanne reached to pick-up and place the youngster securely between both parents: soon afterwards the sobbing stopped as she quickly snuggled down between the two adults.

It was well over an hour before the family of three were enjoying a traditional French petit dejeuner in the bar area, they were alone and had the undivided attention of Madame Dubois.

"Can I get you anything else?" Asking as she

re-entered the room "More tea or coffee? Maybe some milk for la jeune fille?"

"No thank you so much, that was fine," David replied. "I must come and settle our bill and then be on our way. There is much more driving to accomplish before the day is done and the sooner we get on the road the better."

The French woman raised her eyebrows as she responded.

"The weather is good for this time of the year, often the mistral, the wind from the North you understand, can play havoc. Which direction are you heading today? Whereabouts are you…"

Before Madame Dubois could complete the next question, Suzanne, fearing the way the conversation was progressing, cut her off.

"Madame, your English is so much better than our French. We really aren't sure where we are going to find ourselves at the end of the day, but what I do know is that in two days time we have a ferry to catch in Saint Malo and have very little time to waste."

She reached and took Emily into her arms.

"Thank you so much for your hospitality; it was just what we needed."

"You were all more than welcome and I am so pleased you enjoyed your overnight stay. You must come back here one day when you have more time to…spare. Is that how you say it in English?"

Once again, Suzanne gave a warm smile.

"Perfect! But now I really must go and finish the little packing we have left to do, my husband will settle the bill."

With Emily in her arms she turned and quickly left the room, David remain seated, smiled to himself, and finished his nearly full cup of coffee before making his way to the door leading into kitchen to seek out Madame Dubois.

While Suzanne finished fixing their daughter into her

safety harness on the back seat of the car, David was placing the final piece of overnight luggage in the rear, but it was only when both parents were seated and strapped into the vehicle that Emily let out a piercing scream.

Knowingly, Suzanne twisted around to see what the reason might be for her daughter's sudden and apparent unruly behaviour; David looked into the rear-view mirror to witness a very distraught young lady.

Unbuckling and smartly jumping out of the stationary car, she opened the rear passenger door to comfort her daughter, but it was more than apparent to Suzanne what the problem was.

"David, will you please wait here with Emily, it seems Teddy has been left behind, I think we must have missed it."

"Strange, I was sure I checked everything before I came down to the car," he replied and daughter duly obliged when father added, "Calm down Emily, mummy is going back to find your teddy bear."

As she made her way back to the front entrance, Suzanne found it hard to listen as he started to gently scold Emily for not looking after her teddy and leaving it behind because in truth it had been Suzanne herself who had earlier hidden the toy behind the wardrobe in the bedroom as an excuse to enable her to return and speak alone with the owners of *Auberge du Tarn*.

In haste she took the stairs up to the first floor two at a time and was pleased to find the door to their overnight room ajar. Without hesitation Suzanne went directly to the place where earlier she had surreptitiously hidden her daughter's toy, but as she bent down to reach behind the dark oak furniture someone entering the room startled her.

"Madame Burge! I thought you and your family had left, I heard someone running up the stairs and I came to investigate whom it might be. Is there a problem? Is everything OK?"

With a look of relief spread across her face, Suzanne

got to her feet clutching Emily's teddy bear.

"Don't worry Madame Dubois, everything is just fine. As you can see my daughter left this behind, she must have lost and then forgotten all about it. It is a good job we remembered before leaving, I looked everywhere and found it down behind the wardrobe here; goodness knows how it ended up there."

"C'est bon! I am so pleased you found it, your pretty daughter would have been very upset if she had lost it."

Suzanne could not summon the courage to ask the question and moved towards the bedroom door to leave.

"My husband and daughter are waiting in the car, I really should go, thank you once again for your hospitality."

Closely followed by the French woman, Suzanne made her way down the narrow staircase for the final time. At the bottom she abruptly stopped having suddenly realized this was likely to be her last opportunity to discover the truth, Suzanne turned to face the still descending Madame Dubois.

"Maybe there is one more thing you can help me with."

She reached into her blue shoulder bag and withdrew the now neatly folded but crumpled copy of *Journal de Mende*, arranged so it opened to the headline story appearing on page three.

Handing the old newspaper to the French woman now standing beside her, Suzanne pointed to the photograph which appeared above the article.

"Madame Dubois, can you tell me who this man is? My understanding of the French language tells me it is one Jean LeRoux, with a wife called Claudine, is that correct? Did you know them?"

Madame Dubois looked long and hard at what she had been handed before answering the question.

"You are correct Madame in what you say, it is a very bad, some say very sad, affair. I know you are in a hurry, but if you are interested and have a few minutes I will let my husband tell you the story, he is better acquainted with the details," adding with a smile, "You see, Roland spends too long with his friends, as you say in England, 'gossiping' in the bar."

The beckoning French woman hurried down the passageway before eventually disappearing at the end through a beaded curtain.

Suzanne followed and entered into what seemed to be the Dubois' living quarters and even before the brief introductions she had presumed the old and portly gentleman sitting on the sagging easy chair in the far corner of the beamed room to be Madame's partner.

"This is Roland, my husband; he will be able to tell you everything you want to know."

Putting the chipped mug he had been drinking from on the table beside him, the Frenchman, without rising from his chair, grunted an informal welcome.

"Bonjour Mademoiselle!"

"I am sorry my husband speaks so very little English, but I will explain to him that you and your family were our guests last night and before leaving would be very pleased if he would be happy to talk and answer a few questions that you have."

Suzanne once more removed the old newspaper from her shoulder bag and passed it to Madame Dubois.

"Please can you ask him about the person in the photograph and what, if anything, he knows about him?" Not wishing to display her ability to speak fluent French, adding "Perhaps you will be good enough to translate for me what he says?"

"But of course, perhaps you would like to sit down."

She pulled an upright chair from the corner of the room, all the time tentatively waiting as Madame Dubois spoke in a rapid whisper to her husband. With the exception of his opening exclamation of 'Il est impossible' Suzanne found it hard to follow what he was saying.

313

After five more minutes of further exchange between the married couple, a frown upon his weathered face, Roland retrieved the mug he had been drinking from and slumped back into the worn leather chair.

As he took a hearty swig of whatever was contained in his earthenware cup, Françoise Dubois looked to her husband settling back into his retiring position and did not turn to face Suzanne until a single nod of the head by Roland Dubois indicated he was ready and she could commence telling their English visitor what he knew about the old newspaper article laying on the table before them.

"Although the story is long and complicated, my husband says I must be brief; it is one the locals are, as we also say in France, 'hesitant' to talk about. You must forgive him, but we have very few English guests staying with us so he was very surprised you were asking questions about such matters; I told him to be quiet, your business has absolutely nothing to do with him."

Breathing a sigh of relief, Suzanne sat motionless as Françoise Dubois started to re-tell what her closely watching husband had just told her.

"The picture of the man in the newspaper is one Jean LeRoux, he was very well known in the area as a no good person, a thief, confidence trickster and a very violent man. Lefeuvre…Martinez…Le Roux is only one of the many names he had used over the years, the photograph is one taken nearly two months ago in Montpelier of police arresting him; as the paper says, he was wanted for allegedly murdering his wife and they had been after him for over six months."

Holding her breath, Suzanne asked the vital question.

"And what was his wife's name?"

"Ah, Claudine, she was such a sweet person, nobody knew if they were really married, but they had been together since she was a young girl, such a waste!"

Madame Dubois had Suzanne's undivided attention.

"This man was terrible and over the years had had

many women, but Claudine never possessed the courage or the means to escape his evil influence. From time to time he would pass through Pont de Monvert and always found his way here, the bar being the attraction. His reputation went before him and wherever he went the locals hated him. My Roland always warned me to be so very careful, although when he was around you can be sure his woman was always not very far away watching from the shadows. Jean LeRoux's undoing finally came about one stormy night not so many miles away from here in Nimes."

Chapter 31

The French woman stopped talking, despite the early hour of the day her husband, chin resting on chest, had fallen asleep in his chair.

"There is more, but I fear I have kept you long enough, you must be on your way."

There was no effort by Suzanne to move from her seated position.

"No Madame, please continue I would like to hear the end of the story. My family is in the car and will not mind waiting a little longer, adding as she turned her head towards the sleeping figure, "We need not disturb Monsieur."

Françoise Dubois hesitated before carrying on.

"Very well, this is what my husband was telling me earlier. That particular night it was very windy and rain had been falling non-stop for several days, it was shortly before midnight when a female walked into the Gendarmerie Office in the centre of Nimes. The woman was in a sorry state, the clothes were all torn and hung from her as rags and it was apparent from the cuts and bruises to the face her claims to have been assaulted were probably valid. She told the young police officer on duty behind the desk her name was Claudine LeRoux and lived in a village just four kilometres outside of the City, where she had just walked from in the pouring rain. Madame LeRoux said she had something to tell the police about her husband, Jean LeRoux, and also wished to report that earlier in the evening she had been viscously attacked and assaulted by him."

Suzanne sat in silence, spellbound by the story.

"Unfortunately, the young police officer was alone and did not call for immediate help, instead he listened with incredulity to what she had to say, the entire district's police were only too aware of this woman's past history. Eventually, sitting Claudine on the wooden bench in the entrance hall, he telephoned his off-duty superior for guidance.

What happened next is not totally clear, but it appears after forty-minutes of waiting for the appearance of someone else to help her, Claudine decided the better option was once more to throw herself upon the mercy of the elements rather than a disturbed and unbelieving Police Inspector. Claudine must have asked herself why she ever decided to go to Nimes in the first place and think the Police would be able to help. She probably answered her own question with the thought that the only intention had been to get even with Jean. The years of suffering and humiliation had finally broken her and this latest outbreak of violence had been the final straw.

Tired of waiting, while the watching policeman had his back turned and an hour after she had entered, Claudine quietly slipped out of the building."

There was another pause.

"Madame, should you be joining your family? They will be worried and wonder where you are."

She was a little annoyed the French woman appeared to be taking her time, but was desperate for her own peace of mind to hear the end of the story, Suzanne petulantly replied.

"Please let me be the judge of that, Madame the sooner you finish the sooner we will be on our way. Do you hear them complaining?"

Pleased there appeared to be no audible cries of dissent coming from David or Emily about the delay, Suzanne quickly answered her own question.

"No, they appear to be quite happy – unless you have reason not to just finish, please."

Françoise Dubois looked surprised at Suzanne's reply; perhaps the attractive English woman had another side to her apparent sweet nature.

"Before Claudine left the house in all that atrocious

weather to walk to Nimes, Jean's drunken stupor had caused him to fall asleep, only to awake four hours later to find his wife gone. He guessed she had decided to walk to the City because from past experience that is always where she fled when trying to escape his unwanted attention"

Roland Dubois stirred in the chair, but did not awake.

"Jean immediately went in pursuit of his wife, driving around Nimes in the early hours he eventually found her taking refuge from the stormy weather in a bus shelter close to the main Square.

The evil man must have bundled Claudine into his car and taken her back to their house and because of his earlier violence she must have been in much pain, wet and exhausted. Probably physically too weak to resist, but already having confessed to him what she had told the young police officer, Claudine sealed her own fate.

Aware of where the couple were currently living, in the morning Gendarmerie from Nimes went to their village to investigate if there was any truth in Claudine's accusations. Besides the physical abuse, she had alleged a number of years previous Jean had committed a murder which the authorities were unaware of and had never been discovered."

Suzanne, fearful of what might come next, held her breath.

"Alas, the three policemen were too late; they should have given her the protection when she needed it the most. Arriving at the house, at first Jean denied them access to the property by barricading himself in and it was only when reinforcements arrived, including a trained negotiator, Jean peacefully emerged and was promptly arrested.

On entering the building the police team went carefully from room to room searching for who knows what. It wasn't until they got to the top floor and the locked door of a small bedroom did they make their grizzly discovery, after forcing entry into the room they found the mutilated body of Claudine LeRoux. She had been gagged, bound by the wrists and ankles and stretched-out across the bed and apparently bludgeoned to death by the madman who Claudine had chosen to call her husband. Later the police confirmed she had died before their arrival."

Immediately Madame Dubois whispered to herself, "Dieu reste son ame!"

"That is simply awful, I was obviously mistaken in thinking I knew the man, how silly of me. I am so sorry to have bothered you, now it is really the time I was on my way,"

Suzanne rose to leave.

Husband Roland still asleep in the chair and, having had an unexpected audience for the previous ten minutes, Françoise Dubois still wanted to talk.

She reached out and touched Suzanne on the arm. "

Madame veuillez vous s'asseoir - there is more to this sad tale."

Having no wish to upset her French hosts and curiosity warningly aroused, Suzanne duly obliged.

"It is said that when she first went to the Gendarmerie because of her past reputation her allegations were not taken seriously. Claudine gave them sketchy details of a murder Jean allegedly committed ten years ago and to which she had been the only witness, claiming her husband had in temper shot dead an older English man and his daughter before burying their bodies on the Englishman's land. At the time Jean and Claudine lived close by and in return for their accommodation used to help the man and his daughter with duties around the farm.

When police arrested Jean for the murder of Claudine, of course, he denied the earlier charge saying she was completely mad and delusional, but it didn't matter really as he was already in enough trouble with the death of his wife and was in total self denial of everything else.

For his own safety, as much as anything else, while awaiting trial for the murder of Claudine he was held in solitary confinement and transferred to a high security prison near Lyon. One morning la prison laissais took Jean his breakfast only to find him dead in his cell; he had taken his own life. Again, no one is really sure, but it is said he hung himself using the blanket from the bed and although many questions were asked of the prison authorities of how it was allowed to happen, I think the general consensus of opinion was bon debarras or as I think you English say 'Good riddance to bad rubbish!'"

"Yes, I was truly mistaken, I certainly never met the man," Suzanne said, asking quizzically "…and that was the end of that?"

"Well not quite, after Jean's arrest police did establish whereabouts the farm was situated that Claudine had spoken of and promptly did a search of the area around the ruins of the former farm buildings. It was all very low key and following Jean's untimely death the whole thing was called off and the deceased Claudine was accused of lying about the whole thing in order to get even and make trouble for her abusive husband. In France we say les morts ne parlent pas!"

"I understand what you are saying, it is very true, but out of curiosity I have just one more question Madame, whereabouts in relation to here is the farm you talk about?"

"'Was' rather than 'is'!" Madame Dubois exclaimed, "Unfortunately here in the Cevennes hill farming as a livelihood is dying and people are leaving the land and moving to the big cities, sadly that particular isolated farm was one such victim. I am told today very little remains of the buildings – it is at the end of a very long and exposed valley, however some of Claudine's story is known to be true because at around that time an Englishman did come with his beautiful young daughter and bought the derelict buildings together with the surrounding land. Where in the past others had failed, they spent some years trying to make a success of it; if you know where you are going it's less than an hour's drive away from here."

Momentarily Suzanne did not have a ready response to what Françoise Dubois was saying, the only thing that mattered to her was the dawning realization the burden of past guilt was about to be lifted from her shoulders.

"What is so strange about all those years ago, and what people for miles around still talk about, is the way the English couple just seemed to disappear; some say they both died from a serious illness, others that they both left here for pastures new – maybe they left France and went back to England who knows? At one time she was known to have tried to sell the property, but there was no interest, it is all a mystery from the past. One day they were here, the next day they were gone.

For a while the father was a well-known figure around the local weekly markets selling produce from the farm. The daughter, much to the male population's displeasure, was not seen around so much, she was very attractive and all the men would turn their heads as she passed in the street. It is well over ten years ago and is now mostly forgotten, but Roland still talks of this gorgeous English girl he once saw walking through the Square in Florac."

Suzanne sighed.

"Yes, a lot can happen in ten years…anyway, thank you for putting my mind at rest, thinking you know someone when you really don't can be quite embarrassing!"

She glanced at her watch.

"Gosh! Look at the time, my family really will be wondering where I am."

As Suzanne went to leave the room she affectionately hugged Françoise Dubois.

"Thank you Madame, thank you."

"I am sorry my dear it wasn't the person you were looking for."

Turning towards the figure slumped in the chair, "I should wake him otherwise he will be sad he missed saying goodbye, earlier Roland said he thought you were very pretty and reminded him of a young English girl he had once met." She rolled her eyes, "Vieux bouffon!"

Leaving the building, Suzanne heard the Frenchwoman call after her, "Au revoir Madame, ont un voyage sur!"

*****

As they left Pont de Monvert and *Auberge du Tarn*, looking out of the car window at the passing stark countryside, Suzanne was trying to understand the full implication of what Madame Dubois had just told her.

Returning she had found David and Emily had long left the car and made their way down to the rocks alongside the clear flowing river. He had tried to understand what Suzanne was telling him, but Emily's excitement at seeing the return of her mother, together with being reunited with her beloved teddy bear, had trumped everything else and with an exchanged smile the two adults knowingly agreed then was not the time and her news would perhaps be better shared when their daughter was perhaps a little less animated.

Breaking from studying the road map resting across her knees, Suzanne looked across at her husband who was carefully following instructions as he negotiated the numerous bends in the narrow bumpy highway.

"Thank you for being so patient and keeping the little one occupied, I had no idea when I began talking to Madame Dubois it would take so long."

"Over thirty minutes actually, Emily was getting beside herself…for Teddy…not her beautiful mother you understand," momentarily he took his eyes off the highway and lent-over to kiss his wife lightly on the cheek, "I very nearly came looking for you, but somehow I guessed right that you were best left to your own devices, it was sealed when Emily asked to go down and look at the river. It seemed to keep her occupied before you re-emerged, but tell me, did you plan it all it on purpose? Did you or Emily leave Teddy behind?"

Quickly glancing round to see if the silence from the back of the car was an indication their daughter was happy, Suzanne could not help but smile to see Emily cuddling her favourite soft toy tightly as if to make sure it did not escape again whilst she was taking an unscheduled nap strapped into the car seat.

"Slow down David and pull in here!" Suzanne suddenly exclaimed, "I feel sick and you need to hear what I have just learnt, if you don't mind I would rather tell you now right-away and before we get there."

He braked hard and pulled into a gateway on the right hand side of the road. The sudden stopping stirred, but did not wake Emily.

"Please will you tell me what exactly is going on?" he asked, as the vehicle came to a complete halt.

"I am confused, after agreeing in the first place it was a good idea we should make this trip together, you then start acting in a strange and secretive manner, it's as if..."

Before he could finish his sentence, Suzanne had opened the car door and in one movement left the vehicle, managing to make it to the scrubby hedgerow before she was violently sick.

David quickly followed and soon had his comforting arm around Suzanne's shaking shoulders; he could see that tears were now running down her face.

"What is the matter my dear, are you unwell? Has all the travelling been too much? Perhaps we were wrong in attempting to revisit here, nobody knows what you have suffered and I am sure whatever sinful deeds happened over ten years ago your conscience should now be more than clear."

She turned to face her husband.

"David you don't understand, my years of running and trying to hide from myself are over. The anxiety and

323

stress I have suffered you have tried so hard to understand, for that I am truly thankful, but I can never expect you to fully comprehend what really happened to me ten years ago. Suzanne took him by the hand and started to lead him back to the car.

"What Françoise and Roland Dubois have let me know today, although it will never replace my dear father, brings a necessary closure to the sad events surrounding his death."

"Do you still wish to continue to the end," David sombrely asked.

"Yes, of course I do, put my vomiting down to a strange mixture of relief and worry, I'm fine, but before we move on any further I have to tell you the story of Jean and Claudine LeRoux."

*****

"Are you sure we are following the right track?" the driver asked as they lurched forward over the bumpy surface, having long lost count of the deep ruts he had failed to fully negotiate going up the seemingly endless twisting valley, David was not totally sure they were in the right place anyway.

"Just around the next bend, it's not too far" came the far from convincing reply.

"I am not sure I believe that, you have been saying the same thing for the past fifteen minutes," nodding towards the back of the car, "At least Emily seems happier than she was earlier today, but with all this bumping around how are you feeling now?" David asked.

"With all the miles we have covered and all the strange beds she has slept in over the past ten days, I think Emily has been marvellous and as for me, as I said previously, I think my worries are all in my head and back there my body was trying to tell me something, no, I'm fine, don't worry."

"But I do, after all you are my wife and…" Before

324

David could finish his sentence he had to bring the car to an abrupt halt. They had reached the end of valley and the track they had been following petered out into a grass overgrown flatter area on which several ruined stone buildings were standing; he gasped.

Immediately Suzanne jumped out of the vehicle, whispering in disbelief.

"David, this is it, we are here!"

Suzanne ran away from the car towards the derelict structure she remembered as the main farmhouse, leaving her husband to tend with their daughter.

Arriving at the old building it was soon clear to her that due to the collapsed roof and part of the top floor, entry would be very difficult and dangerous, undergrowth remained undisturbed and after the lack of attention for so many years the scrub had seemingly spread everywhere. The nearby barn, once both her studio and sanctuary, had fared no better; the wooden frame was barely standing, very little siding remained and there was no sign of the glass which had once covered one wall. The cottage where the fateful event had occurred, surrounding outbuildings, pathways and fences, all were in a desolate state of repair or lost for ever, all gone, all that remained were memories.

The afternoon sun came from behind a lonely cloud as Suzanne walked slowly towards the one apparent remaining constant, the still standing old fig tree, even thicker than when she sought solace under those spreading branches.

Sitting in the shade of the tree by the ever flowing stream, Suzanne surveyed the scene before her and tried to sum-up the courage to do what she knew, having come this far, must be done. She was disturbed from her deep thoughts by the arrival of David carrying Emily in his arms.

"Mummy, look what I have for you!" Sitting down on the ground next to Suzanne, Emily presented her mother with the small bunch of wild lavender she had just picked.

Kissing her daughter on the forehead, Suzanne thanked Emily for her kind thought.

"It is so beautiful, you must have been so happy here, the colours of the abundant wild flowers, the scent of the lavender, it is all so stunning and yet so peaceful."

"My father's feelings exactly, he worked so hard to try and make it home for us, heaven on earth he used to call it; all gone." Suzanne fell silent.

"Whatever you are thinking about my dear, you must forget and move on, we are everything to you now." He waited for her reply.

"David, I have seen all I want to see here, but there is just one more thing I have to do before we leave. Please will you take Emily back to the car and wait for me there, I promise not to be too long."

"Take as long as it takes, but just remember we both love you very much, we will be waiting for you."

Without turning around, gathering his daughter into his arms and despite Emily's minor protestations of not wanting to leave Mummy, David started to walk back to the parked car.

He stood by the vehicle and watched closely as the lone figure climbed up the side of the valley, in her hand he could clearly see the bunch of wild lavender Emily had picked minutes ago and then proudly presented to her mother.

David observed Suzanne had stopped her upward climb and was now crisscrossing the ground in front of her, head bent as if looking for a clue, nearly two hours passed and it was well into the afternoon, still the lone figure searched. He had fed and watered Emily who, bored with playing with her travelling toys, was now fast asleep curled up on the back seat, while her father slouched in the front.

Suddenly David was up and standing to pay closer attention, Suzanne was stopped in front of what from distance to him seemed just another patch of undulating ground. He watched as Suzanne knelt and placed the wild flowers on the ground, twenty minutes passed before she got to her feet again.

Hands clasped in front of her, Suzanne stayed a short while longer staring at the lavender in front of her before eventually turning away and starting the descent into the valley below.

As she approached David ran forward to greet his wife; he threw his arms around her in comfort. It was clear from the red eyes Suzanne had shed more than one tear in the time away.

"I found it; I found my father's gravesite! David I have told him everything, about my life experiences, how we met and how proud he would be of his granddaughter and about what happened to Jean and Claudine; there was so much to tell him." Suzanne lowered her voice, "I also asked for his forgiveness – it was so mean of me, I did not mean to kill him."

As she tearfully continued, David took her back into his arms.

"But all that is in the past, I have no need to return here, ever. Father told me not to comeback and he fully understands."

Their long warm embrace was interrupted by a waking voice calling from the car. "Mummy, mummy, there you are! Where have you been? Teddy and me have missed you; we both want a hug too!"